PROPHECY

The Wizard Hall Chronicles

SHERYL STEINES

THE WIZARD HALL CHRONICLES

Cover Art: Damonza
Editor: Rachel Porter
Prophecy

Copyright 2019 Sheryl Steines
All rights reserved.

ISBN 10: 0-9858652-8-8

ISBN 13: 978-0-9858652-8-3

PROLOGUE

One week after Annie returned home from Paris...

SINCE RETURNING FROM France, Annie couldn't help but think if Sturtagaard hadn't let her know that Amelie was a vampire, she would have spent the week deliriously recovering from her recent injuries, watching television, baking, or enjoying some other mindless activity rather than chasing and killing the vampire. She shuddered at the thought.

She had little time in France to dwell on the loss of the Black Market or of its connection to her father's eight-year-old murder investigation. But, in the end, the journey across Europe left her exhausted. She moved the heating pad to a new location and snuggled into the corner of her sectional sofa, wrapping herself in a thick, warm blanket. It didn't take long for sleep to overtake her, leaving her blissfully unaware for the entire afternoon.

When she woke, she was enveloped in Cham's arms. He was sound asleep.

Of course and I'm not anymore.

Annie slid out of his embrace, pulled the blanket to his chin, and left him sleeping in the corner. She walked through the dark house and switched on the kitchen light, which blinded her momentarily. When she gained her bearings, she was immediately drawn to the dusty box that had been sitting on her kitchen table since before she left for France. After searching her house and garage, she had finally found it in the crawl space in the basement, where her father hid it eight years prior. But the newspaper from Sturtagaard, letting her know Princess Amelie was still alive and living as a vampire, had put going through it on hold. Though Cham was curious, he had left the box alone. Now that Annie felt better and more rested, her curiosity was overwhelming.

Annie was fairly certain that, in it, she would find the missing file for the case her father was investigating when he died. She sighed and glanced at Cham sleeping in the other room; his chest rose and fell peacefully.

She lifted the lid and peered inside. Sure enough, she saw a file and pulled it from the box. Her father's handwriting was slanted and square, scrawled across the spaces for guard name, case name and number. She could still feel the grooves left from where he had pressed the pen into the folder. Her stomach roiled with relief and uncertainty.

Is this still important?

With a tentative sigh, Annie opened the folder. It had been partitioned into several sections; the first item she saw was a note addressed to her in the same familiar writing.

"What the hell?" she asked no one as she unclipped the note.

My dearest Annie,

If you are reading this, I am dead. And as I write this, that realization hits me hard with the things I will miss or have already missed. For that, my angel, I am so very sorry.

But sometimes as a wizard guard, there are cases so challenging that you are forced to do things that you otherwise would not do. Sometimes the rules can no longer apply. There is too much at stake to risk our way of life and the lives of our family.

I have to make a choice. I have to choose being with you and Samantha for as long as I can, or I can save the world from ourselves. It's a choice that I deeply regret that I have to make. Sometimes our choices lead us to this very place and time.

I came across Wolfgange Rathbone in the course of this case. The Chintamani Stones that once belonged to King Solomon have been stolen and are sold in the Black Market. They are a danger to our people, and to the nonmagicals that we share this world with.

So sorry my love, but they asked me to stop. They asked me to hand over the stones that I was able to retrieve. They belonged to the Wizard Guard, to the Wizard Council but I did as they requested because they threatened my child. They threatened you, Annie.

My dear, sweet Annie. It wasn't the first time that your very existence has been threatened. I regret that I will not physically be there for you at any time to protect you. But there is a reason why I so diligently trained you, my dear. Because there will be a time in your future when you need to know what to do, how to keep yourself alive. I gave you all that I could in the short time that I had with you.

I promise you, Annie, that I gave them back all of the stones I had in my possession. But when you deal with secret societies such as the Fraternitatem of Solomon, which hide themselves away and don't participate in the world as it is, you find that you can't trust them. They are paranoid, distrustful, and have many secrets I wish I could have shared with you.

They had Rathbone in their employ, and it's him I fear the most. Not because I can't defend myself against his weaknesses, but because I have you in my head, and your safety blinds me. I will die before I let them get to you. Because there is a prophecy my love. You are at the center, and I will do whatever I can in life and death to ensure that the prophecy doesn't come true.

This might seem to be the ramblings of a man who

knows his death is imminent, but I assure you, this is real. If I am dead, it was at the hands of Rathbone on the orders of the Fraternitatem of Solomon. They will still be after the stones that I promise I no longer have.

Please believe me that I will do everything in my power to keep myself safe, to keep my friends and my children away from this difficult case. I do this for all of you because it was I who dug myself into this mess.

You deserved so much better than what I gave you. I wish that I could have raised you more like I did Samantha, but I couldn't. I had to protect you.

Rathbone knows this prophecy, and he is using it against me to get what he wants. Be wary of him.

I didn't die in vain. I died to protect you and the powers you will someday have.

You are so very special, my love, so strong, so beautiful. I wish you happiness, security, and safety. May you remember all that I taught you. Be safe, my darling. I love you always.

Dad

Shaking, Annie placed the folder inside her blood-lock cabinet and slammed the door shut. As she reread the letter from her father, she slid herself to the floor, lowered her head, and cried.

∽

She hid the letter in her thick sock. Throughout the evening, the paper would scratch her skin whenever she moved. Annie still hadn't shared what she discovered with Cham. There were too many questions, and she hadn't wrapped her head around the information. He clearly knew something was bothering her; it made him overly attentive and patient as he held up the conversation. In that, she felt guilty and anxious. All Annie wanted to do was pull out the folder and dig into its secrets.

Even though she was exhausted, Annie couldn't sleep. She sat on the window seat beside the bed and watched the moon travel across the sky, but it didn't calm or help quiet her thoughts. She broke down and snuck through the dark house, retrieving the folder from her locked cabinet. She held her breath, burning her lungs as she opened the well-organized folder. Jason had broken the contents into sections that were each separated by a sheet of colored construction paper. She slowly let air out of her lungs, took another deep breath, and noted each section: photos, notes, and a plastic bag stapled to the folder, containing a small cassette tape.

What the hell?

She forced herself to breathe in and out, in and out, as she opened the binder clip that held a large stack of photos. Her jaw dropped violently and her heart hammered; the pictures slipped to the table.

"No. No. No. That..." Her voice cracked.

"Annie, what's wrong?"

She had been so lost in the first picture, she hadn't heard Cham enter the kitchen.

"It can't be," she murmured.

"Annie?"

Though she hadn't acknowledged him, he sat beside her and grabbed the first picture. His jaw went slack. "This is... this is your mom," he said and turned the picture over. "With Arden Blakely?"

Annie shook her head, unable to speak. The shock was so raw that she ached.

But what is it really?

Reluctantly, she picked up the next picture and forced herself to stare at it, focusing on what she might learn from it.

The faces, so familiar, so young—and yet to Annie, there was nothing in their expressions to make her think they were friendly. Her mother's eyes were squinting, possibly by a hot sun. They appeared empty, sad maybe. But it was her jaw that stood out to Annie, clenched tightly as though she would vomit or was under great stress.

Eight years ago, Dr. Arden Blakely had less gray in her short hair, fewer wrinkles around the mouth, and her eyes appeared focused and determined, not hazy with post-traumatic stress. Annie guessed she was probably a full-time assassin for the secretive Fraternitatem of Solomon back then.

Mom? Why?

Seeing the pictures of her mother, alive when she was thought to be dead, brought up a swirl of memories of her father's death, and each memory socked her in the stomach a second time.

Annie remembered the days when Jason Pearce didn't make it home due to a hot lead on an investigation. When she and her sister, Samantha, were young, babysitters or friends had been lined up. When they were old enough, he'd send word that he wouldn't be returning until late—or early, depending on one's view point.

But the night he died, there had been no contact. As the hours stretched without word, Ryan Connelly, his Wizard Guard partner, grew worried. After twenty-four hours, several Wizard Guard colleagues—Milo Rawley, John Gibbs, Ryan Connelly, Trish Buck, and Kirby Winslow—began a frantic search of the Black Market. When they hadn't found Jason at the market, they searched for him at all of his usual haunts, called and visited his contacts, and even interviewed Archibald Mortimer. There had been no clues as to where Jason Pearce had gone.

Kathy Connelly and her son, Robin Price, had come to the house to sit with Annie and Samantha to keep them occupied while they waited to hear from Jason or the team.

By the end of the second day, the telecom manager, Melissa Swiss, came to Ryan with news of a John Doe in the Chicago morgue. The dead man's description was uncannily similar to Jason.

When Ryan came home alone, his face was pale and forlorn. Annie's heart sank, her stomach roiled. She couldn't see Samantha through the flow of tears that she couldn't stop.

The days passed in a blur. People arrived with food and condolences. Janie Parker, Dave Smith, and Cham Chamsky sat with her. When she couldn't speak, they stayed anyway.

Eventually, Annie would move on and live her life, graduating from high school, becoming a wizard guard. In the years since Jason died, she had gone to the records room at Wizard Hall and copied the contents of his death investigation folder.

Sometimes she wished she hadn't; the crime scene photos of where he died had left her shaken. He died alone, battered and broken, only discovered when employees returned to work on Monday morning. She could never un-see those images. They would be with her forever, and when she thought of them, she would feel numb and cold with an anger that would fill her all over again.

While it was the common belief that Wolfgange Rathbone had killed him, there was a lack of evidence until they convicted him of the murder of Princess Amelie of Amborix. To rattle Annie and attempt an escape, he admitted his role in Jason's death. Though Annie knew it was a ploy, she also knew that he indeed killed her father.

"Annie, please say something," Cham said, his voice filled with such anxiety that she finally pulled herself away from the dark memories.

"I'm sorry," Annie whispered. "I just opened the folder now." Her voice was parched. She summoned the note with trembling hands. "The newspaper article with Amelie pushed this all away. You were sleeping, so I finally decided to tackle it." She was breathy, it was difficult to suck in the air and release it. She passed him the note. "I found that earlier today. In the folder." Since finding it, she had clenched it tightly, folded it and reopened it several times. It was almost as worn as she felt.

Annie rested her elbows on the table, her head fell in her hands and she cried. There was no point in hiding the bitter emotions that had been violently stirred within her.

Cham slid the folder back across the table and wrapped his arm around her shoulder. "Take your time. We'll go through the folder when you're ready," he said. "I can call Ryan if you'd like."

Annie pulled away from him, sat straighter, and summoned the folder. "No. Not yet. Not until we know what this is." She wiped her eyes, her hands still quivering.

"We don't have to do this now."

She reached for the letter. "Read this. Now," she demanded. While he read, Annie picked up the next picture. The images of her mom took her breath away. She pulled the next picture, a blurry image of her mother in what Annie knew to be the Cave of Ages in southern Israel.

The Fraternitatem!

She pushed the photos to the side, unable to look at them any further, and fumbled with the notes, not sure she wanted to read the contents.

"A prophecy. He's implying you're in danger," Cham said with much anxiety in his voice.

"Apparently," she responded coolly. Her emotions seemed to burn hot and cold as she attempted to grasp what it all meant.

Cham shuffled through the additional pictures. "I don't even know where to start asking questions," he admitted, still stunned by the images and her father's explanation.

"Who's buried in her grave? Did Dad know it wasn't her? Did she leave willingly, and why? If she's with Arden Blakely in the picture, does that mean she's a member of the Fraternitatem? Is she one of their assassins?" Annie asked, all in a rush.

"Yeah, those questions." He sighed.

When Annie glanced up, Zola, her Aloja fairy, stood in the shadows. Her emerald green eyes were shaded with gray, for the sadness she was unable to hide. Zola had been magically linked with Annie since she was a baby. What Annie felt, Zola felt.

"You knew about Mom." Annie didn't mask the accusation.

Zola glided across the wood floor. Her transparent wings were like wisps of fragile skin, fluttering when she walked. She took a seat across from Annie, her expression determined and thoughtful.

"There was something…" her eyes crinkled in concentration "… odd. Her body felt odd. But she wasn't magical, so I couldn't trust the reading." Zola saw the folder on the table top and pulled it close. A small squeak escaped her lips when she saw the photos. Her hands shook.

"Don't tell Samantha until you know when these were taken and if she's still alive. Your pain is more than I can bear right now," Zola said as she placed the pictures away in the file.

⟡

Annie promised Zola she'd keep the pictures to herself until she knew for certain what the images meant. Before returning to work, Annie did an internet search for Emily Pearce, but she discovered she wasn't as creative or as knowledgeable as Bucky Hart, the computer guru at Wizard Hall. Rather than fumbling aimlessly through the internet, she thought she'd ask Bucky to take a crack at the search.

She held her breath as she knocked on Bucky's cubicle wall, knowing asking him to do this would open up so many more questions, but Annie needed to know. While Jason had hidden the files to protect them, he must have known that Annie would eventually find the box in the crawl space.

"Hey, Annie Pearce. Come on in," Bucky said as he cleared a chair for her.

She took in a deep, slow breath which did little to ease the nausea in her belly.

"What's up?" he asked. He frowned when he saw her pale face.

"How much do you know about my dad's murder?" Annie whispered. Instinctively, he placed a hand on the wall and sent a muffle spell across his small cubicle, enveloping them in privacy.

"I know Rathbone did it. It's related to the Fraternitatem and the Chintamani stones. Beyond that, I'm clueless," Bucky said.

Annie shook her head. "This needs to stay between you and me. If I'm not around, find Cham. He's the only person who knows this." Bucky understood her stern, serious expression and nodded in agreement.

She handed Bucky a picture of Dr. Arden Blakely with Emily Pearce. He examined the picture and glanced back at Annie. "Isn't this that doctor? The assassin? She looks younger, but…"

"It's Dr. Arden Blakely," she said quietly.

"That's not why you want me to see this," Bucky said.

Annie nodded.

Bucky grimaced and reviewed the picture again. This time, he couldn't ignore the striking similarities between the other woman and Annie. He stared back at Annie. "If I didn't know better, I'd say the other one is related to you," he said guardedly. Bucky, all of twenty years old, had been a child when Annie's father had worked in Wizard Hall. He had heard about Jason Pearce and his skills as a wizard guard and only knew from others that Annie's mom died when she was very young. Until now, it probably hadn't occurred to him that he had never seen a picture of her mother in her cubicle. Bucky observed Annie carefully.

Annie cleared her throat to find her voice. "It's my mom, Emily Pearce."

Bucky turned the picture over, and noted the date—July, 2011—and the name of the two women: Emily Pearce, Dr. Arden Blakely.

"Annie, I'm not sure what to say except I'm sorry." His concern was overwhelming.

"Thanks. I found this in a folder hidden in my crawl space. Dad was protecting someone… her, us. I don't know why. This was taken eight years ago. I looked for her online, but I'm not you," Annie said.

Normally Bucky would have made a smartass-y joke, but he sensed Annie's pain and said, "I can do a search. Find out if she's still alive." He stared at the picture again. "Maybe the Middle Eastern Guard… never mind that. Everything about the Fraternitatem is very difficult to find. She might have gone dark."

"Weirdly, they still used Arden's real name. Maybe they are with Emily? I get that I'm asking for the impossible. That's why I'm coming to you." Annie sighed and her hands shook as she took back the picture.

"I appreciate your confidence. Just so I know, is there anything else in the folder that might help?"

Annie shook her head. "I haven't gone through it all yet. I'll pass along what I can when I find it." Annie grimaced and wrote down some names. "I'm assuming if Emily's alive, she's in the Middle East. Though Arden Blakely was eventually released. Emily could have come home. I have a grandmother here. I haven't seen her since I was three, but her name is Gloriana Worthington. Maybe Emily got in touch with her. Maybe?"

"I'll do what I can. Though I can't help but wonder if you really want to do this," Bucky commented.

Annie chuckled. "I don't, but I can't not look."

Bucky pulled out a folder, marked it *data search, Lady Elizabeth* in honor of Annie's middle name, and placed the note about Annie's grandmother inside. He held out for the picture. Annie stared at it before handing it over. He quickly made a copy and handed the original back to her. Once he had the folder created, he punctured his finger in his blood lock and placed the folder inside, closing the drawer. "It's lucky I like you," he quipped.

"Yeah, I know."

⁓

By three in the afternoon Annie received the following text: *Nothing yet. But it's the Fraternitatem. I will keep looking. It may take time. B*

Annie pocketed her phone and sighed. She pulled up the folder she was reviewing on a cold case, but she couldn't concentrate on the new lead. Restless, she decided to share with the one person who was there when the events happened and who could remain detached if needed. She knocked on Gibbs's cubicle beside hers. Each tap jiggled the wall.

He glanced up from a picture he was reviewing with a large magnifying glass. "Girl," he said and motioned for her to sit. "You look like hell." He observed her carefully.

"Not sleeping." She pulled out the file and slid it across his desk. Gibbs of all people recognized the handwriting, the case number, the folder.

"You found the missing file." He pulled out the contents. Annie had left Jason's note on the front of the contents. He picked it up and read.

His hands shook as he read Jason's words, his warning to Annie, her imminent danger. Gibbs said nothing as he continued through the folder, stopping on the picture of Emily and Dr. Arden Blakely. He turned the picture over, noting the date.

"Who else knows?" Gibbs asked.

"Cham, Zola, and Bucky," she said.

"Has Bucky found her?"

Annie shook her head. "Not yet."

Gibbs returned to the folder, quickly perusing the rest of the images, and stopped at the cassette tape. "Have you listened to this yet?"

Again, Annie shook her head. "I need a tape deck that small. I don't have one. I'll listen soon."

He reassembled the documents and slid the folder back to Annie. She placed them back in her field pack. "He never told me he found her. Who did we bury?" Gibbs asked mostly to himself as he turned around. He, like most wizard guards, had a blood lock on the credenza. He punctured his finger, opened the drawer, and searched for his personal folder on Emily's death.

"Zola thought there was something odd about her body," Annie said.

"We didn't see a glimmer on the body. We couldn't find any

distinguishing magic that would tell us how she died. While we found inconsistent magic on her, we thought she was killed by a nonmagical."

"So what happened?"

"Someone with an agenda, with complex magic, needed Emily for some purpose," Gibbs said softly.

And who would fall into that category?

"I have my notes here." He slid the folder to Annie, who placed it in Jason's file. "When Bucky finds her, let me know. Okay?"

Annie nodded. "I will."

CHAPTER 1

ANNIE SHOT AWAKE as the sound of a text message pierced the darkness. Her breathing was heavy and her hands trembled as she read the message. It was sent by the telecommunications rep, Max White, one of the hundreds of reps across the United States who managed the 911 emergency call systems, searching for hints of wayward magic, creatures, or evil wizards.

Multi cls. 2 Poss dmn Howard St. Evanston.

Annie put down her phone and contemplated the report. Multiple calls, 2 possible demons on Howard Street in Evanston, Illinois. Depending on the police reports, odd calls were sorted and turned over to the appropriate department, whether it was the on-call wizard guard or to the Vampire Attack Unit. Tonight, the call was routed to the Wizard Guard department, specifically Annie and her partner Spencer Ray, who were on call for the night.

Rolling her eyes, she knew it could be a number of things from vagrants to teenagers pranking local residents. While many calls were legitimate demon reports, Annie wasn't expecting much of anything at three in the morning during summer vacation.

She raced through her morning routine, dressing in her demon-chasing clothes: jeans, T-shirt, thick hoodie, and gym shoes. Observing herself in the mirror, she gathered her thick, chocolate-brown curls into a messy bun, clipping it with an etched golden protection amulet Zola had given her when she was a young girl.

Checking her phone, she groaned before finishing up; dropping eye drops in her red eyes caused from another sleepless night, dotting concealer around the dark circles that she couldn't erase, and running lip gloss across her lips.

"Ugh," she murmured and shut off the bathroom light. Stopping at Cham, she bent over him and kissed his cheek.

"Everything okay?" Cham murmured, wrapped tightly inside the blankets.

"Mysterious demons near Howard Street," she said.

He sat up and held her wrist. "You okay? You tossed and turned a lot last night."

She hesitated. It wasn't the moment to let him in on her night's musings because it was the same thing that had kept her awake for the last three months: no news from Bucky regarding her mom. She sighed softly. "I'm fine. We'll talk later. Gotta run." She kissed him one last time before racing down the stairs for the demon.

✍

"This is the neighborhood," Spencer said as he re-checked the coordinates left an hour ago by Max White.

They had walked up and down Howard Street for several blocks in either direction and began making a large circle around the neighborhood.

"And Max heard these calls on the 911 call system? I don't see the police," Annie commented dryly. As she expected, this looked like it would end up being a wild goose chase. "Why are we here again?"

"More than one call came in. Buck it up," Spencer teased.

Their flashlights swept the sidewalk as they turned down an empty alley, a perfect place for teenagers to cause trouble.

Each house stood silent as families slept, their side yards empty and their backyards filled with swing sets, barbeques, and the occasional blow-up pool or trampoline. Up ahead, Annie spotted a trail of overturned garbage cans, used food containers, ripped plastic bags, and rotted food.

"Looks like we found something." Annie pointed her flashlight down the road as another garbage can was tossed into the alley with a loud crash.

Annie and Spencer glanced at each other, bemused. Both shut off their flashlights and cautiously crept along the alley, following the sound of garbage cans being clacked together.

Stopping short, they listened to angry grunting and plastic bags being ripped apart, with unwanted items strewn into the road. Slowly, they stepped beside the garage door and poked their heads around the wall, expecting a gaggle of bored teenagers. Annie's jaw dropped.

In the bright moonlight, they saw a man… but not a man. He was easily over seven feet tall, very thick and muscular. Whatever he was, he lifted the can above his head with no effort and dumped the contents on the ground.

"That is one big… what is it?" Spencer asked.

Annie flashed her light in the creature's eyes, temporarily blinding it. She took in its face, its pockmarked skin covered in battle scars, its delicate features for a creature of that size and girth, a long, thin nose, close-set eyes, and squared yellow teeth. To Annie, the creature's face seemed nearly human. Though he was bigger than even a large human man, she could see his human-like limbs, long and thick, and five fingers on each hand.

"I think he's a large demon?" Annie asked. But there was something in his quizzical expression, his lack of communication.

Is he human or demon?

"What are you doing, sir?" Spencer asked cautiously, his palms facing the being that he too had been struggling to identify.

There were two basic classifications for demons: humanoid or animal-hood. A humanoid demon had delicate human features, relatively hairless skin, and independent thought. They were vampires, furies, succubae, banshees, and the like.

The other demons, animalhood, seemed less like people and were covered in fur or scales. Some had four limbs and a head, but they lacked speech and independent thought. Usually, that particular demon lived in the wilderness, away from civilization and hunted prey.

Both Annie and Spencer saw this creature as something different.

The demon grunted in surprise, offered no explanation for his presence, and in one easy motion, tossed the garbage can at them and ran down the alley.

"Crap, that thing is huge," Spencer noted as he and Annie charged after it.

For his size and girth, he lumbered down the alley quickly. Fearing exposure if they teleported after it, Annie and Spencer pumped their arms and picked up their pace to keep from losing him in the darkness.

The demon turned left at the next intersection as if he knew where he was going, running faster without tiring. Annie and Spencer followed and were soon dripping in sweat, with cramps in their legs and sides.

Without warning, the demon slid to a stop. Annie and Spencer slowed and crept along the edge of the sidewalk, trying to ascertain what had stopped him so quickly. Blocking its path was an equally tall and sturdy man, his eyes glaring at the creature. Annie observed him quickly but in the dark could only see his tunic, tied at the waist with a thin string and a sword hanging at his hip.

"What the hell?" Spencer murmured

They observed the man with the sword intently. He removed long, thin hair from his face as his eyes darted from the demon to them. He shouted harshly at the demon.

"What did he say?" Spencer asked Annie.

"I don't know," she admitted. In an instant, the demon ran one way, the man the other.

"Go!" Annie pointed. She followed the demon, leaving Spencer to chase the man.

∽

For an hour, Annie pursued the demon, slowly winding closer to the center of the neighborhood. His longer strides kept him several blocks ahead of her. While she quickly grew tired, the demon continued to run without slowing.

Streetlamps stood like soldiers on both sides of the street; some flickered but others lacked bulbs entirely. The demon ran either through beams of light or into the shadows. Annie listened to the heavy pounding of his thick feet against the cement sidewalk and followed.

An early summer rain spattered the sidewalk and stuck to Annie's curly hair. She pushed several strands behind her ears and wiped her face with a moist sleeve.

This is getting ridiculous.

Still several blocks from the demon, she anxiously glanced down both sides of the street, crossing into an older and more familiar commercial neighborhood. With dawn nearing, the small, independent businesses were still boarded up for the night, metal bars hanging protectively against the windows and doors.

The wizard-only store known as the Snake Head Letters, came into view. It traded in magical objects, potions, books, and other trinkets that ran from highly questionable to purely evil. Annie spied the owner, Archibald Mortimer, observing her with some interest as she ran past the grimy front window of his store. He neither helped nor hindered her efforts, nor reacted in any way. It was clearly a change in his attitude where she was concerned.

Annie assumed he hadn't gotten over the beating he received at the hand of Gladden Worchester three months ago. Gladden had beaten Mortimer, forcing the older, weaker man to give up information on Annie. Although he had tried to keep quiet, a few well-placed, devastating blows convinced him to reveal what he knew about her.

The beating caused a string of events to occur, which all together led to the destruction of the Black Market. While that loss was a boon to Mortimer's business, he was a changed man, withdrawn and nearly silent. It was still too early to determine the repercussions to the wizarding world.

Annie put Mortimer out of her mind and slipped between two buildings as sharp pricks of pain seized her side, belly, and chest. Although she exercised regularly, the extended chase left her exhausted and doubled over, searching for breath.

While listening to the demon's clumsy footsteps, she realized how much farther away he was now. She peered around the wall and saw him run through the light of a streetlamp and turn down the next street. Annie sighed, glanced down each side of the empty roadway, and teleported herself a few blocks ahead of the demon.

He barreled toward her. She calculated her timing and threw a jinx. The magic hit the demon in the shoulder, jerking him backwards. He growled.

Cautiously, Annie shone her bright flashlight into his eyes.

"What are you doing here?" Annie asked. A humanoid demon would have answered, but this one only grunted, sniffed, and snorted.

Human features, animal mannerisms?

She removed the flashlight from the demon's eyes and saw something else there. As the creature clamored away from her, she realized she saw terror.

The sky turned a dim gray with hints of orange as dawn approached. Annie watched the demon hobble across the road, heading for a narrow two-story home at the end of the block. Reaching its destination, the demon shuffled up the stairs, yanked the front door open, and ran inside.

What the hell?

With the demon confined to the house, she slowed her pace, giving herself time to catch her breath and take in her surroundings. Thin houses on small plots of land lined both sides of the street; each house was similar in size and design. The houses in this older neighborhood appeared well maintained, all except for the house at the end of the lane. She stood on the sidewalk and stared the building, which leaned to the left.

Annie cautiously stepped up the cracked sidewalk, thin chips of cement cracking under her shoes. The small porch felt sad and neglected, with several rotted boards and an overhang that had separated from the house. She stood at the open door that hung limply on the hinges and listened to the sounds of ripping and thumping above her. She flashed her light inside the room without entering the house.

The narrow room was cluttered with abandoned furniture: a ripped sofa, a spindled chair missing its fourth leg, and a low coffee table with a scratched top. Beyond the room, she saw a darkened hallway that she could only assume led to a kitchen.

The walls were dirty, with peeling paint and a lone picture of a boat on the ocean hung askew. The worn carpeting had a large scorch mark at the center. She raised her eyebrows.

"Why do these buildings always look like this?" she murmured.

Something heavy crashed inside, causing the ceiling to shake. Annie glanced up.

"Going inside by yourself?"

Annie jumped at the familiar voice. She spied Sturtagaard leaning against a tree just outside the property line.

"What are you doing here?" Annie scowled. She hadn't seen the vampire since returning from France, and it had been a pleasurable three months without his sniffing, sneering, and ill temper. She didn't even care that he had assisted in the capture and staking of the vampire, Princess Amelie. Frankly, Annie was glad he hadn't been around.

Annie debated if she should engage in conversation with him, but as always, he piqued her interest. She strolled off the rotted deck and stood in the small patch of front yard.

"I'm just making sure you're doing your part," he mocked.

"My part in what?" she asked guardedly. Another thump echoed from the upstairs; she turned back to the house quickly.

"That one's too stupid. You have time," Sturtagaard said. He glanced at his fingernails as though checking his manicure was still intact, pretending he was uninterested in her presence there.

"That's not a typical demon, is it?" Annie asked. She was curious as to Sturtagaard's real purpose.

How deep is he in this?

"No. It's not. You will find out in time." His lips turned upwards. He appeared bored, like he couldn't be bothered with this conversation.

"What part am I playing?" she asked him.

Sturtagaard shrugged. Angry he was pushing her buttons, Annie summoned a stake and flipped it in the air, catching the hard ash in the palm of her hand. As it landed, Sturtagaard jumped at the sound, but he didn't look at her immediately. When he was done checking his nails, he rooted around in the dirt beneath his usually well-groomed leather shoes. When he finished stalling, he glared at her.

"I've said too much already. I, like everyone else in this, had a role and this was mine."

What roles?

"What the hell are you yammering about?" Another crash boomed inside the house. "Unless you have something useful to say, I'm leaving." Annie returned Sturtagaard's glare, but he simply shrugged.

"You'll be safe when the thunder comes," he said.

The ominous advice made little sense to Annie. She clearly wore her anger and confusion on her face. Sturtagaard couldn't help but laugh.

"What are you playing at?" she shouted at him, losing all patience with the vampire.

"I'm not playing at anything. I'm giving you, shall we say, helpful advice." He crossed his arms against his chest and leaned into the tree.

"Why am I wasting my time?" she mumbled. But Sturtagaard, thanks to his vampire hearing, heard the words through her semi-closed lips.

"Because you are curious as to why I'm here and the meaning of my message. I know you, girl. I've known all about you from the minute I first met you. You aren't as complicated as you think you are. You are still trying to please your daddy, and you won't stop until you're dead like him," Sturtagaard hissed.

Annie ignored the noises and marched to the vampire, who seemed unnerved by her. This bothered Annie. She held the stake against his chest.

"What the hell do you want?" she asked through gritted teeth.

"I'm responsible for making sure you came here, to this house, on this day. You need to follow the plan just as much as I do. This will all make sense to you in a few days. Oooh, I fear I've said too much," Sturtagaard said nonchalantly, as if that would make it all better.

"Why shouldn't I stake you now?" She pressed the sharp point into his chest; he pursed his lips.

"You can't because the Wizard Council says so." He offered a crooked smile exposing his fangs. "Besides, I know where the new Black Market is."

She held the stake tightly in her grasp. "Really… and where's that?" she taunted.

"Now, now girl. One problem at a time. It's time you deal with that demon up there. Otherwise, this whole exercise will be useless." He pushed the stake away, glanced at the lightening sky, and rolled away from the tree, skulking into the nearby forest.

That damn vampire!

CHAPTER 2

FOR A BRIEF moment, Annie stared into the trees, debating if she should run after Sturtagaard and force him to explain his cryptic messages. It was the next crash that caused her to return to the house.

Immediately upon entering, a rancid, rotten smell assaulted her. There was something else…

Mullein?

Odd that she should smell the burnt stench of an herb used to conjure black magic or demons.

Annie set her flashlight on dim and scanned the walls, ceiling, and floor, stopping on the burn mark across the musty carpet. She knelt beside the scorch mark, touched the soot, and sniffed the silky power.

"It *is* mullein," she said to the empty room. "Is this where the demon was conjured?"

Thump! She looked up at the ceiling. The center chandelier swayed from the crash on the floor above.

In hopes of avoiding a hand-to-hand fight with a demon twice her size and three times the weight, Annie summoned her crystal and took a reading of the magical energy found in and around the soot on the carpet. The crystal glowed a deep black. She looked inside, reading the dark magic that appeared about a week old.

The ceiling continued to shake as the restless demon tossed several hard objects. Annie sighed, pocketed her crystal, and checked her phone, leaving a message for Bucky Hart.

Who owns this house? she texted him, sending him the coordinates immediately.

When she finished, she took one last look around the room before heading up the stairs.

It was a crappy house, probably long abandoned. The treads were uneven and squeaked with each step. The entire staircase felt as though it leaned to the left. Annie took cautious steps reaching the top and stepping on the second floor.

The hallway contained two bedrooms and a bathroom. She tried the handle on the door to her right; it was locked.

I'll check it later if there's time.

Currently, her perceived assumptions about demons were jumbled. This demon was perplexing; different than any she had ever chased before. While he acted much like a low-level demon that lacked speech and thought, he ran with purpose toward this house, to that room, and proceeded to search for something.

But Sturtagaard called it a stupid one.

Guardedly, she walked to the front bedroom and poked her head inside. The demon had toppled a large armoire, which now lay front side down. There was a large footprint on the back panel, which lay in pieces. Wall boards were haphazardly piled on top of it, with additional thin bits of dust and two-by-fours contributing to the growing pile of debris.

Annie stared in horror as the demon continued to yank large pieces of wall board and studs from the side wall. He had already removed a large hole.

What is he looking for?

Annie froze when her phone buzzed, but the demon, preoccupied with his work, seemed unaware he was being watched. She breathed a sigh of relief, then waved her hand across her back pocket and shut off the ringtone.

Agitated, the demon reached inside the hole; whatever was hidden in the wall was still out of its reach. The demon grabbed another handful of wall and pulled. It cracked and ripped as the board gave way, detaching from the studs. The demon tossed the section of wall on a pile.

Again, the demon stuck his head into the hole and squealed. He still didn't seem to comprehend why he couldn't reach whatever he was searching for. In frustration, he punched at the stud like a punching bag.

Fearing the instability of the old house, Annie raised her palm and shot a jinx, sending yellow sparks flying through the air and hitting the beast in the upper arm. His arm jerked forward. The demon growled and clutched his shoulder.

Spotting Annie, the demon barked and then lunged. Her hands shook as she cast a stronger jinx, but either she missed or the curse was weaker than expected. The demon seemed unaffected by the blast. He clipped Annie's shoulder, knocking her to the ground.

Before she could react or turn away, the demon sat on her, crunching his thick legs around her petite frame, squeezing her and shoving her head into the musty, dirty carpeting.

Annie flailed her arms, landing feeble blows to the demon's body. No matter how much she stretched, her short, thin fingers couldn't wrap around the creature's neck. The demon bent close to Annie's face. His breath and general body odor made her gag.

Since he was close enough to her now, she found the base of the demon's neck and pushed with her thumbs, irritating the large creature. He howled.

Annie attempted to twist away, but the demon had her secure. Growing anxious, she threw her hands upwards and cast the strongest jinx she could muster. It hit the demon's head, sending him flying backwards.

She scampered off the dirty floor and ran toward the door. Two large hands yanked her up. As Annie hung in the air with her arms pinned to her side, she kicked out her legs in vain. Panicked and growing weak, Annie finally took one last kick. This time, her boot made contact with the demon's ribcage. The demon growled and smiled, easily tossing her down the hallway like she was a rag doll.

"Ahhhh!" Annie flew through the air; her head hit the wall and she flipped over, landing face first on the musty carpet. "Ooooff," she moaned.

Her stomach churned at the stench deeply buried in the wood floor. Her head felt heavy and filled with ringing and buzzing. As she came to awareness, the distinct sound of a deep-throated laughter came to her.

Sturtagaard?

Annie turned her head and opened her eyes. Shapes and colors swirled before her. Gingerly, she raised her head, then violently heaved what little acid she had in her stomach. The bitter taste of bile burned her tongue.

She struggled to sit, pushing herself up with rubbery arms. As the world spun around her, a new wave of nausea attacked her. She turned and dry heaved again; there was nothing left in her stomach. Exhausted, Annie slumped against the spongy wall and took a deep breath, shivering at the pain shooting through her body.

The demon continued to laugh, to hiccough, to grunt as though Annie's pain was the funniest thing he had ever seen.

Maybe it is funny.

Normally, this reaction would have angered her and she would have felt like a fool. But this demon, one that she had never seen before, intrigued her.

Though still fuzzy, she could see the human-like features of the face and the shape of the body, the mannerisms, the clothes. For Annie, the demon just didn't add up. Nothing seemed to fit.

A hybrid? Where does that come from?

She shuddered at the thought.

While the demon remained preoccupied with his own amusement, Annie pressed herself against the wall and pushed up. Weak and trembling, she twisted her palms outward, took whatever energy she had left, and let the jinx fly from her hands. Large green sparks flew from her palm and landed in the demon's mouth. His eyes widened, and his body sputtered and jerked violently. Annie watched in amazement as smoke billowed from his mouth, like a volcano about to erupt. The demon howled as the spell ripped him apart. Annie ducked low, covering her head with her arms as creature parts flew across the hallway and bedroom.

When she looked up again, she saw slimy remains covering the ceiling, walls, and carpeting. Blood and sinew hung from the hallway light. Wet pieces plopped to the carpet and slid down the walls. When she felt monster guts run down her cheek, Annie blanched and wiped away the gore. She pulled parts from her thick hair, flinging them to the ground in disgust. Again, Annie's phone buzzed. She raised her eyebrows, surprised the phone hadn't broken in her fall, and answered the call.

"Yeah," she breathed heavily. It hurt to take in the air.

"It's me. Where are you?" Spencer asked with an anxious tone.

She leaned against the wall and closed her eyes.

"I got it," she wheezed, trying to take a deep breath. "Demon parts everywhere." She lips curled in disgust when a demon finger plopped in her lap.

"I thought it was a retrieval, not a kill," he said.

"A little change in plans. Sorry." She threw the demon finger on the floor.

Spencer repeated, "So, where are you?"

"I'm at the end of Keeney Street near the trees. It's the only house that looks abandoned," she answered.

Demon parts continued to fall to the floor.

Ugh.

"Did you catch that man?" she wheezed.

"No. He got away. I'm coming for you. You sound horrible," he said.

She couldn't argue as she pushed back against the wall and pulled herself up. "I'm going to collect samples," she said as she limped down the hall. "And figure out what the hell he was searching for when I found it. I'll see you soon." She slipped in a pile of demon slime. "Ooooff. Shit!" she said as she grabbed the door jamb.

"Are you okay?" Spencer asked. "You sound hurt."

"I'm fine. I'll see you later. Okay?" She entered the room and headed to the hole in the wall.

"On my way now," he said.

She directed the flashlight between the studs and stuck her head inside the hole.

"Oh," she said.

"Annie? What's happening?"

"Later," she said and placed the phone in her back pocket without saying goodbye.

A white object was nestled between the studs at the floor. She summoned it and let the object hang in the air above her palm. She trained her flashlight on the four-inch-long artifact that appeared to be a hand-carved piece of…

Bone?

The design was old, grotesque, a human shape with an ugly face and a long beard, carved to a point. A triangle-shaped hat sat on top of wild hair. Someone over time had drilled an uneven hole through the top point of the hat.

A necklace? Amulet?

She ran a palm across the small totem and chanted a reveal spell. The statue radiated a shimmering white light.

At least it's good magic.

The statue vibrated against her skin. When she held it to her ear, it hummed softly and tickled her skin. She quickly realized it was a talisman —an object strong enough to create magic or conjure an object or possibly even a demon.

"So where did you come from and how did my demon know you were in the wall?" Annie asked aloud. She placed it back to her ear as if it could reveal its secrets.

Her attention shifted when she noticed unusual noises around her. When she turned around, she saw demon parts roll across the floor and slosh and plop from the ceiling. Slimy and oddly colored muscle and sinew slid across the carpet, carrying with them bits of dirt and carpet fibers. Wet muscles, organs, fingers, and legs found each other as if they were magic. They reformed, taking their original shapes. Slowly, a body grew. Arms and legs sprouted from its massive trunk. Feet and hands shot out from the end of the limbs.

Confused, agitated, frustrated, the demon thrashed about on the floor, flaying and jerking, his thick hands feeling for a missing head.

Annie jumped back in horror as the regenerated, headless demon thrashed about. She gawked as a tiny head developed from the stocky tree trunk of a neck. Gradually, the head blew up like a balloon. The same ugly face appeared; long, stringy hair sprouted from the scalp and down to the shoulders.

The demon's eyes, wild with anger, darted back and forth until they found Annie. With the talisman in hand, she teleported from the room. The demon grunted, pulled himself up, and stumbled as he lumbered out the door.

Halfway down the stairs, the demon, seeing Annie in the front room, slipped and dove for her. She lunged out of the way; the demon hit the floor, which shook at the crash.

Panicked, Annie cast a strong jinx, hitting the demon in the chest. Weakened from being blown apart, the demon fell through the bay window, shattering the glass across the overgrown bushes beneath the window.

Annie ran outside and cast another jinx. She missed the escaping demon, instead hitting the dry bushes which began to smoke.

"Damn." She conjured a water bottle, dousing the small fire.

The demon rushed her. Both fell against the hand railing. All of the demon's weight pinned Annie against the weakening wood. When she cast another spell, she sent them both through the front door.

Propelled by adrenaline, Annie rolled away as the demon clambered up and lunged for her. She teleported to the end of the hallway, which was just dark enough to keep her hidden from the creature. She pressed against the wall. With her palm out, she lifted the spindly chair and threw it at the demon. The creature looked around, still unable to see Annie, and stomped on the chair, breaking it into smaller bits.

The demon grew angry and growled loudly. He sniffed several times before walking to the hallway. Annie cast the next spell, lifting the end table. It only grazed the beast in the chest and fell to the floor. The demon stomped it to pieces.

Annie stepped further into the shadows toward the kitchen. She could smell both the demon's stench and her own. It smelled like fear.

With one more spell, she directed the sofa toward the demon, knocking it to its knees. Nearly out of energy, she stepped in front of the demon and launched another attack with successive spells, not letting up until the creature keeled over, unconscious.

Exhausted, she leaned against the wall and slid to the floor, wincing with pain.

"What the hell?" Spencer said as he entered the house. He glanced around the room at the broken window and the oddly placed, broken furniture. "Annie?" he shouted.

"Here!" Her voice was small; she had difficulty breathing.

Spencer shined the light in the room and ran for Annie, sidestepping the unconscious demon.

"What the hell happened?" He knelt beside her.

"The demon regenerated. Did you know demons could do that?" Her breathing was shallow. She winced.

"I need to get you out of here." He offered his hand. She waved him away.

"No. He's strong and dangerous. You need to get him to Tartarus. I can wait."

He shined his light in her eyes. She turned away. "No, you can't," Spencer said.

Spencer pulled out his phone and explained the situation to the voice on the other end. Annie knew it must be Graham Lightner, manager of the Vampire Attack Unit. A team would be here soon.

"I'm going to secure the demon and then get you the hell out of here." He assessed the sleeping creature, lifted a heavy eyelid, and placed a finger under the demon's nose to feel the air rush in and out. Certain that he was only knocked out, Spencer started tying the demon's feet with magical rope, ensuring he couldn't escape.

"Clothes and no shoes?" Spencer pulled on the rope to make sure he couldn't make it budge and began to tie the demon's hands behind his back. "Has he said anything? He doesn't seem to be of the talking and thought type," Spencer said as he continued to tie the demon with magical rope.

"No. He's only grunted and howled. This is the most bizarre demon." Annie stopped to take a shallow breath. She watched Spencer finish securing the demon; quickly and efficiently, the large beast was bound in magical rope that nothing could escape. "I watched him act like an animal, digging through the garbage, and sniffing the air. Plus, he stinks. But then I swear he was thinking and working out a problem." She coughed. Pain seized her body, and she shuddered.

As the successive spells to the demon began to wear off, he growled a low guttural sound.

"And he doesn't speak," Annie added.

"Just the growling? Grunting?" Spencer pulled the last of the rope taut around the demon's wrist.

"Just sounds. No words," she said and took as deep of a breath as she could. Spots popped out before her eyes.

"Regeneration is new." He pulled the demon's chin to study the face and cast a sleeping spell over the creature.

"I blew him up. Pieces flew everywhere. But everything regrew in the time I talked to you," Annie explained.

To be sure the demon was contained, Spencer summoned additional magical rope, and tied the demon's arms to his very thick body. Even he couldn't release the magical knots. "I think it's secure," he said and pulled the demon in the air, letting him float.

At a sound from behind them, Spencer and Annie both turned around to see Graham Lightner approaching.

"Hey, Graham," Spencer said.

"What a mess." Graham walked to the demon and saw Annie still sitting on the floor. "You need the hospital," he said as he touched the demon, assessing his condition.

"Yeah. In a minute. I blasted a spell, but the demon blew up and regenerated," Annie informed him.

"You used multiple spells?" Graham said as he noted the number of spell marks across the creature's face and arms.

"He was pock marked prior to my spells. It looks like he's seen a lot of battles," Annie said.

Skye Starling, another member of the VAU entered the room and nodded at the small group.

"Take Annie to the hospital," Graham told Spencer, waving Skye over.

"Hi, Spencer. Well, get a look at this demon. Tried to take it yourself did you, Annie?" Skye joked. "Wow. Go to the hospital. We've got this."

Annie stumbled as Spencer helped her up. "On our way. When you get the demon to Tartarus, can you take DNA and have Perkins Abernathy try and date the demon…" Annie touched his shirt; roughly woven, nearly gray from dirt and out of place. "And the clothes? The demon didn't get these from a garbage can. They're odd to say the least."

"Almost looks like what my man wore. Though without shoes and a weapon," Spencer said.

"We have no idea what the demon is or where he came from. Blowing him up didn't work." Annie faltered with her first step, nearly falling in Spencer's arms.

"Annie, go. We'll take care of this and let you know what we find," Graham said patiently. "Go." He and Skye watched as Spencer teleported Annie to the hospital.

CHAPTER 3

"SO I CAN leave when you're done?" Annie asked Dr. Christine Andrews, head of the Black Magic Medicine Department.

The doctor was well familiar with the wizard guards, having treated all of them at least once. She ignored Annie's question as she took her blood pressure and recorded the results in Annie's chart on the electronic tablet. She bit her lower lip and looked at Annie quizzically. "Seriously? Have you looked at yourself? You're a mess!" She placed the tablet on the long rolling table that crossed the end of Annie's bed. Whether Annie liked it or not, she would be using that table later that evening for her dinner. "That's the second concussion you've had in three months, and now you have at least one broken rib. I'm grounding you," Dr. Christine advised.

"I can't get any work done here," Annie grumbled.

Dr. Christine placed her hands on either side of Annie's head and chanted a healing spell to reduce the swelling to Annie's brain. Annie closed her eyes; the warm tingly sensation spread across her forehead and to the back of her head, easing the pain and nausea. When the spell was complete, Dr. Christine lifted Annie's eyelids and checked her sight. "How does that feel?"

"Better. I'm fine. Just put that in the chart and let me go. Please."

The doctor laughed as the door to the room opened. Cham entered cautiously, taking a seat beside Annie.

"Hey, babe. Hi, Dr. Christine." He sat patiently beside the bed as the doctor finished her assessment.

Annie closed her eyes again, feeling the warmth of the spell as it continued to work the magic. "What did Spencer say about his target?"

"I said no work," Dr. Christine reminded her as she returned to fiddling with Annie's chart, making adjustments to the course of treatment.

Annie rolled her eyes.

"The man you saw got away. We'll do another sweep of the area tonight," Cham told her. He began rubbing her palm with his thumb. The simple motion always comforted her. "He said they knew each other."

When Dr. Christine finished adding to Annie's medical chart, she continued the examination by poking Annie's ribs. "How does it feel?"

Annie winced and sucked in air, holding it in her lungs. "Hurts." She slowly let out her breath.

"I think you have two broken ribs. I'm ordering an X-ray." Dr. Christine tapped the end of the pen against the tablet before making notes. She exited the room. Annie could hear her low voice mumbling to someone in the hallway, but she was too tired to figure out what Dr. Christine was saying about her.

"You look like hell, by the way," Cham said. He kissed her hand.

"Every girl likes to hear that from her boyfriend," Annie mumbled.

"The point is you need rest. Stay tonight. Let them take care of you," he offered.

"I'd rather go home and let you take care of me." But Annie knew the broken ribs and concussion meant she'd be stuck here for the night.

Dr. Christine returned, picked up the chart again and made additional notes.

"If you know, can't you just heal them?" Annie asked.

Dr. Christine smiled and patted Annie's hand as a portable X-ray machine was wheeled into her room. While it was being set up, Dr. Christine said, "You know I can't just do that. I need to know exactly where it's cracked. You need rest. It'll take a lot of magical energy to heal."

Annie sighed as the bed was laid flat and the X-ray machine placed above her. Cham hid in the hallway as they took several pictures of her ribs.

When they finished, Cham returned and the X-ray machine was wheeled out.

Cham handed her a scroll. It was sealed with the Wizard Guard seal, a triangle with a wand at the center. Annie knew what it was and tossed it in her lap.

"Tired?" he asked.

"You have no idea. This isn't what I expected today," Annie said. She played with the functions on the bed and raised herself to a more or less comfortable sitting position.

"Not gonna read that?" he asked.

Annie chuckled. "Don't make me laugh. I'm off. I figured as much." For his sake, she pulled apart the scroll and read the order, signed by Milo Rawley, Wizard Guard Department Manager, giving her the next week off.

"The demon's at Tartarus. Gibbs and I will go off and find the other man that you saw. All your other cases can wait," he reminded her. She began to drum her fingers against the safety railing on the bed. "You really can't sit still, can you?" Cham asked. He took her right hand and held it.

"If I can't do anything anyway, I'd rather do nothing at home."

Dr. Christine entered. "Two ribs. I'll start the healing spell now. You're staying overnight and I really hope you don't work while you're here," she said. She handed Annie her X-ray and, as Annie reviewed the cracks on her two ribs, the healing spell warmed and tingled and knitted her bones back together. Absorbing the magical energy and using her own to heal was an exhausting experience. Annie held her breath as the doctor held her hand above Annie's ribs and cast the spell.

"So this round is complete. The pain should ease in a few minutes. I'll, come back later for more healing and, in the meantime, no magic, no work. I'm serious about that," Dr. Christine fervently reminded Annie.

"I'm too tired now anyway." Annie yawned and pulled the blankets to her chin.

After scratching notes on Annie's chart, Dr. Christine left them alone in the sterile, white-walled room. Her soft voice discussed patients with someone in the hall. A soft comfortable din wafted to Annie.

"You should go home, too," she told Cham. "I'll be fine."

"Really? I'm staying until they kick me out. Besides, you'll be getting calls soon, I'd like to know what's going on."

Annie nodded. "The man spoke a language I didn't recognize." She stifled another yawn just as her phone buzzed beside her on the table, vibrating against the metal top. She summoned the phone and turned to him. "And you knew that how?"

Cham shrugged and offered a smile as she answered the call from Bucky and put it on speaker. "Hi, Bucky. Find out about the house?"

"Firstly, how are you feeling?" he asked.

"Eh. You know. Concussion and two broken ribs. The usual," she said. Bucky offered a friendly chuckle.

"Good to know. Feel better. And as to your question, that house was recently purchased by a Gila Donaldson."

"Huh? Any relation to Emerson Donaldson?" Cham asked, clearly thinking immediately of the researcher for the Wizard Guard that he and Annie both worked with.

"I knew you'd ask that. So I pulled all Gila Donaldsons. There's only one in the United States. Based on age, birthday, address, etc., it is Emerson's grandmother."

Annie and Cham exchanged surprised glances. "Thanks, Bucky. Was there anything else?" Annie asked.

Bucky typed away at his keyboard as he always did when they spoke. "That's it. I have copies of the mortgage and note for confirmation. Was there anything else you need me to search for?" he asked.

Annie looked at the phone. "Nope. The Donaldsons are descendants of the original coven so we'll have to play it differently. It's odd though," Annie said thoughtfully.

"Yeah. I thought so too. Bit of a coincidence if you believe in them. Anyway, if you need something else, let me know. And feel better soon," Bucky added and hung up.

Annie played with her phone for a moment, assigning a meaning to the new information. "What do you think?" Cham finally said.

Before she could answer, Spencer and Gibbs entered the room.

"You look marginally better." Spencer sat in the chair to her right. "You were about to answer?"

Annie chuckled and grimaced as she shifted positions. She was growing stiff in the neck, back, and legs from the fight with the demon. "Get a load of this. The house is owned by Gila Donaldson, Emerson's grandmother," Annie said.

Both Gibbs and Spencer took a moment to digest that tidbit. Annie bent at the waist and touched her toes. Still uncomfortable, she leaned against the bed again, struggling to find a comfortable spot.

"So, if we don't believe that's a coincidence, what are we thinking?" Gibbs asked. He leaned against wall of the room, his thick arms folded across his chest.

"I smelled mullein in the front room." She summoned her crystal and tossed it to Cham. "It's definitely black magic."

Cham looked inside the crystal before handing it to Gibbs. He waved his palm once before giving it to Spencer.

"You think Gila Donaldson summoned a regenerating demon?" Gibbs asked.

Spencer handed the crystal to Annie, who tossed it in her lap. "Someone conjured a demon. Was it her? It's not a stretch, seeing that she purchased the house," Annie concluded.

Annie closed her eyes when she saw spots floating in front of her. A dull ache formed at the back of her head and was creeping to the top of her head, threatening her forehead. She touched the hard knot at the center of her forehead and grimaced.

"You're tired. We should go," Spencer said.

"No, it's fine. Just a bump and a dull ache," she said.

"No, we'll go. I'm heading to the library to get a handle on the regenerating demons," Spencer said.

"There's more," Annie said. Exhaustion finally had a grip on her, but she needed them to know this. "Sturtagaard was outside the house when I got there." It wasn't good news; the three men looked at her with surprise, worry, and anger.

"Now, why is he involving himself?" Cham asked, his jaw clenched. He tightly held the arm rests of his seat.

Maybe I shouldn't have brought it up.

"I'm not sure how he's involved. He said a few weird things. First, he told me I have a part to play in this," Annie began. She looked at Spencer. The two of them were fond of each other and enjoyed working together. At the mention of Sturtagaard, he seemed rather upset, his hands balled into tight fists.

"A part to play in what?" he asked. After spending a week in France babysitting the vampire, neither he nor Annie was happy at the prospect of doing it again.

Annie shrugged. "Beats me. He wouldn't elaborate, feared he said too much." She rolled her eyes before looking at Cham. Annie had only shared the next piece with Cham and Gibbs, and couldn't bear to look at Spencer.

She carried the letter from her dad in her field pack. Now with Sturtagaard's words, she wondered if her part in whatever this was had something to do with her father's warning of a prophecy.

"He also said I would be safe in the thunder," Annie said.

Gibbs and Spencer looked at her suspiciously.

"What the hell is he planning this time?" Gibbs asked.

Annie summoned the letter from her dad and handed it to Spencer. "I found Dad's missing case file. This was in it." She glanced quickly at Gibbs and dropped her gaze.

Gibbs pretended to read the letter over Spencer's shoulder. When they finished, they exchanged glances.

"I would've ignored the vamp until reading the letter," Gibbs admitted. "Outside the house owned by Donaldson, a descendant of the original coven. Odd coincidence."

"You don't believe in those," Annie reminded him.

"I don't either. I wonder though, if this has something to do with why we can't stake him," Spencer said.

Annie hadn't thought of that. It was a bone of contention with the wizard guards; after all of the problems he caused over the centuries, it was forbidden to stake the vampire and no one knew the real reason.

Annie yawned.

"We should go," Spencer said and handed her the letter.

"Girl, get better." Gibbs kissed her temple.

She watched them leave.

"It took a turn for the odd," Annie mumbled.

"Worry about it in the morning. Get some sleep." Cham ordered with a smile. He watched as Annie fell into a restless sleep.

∽

Familiar, worried whispers tempted her to consciousness. Annie's eyes flickered, their images became clear to her. She kept her eyes closed, feigning sleep; she wasn't ready for family just yet.

But Annie couldn't hide from Cham. "You're awake," he said drawing all attention back to her. She pouted for his benefit as they descended on her, the family that she and her sister Samantha created after their parents died. Kathy and Ryan couldn't help it; she was as important to them as they were to her.

"Good, sweetie. You're awake." Kathy planted a kiss on her cheek and pulled her into a hug. "I hear it's not so bad. They'll release you tomorrow." She smiled at her goddaughter. Kathy and Ryan had been her dad's best friends. Annie had known Kathy her whole life, and had anyone ever asked, Kathy's face was the only face Annie saw when she thought of "mom."

"Feeling better?" Kathy asked hopefully.

"Yeah. Tired is all," Annie said.

Ryan sat at her feet. He was the man who kept her from falling to pieces when her father died. He hid his emotions behind his smile; all she had to do was look in his eyes to know he was worried.

"Annie." Ryan squeezed her foot. "I thought this was a quick capture," his voice quivered though he joked.

"Why shouldn't I have any fun?" Annie replied.

Though she felt better, her body ached from her feet to her head, something a strong pain potion would eventually take care of. She fidgeted with the bed controls, trying to find relief as well as avoiding eye contact with her sister, who glared at her uncomfortably.

"You had to go up against a seven-foot-tall demon?" Samantha finally said.

Annie stared at her sister, frowning. "If I knew my magic wouldn't affect him, I would've waited for backup. We took him down, so he's off the street. Besides, I'm fine. You guys came and visited. Go home, eat something good. Think of me."

"We just wanted to make sure you were okay. And you're relatively okay. Though you really need to stop falling on your head." Kathy winked.

"I'll try and remember that when the next demon throws me across a room." Annie held Kathy's hand, letting her mother her.

"And just to let you know, Robin is coming home in a few days. I want you well enough to come to dinner," Kathy said. Her son was, by trade, an adventurer traveling the world in search of rare and dangerous magical artifacts. He always came home when he found something or if his mother harangued him. Annie wondered which it was this time.

"That'll be fun," Annie said. "Anyway, before you all berate me for working or to get me to take care of myself or yell at me, go home. I see it's night, and I'm fine."

"Fine, we'll go. You sleep and rest." Kathy offered another hug and kiss. "I love you, honey. Sleep well." Reluctantly, Kathy pulled away. In the time since Annie had found her father's file and read his note, she missed her parents even more and, in that moment, would have preferred Kathy to stay. She resisted the urge to beg her to spend the night in the hospital room with her.

"Make sure you don't go to work too soon. Though I know you." Ryan touched her hair and kissed her forehead. "Love you, sweetie."

"I love you," Samantha whispered. It was all she could say. Annie knew that every time she got hurt on the job, it reminded Samantha of all they had lost. Annie felt a tinge of guilt.

Annie waved and waited as they reluctantly left the room, their footsteps growing softer as they left the floor.

"They could've stayed," Cham said.

"When I'm hurt, it causes them pain and I feel guilty," she said. "Much like how I feel when you first see me here."

To avoid his gaze, she picked up her phone and checked for messages.

"Expecting a call?" Cham asked.

"Seeing that it's 8:00 PM, I expect there's no news from Graham or Perkins yet." She dropped her phone on the table, it pinged against the metal. "I'm going to Tartarus tomorrow. I want to study that demon," Annie said.

"I figured you would." He sat back in his chair as the door swung open once again as Dr. Christine entered to resume Annie's treatment.

∽

Annie finally convinced Cham to leave, albeit reluctantly.

While she felt better, the room was dark, cold, and lonely; she missed his presence, his scent, his touch. But Annie needed time alone to process the connections.

Finding her father's file, reading his notes, seeing the pictures, and once she found a tape recorder and listened to the tape, forever changed her. She couldn't un-see or un-hear what it contained. While she was glad to have found the missing folder and know what was inside, she ultimately knew that loading the information on the cassette tape to her phone would be a bad idea. It was filled with such pain, emptiness, and anger that was more than she could bear—and Annie was bearing it alone.

She snuggled under thin covers, inserted her ear buds and tapped on the recording to hear her mother's voice for the maybe the hundredth time. It didn't get easier.

"Emily. You died. I saw your body. You were dead!" Jason's voice rose with emotion.

"And now I'm not," Emily said.

"Emily, how are you here? *Why* are you here?" Jason asked, such deep sadness in his voice.

There was a moment of silence between Jason and Emily. Footsteps clicked in the distance.

"Because they… they told me they would hurt Anne Elizabeth if I didn't come. I couldn't let that happen. I went with them." Emily sighed. "Jason, there is so much even you don't know."

"Why didn't you tell me? I could have helped you."

Emily laughed coldly, robotically. "They're powerful. They had ways to make me see that I needed to leave. Even you, the great Jason Pearce, Wizard Guard, is no match for them. What could you possibly have done?"

Metal scraped against glass. Someone slurped. "You shouldn't be here," Emily said.

"I can take you back with me. Now," Jason pleaded.

"No. What's done is done. I have a life here. Family who needs me. Even if I wanted to leave with you, I couldn't. There's something I'm meant to do. A greater purpose for me. I can't leave. I don't want to."

"You left a family who loves and needs you. Don't you care about Sami and Annie?"

"If you had left well enough alone, left *me* alone, we wouldn't be here now. All you had to do was give them the stones and leave. Why must you make things more difficult than they need to be?" Glass clinked against glass.

"Emily, what did they do to you?" A chair scraped against a floor, a table rattled.

"Let go of me!" Emily's voice sounded cold, bitter, possibly angry. "Go home. Be with your children before the Fraternitatem kills you. I won't be coming with you." Another chair scraped across the floor and footsteps grew softer as Emily seemed to leave and the tape ended.

Each time Annie listened, she shuddered and grew colder. "She didn't even ask how we were," she said to herself softly. She wiped away a tear, as she had each time she'd listened. Fewer fell now than when she first listened to the tape. Replacing the sadness was a new round of anger she couldn't control.

CHAPTER 4

TWENTY FEET BELOW the human basements of Tartarus Prison were the demon pits, a noisy, dark, and smelly space created to securely house all demons captured by the Wizard Guard or the VAU. Each individual pit was a ten-foot-by-ten-foot square and ten feet deep. The stone walls and floors were covered in a slick, oily substance that kept demons from climbing out. Ever since the prison was built in 1692, no demon had ever been able to leave.

Anyone who entered the stairwell was immediately hit with humidity and an unbearable stench that saturated their clothes and hair. Only the very determined came down to the pits and stayed for any length of time. Most witches and wizards never came down at all, if they even knew it existed.

Annie grimaced as the guard from the Wizard Zoological Society steered her to her demon's pit. Noomi, a petite woman with long brown hair and light-blue eyes, flashed a smile as she led Annie across slimy, dung covered stones and rotted food. Low growls, angry grunts, and frenzied cries wafted up to them.

"Here you go, Annie. Not sure why you want to see it," Noomi said. She was dressed for the job in dark coveralls and heavy gloves. She placed her hands on her hips as she waited to escort Annie back out.

"I've never seen a demon that could regenerate. I was curious." Annie crouched low and peered at the creature as he paced wildly. He stopped suddenly, glanced at the smooth stone walls, and felt for a hand hold to pull himself free. The stones, however, were cut in such a way there were no spaces between each rock, and any cracks were self-repairing. In frustration, the demon kicked the wall and continued the dizzying pacing.

"He's been doing this all day," Noomi advised.

"Has he said anything?"

"No. He acts humanoid and animalhood at the same time. It's the damnedest thing."

Annie took a breath and shuddered. Her body still ached from tracking and capturing the creature. It had been all she could do to convince the hospital she was ready for release, but now that she was down in the pits, she wished she had stayed in the ultra-clean and quiet hospital room.

"Do you mind if I stay for a bit? I'd like to see what he does," Annie said.

"Suit yourself. I'll be in quadrant four working on another demon if you need me." Noomi walked from Annie toward the back of the large pit area; her flashlight bounced as she walked.

Annie sighed, summoned a blanket, and laid it flat on the top of the pit where she took a seat. No matter how hard she tried, she couldn't stop observing and studying the creature.

Where did you come from?

The more the demon paced the pit, the more frustrated he became. With nothing else it could do, the demon ran at the wall and gave it a heavy punch. The force was so strong the stone cracked and loose debris clinked against the floor. Seeing the foothold, the demon punched the stone several inches above the first hole.

But this was Tartarus Prison, a structure designed to hold evil wizards, vampires, and the most dangerous demons of the magical world. Within minutes of the stone breaking apart, the magic inside caused it to promptly repair itself. The demon yelped and shook out the pain in his hand.

"Hey, Annie," Spencer called out from behind her. He joined her on the floor. "How are you feeling?"

"Stiff and sore, but otherwise I'm good. No more concussion, no more cracked ribs." Even as she spoke to him, she couldn't take her eyes from the demon. "He's restless," Annie offered and placed her chin in her hands, resting her elbows on her knees.

Spencer bent at the waist and watched with curiosity. "My target is human," he said.

"Hmmm," she murmured. The demon looked at his hands and back to the wall as if planning escape.

"So, what do the human and the demon have in common? Do you think they're here together?" Spencer asked.

"Well, it appears your target knew the demon. What the hell language was he speaking anyway?" Annie asked.

"I recognized nothing he said."

"Look at what the demon is wearing? It's so..."

"It's not modern. The long tunic, loose pants, primitive shoes. Mine wore boots that were higher on his legs, not these bootie things. Actually, they're both dressed in similar clothes," Spencer said.

"Who wears that?" Annie said. She desperately tried to connect the dots and she feared there wasn't enough information to do that yet. And no matter what ideas she came up with to explain the demon and his presence here, she just couldn't place the regeneration demon in the pit. She was stumped.

"Cosplay?" Spencer asked.

Annie glared. "Next guess." He chuckled.

The demon marched along the walls of the pit, turning left at each corner and continuing down the next wall.

"Clothing notwithstanding, maybe your target was the one who conjured the demon with mullein, and it escaped and he was out searching for it," Annie suggested.

"When we meet with Gila Donaldson, we'll have to ask her if she knew him and why he'd be doing that in her house," Spencer quipped.

"Ugh. This demon's making me dizzy." Annie finally pulled away from watching the creature and turned to Spencer. "How about we pay a visit to Gila Donaldson and find out what she knows?" Annie's phone buzzed. She glanced at it. "Actually, Graham and Perkins have something for us. I hope they don't mind the stench."

"The smell's worse once you're out of the pits." Annie grimaced at her smell as Spencer held the lab door open for her. Graham Lightner, manager of the VAU, and Perkins Abernathy, the Wizard Hall lab manager, were discussing the clothing samples laid across the farthest stainless steel table in the large laboratory. "Oh, good, you're here," Perkins said and waved them to the table.

The lab had been blown to pieces three months ago when a rogue French Wizard Guard attacked Wizard Hall with an ingenious spell. Marielle Beauchamp was now serving time in a nonmagical prison in France after killing several family members for the remaining Beauchamp money and property.

Annie was surprised how much work they'd managed to do with the lab in such a short time. Rather than holding just three stainless steel tables, the room was now large enough for five gleaming tables. The shelves below each table held clear storage boxes filled with implements and tools. Cabinets and shelves covered all the walls, a new door led to the shower room. She noticed the vent to the incinerator was no longer in the middle of the floor, open and exposed. She guessed it might be hidden in the changing/shower room.

The room was clean, smelling of disinfectant and ammonia.

The wall between the lab and gym space was rebuilt, including a window that was thicker than the previous one. She glanced inside the gym. The massive space was partially finished. The floor had been installed, the walls were bare. The wall between the gym and the maintenance department had been blown out in the blast and was now rebuilt.

"It looks good," Annie said as she and Spencer joined the two managers at the table.

"Thanks, Annie. I've got to say, yet again, you bring me the most unusual things," Perkins said as he picked up a vial. "What's your impression of the demon?"

"Well, he seems half human and half demon," Annie responded.

Perkins raised his eyebrows. "Yes. He's a weird combination of the two, and there's nothing like it in the databases."

"Awesome," Annie said without cheer.

"He is a demon. We just don't know the species, location of orientation, or how he was created," Perkins added.

"But he is a hybrid? Please tell me he was created with magic, and not by intermingling of the species," she said.

Perkins chuckled. "Well, I can't say that with any confidence, but I will say it's a bit weird. There is a dark magical trace attached to the demon, but it's old. So old that we ran the trace twice. It's one hundred years old," Perkins said.

"The demon's one hundred years old?" Spencer asked.

Perkins shook his head. "I thought that, too. So I sent Minka and Roscoe back to the demon to examine him best they could. You know freezing him, checking his teeth for wear, taking X-rays. If we look at the demon as if he's a human, the demon would be about fifteen years old. But then, he's a demon. His teeth could wear quicker than a human, or not as much. So we looked at his pelvic bones and how they were formed. Also about fifteen years old. Because he's not magical, we can't measure his trace, but honestly, I think the demon is younger than one hundred years old."

"That doesn't make sense," Annie said.

"The body is young; the magic is old. So no, it doesn't make sense," Perkins replied.

"Could it be that the species of demon was created a hundred years ago, and they have been reproducing," Spencer suggested.

"That's my best guess. I'd have to do more tests if you need an exact age of the demon. But I think if the species was originally created, the demons are now reproducing on their own," Perkins explained.

Annie frowned. "We don't need an exact age. I'm more concerned about where he came from. He had to be conjured from somewhere. And I've never seen a demon like this."

Graham stepped in. "Well, the VAU did a little sweep of the house after you left. Good catch on the mullein. It was recently used, probably to conjure the demon. We haven't determined from where. However, that brings us back to Perkins and the clothing."

She raised her eyebrows in anticipation.

Perkins held up one of the many fabric swatches they pulled from the demon. The first came from his tunic. What had started as a white garment was now dirty gray and covered with black smudges and dark brown spots of dried blood. "This is from his shirt. We dated this to the late ninth century."

"Seriously?" Spencer asked.

Annie and Spencer each donned latex gloves and held the fabric samples. "Late ninth century? And the rest of the items?" Annie asked as she picked up a sample of the leather belt and a sample of the pants.

"All the same," Perkins said.

"So the demon was probably summoned from the ninth century? I wasn't expecting that," Annie said. She rubbed the fabric between her gloved fingers before placing them back on the table.

"Allen and Skye captured the magic. They're trying to reverse the spell to determine the date and time the demon came from. The next bit of help should get us closer." He offered a sly smile.

Annie and Spencer glanced at each other. "What about your target? He was dressed the same, wasn't he?"

"Yeah, he was," Spencer said.

"You can't summon a human," Graham said.

"Is it a coincidence that he was there at the same time?" Perkins asked.

Spencer laughed. "He spoke a language we didn't recognize, and he and the demon at least seemed aware of each other."

"Our best bet is to trace the conjuring energy to find out where he came from. In terms of your target, Spencer, we just need to bring him in. He could clear all of this up as well," Graham reiterated.

"Another thought, I can pull a tooth. There's way to determine where a person or creature grew up by how their adult teeth were formed. I can try that with the demon," Perkins offered.

"Let's hold off on pulling the tooth for now. We can make the leap and assume if the clothes are from the late ninth century, the demon probably is too. At least that will give me a time frame for research into the demon," Annie advised.

"Just remember, if he came from the ninth century, the magic inside him is still a hundred years old. You might want to start in the eighth century and work to the end of the ninth," Perkins suggested.

"Next question then, why summon a ninth-century demon here?" Graham asked.

"And if the man is here for the demon, where did *he* come from?" Spencer added.

"Those are definitely the questions to ask," Annie said as she thought of her dad's letter, the prophecy, and Sturtagaard's cryptic message.

⁓

After a quick shower, Annie and Spencer grabbed their lunches and found an empty table in the Wizard Hall courtyard. The summer day was warm but not too hot, and the bright sun invited several wizards to have an outdoor picnic on what felt like a perfect summer day.

The southwest corner of the courtyard held the elementary school, preschools, and camps. The enclosed playground was filled with young children, climbing on the equipment, laughing, shouting and running around, taking full advantage of their summer break. Annie wondered if Cham's nephews, his brother Jimmy's sons, were out for their lunch break.

Cham and Gibbs joined them, pulling her away from reflecting on the kids. "So what's new?" Cham kissed Annie's cheek and sat beside her. He unwrapped his meatball sandwich and took a large bite.

Annie explained the DNA test, clothing samples, and the mullein trace.

"Should we state the obvious?" Cham asked when he swallowed.

Annie played with her turkey sandwich. "That the demon is wearing clothing dated to the ninth century and was most likely conjured from the past?"

They were quiet for the moment as they continued to eat their lunches.

"You do realize that Sturtagaard was a Viking in northern England, specifically Northumbria, in the ninth century," Gibbs said. He stabbed his steak with his fork and cut off a piece.

"Records are inconsistent. Some magical historians say he was turned somewhere in between 865 and 875 CE, other historians think he was turned in 950 CE. That's generations apart," Annie said.

"You should ask him," Gibbs grumbled.

Annie frowned and turned to Spencer. "I didn't get a great look at your target, but what did he look like to you?" Annie asked Spencer.

"You're going to make me say it aren't you?" Spencer asked. She raised her eyebrows. "He looks like a Viking."

"So you're suggesting time travel?" Cham asked.

Spencer chuckled. "No. I'm not suggesting anything." He took another bite of his salad.

"Ugh." Annie summoned the talisman she found in the house. "With everything else, I nearly forgot. The demon was looking for this." She lay it on the table.

The three wizard guards stared at the talisman. "It's weird. The Vikings started invading England in 793," Annie began. "The coven came here at the end of the ninth century or early tenth century. The dates aren't completely accurate."

Spencer picked up the talisman. "These and mullein are used to conjure demons. So again I ask, why conjure a ninth century demon?"

Annie took a bite of her sandwich and chewed slowly.

"Think back to Jason's letter. He mentioned a prophecy. Sturtagaard is at the house when you get there. Let's say he knows what's going on, that you need to find the demon. Conjuring a demon and leaving it to terrorize a neighborhood would bring out the Wizard Guard," Gibbs said.

"It's all too... perfectly planned and executed," Annie said.

"Why? Because he got you to the house when he wanted you to be there? It did take a week for us to be connected with the demon." Spencer said.

"Okay. So not perfectly executed." Annie took a swig of water from her bottle.

"I can't see Sturtagaard conjuring a demon. Too much work, too little reward. I wonder what his role is?" Cham frowned.

"Annie. How long have you had that note?" Spencer asked.

She glanced at Cham and quickly at Gibbs. "I've had it for three months."

"Have you tried to find the prophecy your dad mentioned?" Spencer asked.

Annie had spent the last three months not sleeping well as she waited for Bucky to find her mother. It had seemed more pressing than finding a prophecy. But now she realized Spencer was right. "Honestly, there were some other things in my dad's missing file I wanted to investigate first. I hadn't thought to search for the prophecy," Annie explained.

"So what should we tackle first, the prophecy, Sturtagaard, or Gila Donaldson?" Spencer asked, rolling his sandwich wrapping in a ball and stuffing it in his bag.

"Sturtagaard won't give us an honest answer. Let's find out what Mrs. Donaldson knows. Maybe she can clear it up and we can send the demon back to where it came. If we need to, I can have Mrs. Cuttlebrink look for the prophecy," Annie said.

"And the other one?" Spencer asked.

"Gibbs and I will go and find a tall man dressed in ninth-century clothing. What could go wrong?" Cham teased.

As the Wizard Guard department manager, it wouldn't be odd for Milo Rawley to come to Tartarus Prison to interview suspects or to conduct other Wizard Guard business. He mostly chose not to come unless absolutely necessary. Today wasn't, but he couldn't stay away from a demon far too interesting to not observe for himself. He sat on the edge of the pit as the creature paced, scratched feverishly at the stone wall, and grimaced at the blood dripping from his raw fingertips. Milo wanted to cast the spell to blow him up, but refrained.

When the demon wailed a slow, anxious cry, Milo inched closer for a better look.

Very strange.

The demon paced, glanced around the empty pit, and appeared to be thinking of something.

Milo moved his palms, thinking about blowing the demon up, but for a second time, he rested his hands on his knees.

"So, have you seen him regenerate yet?"

Milo smiled. Ryan Connelly, the Grand Marksman of the Wizard Council for America, was standing behind him and looking into the pit.

"I haven't seen you at Tartarus in a while. What brings you here?" Milo asked.

Gracefully, Ryan lowered himself to the edge of the pit and crossed his long legs, taking a look at the regenerating demon. Ryan rarely ventured to Tartarus Prison unless it was of great importance. This wouldn't normally be considered important.

"Well, I must admit, I'm very curious about this demon." Ryan said, sounding nearly giddy. As a former wizard guard, he rarely came across something he hadn't seen before. "And that is the creature Annie went up against. I'm surprised she wasn't more injured."

"She can fight," Milo said. He was reflective, silent, his usual gruffness not present.

"What are you thinking?" Ryan asked. It was unlike Milo not to share.

"They think the demon is from the ninth century," Milo said.

Ryan raised his eyebrows. "Have they caught the other one yet?

"Cham and Gibbs are going out later today." Milo sighed.

The demon, tired from pacing, from the chase yesterday, and from the present day demon pit, sat in the center and stared at the blood-stained wall.

"What's he doing?" Ryan asked.

"Thinking," Milo said sardonically. "You ready to see this?" Ryan offered a nod.

As if they were kids in a toy store, the two men excitedly stood. Milo grinned as he jinxed the demon. At impact, the creature blew apart. His innards flew across the large pit; bits and pieces of the demon covered the walls and the floor, some landing beside Milo's foot. Yet, as quickly as the creature blew up, body parts—muscles, sinew, fluids—inched together, reforming the large creature. Arms and legs sprung out of the torso, and hair grew from the new head. The demon shrieked; his voice reverberated across the basement.

Other demons throughout the prison reacted with grunts, cries, and barks.

"That was cool," Ryan said. "Buy you a beer?"

CHAPTER 5

ANNIE AND SPENCER landed in the side yard of the house belonging to Gila Donaldson, a corner lot along Sheridan Road in Evanston. At this time of day, most residents were still at work, though the well-traveled street was quite busy.

They separated as Annie strolled to the empty backyard where the pool water glistened and the cushions on the chairs baked in the sun. Annie glanced at the three-story home towering above her before strolling to the front yard, stopping at a side window. The lights were off, and the expensive television above the fireplace was black. She gazed across the yard, along the sidewalk, and to the house next door. She met Spencer at the front door.

"She could be at work," Annie suggested. She and Spencer walked up slate-covered steps and stood before the intricate, leaded glass window on the front door. She pressed the doorbell.

"Nice house," Spencer commented.

"It pays to be a descendant of the original Wizard Council, I guess," Annie said.

They waited the acceptable amount of time before Spencer pressed the bell again. Annie stepped off the porch and peered at the windows. The curtains in the attic window fluttered.

"Someone's home." Annie pointed up. "I saw movement in the attic window."

They waited for a moment longer. Just as Spencer was about to push the bell for a third time, the door squeaked open.

Seventy-two-year-old Gila Donaldson was slim with nicely coiffed silvery blonde hair. Her skirt and blouse were contrasting shades of beige. She looked put together though perhaps overdressed for the hot summer day.

"Hello, Mrs. Donaldson, I'm Annie Pearce and this is Spencer Ray. We're wizard guards." Both held their badges for her to see.

The descendant of the original coven mumbled to herself incomprehensibly, though Annie thought she heard the name Anaise.

"So, how can I help the Wizard Guard?" Gila asked cautiously.

"We have some questions about the house you own on Freeny Avenue in Evanston. Can we come in?" Spencer asked. Gila Donaldson tightly held the handle of the front door, Annie glanced uneasily at Spencer.

"I can't figure what the Wizard Guard is doing with that knowledge. It's really none of your business," Gila said curtly.

"Actually, ma'am, may we come in? There's been some trouble at the house we need to discuss," Annie said.

With her hands tightly gripping the door handle, Gila Donaldson motioned them inside, closed the door quickly, and walked them to the front room. "Please sit. Can I offer you some water or some tea? Coffee?" she asked.

"No, ma'am. Just a few minutes of your time," Spencer said.

Reluctantly, Gila Donaldson sat across from Spencer and Annie and placed her hands in her lap, wringing them. "How can I help you?" she finally asked.

"Ma'am, I chased a demon to that house yesterday morning. He stormed inside as if he knew the house, and he completely destroyed the front bedroom looking for this." Annie held up the talisman, observing Gila carefully as she did. Gila's eyes widened, but she said nothing.

"Do you know what this is for?" Annie asked.

Gila shifted in her seat and pulled a loose strand of hair from her face, tucking it behind her neatly styled short bob. "It's a talisman," she mumbled.

"We found mullein trace and magical summoning spells in the house. Did you or someone you know summon a ninth-century demon?" Annie asked.

"That's private property. You had no permission to enter the premises. I can report you," Gila said indignantly.

Annie and Spencer exchanged glances. "Mrs. Donaldson. We realize that we didn't have permission to enter, but a demon was running loose in the neighborhood, and we were not aware that you owned what looked to be an abandoned home. We as wizard guards are within our rights to investigate a magical creature in a nonmagical neighborhood. We captured the creature and secured him at Tartarus," Spencer told her.

Gila moved her hands to the armrests of her chair. Her hands clutched them so tightly that her knuckles turned white.

"Fine. I'll give you that, but I do not give you permission to enter the property again," Gila said, though her voice was soft and weak. Even she realized that dark magic had occurred there and that the wizard guards indeed had the right to investigate. She sighed deeply.

"I know you're aware that's not true. The house is a crime scene. We can go back to investigate." Spencer watched her reactions closely. Reluctantly, her muscles slackened and she let go of the chair.

"Thank you for informing me about the demon. Is there anything else?"

"We think this demon has something to do with a prophecy that involves Annie, and we would like your help to find out what that is. We think she might be in danger," Spencer said clearly and with authority as he stared at Gila.

She drummed her fingers against her silk skirt. "I'm sorry if this demon caused you problems. I hope it hasn't hurt anyone." She sighed again as if resigned to continue, then looked at Annie. "There are certain things that are going to happen to you. I wish I could say more. I really do, but Annie Pearce, this is your destiny. I am only one small part of this and I did what I was required to do. I can't tell you anymore. It is up to you to figure it out."

Annie stared at the talisman and then back to Gila Donaldson. "So you were required to summon a demon and a man from the ninth century for what purpose?"

Gila shook her head, stood and opened an antique desk in the corner of the long front room. She took out a yellowed, brittle scroll sealed with the wax seal of the Wizard Council. She handed it to Annie. "I was told very little over the years except that I was to summon a demon. I don't know what man you are referring to, but you can't summon a living human. Once you became engaged in the events, I was to give this to you," Gila said and handed the scroll to Annie.

The seal was thick and dry, nearly brittle, but it looked as though it hadn't been touched in years.

Perhaps even one thousand years?

"Is this the prophecy?" Annie asked. Gila shook her head.

"I don't know what that is. All I know is what I've told you. I have nothing else. And thank you for alerting me the house was destroyed. I'll have someone on that soon. I think you need to leave now."

Gila rushed them from her house without saying goodbye.

Spencer glanced at the front door. "Maybe Emerson will be a little more forthcoming. Shall we find out?"

✥

Gila Donaldson watched Annie and Spencer leave her property from behind the attic curtains. It pained her to lie so blatantly, but then, they all their roles and that was hers. She stood over her alter where her familial *Book of Shadows* lay opened to the pages that guided her every action where Anaise concerned.

> *My dearest Gila,* the letter began.
>
> *There will come a time when you will need to set the plan in motion. You, Gila dear, will meet Anaise the Brave and your single goal will be to get her back to us, whatever the cost.*
>
> *All that you need has been recorded here in this Book of Shadows. We all have our roles, yours starts here and will end with Anaise coming to us and returning home…*

Gila re-read the plan as it was laid out centuries ago. Today, she was to give these pages to Annie. But she didn't.

Because her power will be too strong.

Annie was special, the power that would come to her would endanger them all. The conflict had roiled in Gila's stomach when she was given her destiny. For what she was about to do, she could only hope the ancient ones would forgive her for her transgressions.

✥

Before hounding Emerson Donaldson, Annie and Spencer met in the conference room on the fifth floor of Wizard Hall. She stared out the large window and down on the roaring traffic.

"What are you waiting for?" Spencer asked patiently.

"I wanna know, but I don't." Annie stared at the unbroken seal of the scroll and snapped it easily. She sighed and unrolled the scroll.

> *Anaise,*
>
> *We called to the ancient ones for guidance. They sent us your vision in the fire and exclaimed that it will be you who will save us from these wretched beasts that have overrun our home. Blessed be. This is to reassure you of the ancient ones' love and the gift to you for the role you play in this war. The great coven of Northumbria will forever be in your servitude.*
>
> *Wizard Council January, 880*

"Um… huh?" Annie passed the scroll to Spencer.

He read quickly and said, "What the hell are you supposed to do with this?"

"Go to the past and kill the demons, apparently. I didn't know time travel was even possible!" Annie said, her voice several octaves higher than normal.

"Do you see the date?" Spencer asked.

"Late ninth century," Annie said.

Spencer dialed his phone and asked Emerson to join them in the conference room. The young wizard appeared within minutes and nervously took a seat beside Spencer.

"What's up?" she asked casually, though Annie thought Emerson was well aware of what was coming. She handed her the scroll. As Emerson read the ancient words, she fiddled with her hands.

"Your grandmother gave it to me." Annie dropped the case file in front of Emerson.

Knowing she couldn't lie her way out of the situation, Emerson opened the file. Pictures of a house, a scorch mark in the dirty carpet, and of the demon, along with samples of the clothing. She read the report lab results.

"The demon's from the ninth century?" she asked.

"Yes. We found him in that house that, surprisingly, belongs to a Gila Donaldson," Annie said. "Keep reading the file."

Emerson continued to peruse the notes, finding the computer search results and a copy of the mortgage signed by Gila Donaldson.

"It could be another Gila Donaldson," Emerson said. But after reading the date and place of birth and the primary mailing address, she clearly knew it was her grandmother. "Why would my grandmother buy this crappy house?" Emerson closed the folder and handed it to Annie.

"She is responsible for some part of a larger plan. While she didn't completely verify it was her, someone conjured a demon in the living room of that house. We want to know why, but she wouldn't elaborate. Would you be able to?" Annie shoved the folder in her field pack.

"I only know that something is coming, but I'm not privy to what that is," she said.

Annie pursed her lips. "So they've been passing information from generation to generation but not to you?"

Emerson blanched. Annie thought she might have struck a nerve. "It's coven business, and I'm not part of that," Emerson said.

"So what's your role in this? Did they force you into the Wizard Guard to spy on us? Make sure we're doing our part?" Annie raised her voice but backed down when Emerson hunched over. "I'm sorry. That was uncalled for," Annie murmured.

"I wish I could help you, but I had no role in this. I wanted to be a wizard guard because I want to help people. I just couldn't hack it. Now I'm just a researcher." Emerson sighed.

"If it helps, you're the best researcher we have," Annie said.

"It doesn't, but thanks for the vote of confidence," Emerson said.

"I'm sorry if you're unhappy, Emerson, but we need to keep moving on this. If you can find out anything, please pass it along. What we think we know makes no sense," Spencer said.

CHAPTER 6

WHEN THEY BECAME a couple, Annie and Cham could no longer work together as wizard guard partners. The ripple effect meant there was a partner switch: Annie with Spencer and Cham with Gibbs. They were productive partnerships until Cham was promoted to Wizard Guard Assistant Manager, leaving him to split his time between administrative duties and field work. This left Gibbs time to work alone, which is what he preferred. On occasion, however, Cham and Gibbs returned to their partnership as though there had never been a break.

"We'll spiral from the outside and meet at the house," Gibbs said.

Heading in opposite directions, they wound their way through the residential neighborhoods by walking the outer streets and methodically turning inwards, searching all alleys, peering inside open garages, and scanning back yards, front yards, and the spaces between the houses.

Cham moved through the streets quickly. There was no sign of the mysterious man: no destroyed foliage or houses, no garbage strewn about, no camping gear or dead animals. Reaching Keeney Street, Cham turned left toward the house at the end of the block.

Hypervigilant, he checked carefully from one side of the street to the other. He sensed anxious neighbors when he glimpsed a flash of curtains being pulled together and the resident who jumped in his car and peeled out.

Knowing he was just an unassuming wizard guard in his T-shirt, jeans, and gym shoes, Cham chuckled, glanced down the street, and was surprised by the footsteps clacking against the sidewalk behind him.

"Excuse me," a man said. His short legs and short stride made him look as though he were hopping to meet Cham.

Cham smiled patiently.

"Excuse me, are you in charge here?" the man asked.

Cham nodded and pulled out his identification, an expertly crafted Cook County sheriff's ID that only the Wizard Guard could manage.

Uninterested in whether Cham was who he claimed to be or was even with the police department, the man nodded and said, "It's about time. We've been trying to get the police to listen. They come and take notes but don't search. First, it was that vagrant eating out of everyone's garbage cans, and then that drunk staggering through the streets at all hours of the day."

"The drunk?" Cham began to take notes in his mini notepad.

"You know, the one dressed as a Viking. To be honest with you, the costume isn't very good. I saw him the other day when he tried to steal food from the Dinkers' garage. He wasn't even wearing the hat with the horns. Did ya find him yet?" the man asked.

Cham noticed a tiny piece of salad lodged between the man's teeth and averted his gaze. "That's actually why I'm here now. He appears to have moved on, but we're sweeping through the area just in case. When was the last time anyone saw him, Mr...?" Cham held his pencil expectantly.

"I'm Peter Pinkerton. Your police friends stopped here last night. Walked up and down the street and left. The guy went that way. Everyone's afraid to walk in the trees." Peter Pinkerton tried to peek at Cham's notes in his notebook.

Cham glanced in the direction of the forest, where a rough, narrow path had been chopped through the branches.

I wonder if he's back there.

"Have you met the owner of this house?" he asked, pointing to the abandoned building.

"Oh, yeah. A nice old lady bought it a while back, two, maybe three months ago. I think she said her name was Gilda. No, that's not it. It was a strange name I'd never heard of. Something like Gerta or Githa. Nice lady, pretty blue eyes. Saw her just that once, never seen her since. Doesn't look like she's been back," he said, then added, "The vagrant went in there, too. Saw him go in there a few times." The man looked at the building. "Looks like he ripped the door off. Someone needs to tell that woman."

Cham pulled out a business card and handed it to him. "We have contacted the owner, so she's aware. If you ever see the man in the Viking costume again, please call me directly."

Peter Pinkerton tucked the business card in his shirt pocket. "What about that vagrant? Do you know where he is?"

"The vagrant is safe in Tar—um, jail right now. We'll be looking for a better place for him to live as soon as we can. Thanks for your time, but I should go." Cham nodded once and turned to leave.

"You're not so scary," Peter Pinkerton yelled out.

Cham turned. "Excuse me?"

Peter fidgeted and glanced at his hands.

"It's just, it's… I mean, you're not like the other police. Some think you're with a secret police. They're afraid of you." The man's eyes darted across the street.

"Sorry. I didn't mean to scare anyone. I promise, I'm just the regular police," Cham smiled. "Thanks again."

⇜

Gibbs glanced down the alley lined with garages. Some were open, but most were closed. He could hear metal clanking as though someone were fixing something, *or maybe…*

He headed toward the noise, glanced in the first open garage, and was met with a space packed full of broken lawn chairs, bicycles, and one jeep that was so dirty, someone had written "Wash me" on the window. Grimacing, he stepped out and continued to the end of the alley.

He checked the side yards, bushes, and behind sheds, methodically searching each street and alley until he, too, reached Keeney Street and turned right.

Thump, thump, thump.

Heavy footsteps echoed behind him. They lacked the clickety clack of hard soles against cement, sounding more like a hit to a punching bag. He turned just as a tall yet stocky man ran across the residential street.

Gibbs stared with interest at the man who could very well have come from the ninth century. Spencer had been adamant about this, and the collected evidence suggested the same. Gibbs took in his appearance. A thin, lightweight shirt, possibly cotton or linen, hung low on his body and was tied at the waist with a thin strip of fabric. The man also wore high leather boots and a thick fabric tied around his neck that fell askew and bounced with each step. As the man ran, his belt slipped from his waist.

It's a good costume if that's all it is.

But Gibbs didn't believe in coincidences. If the demon's clothes were dated to the ninth century and this man dressed the same, he probably came from that time too.

How did he get here?

Fearing exposure, Gibbs ran after the man, whose much larger stride gave him a huge advantage. Pulling away from Gibbs, the man crossed the street, jumped the curb and clipped a woman walking her dog. She fell hands first into the grass and the dog barked wildly, attempting to frighten the man who was now half a block from the collision.

"Jackass!" she shouted; Gibbs finally caught up, reached out, and yanked her up.

"Ma'am," he said in acknowledgment and continued to run after his target.

After several blocks, Gibbs's lungs burned and his heart pounded. The man turned onto Keeney Street toward Gila Donaldson's abandoned house. The Viking ran at Cham and, to avoid a collision, Cham pulled Peter Pinkerton from Viking's path. The force landed Peter Pinkerton in the grass. Gibbs ran past.

"Hey, watch it!" Peter shouted feebly.

"Sorry. Thanks again for your help!" Cham shouted, following Gibbs and the mysterious man into the trees.

Once tucked safely inside the thick foliage, away from prying eyes, Cham teleported himself a few yards ahead of the man. He was shocked by the costume the man wore.

Before he could fully process what he was seeing, Cham slammed a heavy jinx into the stranger. Rather than sending the man flying through the air, the spell bounced off of his shoulder. Without missing a step, he ran at Cham, knocking him off his feet. When Cham opened his eyes, he was several yards from where he started, and the agile man was headed deeper into the trees.

"What the hell?" Cham yelled.

Gibbs ran past Cham and shot a jinx. It, too, bounced off the scarf and flew back at him. Gibbs slid into a muddy spot on the trail and landed on his back. "Shit!" he yelled as he stared at the canopy of trees above him.

Detangling himself from the undergrowth, Cham watched the trees as they sputtered in the man's wake. After estimating the speed, he teleported. The force of landing on the Viking's back knocked them forward. Quickly, Cham cast the freeze spell, it only served to irritate the man. The stranger rolled over, picked Cham up by the collar, and tossed him against a tree.

Gibbs slid to a stop after teleporting near Cham and aimed a powerful spell at a hefty branch hanging above. It creaked and groaned before crashing to the ground. The Viking ran from the falling branch, tripped in the tangle of roots, and fell. Gibbs and Cham raced to the man.

The Viking proved to be difficult to roll on his back. Gibbs grunted until he had him pinned to the ground and knelt beside him. "So, what do you think?"

"Shaggy, unkempt beard, shaved head covered in tattoos that look like ancient runes. And look at that scar from his chin to his temple. That was some injury," Cham commented. "The original Wizard Council used ancient Viking symbols. They're all over Wizard Hall," he added as Gibbs conjured magical rope.

"You think he's a real Viking?" Gibbs asked as he tried to tie a magical rope around the man's wrists. The rope disappeared when it touched the man's skin. Gibbs and Cham exchanged concerned glances.

"He's immune to magic?" Cham asked.

"Explains a lot." Gibbs patted the man down, searching for the amulet or talisman that was blocking their magic.

The man's eyes darted between Cham and Gibbs, finally landing on Cham.

"Do you have a name?" Cham asked.

If he understood the question, he refused to answer. He averted his gaze and watched clouds float across the sky.

"It'll be better for you if you tell us your name, man," Cham advised. The man closed his eyes.

"Suit yourself. Anything on him?" Cham asked. He observed the man carefully, surprised how calm he was under the circumstances.

"Nothing obvious. Potion maybe?" Gibbs held his palm up and summoned a crystal and maneuvered it across the man's chest.

Curious, the man sat up and surveyed Gibbs.

"Got something to say?" Gibbs asked.

The man pushed his arms out, punching Cham and Gibbs each in the chest. The force of the blow knocked the wind from their lungs, and both fell to the ground.

They lay on the ground, struggling for breath; branches rustled as the man ran off into the distance. "You okay, Gibbs?" Cham asked as he groaned and gingerly pulled himself up. He glanced into the trees; the man was long gone.

"Great," Gibbs grumbled as he lay in the twigs and watched the sky. Hot, muggy air hung around them uncomfortably. The forest was quiet as animals hid in the shade.

"That… hurt," Cham said through shortened breaths. His chest felt heavy. He got up and bent over Gibbs. "You okay?" he asked again.

Gibbs grimaced as he struggled to breathe. Cham offered a hand and pulled Gibbs to a seated position in the brush. "He's a lot stronger than I expected."

Cham sat beside Gibbs. "That wasn't a costume."

"No, it wasn't. He's definitely not from around here."

Cham rubbed his chest, trying to inhale evenly. "Think we're looking at a real Viking?"

"The costume's good if he's not," Gibbs said.

"It's a lot of work to bring someone across time. Even for a prophecy," Cham said. He glanced at the narrow path through the trees. The man had either stopped or was far enough away that the branches had stopped rustling.

"Better let Annie know," Gibbs said as he eased to his feet. They teleported without following their target.

⚜

The rhythmic chopping, slicing, and layering of the vegetables in the salad bowl calmed Annie, giving her something else to think about besides the prophecy, the Viking, and the demon.

Between chops, she watched her best friends, Dave Smith and Janie Parker, engrossed in conversation, laughing periodically, and just living normally.

It's been too long.

"The baby yeti was this big." Dave held his hand four feet above the ground as he regaled them with stories of his recent trip to the yeti colony in the Rocky Mountains. After three months observing and researching the colony for the Wizard Zoological Society, he had many stories about the peaceful creatures.

Annie finished the salad and floated the bowl to the table, which was already set with the rest of their dinner.

"So, tell us about your creature." Dave looked at her expectantly as he took the bowl and helped himself to a heaping pile of salad.

"Well, the demon is definitely unusual," Annie admitted.

"How so?" He stabbed a steak and set it on his plate.

"He grunts and growls like a low-level demon and is otherwise nonverbal. He stinks like the demons that live in the wilderness but looks human and wears clothing." Annie scooped a spoonful of rice onto her plate, but realized, she wasn't hungry.

"So, it's what – a hybrid?" Dave asked.

"Half human, half demon?" Janie frowned. "Eww, gross."

Annie chuckled. "It's not quite that. The samples do show human and demon DNA. I found pretty strong dark magic in the house where I found him. We're not sure what that means. When I was in the hospital, Spencer did a little digging in the library. So far he hasn't found anything about demons that can regenerate, and the books I have here don't produce any info," she said.

"Sorry I'm late," Cham said from the hallway. He offered a wan smile as he gingerly walked in.

She smiled. "I was wondering where you were."

Cham grimaced when he sat.

"What's the matter?" Annie asked.

"I'm fine. Just a bit of a struggle with our man," Cham said and filled his plate with food.

"Same place as Annie's?" Dave asked. He was nearly finished eating and reached for another roll.

"My target was in the same neighborhood. It's definitely not a coincidence they were both there."

"Anything good on this one?" Annie asked.

Cham cut off a piece of meat and chewed slowly. "We got a good look at him. He's dressed in clothing that is reminiscent of the Vikings. Tunic, natural fibers, leather shoes."

"So, what is yours? Human or demon?" she asked.

Cham frowned.

"What?" she inquired.

Cham took a breath and winced. "He escaped." He shifted in his chair.

"So what's really wrong with you?" Annie asked.

"He's strong. He's big and he punched his way to escape. And he did this." Cham raised his shirt. Already dark purple, the bruise was five inches in diameter at the center of his chest.

Janie squeaked in surprise.

"Whoa," Dave said.

"Damn." Annie walked to his chair and touched the spot, poking at the injury. He grimaced.

"Any broken bones?" Cham inquired.

"I don't think so. I can heal the bones; the bruise won't heal so quickly." She summoned her water. The liquid rose from her glass and hung above her palm. She warmed it and placed it over his chest. He closed his eyes.

"Just curious, but why couldn't you use magic to capture this man?" Dave asked.

Annie floated the water to the sink and let it splash. She began touching the bruise, feeling his ribs. "Anything?" she asked.

"Just a little tight." He lowered his shirt and turned to Dave. "He was immune to all our spells. We did a thorough search, but didn't find anything that could resist the magic."

"It would take incredibly strong magic to come from the ninth century and to resist a witch's magic. Why didn't he cast a spell on you?" Janie asked. She began stacking the dirty dishes in a pile.

"He had plenty of opportunity to cast one. I don't think he's magical," Cham said thoughtfully and pushed his unfinished dinner aside.

"So a man and a demon seemingly from the past arrive in the same location. What are they doing here? Scouting to attack?" Dave half teased.

"That's not funny," Annie said. She thought of the prophecy and Sturtagaard's message.

What do they have to do with each other?

Her stomach roiled as she debated telling them about her dad's letter and the prophecy. But she couldn't, not until she figured out how to tell her sister. She sighed heavily. "Once we find Cham's target, we should have a better idea of what they're doing here." She let her fork settle against her plate.

"Better finish dinner before we're attacked," Dave joked.

CHAPTER 7

THOUGH SHE WAS ordered to take the week off, Annie had spent the previous morning at Tartarus Prison and now was at Wizard Hall. Milo stopped at her cubicle door. "I told you to stay home," he grumbled as she sorted through the mail and folders in her inbox.

"Just catching up. I'll leave soon," Annie said.

"Humph," Milo mumbled and continued to his cubicle several away.

She placed work-related folders in one pile after she made notes on each, placing a priority number on those she needed to work on immediately and those she could wait on.

The rest of the pile was miscellaneous items, memos, and brochures that were all unnecessary; she tossed those into the garbage can. She then opened and assessed the remaining envelopes. The outside of the final envelope contained only her name in shaky handwriting.

Annie opened the envelope and peered inside. Nestled in the bottom of the envelope was a plastic bag. She pulled it out and stared at the blood-covered atomie bean inside. She couldn't know for sure, but Annie thought it might be the bean they had placed in Sturtagaard's shoulder a year ago.

Quickly, she grabbed a map and the atomie bean they used to search for Sturtagaard over the last year. She scried for him and, as she expected, the crystal lit up over Wizard Hall. Annie sighed. In that moment, she realized the only creature who knew anything about what happened in the past was gone.

٭

The Snake Head Letters was open twenty-four hours a day, but visits between 10:00 p.m. and 8:00 a.m. required an appointment. As it was 7:30 a.m. and Annie didn't have an appointment, she knocked on the locked door and hoped Archibald Mortimer would open up.

A dim light at the back of the store switched on, casting shadows across the rotted floors. Archibald Mortimer shuffled down the main path to the entrance. He glared at her briefly with cloudy, gray eyes, and hesitated before deciding to let her in.

Without greeting Annie, he turned and walked to the back of the store. The door rattled when she closed it. She followed him to his office.

The destruction of the Black Market had been a boon to Mortimer. He was the only magical store with contacts in the black magical world that could locate whatever a wizard might need. While he should have been busier than ever before, his store looked much the same: still jam-packed with books and artifacts that spilled into the aisles and weighed down the many wooden shelves; the same rotted floorboards; the same dirt and grime covered the walls as it had for decades. Annie frowned as she watched him sit himself in an armchair in the corner of the store.

Graciously, he picked up a plate of scones and offered it to her; she shook her head. He took a sip of his tea.

"Whaddaya want," he grumbled as he put his mug back on a thin table that creaked with the extra weight.

"How are you feeling?" she asked expectantly. Though it wasn't her fault he was attacked by Gladden Worchester, a part of her felt guilty because the man had been looking for her.

Mortimer looked at her, his thick gray-and-black eyebrows turned downwards. He waved her off. "Whaddaya want?" he asked again.

"Well, you look just as shitty as always. I hope you're feeling better at least." Annie leaned against the reception desk and observed him carefully. "I have a question I thought you might have an answer for."

Mortimer looked at her patiently.

She continued. "I'm assuming, as you hear everything, you know about the demon and the Viking from the ninth century."

He smiled.

"Having said that, are you aware of a prophecy about me?"

He shook his head with a confused expression on his face. "I am not aware of any," he said.

Annie summoned her dad's letter and handed it to him.

He squinted as he read the letter. Without reaction, he returned it to her. "What's it got to do with me?" he murmured.

"Sturtagaard's gone. He knows something about the Viking and the demon because he's from the same century as they are." Annie left the desk and walked toward the bookshelf, absently staring at the old bindings without really processing the titles. "He told me I had a role to play in this. Whatever 'this' is."

She glanced at him, but couldn't read Mortimer's expression as he shifted uncomfortably in his chair. He picked up his tea and took a long sip before answering. "I'm not familiar with the prophecy. Yours or anything having to do with the Viking and demon. I will... I will see what I can see," he said cautiously.

Annie's fingers trailed against the rough spines of the books as she walked back to the desk. She lingered there, surprised that he might bring it up to his counterparts.

It was his turn to observe her. "Got somethin' to say, girl?" he asked.

"Anyone order mullein from you recently?"

He smiled and shook his head. "You can get that anywhere."

While she knew that to be true, she had hoped it would lead her to Gila Donaldson. "You're not going to share?"

"My clients rely on me keeping their privacy. However, I can tell you that I didn't sell the mullein that conjured your demon," he said. He crossed his legs and sunk back into his chair.

"I found the mullein in a house belonging to Gila Donaldson, a descendant..."

Mortimer held up his hand to stop her.

"Everyone knows who the Donaldsons are. You have your answer, then," he said.

Annie was disappointed with his cryptic answers and the fact that everything was pointing to Gila Donaldson. She drummed her hands against the counter.

"And?" Mortimer asked patiently.

If she'd had any welcome in the store, Annie had overstayed it. At this point, she wasn't sure what she was planning to accomplish by continuing in Mortimer's presence, and yet she couldn't leave. "My mom was alive eight years ago," Annie blurted out.

His face remained stony. He pulled himself out of the chair and stood behind the desk. "The Fraternitatem?" he asked.

"Good guess."

"Not a guess. Jason was investigating them when he died, yes?" Mortimer asked.

Annie nodded.

"Could never figure why they killed 'im for them stones. He musta found her there," he said thoughtfully.

"You read my dad's letter. I'm supposed to do something and receive powers for it. He warned me that the Fraternitatem will come after me for those powers," she said.

Archibald Mortimer grumbled as he pulled himself up and shuffled to his back office. Annie followed and watched him as he stuck his index finger into the lock of his safe and pressed down. It punctured his skin and the blood dripped into the lock, releasing it. The door swung open, revealing a thick pile of documents and a dark tome sitting on top.

He pulled out the book and slammed the safe door shut. "Here."

She held an ancient tome, covered in dark leather, embossed with the familiar symbol she knew so well: the six-pointed star surrounded by four dots that formed a square.

The Fraternitatem.

Her hands shook as she opened the front cover. The pages were written in Hebrew. Holding her palm above the page, she cast a translation spell and watched the words shimmer away and return in English. The first spell of the book was a mind-control spell. Annie shuddered. "This is really their grimoire?"

"Yes."

She turned another page. Each spell was typical of a grimoire: spells, potions, and notations regarding evil magic. "How did you get this?" Annie demanded.

"I won't tell you that. I warned you three months ago not to mess with them. I warned your father, too. But if he knew she was still alive and he pushed… I issue you a strong warning. Run away if you must. But if you can't, that grimoire might give you insight."

"Why didn't you give it to me when I asked for help three months ago?" Annie asked incredulously.

Mortimer's crooked smile exposed his yellow teeth. "I know you, girl. If you'd had this, you would have run off after them."

Annie looked at the book and back to Mortimer. "How much for the book?"

He waved her away and grunted something unintelligible.

Annie began to pace across the linoleum floor, so worn in areas she could see the plywood underneath. "Do you know about regenerating demons?"

Mortimer seemed to be growing tired, whether from his age or the beating or because he just wanted her to leave. Still, he sat on the desk chair. "You are full of questions this morning."

"It's a strange case," she admitted and placed the book in her field pack.

"My guess is that the demon was conjured to get you to the house. Your best course is to find the prophecy and find out what you're supposed to be doing."

"It's all pieces to the puzzle." She turned toward the books. "Mind if I look?"

Mortimer shrugged.

The demon aisle was packed with books but was not as comprehensive as what she would find at the Wizard Hall library. Annie couldn't understand her pull to this store or to Mortimer, except that she thought he knew more than he let on.

"Why would they have taken my mother? She was—is—a non-magical. What did she have that they wanted?" Annie asked.

Mortimer stood at the end of the aisle and shook his head slowly. "I have no books on this regenerating demon. And the Fraternitatem… they only take people who can give them what they want or need. If they want these powers you're to receive, what use would she have to them?"

Annie stared at the weakened man, surprised by how long he had been willing to speak with her let alone giving her the book. "She comes back and tries to bond with me. Get me to trust her and then…" Annie said.

"Go and protect yourself," Mortimer said.

"How?"

He shrugged his shoulders and walked into his office, leaving her alone.

✧

Although Annie had promised she'd go home and rest, she returned to Wizard Hall. As always, she was greeted by the day security guard named Manny. He smiled brightly when she entered.

"Annie Pearce. You're late," he quipped as she tossed her spell into the security box on his desk.

"Actually I was here at six in the morning and left again," she teased back with raised eyebrows.

"And here I missed it. I will miss this back-and-forth, Ms. Pearce," he said and held the door for her.

She looked at the familiar face she'd seen every day for the last four years. "Why? You're not leaving us, are you?"

Manny chuckled. "Nope. I am, however, the new assistant manager of security. I'm moving up!" He beamed proudly.

"Congrats! At least you'll still be around." Annie shook his hand and slid through the door. "Don't let it go to your head," she said as she entered the buzz of the hall.

The back entrance led to a narrow hallway where the walls were covered in ancient maps, diagrams, and shadow boxes filled with artifacts. It opened to the human resources department. Annie turned down the center hallway that split the department in two and headed for the Legal Department.

Modern glass doors to the department were currently closed but not locked. Annie entered and took the center aisle to Samantha Chamsky's cubicle. As she expected, Samantha was at her desk, a thick tome open as she took notes on a yellow lined pad.

"Hey, Sami, got a minute?" Annie asked, startling her sister.

"Jeez, you scared me half to death." She pointed to the only chair in the cubicle and removed the stack of folders covering the seat.

The two women were so close in appearance from their long, curly brown hair and brown eyes to the shape of their lips. Anyone would have assumed they were sisters. The only difference was how they dressed, and that was dictated by their professions. While the lawyer in Samantha favored suits and heels, Annie wore a sweater, cargo pants and boots.

Samantha observed her sister carefully. "You look like hell. Why aren't you home?"

"Thanks. I love you, too." Annie leaned against the back of the chair and summoned their dad's last case file. She held it tightly with shaky hands.

"Sorry. You just need to rest. There's been so much since the Black Market." Samantha eyed the folder.

"I'll rest when I'm…" Annie was about to say dead and refrained for its inappropriateness. "I'm on my way home after I talk to you."

"Okay?" Samantha dragged out the word, concerned.

Finding out Emily Pearce was alive eight years ago had been such a shock for Annie. When her mom died, she had been three years old and had no real memories of her and really never missed her. It would be different for Samantha, who had been five when Emily died and who still had memories that haunted her.

Annie took a deep breath and slowly released the air as she held the folder; her grip was so tight, her knuckles were white. "I found the missing folder from Dad's final case. Before I left for France, actually." Samantha's look of concern made Annie's stomach churn, yet Samantha remained silent as she waited for Annie to continue.

"Dad's last case involved the Chintamani stones." Annie tapped the folder restlessly. "He'd been tracking them in the market, and that was where he met Dr. Arden Blakely and eventually the Fraternitatem of Solomon.

For Annie, her father's death had been almost harder on her than on Samantha because they shared a love of learning black magic, understanding it, and stopping it. She had spent so much time with him at work and in the field, learning what she could. Remembering that time broke her heart; she wiped away a lone tear.

"His notes are very specific. He said they threatened him, forced him to return the stones, which he did. They killed him anyway."

Samantha visibly shuddered. "I thought it was Rathbone," Samantha said.

Annie shook her head. "He did their bidding. They were behind it." Tears welled in Samantha's eyes. Annie pulled out her dad's note and handed it to her.

As Annie's hands did the first time she read the letter, Samantha's hands shook as she read her father's words. She wiped her tears from her cheeks. "Why didn't you show me this earlier?"

"Because of what else is in the folder. Because I didn't want to bring up all of this shit until I knew for sure, but now I don't think I have a choice."

Samantha sighed. "Prophecy? Does he say what it is?"

"No. I didn't think anything of it until Sturtagaard was at the house when I caught the demon. He said I was supposed to be there and that I had a part to play in this," Annie said.

Samantha glanced at Annie. "So how long has he known about this? And what are you going to do to stop this?"

Annie held the folder out for Samantha to take. "It's not that simple. I'm supposed to receive a power for completing the prophecy. I think the Fraternitatem is going to come back for the power," Annie said. She pushed the folder at Samantha. "There's more."

Samantha reluctantly took the folder and opened the front cover. Her face blanched, and her jaw fell when she saw the first picture. Her hands shook and lips trembled as if she were holding back an ugly cry. She picked up the eight-year-old picture of their mother with Dr. Arden Blakely.

"I…" Samantha's voice squeaked, she looked at Annie. "When?" she managed to ask.

"Those were taken eight years ago. I didn't tell you because I haven't found her yet. If I found out she was dead, I'd say nothing and leave it alone. Bucky still can't find her, and now everything is falling into dangerous places. I needed you to know."

Samantha shuffled through the pictures, taking in the face of her mother, the woman she often dreamed of and still longed for. Annie knew Samantha couldn't understand why she didn't feel the same way. But Annie couldn't miss what she didn't remember.

"Dad noted every contact he made with the Fraternitatem. He was meeting with them to turn over the stones, and that's where he saw her. He thought the shimmering blue of the Cave of Ages made him hallucinate, but he knew. He knew it was her. When he approached her, she pretended not to know him."

Samantha was still trembling and now crying, "Why didn't you tell me?"

Annie lay the folder on the desk and held Samantha's hands. "I didn't tell you because of the initial shock. I couldn't wrap my head around it," Annie said. "Honestly, I was hoping we'd have something tangible by now, but if Emily's alive, they're hiding her well."

"Mom died! I remember her body lying in the casket. They didn't want me to see her. But I did. She was dead!" Samantha insisted. "How did they not know it wasn't her?"

"Zola knew there was something off. But because Mom is nonmagical, she couldn't get an accurate read on her."

"Why didn't you tell me? What the hell were you thinking?" Annie jumped at Samantha's uncharacteristic shouting.

Annie stood and grabbed the folder, shoving the contents inside. "I'm sorry. I'm sorry I couldn't tell you until I knew for sure. I'm sorry I hid this from you until…"

Samantha reached for Annie before she turned to leave. "I'm sorry I yelled. I'm just so furious at you. At her. At Dad for not doing something. It's just this is a bombshell."

"It's a lie of omission. I'm sorry. I was always going to tell everyone. I just needed time to figure out what to do," Annie admitted.

Samantha grabbed the folder again, opened it, and took out the pictures. "Where do you think she is?" Samantha continued to stare at a picture of Emily at the market. The girls looked so much like Emily except for her red hair. "She was beautiful," Samantha murmured.

Annie sat back down and bent forward. "Bucky's searched for credit cards, mortgages, library cards, college degrees, death certificates, birth certificates with her name. There's nothing. I didn't expect there would be." She shifted in her seat.

"You okay?"

"Yeah. I'm going home next. I just wanted to let you know what was going on before I did. I should go." Annie packed her items away and stood up.

"So she pretended to not know him. Why would she do that?" Samantha asked.

Annie summoned the cassette tape. "When Dad finally got her alone, she admitted to leaving willingly. He begged her to come back. She said she couldn't, she wouldn't. Something about a greater purpose." She pocketed the tape and sighed. "I listened to that fucking tape over and over again. She never asked about you or me. Even after Dad told her about us." Annie wiped away tears. Samantha wrapped Annie in a hug.

"Why did she leave? Did she tell him why?" Samantha asked.

"She didn't. According to Dad's notes, he spoke with the Fraternitatem and begged them to let her go. That's when they told him of the prophecy and basically said she was staying. That was the end of it."

"So she refused to come home? I'm not sure how that makes me feel."

Taking Samantha's hands, Annie looked her square in the eyes. "Dr. Blakely was brainwashed and became their assassin. That's probably what happened to Mom. They went to a lot of trouble to kidnap and doctor up a body. She won't be the same woman after twenty years."

Samantha let the tears run down her cheek before she wiped them away. "I'm still furious with you."

"I know."

"Maybe someday you'll find her." Samantha reached over and kissed Annie's cheek.

"Maybe."

If she doesn't find me first.

CHAPTER 8

"YOU'RE HOME?" CHAM asked Annie over the phone. She plopped on the sofa in her den and rested her head against a pillow.

"Yeah. Yeah. I had some things to do. I'm home now." She stared at the grimoire from Mortimer's that lay on the sofa beside her. "I told Samantha about Mom."

Cham was tapping his phone screen lightly but stopped. "How did she take it?"

"She's furious at me for not saying something sooner. I think it's her way of dealing with the bombshell that Mom didn't die when we thought she did."

"The two of you have a strong relationship. She'll come around." Cham began typing again.

"Maybe." Annie held the book; it vibrated lightly. "I'm tired. I'll talk to you later, okay?"

"Yeah. Sure. Call if you need me."

"Love you." Annie hung up before he could answer and tossed the phone on the sofa.

She stared at the cover of the grimoire.

It's very old.

Still stinging from the bomb sent to Wizard Hall three months ago by a rogue French wizard guard, Annie remained distrustful of Mortimer's motives for giving her the grimoire, regardless of what he previously had gone through to protect her identity. Cautious, she scanned the book with her crystal and was surprised by the good magical trace that seeped inside the pages. Grimoires weren't meant for practitioners of good magic; they were created by those wishing to perform or control evil.

I wonder if he knew this.

While the grimoire was marked with the symbols of the Fraternitatem, it carried good magic. Annie supposed it could be because their initial purpose was to protect the world from the magical artifacts of King Solomon. Somewhere in the group's long history, their motives changed. Annie distrusted the good magic, thinking it might be a ruse for the unsuspecting witch. The book generally made her uneasy and reluctant to own it.

But then again...

She shuddered briefly, took a deep breath, and opened the book again, returning to the last passage she read.

Her hand shook as the passage explained what to do with the poisonous herb called "foxglove," used to ward off evil spirits.

"There's plenty of non-poisonous herbs that do that," she said to herself.

As she read the explanations on how to control lower magical creatures, her skin began to prickle and her stomach churned at the ease for which these spells were created and used by the Fraternitatem. Her head ached and she felt sick, yet she couldn't stop. She felt as though she needed more— she needed to know how they "killed" Emily. She began to skim rather than read, searching for any clue how they might have done it.

Soon enough, she found it there within the pages, how they ferried her mother away from her and Samantha in such a calculated way. They had used the drug potassium cyanide, which was easy to administer to fake her death. That, combined with clever magical glamours, meant that all of them—Jason, Ryan, Milo, the Wizard Guard, and Wizard Council—believed that Emily was dead. Annie reread it in the grimoire; whoever wrote the passage did so with pride and almost glee in how they pulled off the bold move by stealing a beloved mother away.

She thought of the cassette tape and the coldness in Emily's voice as she spoke with the man who was once her true and only love. She shuddered and cried.

"What is that?" Zola startled Annie but gracefully sat beside her; her fairy wings gently waved and kissed Annie's skin. "It's a Fraternitatem book," Zola added as she handled the leather-bound tome.

"Mortimer claims it will help me face them. I feel a bit tired from the magic inside."

"You ought to not trust that man."

Annie showed Zola the passage. Zola read the words and asked, "You really think they're coming for you?"

"You were alive in the ninth century. What do you know about this?"

Zola held her hands in tight fists as she stared out the window to the backyard. "I was in Spain at the time." Wind blew through the yard, bending flowers and bushes in the backyard. Zola sighed. "I... I can go back home and find out what happened in the past," she offered reluctantly.

Since the magic in the grimoire left Annie tired, she placed the tome on the floor and snuggled into the corner of her sofa. Zola pulled the blanket up and around her.

"Maybe. Not now. I do believe they're going to come whenever I fulfill the prophecy. I'll need you then," Annie said. "Unless you know how I can stop the powers from coming to me," she murmured.

Zola ignored the request and instead smoothed out Annie's blanket and held cool hands to her charge's temples, cradling her head like she had done when Annie was young. She had cared for Annie when the girl cried out for her dead mother, until she stopped because she no longer remembered Emily's touch or the sound of her voice. Eventually, the only mother Annie remembered was Kathy.

Zola let the spell warm Annie and wash away the conflicted feelings. She gave Annie a good healing nap because she knew that in a few days' time, Annie would not have this sleep or warmth or food.

Annie's breathing slowed and evened out as she slept. Zola watched her at rest and wondered how much she should tell Annie about what was to come.

❧

When Annie woke, the sky was filled with thick, gray clouds. It was nearly time for the workday to end. She felt rested, and yet there was something gnawing at her that she couldn't quite place.

Zola's gone.

It was like a hangover that lingered long after it should. Annie listened for any sound of Zola, but the house was empty. All she could hear were the raindrops that pinged against the window.

She rested her chin on the back of the sofa as she watched the rain spatter across the deck and muddy the flower garden in the far corner. Hiding in the manicured patches of daisies was a billdad, a rabbit-like creature with the tail of an otter. They were attracted to her magic and spent years digging in the backyard, eating bugs. As a child, Annie had often chased after them, scaring them away and sometimes playing with them, all the while ruining her clothes and getting scolded by the fairy.

The thick clouds rolled over the house, and the rain became a deluge. A bolt of lightning lit up the sky and the thunder crashed. Annie's heart pounded as she remembered Sturtagaard's cryptic words. *You're safe in the thunder.*

She sniffed the humid air and thought she caught a scent that was musky and spicy, warm and familiar. "Dad," she murmured and turned to see a dark, empty kitchen.

The clock pinged as the minutes passed. She scratched the sock where she hid her dad's letter. She pulled it out and reread his words, mostly to see the familiar handwriting, to touch the paper that he once touched. The scent of cologne grew stronger. It was his scent; she would never forget it as she kept his half-filled bottle still in her bathroom.

She teleported upstairs and opened the medicine cabinet above her sink. The green glass bottle was dusty; it was where he had left it before he died. She picked it up, dusted it off, and took a whiff of the scent. She could almost feel the weight of his hand on her shoulder, the warmth of his touch, the love he had for her and Samantha. She dabbed the top and let the scent linger in the air, then placed one drop on her wrist, and put the rest away for fear she might spill even just a little.

The thunderstorm raged on. She sat on the window seat in her room and watched the rain pour, watched the lighting. It no longer felt danger-ous. It felt... *safe.*

Maybe he's the thunder. *Dad?*

But something still lingered in her gut and she couldn't quite reach it, see it, or determine what it was. Maybe it was that Zola who hadn't yet told her whatever it was that she was hiding.

Why do I think that?

Annie sighed and rested her head against the cool window. The water dripped against the glass.

"Hey."

She turned, a smile spreading across her face. "You're home!" she said as Cham entered, soaking wet from the rain.

"How are you feeling?" he asked and kissed her forehead. He frowned. "You okay?"

Annie wiped water from his face. "I'm fine. Sturtagaard's gone, and Mortimer gave me a Fraternitatem grimoire to help me fight them when they come. And Zola... I think Zola knows something she's not telling me. Otherwise, all is good."

"You were supposed to rest." He touched her cheek and ran his hands through her hair. "Mortimer gave you a grimoire?"

Annie laughed. "Yeah. I'll show you later. Go dry off and we'll scrounge for food."

"You sure you're okay?" he asked again.

She nodded and let him kiss her deeply, his hands still in her hair. She had no more pain, no more discomfort as he carried her to bed and huddled with her under the covers. His hands and his kisses warmed her. She trusted him as they made love.

Tomorrow she'd worry.

CHAPTER 9

I T WAS ONLY 8:45 a.m., which meant the library wouldn't open for fifteen minutes. Annie didn't mind. It gave her time to take in the carvings on the library doors. She always found something new when she did.

The doors had been originally crafted and hung on a Viking longhouse in Jorvik, Northumbria, in what later became northern England. The carvings on the doors were the earliest recording in the Wizard Council of America. Annie always wondered how it had passed ownership from the Viking longhouse to the coven.

They tracked the history, starting with a battle so bloody and so deadly that the coven left Northumbria for the new world, a little over a hundred years before the first Viking settlement came to Newfoundland in 1000 CE. They remained hidden, their remnants destroyed. The early coven and Vikings had wanted it that way. Over the decades, their ghastly start became folktales, complete with the full, rich images of the Battle of Checkgou, until they established the modern Wizard Council. The story of the Day of First Sun, the mythical magical holiday on September 1, celebrated the closure of the portal between the magical and nonmagical worlds. While the carvings were so accurate and beautifully created, there was one carving that always piqued her curiosity, partially because she was unfamiliar with the tale but mostly because the girl carved in wood looked exactly like her.

Annie observed the face, the detail of the eyes, the hair, and the mouth. For the first time, she really took in the scene surrounding the girl. The demon lying at her feet appeared to be Annie's demon that was locked in Tartarus.

The regenerating demon?

The girl stood alone, her left foot resting on the demon, her arm raised as she held a long sword.

Am I to go to the past?

"Good morning, Annie. Find something interesting?" said Mrs. Cuttlebrink from behind her.

Annie started. "Hi, Mrs. Cuttlebrink. I think I'm just staring at myself."

"It is remarkable how much that depiction looks like you." Mrs. Cuttlebrink pulled out the heavy iron key, placed it inside the thick lock, and opened the library doors.

"Actually, I think it really is me," Annie said.

Mrs. Cuttlebrink stopped and stared at the carving.

"Look at the demon. That's my demon locked in Tartarus Prison. The ugly face, simple clothes, stringy hair," Annie said.

"I'm assuming you're here because of this prophecy I've heard about," Mrs. Cuttlebrink said as she motioned Annie to join her inside.

Soft candlelight from antique sconces lined the oak-covered walls and cast an ethereal glow around the edges of the library. While Mrs. Cuttlebrink switched on the overhead lights, casting harsh white light across the library, Annie found a worktable to the left and sat in the first chair.

Annie summoned her field pack and expanded it to its original size, pulling out several items.

"Now, dear, how can I help you?" Mrs. Cuttlebrink asked.

Annie sighed. "I have several things today actually. It's quite a weird puzzle." She lay out the letter from her father, the talisman, a photo of the demon held in the basement of Tartarus Prison, and the Fraternitatem grimoire.

"Well, dear, you know I love puzzles." Mrs. Cuttlebrink smiled. Looking at the objects, she noted first the picture of the demon in prison and held it close, examining the creature from its clothes to its face. "Now I see what you're referring to. It is remarkably similar."

"It started when I found the demon searching for this talisman," Annie explained.

Mrs. Cuttlebrink put down the picture and held the small statue. While it buzzed against her palm, she studied the underside, the face, the body, and even held it to her ear, listening to the light sound. Finishing a precursory examination, she turned back to the picture. "The two look very similar," Mrs. Cuttlebrink said. "Having noted that, I would begin by suggesting they are related. Though why would a demon be searching for an object that conjures demons?" she asked.

"That is the first question," Annie said.

Mrs. Cuttlebrink made notes on a pad of paper, circling the word AGE.

"The demon's clothing was dated to the ninth century. Most likely, the demon is from that period, as well as that talisman," Annie said. She explained how they dated the demon clothing in the lab.

Again, the librarian made notes on her pad. "Okay. The next item. What about the letter?" she asked.

"First…" Annie explained what Sturtagaard told her at the house.

"And why are you taking stock in what he says?"

"Because of the letter." Annie handed the librarian the note from her father.

When Mrs. Cuttlebrink recognized his familiar handwriting, she glanced at Annie with raised eyebrows and pursed lips. She began reading. Mrs. Cuttlebrink had known Jason, worked with him on a fair share of cases, and assisted with research, much like she did with Annie. As she read each sentence, the lines in her forehead deepened and her jaw clenched tighter. The letter slipped from her fingers when she finished reading. She sighed deeply. "This could support Sturtagaard's message." She placed her hand across her chin, seemingly working through something important. "Where was this found?" the librarian asked.

"In Dad's missing folder from his last case. I found it three months ago." Annie pointed to the folder and left her hand on it as if protecting the contents.

"Now tell me why you think this is related to your demon and the man who's been running around," Mrs. Cuttlebrink said.

Annie summoned her own case file that was quickly growing with test results, notes, and samples. She passed it to Mrs. Cuttlebrink.

"Well, we have what we think is a rough date for the demon. Cham, Gibbs, and Spencer swear the man is dressed like the demon. And then there's this." Annie pulled out the DNA test results, sliding the sheet to the librarian. Mrs. Cuttlebrink read the test results and frowned.

"Really? A hybrid? That might not be in the records at all."

"Funny you say that. I would check with Sturtagaard, but he's removed the atomie bean from his shoulder. I have no way of finding him."

Mrs. Cuttlebrink broke into a hearty laugh. "Leave it to that bastard." When she regained her composure, she said, "I'm sorry, Annie dear. I shouldn't laugh, but he's always in on your cases. He's always around. It occurs to me that some believe he was turned to a vampire at the end of the ninth century. You think he knows something?"

"I think he was there. Unfortunately, it doesn't matter right now since he's gone." Reluctantly, Annie placed her father's note in the folder, still guarding it as if it would save her life.

She stared at Mrs. Cuttlebrink. "So. What do you make of this puzzle?"

Mrs. Cuttlebrink made some more notes on her pad and studied it carefully. "Firstly, how did your father find out about the prophecy?"

Annie held her breath and slid Jason's case file to Mrs. Cuttlebrink. The librarian opened the front cover. "Oh my," she exclaimed, and quickly turned the photo over searching for a date.

"He took these eight years ago. During the Chintamani stones case," Annie said. Nervously, she paced between two tables. Mrs. Cuttlebrink found his notes, and perused them twice for clarity. Her hands shook as she shuffled the papers and the pictures into a neat and tidy pile.

"Annie. Come sit."

Annie did as requested and picked up the notes and photos.

"He doesn't say in his notes that he stopped pursuing your mom for the information about you. My guess is that the Fraternitatem found his presence distracting for her, that it would undo whatever they did to her. They didn't have him murdered over the stones. Rather, it was likely because he found her. If I were the Fraternitatem, that's what I would do. It also occurs to me that this leaves you especially vulnerable."

Mrs. Cuttlebrink had been with the Wizard Council for over twenty years. She had seen just about everything as a Wizard Hall librarian and understood how the game would be played.

"You should've been a wizard guard," Annie joked.

"No. You all work too hard," Mrs. Cuttlebrink said. "So, you're here for my take on all these pieces so we know what you're up against."

"In a nutshell," Annie said.

"Have you spoken to Emerson's family? They are original coven members." Mrs. Cuttlebrink advised.

"Gila Donaldson wasn't exactly forthcoming. I get the feeling she knows more than she admitted. We'll double back at some point because what I really want to know is why she bought the house where I found the demon and who conjured it," Annie said.

"And why." Mrs. Cuttlebrink pulled her notepad to her and took additional notes. "I'll search for any books on this demon as well as anything that might be related to you and a prophecy. Folktales are often stories based on real events, so I'll see if there are any tales that resemble this."

"Prophecies aren't real or destined to happen, are they?"

Mrs. Cuttlebrink put her pen down and looked at Annie. "Seers, runes, fire reading, crystal balls, have all been used with magic to learn about the future. Spells, trances... even the oracles of Ancient Greece relied on gases to prophesize about the future. Are they real? Some believe they are. I guess it's up to you to determine if it's real or not."

"So, if there's a prophecy with my name on it, do I have to follow through with it?" Annie asked.

"Only if you want it to be a self-fulfilling prophecy. Listen, Annie. You have free will and can decide what course of action to take with any prophecy. You can change predicted outcomes. Until we discover exactly what this prophecy says, remain alert and stay safe."

"Any other thoughts I'm missing?" Annie asked as she picked up her things.

"Just one. The Fraternitatem told your father of the prophecy. Who told them?"

❦

Annie's brain buzzed with Mrs. Cuttlebrink's question. *Who told the Fraternitatem?* She knew of only two creatures who were alive at the same time as the demon and the Viking. Sturtagaard was gone and Zola was evasive.

Or was it passed from the original coven to the Fraternitatem?

The question haunted her. She couldn't focus on any other piece of the puzzle and doodled on a pad of paper, not hearing the knocking on her cubicle.

"Annie?" The small voice of Emerson pulled Annie from her musings. She glanced up and waved Emerson inside.

"What's up?" Annie asked cautiously as she turned over her notes, hiding her thoughts. She no longer trusted Emerson fully because of her family connection to Gila.

Nervously, Emerson pulled at her hands as she sat on the edge of the club chair. Annie guessed Emerson had been advised on what she could and could not say. She didn't figure this conversation would end with anything useful.

"Grandma would only admit to purchasing the house and thanks you for discovering it was used for something illegal," Emerson squeaked.

Annie almost felt sorry for Emerson, who started with the Wizard Guard a little over fourteen months ago. While she earned good grades in her training courses and could research with more competency than most wizard guards, Emerson was never able to master the physical aspects of the job. She had yet to pass the final Wizard Guard test.

Emerson looked small and frail in the large chair; the stress of her family's involvement in this situation seemed to be getting to her. Dark purple circled her eyes, which were red and tired. It was this exact reaction that caused Emerson to fail her wizard guard test miserably. Even with Annie as her mentor, Emerson was unable to finish her solo mission to retrieve an ancient magical object.

While Annie tried to keep the girl alive and safe, bending several rules to do so, Emerson couldn't hack it and dropped out due to the stress.

It was that weakness Annie had difficulty understanding. She herself had scored the second highest score of any wizard guard ever – a 638, second only to Cham's 640. In this environment dripping in the stench of testosterone, sometimes you just had to be the best. In Annie's opinion, Emerson was only going through motions. As she watched her now, she could see the conflict in Emerson's face. Emerson needed to choose between her family or the Wizard Guard. Either would be acceptable if you stood by your decision. Emerson seemed incapable of doing that much.

"You do realize she's lying," Annie said incredulously.

"She's my grandma. I can't force a confession from her. She watched me carefully when I was there."

"Listen, Emerson. I could be in danger; the *world* could be in danger. You have to choose one. Either be loyal to your family or be loyal to the Wizard Guard, just choose and stand by that choice," Annie said harshly, and she knew, unfairly.

Emerson wrung her hands raw, turning them red.

"There's an altar room in the attic. I just need to time it right and I can get in… get what you need," Emerson said, finally making eye contact with Annie.

"If you go against them, it could be trouble for you," Annie reminded her.

"My grandmother bought a house and summoned a demon. I know she's lying. I want to know why," Emerson admitted.

In that moment, Annie regretted putting Emerson in the position in which she had to choose job or family. But Annie was growing anxious with the lack of help from those who could help her. "Any other family who might know?" she asked hopefully.

Emerson looked away, her hands still entwined together. "If I know my grandma, she's already told everyone not to say anything."

"I'm sorry I put you in this position. But I'm supposed to receive powers for doing something, and it has to do with that demon and that Viking. I want to know what I'm supposed to do," Annie said.

"I'm really sorry, Annie," Emerson murmured and ran from the cubicle.

Annie sighed and flipped over her notepad as Spencer entered her cubicle.

"I saw Emerson leave. She didn't look happy. Grandma wasn't help-ful?" Spencer asked.

"A big, fat goose egg. And now I've got a horrible thought in my head I can't get out." Frustrated, she summoned a rubber ball and twirled it in her palm.

"What thought?" Spencer asked.

"Mrs. Cuttlebrink is looking for the prophecy, but after I caught her up, she asked me: If the Fraternitatem told my dad, who told them?"

Annie couldn't stop thinking of the work Mrs. Cuttlebrink did for her. Annie always trusted the books, the librarian, the information housed in the miles-long library. It had been her favorite location at Windmere School of Wizardry, and it was her favorite place in Wizard Hall. She could spend hours in study because she simply wanted to know more. After her dad died, she had spent so much time hiding in the stacks reading and trying to understand. Jason had always told her that in order to fight the black magic, you had to understand it. She tried to learn it all.

"Annie, did I lose you somewhere?" Spencer asked.

"Sorry. Just trying to piece it all together at the expense of all of these." She pointed to the stack of case files on her desk.

Spencer chuckled. "You work through those; I have my own paper-work to take care of. Keep me posted." He glanced down to Annie's phone when it buzzed.

"I hate when that happens. It's Mrs. Cuttlebrink. She's got info. Want to come?"

⁐

Several wizards had taken seats at various tables in the library, lost in books, scribbling notes on pads of paper. One pair quietly yet animatedly discussed some topic important to each.

Annie led Spencer to the right where Mrs. Cuttlebrink was busy at the counter, checking out several books. She glanced up quickly, saw Annie and Spencer, and waved them back to her office.

The librarian's office was a roomy space with shelves covering three of the walls. They were packed full of more books, fabric-covered boxes, and artifacts neatly displayed and organized. Annie and Spencer took seats in the open chairs.

"Have you ever been in her office?" Spencer asked.

"Never. But then the library is 'packed' today," Annie said.

Annie observed a pile of books at the center of a clean desk and expected they were related to her. She desperately wanted to reach for them.

"Sorry about the delay," Mrs. Cuttlebrink said and took seat. "I have information."

She handed Annie the first book, a thick tome covered in leather but without a title. Annie opened the book to the first page: *Fifteenth Century Daemon Anthology*.

"It was written by an early English historian and has a wide range of demons inside." Mrs. Cuttlebrink explained.

"Good place to start," Spencer said as Annie opened the book to the location marked by the librarian.

Annie smiled when she read *Regenerato Everto*, the "regenerating demon."

Regenerato Everto (Regenerating Demon)

Regenerating Demons lived predominantly in the area of Jorvik, Northumbria, for hundreds of years. Originally, the demons were half breeds, bred as foot soldiers and forced to work and fight. They were used as an army to defeat the conquering Norsemen.

They have a lack of any negligible intelligence. Therefore, their speech is rather simple, and they lack any ability to create a plan. They are animalistic in their behavior and thought, have no manners, and cannot be reasoned with.

Their diet is raw meat, and their eyesight is poor, especially in low light. They have a good sense of smell and hearing, and can grow to seven feet tall; the female of the species, six feet. They are very strong and incredibly agile and fast for creatures so large. Despite being well built and very muscular, they dislike water as it burns their skin.

Traditional means cannot slay them. Swords, knives, and sharp objects only pierce their hides, making them weak. Beheading does not kill them. Magical jinxes, hexes, or curses will only hurt them. They can be ripped asunder, smashed, or blown apart by a spell, but their bodies will regenerate.

The only way to permanently kill and rid the land of these demons is to destroy them with fire. Any pieces not burned will allow the demon to regenerate. Every piece of the demon must be burnt in order to eradicate it.

Regenerato Everto were destroyed during the ninth century by Anaise the Brave.

Annie quickly read the passage. "Killed by fire? Burning away all the flesh and bones would definitely kill them." Annie showed Spencer the passage.

"This is a good start. Any of those on your desk have additional info?" Annie asked.

Mrs. Cuttlebrink shook her head. "I'm sorry, Annie dear. I have tried several different spells, scrying over a map of the library. I just cannot find any other information regarding these demons. I've looked up early coven history. Whatever happened when these demons were extinguished is gone. I trust that our inventory is substantial and accurate. We have books from all over the world and in many other languages. But you in particular, and this demon, are just not there."

"So the best option is force the descendants to give up what they know," Annie said.

"It looks like it. If anything, you have confirmation the demon is a hybrid, and you know fire kills them," Mrs. Cuttlebrink said.

"Actually, there's something in this passage. The name Anaise. I swear Mrs. Donaldson mumbled it when we were there. I know this name from somewhere, and I can't place it. Do you know, Spencer?" Annie turned to her partner. When Spencer smiled, the memory came back to Annie.

"France. Sturtagaard," Spencer said.

She nodded. "Yeah. Yeah. All his stories about the revenge killings. He wanted to kill Anaise."

"He specifically mentioned her. So he knew Anaise and was there when the demons were killed," Spencer surmised.

Annie smiled. It was another confirmation. What it meant, she didn't fully know yet.

"Not that it matters, but the name Anaise is an old English for Anne," Mrs. Cuttlebrink said.

Annie glanced at her, her brain jumbled with thoughts of the carving on the door, the small passage mentioning Anaise, Sturtagaard, the Fraternitatem.

"The prophecy must say I'm to go back and kill the demons, and for my trouble, I'll receive powers," Annie said, nearly to herself.

Mrs. Cuttlebrink moved closer to Annie and sat on the desk. She held Annie's hands in her cool, soft hands. "Because there are no regenerating demons in this present, I think that is correct."

Annie grimaced. The weight of what she was discovering made her anxious. "You said I didn't have to fulfill a prophecy," Annie said.

"But, what would happen if you didn't go to the past, didn't kill off the demons? Would the demons have multiplied, killed off the human race? And what about the coven? Would they have come here to start over?" Mrs. Cuttlebrink asked.

"Why go through all of this? Why conjure the demon and bring a Viking here to... what? Bring me back when all they need is fire to kill them?" Annie's voice gained several octaves with the stress.

"Maybe they wanted your attention, or maybe there's more they need than just using fire to kill the demons. Yes, it's risky, but it definitely got your attention," Mrs. Cuttlebrink said.

"Besides, you have me, Gibbs, Cham. An entire team to do whatever it is that you're supposed to do. Don't forget that," Spencer said. Annie looked at her partner. It didn't ease the anxiety.

The bell on the reception desk dinged. Mrs. Cuttlebrink looked out the door. "I need to assist. Take all the time you need," she said.

"I might have free will but I have no choice," Annie told Spencer as Mrs. Cuttlebrink left.

"Maybe there's another way to relay the information to the past. We need to talk to Gila Donaldson again. Before this, I didn't know time portals existed. I thought portals opened to another plane of existence only during the same time," Spencer said.

A buzzer sounded as Mrs. Cuttlebrink finished checking whoever it was that required a book and turned her attention to the next in line.

Annie walked back to the library doors. Twenty feet tall and three inches thick, the doors had traveled thousands of miles from England to America over a thousand years ago. They had hung at the entrance of several rooms in the many different American Wizard Halls until the Wizard Council built this current building in 1900 where they had hung ever since.

Anaise was located where Annie always found her, just above her eye line, to the left side of the right door. She touched the carving of her face. Her fingers trailed the smooth wood and found the face of the demon locked in Tartarus Prison. This time, she moved to the right, to the next picture. Always looking for the girl who looked like her, she had never noticed the other carvings. Beside Anaise was a demon, caught in the fire. Behind and to the side of the demon, other demons were also consumed in flames. Dotting the row of pictures were small cottages she had also never noticed, and people dressed in ancient clothing like what the demon and the Viking wore. She continued farther to the right, where a larger cottage stood, maybe a longhouse at the end of town. More demons and more fire.

"Annie?" Mrs. Cuttlebrink touched her shoulder. Annie jumped. Spencer stared at the carvings.

"Sorry," Annie murmured. "I never noticed. It's all here." She barely felt herself being led back to the office.

Annie's stomach roiled as thoughts of the past – her past—and her future haunted her. Sturtagaard…

He knew this was coming!

She leaned her elbows on the table and buried her head in her hands. Sturtagaard, who'd been a pain in the ass of the Wizard Council for centuries—and yet he still lived. He'd inserted himself in many of her cases in both small and large ways. He knew this was coming. He'd known for centuries and waited patiently. The original coven knew. They knew and never said anything, never recorded the event. It was as if Annie was being tested to receive a reward she didn't even want.

"Why me?" she murmured.

"Does it matter why? Annie, they read the prophecy and you were the answer. You're strong and you're incredibly brilliant, as is your partner. You know now," Spencer said.

"Sturtagaard never said our roles in this. Just my role. You're not on the door!" Annie shouted.

"You're not going alone. We'll be there. I don't care what the door depicts," Spencer argued. Annie startled when he angrily jumped from his chair. He ran his hands through his sandy brown, highlighted hair.

"And what if that changes the events? How would that change the future if you came with me? If Cham and Gibbs joined us." Her voice cracked.

They had been partners for a year and they knew each other well. She could see the worry stretched across his face. When his breathing evened out, he sat back down. "We can discuss that later. We don't even know how to open a portal to the past or if we can do that. And if the Viking is here for you, we need to find him."

"Before you get all bent out of shape, there's one more piece of the puzzle you need to see." Annie pulled out the missing file and handed it to Spencer. "I found it in my basement. It's where I found Dad's letter."

Spencer opened the folder. His reaction was what she expected; it's how everyone who saw the photo of Emily Pearce with Dr. Arden Blakely had reacted. Stunned silence. He turned the picture over, looking for a date.

"According to Dad's notes, he took them eight years ago," Annie said. She continued with her explanation of what her dad had left in his notes about her mom and the Fraternitatem.

After perusing several more photos and taking a brief glance at Jason's notes, Spencer closed the file and handed it to Annie. He glanced at her. "The Fraternitatem told your dad. There's no written prophecy. Mrs. Cuttlebrink's question makes more sense. Who told them?"

"And that is today's question," Annie said.

CHAPTER 10

I T WAS LONG past the time Annie should have told Ryan and
Kathy what she knew about her dad's last case, about her mom. She
asked them over but was evasive on the phone, piquing their interest
and worry.

Annie paced alongside her kitchen table. Every once in a while, she'd
stop and stare at the closed folder and then return to pacing. Her palms
were wet with sweat, and her head pounded with a growing anger she
wasn't sure what to do with.

Who told the Fraternitatem?

Annie couldn't let go of the question, even after leaving Spencer in
the library, assuring him she was fine. She wasn't, and her pacing did little
to relieve the anxiety.

Zola had made her chamomile tea; it sat on the table cold.

"You didn't drink your tea," Zola said when she entered the room.

"I should've told them all about this sooner," Annie said. Her hands
shook when she opened the curtains in the kitchen and stared at the patch
of lawn between her house and Mrs. Welter's. Her neighbor had been
there since before Annie was born. She realized at that minute she hadn't
seen her in days.

"I wonder if Mrs. Welter is with her son," Annie murmured and closed
the curtains. The back door squeaked open as Kathy and Ryan entered
the kitchen.

"Annie, we got here as soon as we could. What's wrong, sweetie?" Kathy asked.

Annie couldn't look them in the eyes. She was beginning to realize the depth of her mistake in withholding such difficult news. It didn't speed up her processing of what she had learned; it just made her stomach sour. She pursed her lips.

"It's in the folder on the table," Annie said, keeping all emotion out of her voice. She sat on the window seat and rested her head on the curtain panel.

Kathy and Ryan exchanged worried glances and stared at Annie before placing their attention on the folder at the center of the table.

Ryan slid it to himself and read the letter from Jason, attached to the outside of the front cover.

"Jason's missing case? This letter was in it?" Ryan asked.

"Yeah." Annie couldn't help the tears. "And before you say anything, you need to see the rest of the file." She wiped her tears with the back of her hand.

Ryan opened the folder. Kathy let out a squeal, Ryan said, "Damn!" as he took out the first photo of Emily Pearce and Dr. Arden Blakely together, walking down a street in a magical bazaar, discussing something. He turned the photo, looking for the date.

"Dad took the pictures eight years ago," Annie said.

"Emily was alive eight years ago?" Kathy said incredulously.

"It's all in Dad's notes," Annie began. It came from her in one breath, how Jason had found Emily in the course of his investigation, how he wanted her back, how she wouldn't come, how the Fraternitatem told him about the prophecy, how the demon and Viking were from the past. She heaved as she cried. Ryan and Kathy led her to the den, where she cried with Kathy's arm encompassing her and slumped against Kathy when the tears stopped.

"Does Sami know?" Ryan asked.

"I told her yesterday. She's pissed." Annie shivered. Kathy wrapped a blanket around her shoulders.

"Have you..." Kathy began.

"Tried to find her? Bucky's been searching," Annie said. "There's a tape in the file of Dad talking to her." Annie shuddered. "She… she was so cold as she explained why she left us and why she was staying with them. She didn't even ask about Sami and me. It was like she was focused on them, brainwashed for a purpose. Like Dr. Blakely was. I'm not sure if there's a point to finding her."

"So, she traded her life for yours," Ryan said as he read through his best friend's notes.

"That's what I got from the folder too," Annie wiped tears from her cheeks and sat up straighter. "Mom was a fool. Just because you're not magical doesn't mean you have to be stupid. Why the hell didn't she tell Dad? He could've done something sooner. Protected me. Kept her safe. He could've stopped them. He didn't have to die! She didn't have to leave!"

Kathy and Ryan looked at each other. Zola brought Annie a glass of water. She waved her away, still unsure of what Zola knew and was hiding.

"Maybe Emily thought she was doing the right thing," Kathy said in a soothing tone.

Annie laughed. "That's bullshit," she said.

Cham walked into the den. She looked at him with red, watery eyes.

"They know?" he asked and kissed her, before sitting on the ottoman.

"Yeah. Defending Emily," Annie said.

"Babe, you've had three months to digest this and let it simmer, and you're really pissed. But you have to remember that nonmagicals can be easily influenced when they don't understand our world. The Fraternitatem went to her with the prophecy, and she got scared and believed whatever they told her. That's how they separated her from you," he said.

"Why would they do that? What did they want from Emily?" Kathy asked.

"According to Jason, the prophecy sees Annie receiving powers. They probably want those, and to get to Annie, they had to take out those who protected her, starting with Emily. Annie wasn't close to getting the powers, so take Mom and weaken her. My guess is that running into Jason was an accident and gave them an opportunity to take him out. Jason gave back the Chintamani stones, and yet, they had Rathbone kill him. It was an opportunity."

"Sturtagaard's involved," Annie said.

Ryan glanced up. "How?"

Annie told them how the vampire had waited for her at the house and warned her.

Ryan looked at the folder and tapped his fingers against the front cover. "So Sturtagaard is involved. He said he had a part to play."

Annie nodded.

"The coven reads the prophecy and sends for you." Ryan opened the folder and stared at the picture of Emily. "So how did the prophecy get to the Fraternitatem?"

"The coven knows more than Gila's willing to tell me. Sturtagaard was there. I'm guessing the reason we can't kill him has to do with his role in this." Annie grimaced.

"And which one of them would sell you out?" Kathy asked with condemnation in her voice.

"Most likely the vampire," Annie said.

"I can pull the order that keeps him alive. But that doesn't tell you if he did this. But you're right, the coven knew it too," Ryan said.

Annie held her breath and looked out at the door between the kitchen and den where Zola was listening.

"I didn't sell you out," Zola said with sadness in her voice.

"You were there?" Annie asked.

"Yes." Zola stared at the floor.

"Why can't you tell me what happened?" Annie pleaded.

"I had one thing to do for you and I had eleven hundred years to do it. I couldn't. I failed. I'm hoping after you go to the past, I can rectify it this time." Zola walked away.

Annie tried to call her back. Kathy shook her head. "Let her be for now. If she knows something, she'll tell you." Kathy looked back into the kitchen. Zola had left.

"So what do I do? Do I go back to the past and kill off the demons? What do I do about Emily?"

"One problem at a time. Find the Viking, bring him in, and ask him why he's here. If it's to go back and kill the demons, then you need to figure out how to open the portal to the past and prepare for a trip without the relative comforts of home." Ryan grimaced.

"Is that even possible?" Kathy asked.

"I… honestly, I didn't know you could. But they're here, from the ninth century. Opening a portal like the ones to the Black Market is easy because you tap into the magical energy of that plane of existence. There are so many of those magical pockets everywhere. Chicago is ripe with magical energy. That's why there were four portals in Busse Woods alone," Ryan explained.

"And how do you go back to the exact date and time?" Annie asked. "What can go wrong in that?"

"If you're this Anaise, and you do something different this time, what will you change in the present?" Cham added.

Annie frowned. "That doesn't help. Do I even need permission to go to the past?" She asked Ryan.

"It's never been done to my knowledge," Ryan admitted. "It's something to bring to the Wizard Council."

Annie offered a wan smile as Kathy gave her a necessary, motherly hug.

≪

After Kathy and Ryan left, Annie lay in bed and watched the ceiling fan spin without really noticing it. Her mind spun with other things.

Cham climbed in beside her.

"I can conjure a demon but not a human," Annie said as he pulled the blanket up.

"Yeah, and?"

"If someone conjured the demon, how did the other one get here?" Annie asked. "How did they do this?"

Cham wrapped an arm around her. "We can look for the portal energy. It's got to be close to that house."

"Can I send Lial?"

"If he finds something, he can try and translate the magical energy. It can tell us how it was created. Like you, I had no idea we could do that," Cham admitted.

Annie yawned, exhaustion seeped through her. "I guess if there's residual portal energy, we might be able to trace the exact time and place. Knowing they came from the ninth century, give or take eleven hundred years ago, really doesn't leave me feeling confident." Annie turned and faced Cham.

"If there's a portal spell, maybe we can reverse and reopen it to the past." He sighed. "I don't know." He touched Annie's cheek. "I really don't want you to go back."

"Someone killed those demons, and the clues keep pointing to me being the one," Annie said. She touched his face, her fingers tracing the freckles across his nose.

"I'm hoping it'll be enough to send the Viking and the demon back with what we know, and you won't have to go back," Cham said.

"Whoever conjured them and brought him back got him here in one piece. Maybe it won't be so bad," Annie suggested.

"Doesn't matter. I still don't want you going back. There's too much that could go wrong," Cham responded.

"If someone else was in my position, you would support their trip back. You would do anything you could to help, to make the trip safe, to prepare. It's me, and for the moment, you need to forget that," Annie said.

He pulled away, his eyes moist when he looked at her. "If I can find a way to keep you here, I will."

"For now, I'm not going anywhere," Annie said. She rolled to her back and let his hands search her body as she found his. Her need for him and his need for her created a frenzy they couldn't contain. And for a time, nothing else outside of the room meant anything.

CHAPTER 11

THE LIBRARY WAS packed with employees from the Legal Department. Annie knew some of the lawyers, while others she had never seen before. Mrs. Cuttlebrink rushed around, dividing her time amongst them. She glanced up quickly as Annie walked in, offering her a curt smile while motioning Annie to use the library map to find what she was looking for.

Prior to finding the ninth-century demon and Viking roaming Evanston, Illinois, Annie had had no idea that time portals existed. Needing to know everything she could about them, she stared at the library map, picked up a scrying crystal, and searched for any existing books on portals. When the crystal necklace dropped, Annie used the location number and headed into the stacks of books.

Finding the location number, she was dismayed when she stared at one shelf with ten books.

With little choice, she picked up the first book and scanned for time portals. When the crystal gave her no answer, she replaced the book and searched the next. All but one book contained theories on how to open a time portal. The last book she scanned seemed to be the most comprehensive with actual steps on how to open one. Still anxious about the prospect of traveling to the past, Annie ignored the five-limit book checkout and precariously balanced all ten books on her way back to the reception desk.

Mrs. Cuttlebrink was efficiently pulling and dispersing books to the lawyers. Annie wondered if there had been a rash of cases, deaths, or law changes in the nonmagical world that brought so many magical lawyers here this morning. She wasn't surprised by Mrs. Cuttlebrink's knowledge of books as she returned from the stacks with several more.

Annie sighed as she waited for Mrs. Cuttlebrink and felt some relief when the librarian finally tore herself from the lawyers to join Annie at the desk.

"Hi, Annie dear. I see you'll be busy." She offered a smile as she began to check out each book, forgoing the five-book limit.

Mrs. Cuttlebrink shrunk the pile and pushed the miniature versions to Annie. As Annie grabbed the pile, Mrs. Cuttlebrink reached for her hand. "You always have a choice. Regardless of where the clues lead." She pointed to the door.

"You don't think I should go?"

"I think the magic is dangerous. I don't think you should." Mrs. Cuttlebrink smiled and walked away, returning to the lawyers.

⌘

Annie read the comprehensive book on time portals, spending an inordinate amount of time focusing on their creation and the magic that made up the portal.

"Girl. I've been hearing things. What the hell is going on?" Milo grumbled, entering her cubicle. She glanced up and lay the book upside down, open to her page.

Milo Rawley had been a wizard guard for thirty years, spending his last fifteen as the department manager. Annie wouldn't say he was great or lousy, he was just Milo, and she simply accepted him for all the good he'd done and all of his faults. In the last few months, he had been sickly, making him gruffer and more agitated than normal. While he didn't share the cause of his health issues, everyone believed his imminent retirement was a good thing.

Annie, in no mood to be jovial, matched her mood to his own cantankerousness, "Seeing as I'll be more powerful than all of you combined when this is over, I think you can start calling me 'Annie'," she said.

He glanced at her, a momentary look of shock on his face.

"Fine. You care to share… Annie?"

"See. That wasn't so hard, was it?"

He grumbled, but Annie jumped straight into replaying the events of the last few days, pushing Jason's case file to him. She suspected it was Ryan who had informed Milo, Annie wasn't sure how that made her feel.

While he shuffled through the pictures of her mother and perused her father's notes, she pulled out the Fraternitatem grimoire and opened it to the passage regarding her mother.

"Ryan told me," Milo said as he slid back the folder.

"I figured." She passed him the grimoire. He glanced at the cover and looked at her with raised eyebrows. "Mortimer gave me that," she said.

He read the passage she marked. When he finished, he said, "We had no idea it wasn't her in the coffin. They did a thorough job of concealing her."

"I know," Annie murmured. "I'm gonna send Lial to find the portal the Viking came through."

"Okay." He closed the grimoire, but if he wanted to leave, he made no attempt to stand. He stared at her. "Girl... Annie,"

"Milo," Annie said. She smiled nervously.

"The consensus is that you are this Anaise and must travel to the past. I promise you, we'll find a more appropriate and safe method to resolve this," Milo said. He pulled himself from the chair, though not without grunting and swearing. Annie smiled. She knew this was Milo's way of saying he cared.

"Hey, got a sec?" Annie asked Lial as scried for the Viking using his leather belt. Lial smiled and offered her a seat.

"Yeah. I'm not finding the Viking anyway. How can I help?" he asked. Annie glanced at the map.

"No hits at all, I see," Annie said as she sat.

"Based on the fact he appeared immune to magic and didn't use it, I'm guessing whatever is protecting him is also cloaking him." He pushed the map aside. "So what can I do for you?"

"Well, I'm currently researching portals. They're simple enough if you're opening a door to another plane of existence. What I've found on opening a portal to the past is general. I can go back, but not to a specific time and place. So," Annie pulled out the talisman. "I'm not sure if this has something to do with the portal. I know it's used to conjure a magical being, but maybe the magic inside could be used to track the portal. Specifically, for you to find the portal?" She raised her eyebrows.

Lial chuckled, summoned his crystal and ran it over the talisman, collecting the magic. "Yeah. I'll track it for you. I heard there's a thick patch of trees near that house. I would figure that would be a great place to open one," he suggested.

"That sounds like a plan. Thanks," Annie said.

"No prob. Give me an hour and I'll let you know what I find."

Lial strolled up the sidewalk to the abandoned house. The broken glass that covered the bushes and the porch had been cleaned and the broken window boarded up. The VAU had repaired the door hinges and hung the door, locking it when they left. Lial held his wrist six inches from the door, turned, and heard the lock pop open.

With a crystal in one hand and a flashlight in the other, Lial entered the house and took several passes across the floor. He moved the crystal in front of him, above him, and to each side, searching for any residual magical energy. He reviewed his crystal as it lit up, noting all of the spells, jinxes, hexes, and other magical energy for further examination. Lial followed the magic to the center of the front room, where he picked up a whiff of mullein just above the scorch mark in the carpet. His crystal glowed with a black-and-purple light.

Black magic!

Finishing with the opposite side of the room, Lial climbed the stairs, finding additional wayward jinxes as he reached the top of the stairs. To the right, he came to the closed door and jiggled the locked handle.

Odd.

Again, he popped the lock and entered the dark room. His eyes widened in surprise.

Someone is living here?

The room was small and neat, clean, and painted a soft yellow. The bed was made with a patchwork quilt. Pillows rested against the wall, their eyelet trim crisp, white, and clean. A small chair sat in the corner and a dresser was placed against the wall by the door. The marble top held a water basin and pitcher. He stuck his hand inside; it was still wet.

He summoned his crystal and roamed the small room, around the bed, across the bright yellow rug at his feet, anticipating the crystal would light up.

No magic.

He opened the dresser. The drawers were filled with women's clothing: light summer sweaters, slacks, a jewelry box. Lial snapped a few pictures on his phone, documenting the clothing, the room, and the wet basin, forwarding them to Annie.

Someone is staying here. Basin is still wet, he typed.

With one last scan of the room, he exited and locked the door.

The magic led Lial to the front bedroom, finding the kill spell Annie had used on the demon and the jinxes she had cast on the creature to get him leave and get away from her. He traversed the room, back and forth across the wallboard, through the thick dust, across the damp carpet, capturing all spells, jinxes, and hexes. His crystal lit up white, gray, purple, and white again as it processed the magic.

Wind pounded the old building; it creaked and groaned with an impending storm. When he reached the window, Lial glanced at the gray sky. He took a quick look at his crystal, which was now dull and matching the shade of sky. Believing there was no more magical trace to be found, he exited the house and headed into the trees.

At the start of the narrow trail, Lial immediately found the tell-tale signs of a wayward spell: broken, singed branches. He snapped a picture.

Footprints crossed the trail in all directions. They were unlike anything he'd found that day—smooth at the center and lacking a crisp edge or patterned sole.

Not modern.

He snapped more pictures and followed the footsteps that led deeper into the trees.

His phone rang loudly from his back pocket. He glanced at the screen. "Hey, Annie," he said.

"Hey, Lial. I never tried that room," she admitted.

"You were busy with the demon." He chuckled. "By the way, that house is loaded with magic. From what I can tell most of it is about as old as your kill spell. There were hints of older magic around the mullein, but I based that on the strength of the light. I'll go through all of the magic when I get back. If there's a conjuring spell, it's in my crystal." He took cautious steps down the path. He noted his crystal was glowing with good magic.

"I guess I won't keep you any longer. Let me know what you find." She was short and tense with a quick goodbye before hanging up.

The narrow, overgrown trail was seldom used by humans and opened to a small clearing. Lial estimated it was no larger than thirty feet across and was surrounded by evergreens and tightly packed trees. At the center, he found a cold campfire, charred rocks, and a cooking rack made from sticks.

From behind Lial, footsteps shuffled and the leaves rustled.

Lial turned toward the sound and peered inside the thick branches as something ran through the trees.

Portal first.

After several passes through the clearing, the crystal finally glowed a grotesque grayish green, and then it was gone.

"Huh?"

The color was one he was unfamiliar with, ugly and sickly. He moved the crystal back across the location. The magic was such a tiny spot; it took him several minutes to find the energy again.

Portals to the Black Market had consisted of magic that created a vertical entrance roughly two feet wide and six feet tall. The portal buzzed, hummed, and let off an icy, cold chill. When a crystal was used to find the magic, it would glow a purplish hue. Lial stuck out his hand, but he felt none of those things.

"It can't be that small," he said. Rather than assuming, he raised the crystal upward. A smile crept across his face as the magic trace grew larger.

⚜

Annie was deep in a book about portals, though she still could find no mention of returning to the past, when Bucky Hart knocked on her cubicle wall.

"Hi, Bucky."

He sat without invitation. His collared shirt and clean jeans surprised Annie; he normally wore ripped jeans, sneakers, and T-shirts. She refrained from raising her eyebrows in confusion.

When he settled in, he pulled out a folder and slid it to Annie.

Inside, she found the Donaldson family tree. She perused the first, second, and third pages, learning the tree went as far back as 795 CE. She traced the descendants finally finding another Gila Donaldson around 870 CE.

"So the coven came together around 795?" Annie asked.

"Think of Viking history. They raided England around 793. From what I could find, and it should be in the folder, is that the magicals really were left alone. They lived in the forests surrounded by magic. Something changed that. They seemed to form a more permanent society around 795, probably to protect against the Viking raids," Bucky said as Annie perused the notes.

"Okay. The demon in Tartarus is a little weirder. Its magical trace is from the eighth century, but the demon itself is from the late ninth century." Annie leaned back in her desk chair.

"So, the demons are reproducing?" Bucky asked.

"That's what we think," Annie said.

"Is there anything else you'd like me to do with the family tree or Gila Donaldson? I can work backwards and trace the coven, see if there's coven money and where they're hiding it, search for the other descendants in the area. Tell me where you'd like me to go with this."

"Nowhere in particular. Just run a non-active search and don't waste any time with it, but let me know if something pops up?"

"Just keep an eye out. No problem. I copied the buying agreement for the house. There's not much here."

"Well, if anything appears, let me know. Thanks Bucky," she said. He was looking at her closely. "What?" she asked.

"I want to take a different approach to finding your mom, but I wanted to talk to you about it first," Bucky said.

"Okay. What are you thinking?"

Bucky pulled out a sheet of paper. "Here's the deal, I've searched on Emily Pearce and Emily Worthington. I searched the standard: diplomas, credit cards, mortgages, bank accounts."

Annie nodded. "What's the plan?" she asked hesitantly.

"I'm going to make some assumptions. First, she's living in the Middle East like Arden Blakely was. Second assumption: Arden Blakely used her real name, so I'm going to assume that Emily is using her first name and a different last name, possibly by marriage, possibly just to make it harder to find her. I want to add to the search Emily Potash for your grandmother's maiden name and Emily George for your grandfather's name. I'd like to expand the search throughout the Middle East, and frankly, worldwide. We hadn't discussed how far you wanted me to take this, but I think it's important."

Annie folded her hands together. "Keep going. If I get these powers, I'd like to know where she is before she can surprise me." She sighed and offered a wan smile. She was trying to remain polite even though the more she learned about time travel, the less happy she was.

"I'm going to pull a list of women, first name Emily, who showed up in the Middle East after she died here. I'll continue to search with Pearce, Worthington, George, and Potash."

Annie sat up and leaned forward. "You're amazing."

Bucky blushed. "With your permission then, I'll get started and let you know. Always a pleasure, Annie Pearce."

Her phone buzzed in her pocket. She took it out and glanced at the screen to see a message from Lial.

I found the portal!

⤟

When Lial moved his arm up, he found the magical trace, but it would soon disappear again as if there were gaps in the portal energy.

Huh.

He brought his arm back down, found the beginning of the magical energy, and moved the crystal to the right and left, up and down, finding that the energy was not a large, oval patch of magic. Rather, it wound upwards in a tightly formed spiral. When he couldn't reach any higher, he glanced down the path. After verifying that he was alone in the woods, he levitated upwards, slowly and methodically tracing the spiral that widened with each pass. It ended with a flat, oval energy pool he estimated to be about one-foot wide and two feet long. Lial glanced down. He was hanging ten feet above the ground.

Slowly, he let himself down, following the spiral of the portal until he reached the ground. After finishing a text to Annie, Lial pocketed his crystal and was knocked face first into the earth.

CHAPTER 12

BY NOON, THE sun was hidden under a thick layer of clouds. The warm, humid air already smelled like wet earth after a storm. Another squall was close. Annie glanced at the gray sky as a clap of thunder rattled in the distance.

You're safe in the thunder.

It was an odd thing for Sturtagaard to say, Annie thought as she teleported from the courtyard with Spencer and landed in the clearing beside the house.

Annie scanned the clearing and saw Lial lying in the dirt. "Lial. Hey, Lial," Annie called out as she rushed beside him.

"I'm okay," he said and turned his head. "Someone knocked me out. Wanna guess who?"

Annie helped him sit.

Inside the trees, something or someone moved. Annie pointed toward the other side of the clearing. "The Viking?" she asked.

Spencer watched the trees. "I can't see anything now. We need to get Lial back."

"I'm fine. I'm fine. Check out the portal. It's fascinating." Lial stumbled when he stood.

"You okay?" Annie asked.

Lial grimaced. "Just go look. I sent you the coordinates."

Annie stood at the spot. "Here?" She held the crystal and found the pin prick of magic. "It's small." She glanced at Lial.

Lial grabbed her hand and moved it up and around, following the spiral. The crystal lit up a grayish green. When she couldn't reach any higher, Lial said, "Start levitating." She obliged and followed the magic until she was hanging ten feet in the air.

"This is... wow!" she said.

"I've never seen a spell that color before. And the portal..." Lial said.

She levitated down. Again, there was activity in the trees.

"He must be waiting for us to leave," Lial said.

Annie scanned the clearing, noting the cold fire pit at the center. "He must have stayed here and not in the house." She pointed to the fire pit and walked over. All that remained of his fire was cold charcoal and burnt twigs.

"If he stayed here, where are the rest of his supplies?" Spencer asked.

They broke apart, walking the perimeter of the clearing, searching behind small trees and bushes.

Spencer walked to a small cluster of bushes and knelt at the base.

"Find something?" Annie asked.

Spencer dug at the foliage, releasing a roughly sewn sack. "I'd say he's not magical. He had to hide this." He held up the sack for Annie.

"If he could, he'd have shrunk it," Lial said. Annie dug through the items, pulling out a half-eaten loaf of bread. The misshapen loaf was rough and dry. She took a sniff and grimaced. She next pulled out a second, smaller sack and opened it. The stench was overpowering.

"What is that?" Spencer held his hand over his nose.

"Dried fish?" Annie showed what looked like jerky of some kind.

While she looked for additional items in the bag, Spencer bent low and looked inside the bushes. "Missed something," he said as he pulled out several rolls of animal skin.

"Animal skins and a sack with food. A fire pit over there, so he probably hunted and cooked his food. So they bring him here to come and get me, and then leave him to his own devices in a world he doesn't know or understand?" Annie dropped the bread back in the sack and continued rummaging.

"It does seem like a half-assed plan," Spencer said through his sleeve.

Annie pulled out a lump of fabric and handed it to Spencer. He unwrapped the object, revealing a second talisman, an exact copy of the one Lial carried in his field pack.

"What do we have here?" Spencer asked as he held the talisman for Annie and Lial to see.

Lial felt the talisman in his field pack. "The other one in my pocket is buzzing and jumping." He summoned the talisman from his field pack, it visibly shook in his hand.

"They're reacting to each other? Maybe you should stand apart. That could be an issue," Annie said.

Both Lial and Spencer took a step back.

"Maybe a little better," Spencer said. Lial nodded in agreement. "One to get here and one to leave?" Spencer asked, snatching the talisman. He moved it around, looking at it from all sides, letting it rest in the palm of his hand.

"Maybe you need both to enter the portal," Lial suggested. "You've been reading up on portals. Anything about talismans?" he asked Annie.

"Nothing yet, but then info on time portals is a bit limited. I find it weird that one was hidden in the house and the other out here," Annie said.

"You think it means they shouldn't be stored together?" Spencer asked.

"I'm not saying anything. Just noting that they weren't found together." Annie took back the talisman from Lial and hid it away in her field pack while Spencer holstered the other one in his own pack.

"Anything else in that sack?" Spencer asked.

"I think I've got..." Annie touched the food sack and the bread, and then gripped something hard and smooth.

"A book," she said. "A new book."

It was the kind of journal you could pick up at any department store or office supply store. It was black with a spiral binding, the label still attached. She opened the front cover.

"It's..." she began, quirking an eyebrow in confusion.

"A diary?" Spencer asked, shaking his head. "Never mind. That doesn't make sense."

"No." She flipped through the pages. A map of the area, a drawing of Annie, an envelope stapled to the back cover.

"What's in there?" Lial asked.

Annie explained the contents as she pulled open the envelope. "There's several hundred in cash," she said. "Someone here is helping him."

"Okay. It just doesn't make sense. Why not just tell you that you have to go back, explain the events? Why all this trouble, why the Viking and demon?" Spencer asked.

"Essentially, they've had eleven hundred years give or take to set the plan in motion. It must have been passed from generation to generation, everyone having a role in making this happen, and this is the direction they chose to go?" Lial commented.

"This explains how they knew to come here, to this day and time. Not five years ago or ten years in the future. It explains how he knew where I'd be," Annie said.

She wrapped the animal skins and placed them in the bag and packed the notebook, shoving the sack back inside the bushes. She glanced at Lial. "I have a strange thought."

"They're moving from past to present all the time to make this plan work?" Spencer joked.

"Well, yeah. There's a Gila Donaldson in the original coven. I assumed it was a family name. Maybe it's not," Annie said.

"They had a millennium to get this right. It's time travel. They could, at any point in time, go back and forth and make changes over the years," Spencer said.

"But how did they originally get here and back?" Lial asked.

"They just needed one person to come forward, tell any of the coven members what happened, and set the plan in motion," Spencer suggested.

"Again to the correct time and place?" Annie asked. She crossed her arms against her chest. "I'd say the modern-day coven knew about the plan because they all have their own *Book of Shadows*, and the information was passed through time. They had to have gone back to make this plan work," Annie suggested. She glanced at the portal where the magical energy shimmered in the air.

"I'm not sure if it matters how they did it. We just need to get back and take care of the demons," Spencer said.

Annie glanced at him. "Problem is; I don't trust the coven with the handling of this. I'd like to know how they did it because it might help us figure out how to reopen the portal."

"You're not alone. I already told you this. You have all of us. We're smart. We'll figure out how to get you to the past and back to the future."

"Should we be allowed to, though?" Lial asked.

Annie leaned against a tree. "If we go back, we can change something that shouldn't be changed. Ryan's checking with the council to see if we need permission. But the repercussions are starting to weigh on my mind."

Footsteps pounded across the earth, and trees shook as a heavy body ran toward them. They all turned their eyes to the trail and saw the Viking run from the trees. He caught their stares and slid to a stop where his eyes found Annie. It was the first time she had eyes on him in bright light and observed him as carefully as he did with her. She noted his tattered clothing that looked like the demon's attire: the thin shirt hanging from his frame and the leather boots that were caked in mud, high as his knee, without a sole.

He couldn't take his eyes from her as he took a cautious step and then another. Annie summoned his pack and took a step to him.

"What are you doing?" Spencer whispered loudly. He and Lial raised their palms as Annie, paying no attention to them, stopped two feet from the Viking.

"Anaise," the man said and pulled his sword from his sheath. Spencer and Lial took another step closer as the Viking dropped to one knee, lifted the sword with two hands and bowed his head. She glanced back at Spencer and Lial, confusion across both their faces. She shrugged and turned back to the man.

When Annie hadn't taken the sword, he glanced up at her. "Anaise," he said and held the sword higher indicating she should take it.

Annie recognized the sword, the long thin blade, the decorative hilt, reminiscent of the carving on the library doors. She took the sword from him, holding it in her right hand. She made sideways movements and stared at the thick blade, which looked shiny as if recently poured. She lunged to the side, feeling the balance of the blade, the lightness. The handle felt good in her hands, like it was created for her, and the magic inside tingled against her palm. Annie raised the sword above her head, much like she did in the carving on the library door. It felt like an extension of her arm.

The man was still on one knee, still bowing his head. She put her arm down and tapped him on the shoulder. He glanced up at her, relief on his face. She pointed to herself. "Anaise," she said and then pointed to him.

"Kolgaar," he replied.

She nodded. "We should get him to Tartarus Prison. Keep him safe," Annie said. Cautiously, Spencer and Lial used magical rope to tie his wrists behind his back. This time, the magic was strong and held. The man named Kolgaar was tightly restrained.

"That's odd. Cham and Gibbs said the magic didn't work on him," Lial said.

Annie looked at the sword, touched the blade, and felt the slightest vibration from the metal. Spencer looked at her.

"What?" Spencer asked.

"What doesn't he have now?" Annie asked.

"The sword blocked the magic," Spencer realized.

The longer she held the sword, the more Annie could feel the magic hum through the metal. It vibrated against her skin, along her palm and up her arm. Lial, Spencer, and Kolgaar watched as Annie's magic connected to the magically imbued sword. A soft golden mist billowed from her palm and wound its way around the blade like a snake.

"Annie?" Spencer asked.

She looked at him, her mouth agape, her eyes wide. A spark flew from her palm, singeing her skin. She dropped the sword in the dirt and glanced at her hand. A dull scent of burnt flesh filled her nose.

Spencer ran to her as Lial guarded their "guest." He looked at her hand, summoned a bottle of water and placed water on the burnt flesh, healing the wound.

"I think the sword is yours," he said.

She nodded softly as the rain began to fall.

A thunderbolt flashed, sending a thick tree branch crashing to the ground.

Wind blew the rain horizontally across the tiny island housing Tartarus Prison, pushing Annie and Lial off course when they landed.

"You okay?" Lial shouted as he pulled his leg from the mud.

"This is nuts!" Annie shouted through a thunderclap. She shook violently as the cold rain pelted her body.

"Let's go!" Lial reached for her hand. They ran from the only teleportation location on the island, the clearing at the end of the lane where Jordan Wellington, Princess Amelie's boyfriend, was shot over a year ago.

Sometimes Annie thought she saw his ghost meandering through landscape when she visited the prison. Other times, she vividly remembered the events of that day and her stomach would churn. Today she saw neither a ghost nor the memories with the rain pounding against her.

Lightning flashed, and lit up the field beyond the clearing. Lial grabbed Annie's arm. With her shorter legs, she had to run faster to keep pace with him. A cramp seized her side. Rain continued to deluge the island.

The bird sanctuary that made up the tiny island hadn't been developed. The narrow dirt paths that crisscrossed the island were covered in holes and thick with mud due to the storm. Annie's foot splashed in a long pothole. She slipped, turning her ankle, and fell in the mud.

Lial reached for her as another shot of lightning crossed the sky. Spencer and Kolgaar's forms were visible at the opened gates of the prison.

"Almost there!" Lial shouted.

Annie hobbled after Lial. She lunged through the gates into the courtyard of Tartarus Prison. The gates slammed shut after them.

The rain continued to batter them as they ran through the front doors. The reception area of Tartarus Prison was small; the only window was the front door. Bright overhead lights attempted to add cheer to the depressing location, but only illuminated their flaws: their muddy pants and shirts, their wet, limp hair. Annie shivered in the stone-lined entrance as a heavy stream of air blew from the air ducts.

"Annie, Lial, here. For you," said Vivian, the evening guard, as she handed them towels and dry prison jumpsuits.

"Thanks." Annie rubbed her thick hair with the skimpy towel and peeled off her wet jacket, leaving it on the cobblestone floor.

"That's some storm," Vivian said as she glanced outside the small glass door. The courtyard was nearly empty. One lone tree stood at the edge of the yard. Whatever leaves had grown on it had been ripped off in the wind.

"Yeah. What a mess. Where'd they take Kolgaar the Viking?" Annie asked as she wrapped the towel around her neck.

"The first room on the left," Vivian told her.

Annie and Lial took turns casting a jinx into the security box on the reception desk. When the gate opened, they entered and headed to the bathrooms for a quick change. Leaving her clothes to dry on the stall door, she exited at the same time as Lial.

"You okay?" he asked.

"Yeah." She hobbled across the hall. "Just need some ice."

She stood outside the room as Spencer secured Kolgaar to the chair by his feet and across the chest, leaving his arms free. Once the Viking was secured, Spencer sat across from him and ran his towel through his hair.

"How was the trip?" Annie asked as she sat beside her partner. He dropped the towel on the floor.

"Teleporting's not his thing," Spencer said. Annie looked at Kolgaar and offered a smile. The Viking sat patiently, his face emotionless.

"But traveling through a time portal is?" Annie joked.

Spencer shrugged. "He hasn't responded when I speak with him. I find it odd they didn't send him with some form of a translator."

"Because this whole thing makes sense," Annie said.

Lial brought in a tray with food and placed it on the table. Kolgaar watched.

Annie pulled the sword from her waist and lay it on the table, pushing it to him. "Do you speak English?" she asked.

He didn't respond. She pushed the sword closer and asked him again. Still he didn't respond. "It repelled magic. I thought it might work as a translator," Annie said and shrugged.

"Gibbs and Cham found nothing on him. Maybe there's something in his bag," Lial suggested. Annie summoned Kolgaar's pack and tossed it on the table. He glanced at the bag, pulled it close, and reached inside. Not finding what he was looking for, he turned the bag over and dumped out the contents. Knifes, animal skins, food. Kolgaar looked at them and said something in a language none of them understood. Frustrated, he banged his hand against the table. The food bounced, and Annie jumped.

Kolgaar held his hands about four inches apart and repeated what he had said.

Annie mimicked his hands with her index finger and thumb. She looked at Spencer and Lial.

"The talismans?" Lial asked.

Annie shrugged and summoned the one she carried. Kolgaar's eyes widened; she passed the talisman to him. He stared at the statue with interest, pointed to the hole at the tip of its hat, and held the statue against his chest.

"Like a necklace." Annie summoned a roll of twine that she kept in her field pack, unrolled a strand about a foot long, cut it from the bolt, and placed the string through the hole on the talisman. She handed him the rope.

Instinctively, he tied the rope around his neck and looked at her expectantly.

Annie summoned the tray and slid it to him. "Eat something," she offered.

He nodded and pulled a sandwich from the plate, staring at the oddly constructed food. He pulled the first layer of bread off, took a sniff, and placed the bread back. He took a small bite and chewed and then another bite, quickly eating the sandwich. He reached for another, looking at Annie. "Go ahead," she said.

They watched him eat two more sandwiches before he placed his hand the talisman and pointed to Annie.

Spencer summoned the second talisman and handed it to her. Preparing the second, she slipped it over her head.

"Anaise. I have come a long way to find you," he said. Spencer and Lial glanced at Annie.

"Was that in his language or modern English?" she asked as she pointed to him.

"English," Lial and Spencer said in unison.

"You understand us too?" Annie asked.

He nodded. "I do. This." He pointed to his talisman.

"How can they hear you?" Annie asked.

Kolgaar glanced at her, then at Lial and Spencer, and shook his head. "I am not magical. I do not know how it works. The coven will know."

Annie glanced at the talisman around her neck; a statue to conjure magic, to summon demons, to translate the differences in language separated by thousand years. It had been so much work to bring him here, to have a place to run the operation, to take her back to the past. They could have sent anyone else back in time to stop the demons, once they knew how to kill them.

Why me? Why now?

What was it about Annie at this moment in her life that they would come for her now? Why not two years ago or in five years?

Sometimes she felt like the weight of the world lay on her shoulders, pressing down on her, and whatever move she made next would be the last move she ever made. She had blamed herself for Princess Amelie returning as a vampire, for the loss of the Black Market, for the wizard world almost being thrown into a magical war.

Is this a test? What if I fail?

"Annie? Are you okay?" Spencer asked. She glanced up from the talisman. It had drawn her in.

"Yeah. I'm fine." She looked at Kolgaar. "We need to prepare to go back. I wasn't expecting to find you today. I don't even know what date to go back to," Annie said.

Kolgaar was restless and squirmed against the metal chair. "What do you mean you need to prepare to go back? We don't have time for this. They should have prepared you. You should know how to do this and when to go back!" By the time he finished speaking, he had raised his voice to a shout.

Annie balled her hands into tight fists. She took a deep breath. "Did they tell you that? Did they tell you I would know what to do?"

"Yes. They did. They called on your ancient ones and read it in the fire. They told them it was you and that you would know what to do. We need to go back. My people are dying because of what..." Kolgaar meant to say something but refrained.

At his outburst, Lial placed his hand on Annie's shoulder as if protecting her. "Because of what?" Annie asked cautiously.

Kolgaar shook his head. "It doesn't matter. We need to leave. Now. They are waiting," he implored.

"Listen carefully. This is time travel. We can go back at any time. I just need you to be honest and give me everything you know so we can figure out how to help," Annie suggested.

"We respectfully request that you come with me to my time and rid the land of the demons," Kolgaar pleaded.

"Why Annie? Why not any witch from the future?" Spencer asked.

Kolgaar shook his head. "I do not have an answer for you. The coven..." he grimaced at the mention of the coven. "All that I know is that the old witch came to Jorvik and told us she saw it in the fire. Her face." He pointed to Annie with his free hand.

"How did they find her? How did they know what year she lived?" Spencer asked.

Kolgaar looked at the pile of items he had with him and pulled out the notebook. He slid it across to Annie.

"I saw this already. Did I miss something?" Annie asked.

"It was given to me by someone from your time. She gave me what I needed," he explained.

The wizard guards exchanged concerned glances. "Did anyone odd come to visit you in Jorvik? Clothes like ours? A funny way of speaking?" Spencer demanded.

Kolgaar shook his head quickly. "No. Nothing. Not to Jorvik. It doesn't mean those dirty witches..." He stopped and scowled at Spencer.

"Did they tell you why they were sending a Viking and not one of their own?" Spencer asked.

"I wasn't privy to the discussions. The coven came and offered a solution. King Hrothgar accepted their plan and they asked for volunteers. I know nothing else." Kolgaar glanced at Annie. She could see fear behind his eyes.

Annie pushed herself away from the table. "Kolgaar will be kept here in the prison until I'm comfortable in going back and have what I need in place."

"No! You must untie me. We must leave. Now, before there are more deaths. And those will be on your head!" Kolgaar shouted in frustration.

Annie sternly looked at Kolgaar. "I've already told you, we can go back to the designated date at any time. We don't need to rush out of here. In the meantime, we need a room prepared," she said.

Beyond the door, they heard a heavy thump and several voices shouting. Footsteps marched toward the room. They all looked at the door.

"Hello, brother," said Sturtagaard to a stunned room.

CHAPTER 13

"SHIT," SHE MUTTERED. She, Spencer, and Lial remained shocked by the bombshell. Annie stared at Sturtagaard.

His brother?

She searched for a familial similarity. Their hair—Sturtagaard's was jet black, Kolgaar's was light brown. While their eyes were the same shape, Sturtagaard's had turned black long ago when the demon took over. She wondered if they had once been the blue of Kolgaar's. Their noses were both long and thin, and their height was close, though Kolgaar was wider than the vampire, who was leaner and stronger with the demon coursing through him.

How is this possible?

Kolgaar was the first to speak, "This was my destiny to be here. Why did they send you?"

Sturtagaard stepped inside the conference room, a sneer of distain on his face. "There are many things you do not understand yet. You will come to know that you were not the only pawn in this plan. I have done things..." he looked directly at Annie. "I have done things that led me to this point in time. Because you are too smart," he pointed to Annie. "And you," —pointing to Kolgaar— "are too stupid to get this right."

Kolgaar glared at his brother, unaware that he was a vampire who had been alive for the last 1,100 years. All the Viking knew was that his brother had insulted him. Kolgaar jumped from his seat. Still attached, the chair moved with him. "Untie me!" he shrieked.

"No. You sit." Annie pointed to Kolgaar. "You, come with me." She grabbed Sturtagaard and dragged him from the room.

She threw a jinx, shoving him into the stone wall.

"What the hell's your problem, girl?" Sturtagaard asked. The jinx was so strong, the stone wall cut the back of his head. He touched the injury, sniffed the blood, and licked his fingers.

"You bloody little shit! This is all your fault!" Annie had never lost control around him; she couldn't afford to show weakness. But this was her last straw. Staring at him now, she believed it was Sturtagaard who had told the Fraternitatem about her; she could feel it to her bones.

Sturtagaard felt the chill around her and realized it was no longer fun to jeer with her. "We all have a place in this," he said. He stared at his bloodstained hand.

"You told them. You told the Fraternitatem about me, didn't you?" Annie began to pace.

Sturtagaard sneered. "You're not ready."

Annie threw another jinx, holding it against his throat. Though he didn't breathe, she knew it was tight and uncomfortable for him. Her hand shook as she raised him in the air. She released the spell and he slid to the ground.

Sturtagaard taunted her with a laugh. "You have no idea what you're walking into," he finally said.

"What's going on here?" Vivian asked, coming around the corner.

"Take him to the vampire cells," Annie said and stormed back into the conference room.

"Girl, we need to talk," Sturtagaard said.

"Take him away." Annie didn't look at him as she returned to the conference room.

Kolgaar said, "He... he was there when I left." The Viking seemed confused, working through the logistics, the timing, and the fact that his brother was here.

"He's a vampire. He doesn't age. In your time, he's still human," Annie said.

Kolgaar's eyes were wide, fearful. He looked at them with disgust. "It's not..."

"Possible? It is. That demon you just saw isn't the same man you know. He's a monster and has been for over a thousand years," Annie spat.

"Untie me," Kolgaar murmured.

Annie released the ropes around his chest and the ropes at his ankles. Kolgaar stood and paced along the back wall.

"You're the demons. You're evil with your magic," Kolgaar accused.

Maybe he's not wrong.

"What aren't you telling us?" Annie asked.

Kolgaar shook his head. "I'm here to bring you back, that is all. Keeping me here is doing little to help. I need to get you back before there's nothing to go back to!" He pounded on the table. Spencer and Lial raised their palms and faced him.

Kolgaar backed away. Regaining his composure, he said, "I need to get her back. Now."

"Are we keeping him in this room?" Lial asked.

"Yeah. We'll leave a spell on the door so he can't leave." She turned when Vivian cleared her throat behind her.

"The vampire wants to talk to you now," she said. "Alone." She stepped back and turned, heading for the reception desk.

"Make sure he's okay. Sturtagaard's lucky he's in the cell." Annie stormed off.

⇜

"Why are you here?" Annie asked Lial as he caught up to her.

"To make sure you're okay. Spencer can handle Kolgaar," Lial said. With seven inches on her, he easily matched her quick stride. She didn't hide her displeasure.

Turret Three of Tartarus Prison was a self-contained vampire wing, specially designed to keep vampires in, to deteriorate their metal stability, and keep them in a weakened state. Sturtagaard had lost his hand on an acid window in a cell the year before.

Annie marched to Sturtagaard's cell with Lial following closely behind.

The vampire perked up, smelling her scent as she entered the corridor. He stood against the wall, waiting for her arrival.

"Another new boy? You sure get around," he quipped.

"Your brother-in-arms or really your brother?" she asked.

"No jokes? No quips? No smartass remarks?" he asked and walked to the cell door, careful to not touch the holy-water-imbued bars.

Annie flung a jinx at the vampire. Embers burnt a hole through the thin shirt and burnt the top layer of skin. Lial stared at her, his mouth agape.

"I like this new you," Sturtagaard said as he brushed the fire from his shirt.

"Is Kolgaar really your brother?"

"Damn it, girl. Yes. He's my brother. Same mother, same father." He turned on the water from the sink, drenching the remaining embers. He stayed toward the back of the cell as if that could protect him from her magic.

"What did the Fraternitatem want from you?" she asked.

He leaned against the stone wall, his arms crossed against his chest. "How did you figure it out?"

"There's only two creatures who were alive back then: Zola and you. She wouldn't, and you told me yourself—you hated Anaise so much you wanted to kill her when you turned. Only, I was already gone. Wasn't I? So, what did the Fraternitatem want from you?" Annie asked.

Sturtagaard smiled. "When they found me, I was selling some items of importance to them. They didn't like it very much."

"What did you sell?" she asked.

Sturtagaard stared at her. "When I turned, I did several… things that caused the coven to become very angry with me. But because I was a vampire, immortal, they knew they needed me to make the plan work. To keep out of trouble, I roamed the earth, all of it. But I still managed to find trouble; at times, serious trouble. You see, vampires don't like to die. We want to live, the blood lust and all. While in the Israeli desert, I came across the hidden temple of Solomon. The riches could turn even you evil," he said to Annie, a light smirk on his face. "Gold menorahs, candlesticks, robes, gold pieces, some Chintamani stones. Back then, it was easy to pilfer the items and sell them. It was easier to hide. The Fraternitatem, however, has no sense of humor."

Annie winced at the thought of the Fraternitatem taking her mother, keeping this demon alive for their own selfish needs.

"You didn't hand them over the artifacts, so they decided to kill you?"

"No. They were very forceful. Very…" he bent over and raised his left pant leg, revealing that his calf muscle was nearly gone as if a predator had eaten it for lunch.

I've never seen that!

"They threatened to take me apart piece by piece. I gave them their shit back," he said and lowered his trouser leg. "I had a deal and I had to honor it."

"So, what did you trade your life for?"

"It doesn't do well to give up your contacts. I've never been one to burn that bridge. But I was caught with all of these pieces from King Solomon. And they wanted to know where I got them from. I had to give up my source to not be cut to pieces." His voice took a higher pitch. The vampire was agitated. He started to pace.

"They killed my contact and that made me a pariah. No one in the Black Market would touch me, talk to me, deal with me." He waved his arms in the air.

"Connect the dots. What did you use to bargain for your life?" She was just as agitated.

Again, Sturtagaard glared at Annie. The chill surrounding her was growing stronger.

He continued to pace. "Okay, girl. The Fraternitatem came after me. Wanted to stop the sale of the items. They kill anyone who stands in their way." He glanced at her. "I gave them the only thing I had worth anything. I told them about Anaise, about the demons, and your powers. I was already protected by the coven and was nearly staked by the Fraternitatem. But they… they were intrigued. I had heard about the power before I turned. I had the prophecy and I traded you for my life. Those bastards…" He began to laugh. "Those bastards bound me to them until you were born. Once I let them know that the great Anaise had been born and that your name was Anne Elizabeth Pearce, they took over, did whatever it was they needed to do, and I was completely free of them." Agitated, he sped up his pacing. Annie felt dizzy watching the back and forth. He stopped at the cell bars. "Your daddy did the same thing."

Annie summoned the picture of her mother and shoved it through the door. "No! They used that knowledge against my mom. They took her away from me. I was three years old when she 'died!'" Annie used air quotes and began pacing along the cell doors. "He died because he tried to get her back. The Fraternitatem wouldn't let her go. She wouldn't go."

Sturtagaard stared at her blankly. She summoned the picture back.

"You! You took everything I had!" She whipped the cell door open. It sputtered and squeaked as it slid into the wall. She walloped Sturtagaard across the chin. He floundered and fell backwards. She lunged for him, sitting across his chest, summoned a stake, and held the point to his chest. "Why shouldn't I?"

"Because he's protected until you get back," Ryan said from behind her. He walked casually into the cell. "You can stake him when this is over."

She let the Ryan take her stake and help her up. "Maybe I'll kill his human self when I get there." She shrugged Ryan from her and stormed out of the cell. As she slammed the door shut, locking the vampire inside, she said, "And my name is Annie." She turned and left Sturtagaard stunned and slightly afraid.

❦

"Why are you here?" Annie asked Ryan. He and Lial were both taller than her, with longer strides, and yet they had to jog to keep up with her.

"Spencer let me know what was going on. I need to show you something," he said.

Annie wiped tears from her eyes as she turned down another flight of stairs on her way to first floor conference room. It was getting late, she was tired, and she wanted this to end.

"He did this," Annie said.

"I know." Ryan reached for her, but she pulled away and opened the first floor door. Ryan and Lial exchanged glances as Annie turned right and entered the conference room. Mrs. Cuttlebrink had since arrived and sat with Spencer at the table.

"I'm sorry," Spencer moved his lips without speaking the words aloud. She understood his apology but ignored him.

"Why did you come out in this weather?" Annie asked the librarian as she took a seat.

Mrs. Cuttlebrink held up a scroll. "I wanted you to see this immediately." Mrs. Cuttlebrink placed the scroll on the table and rolled it to Annie. It had been sealed with wax but was now open. "We estimate it's from the fourteenth century."

Annie stared at the seal, the design was the familiar six-pointed star surrounded by four large bumps in the corners as if creating a box. "The Fraternitatem." She unrolled the dry and brittle scroll, which was written in Hebrew. She took a deep breath, waved her hand over the scroll, and watched the language fade out and then back in. She read aloud.

There will be a girl of the future, fair, smart, and lovely.

They will call her Anaise.

She will come to the land of the demons and save the natives there.

For her effort, her time, her sacrifice, she will receive the ultimate power.

Her magic will increase tenfold.

They will revere and bow to her.

They will owe her their lives.

Annie touched the seal. "This must have been when Sturtagaard told the Fraternitatem of Solomon, confirming they're involved. They knew the prophecy. They probably trapped my mom with this."

She sat back in the chair. Images rolled through her brain as she pieced together what they had. Her role, Sturtagaard's role. She couldn't understand the coven's disjoined actions.

"Why go through all of this?" she finally shouted. "Why send him to the future to bring me to the past? Why hide it? Why not just tell me what I had to do, let me prepare, and get it over with?"

Those in the room remained silent. There was no acceptable or reasonable answer.

"We need to go," Kolgaar murmured.

"I don't see any sightings of the regenerating demons yet. We have time," Annie said sardonically.

"Annie. This is serious. We don't need demons reappearing right this instant for you to go back. As much as I don't want you to go back, I can't help thinking that if you don't get back now, the past will continue without the benefit of your actions and the demons might start appearing. That will most certainly expose magic," Ryan said.

"That makes no sense. I can go back any time to the right place and time, and it won't matter," Annie argued.

Ryan held his hands together and touched his lips. "You'd be correct if the plan hadn't been set in motion yet. But it has. They called for you, and time has caught up to you. The plan is in motion. We're on a clock."

Annie shuddered, her hands shook as she stared at the words on the prophecy without reading them.

He glanced around the room. "Okay. This won't resolve itself tonight. We need to cool off and get back at it in the morning. Lial, Spencer, you look into the portal with the help of Sabrina. See what else you can learn. Go home and rest. Kolgaar, I promise we will get you back," Ryan said.

"We need to go now," Kolgaar reiterated.

"We don't know how," Annie said. A prison guard named Matt entered the room and set Kolgaar's room for the night. Annie took one last look at the Viking and left with Ryan.

They took a leisurely stroll down the lane to the teleportation clearing.

"I don't need you to protect me," Annie said as they entered the clearing. She sat at a picnic table that had never been used. No one knew why it was even there.

The sky was orange at the horizon and dark blue above them. She glanced at the moon and sighed.

"If I could, I'd have Milo put someone else on this. You're much too close to this case to be useful," Ryan said.

"I'm fine," Annie said.

"Really? Spencer said you pushed Sturtagaard against the wall, I saw you nearly stake him. We're restricted with him," Ryan reminded her.

"Blah, blah, blah." She knew she was acting like a petulant child. She no longer cared, and yet she knew she needed to get a grip if she were to go to the past. Her life depended on it.

"You're not sixteen anymore," Ryan said.

"You're not my dad," Annie replied. She shuddered. "Sorry, that wasn't nice."

"I have no idea what it's like for you. I didn't lose my parents. I don't have the weight of the world on my shoulders, dragging me down. But I do know you need to get over it and do it quickly," he advised.

Ryan handed Annie another scroll. The parchment had been stored in the records room since this version of Wizard Hall had been erected. Prior to that, it had traveled in boxes and baskets, and been hidden in dark dungeons and scattered across the United States for centuries. The parchment was darkened with age and ripped at the edges. The seal of the Great Wizard Council of America, a Valknut a design of three interlocking triangles, had been placed into the heated wax holding the scroll together. It was no longer shiny and looked cracked, as though it would break upon opening it.

Annie glanced at Ryan, who nodded his approval. She slid her finger under the top layer of parchment and broke the seal. She held her breath as she unrolled the scroll. Ryan shined a flashlight on the paper.

> *This is to decree that for his knowledge of past events, of the prophecy of the future Anaise, and the knowledge and power she will receive after defeating the regenerating demons of Northumbria, now England, for setting the coven of Northumbria free from the terror and power, allowing us to start the Wizard Council of the New World, Sturtagaard the vampire shall retain his freedom. He shall be allowed to roam the earth until his role in the event shall be fulfilled. He will, for this freedom and information, give help when asked and assist when necessary in all endeavors of the Wizard Council in the New World. When his time comes and his task has been completed, he can and will be terminated by the Wizard Council as they determine necessary.*
>
> *This is deemed effective immediately.*

Signed,

Wizard Council in the first

Etheldreda Browne

William Cockburn

Gila Donaldson

Henry Debenham

Anaise Gladwyn

Jacob Reeves

Jacob Rhodes

Gila Rutherfurd

Henry Turnbull

Samuel Vahn

Gwendolyn Townsend

Angus Wickham

Alastair Willoughby

Callum Wortham

Bryony Voxall

Rhys Younge

Annie's hands trembled. The scroll slipped and rolled into itself. She glanced at Ryan and teleported away.

⏳

"He told the Fraternitatem about the prophecy. He went to the house to make sure she gets to the past. That's his role," Ryan said to Cham. Annie sat at the top of the stairs, listening to their conversation. She wasn't interested in joining them.

"She's not safe," Cham said.

"He can't kill her. Not now. He knows what's at stake," Ryan said.

"She can't go back." Cham sighed.

Annie let her tears flow.

"She has no choice." Ryan handed Cham the scroll Annie had left behind. "We have no choice. We can't kill him yet."

Cham read the decree that had kept Sturtagaard the vampire alive for centuries. He could remember all the times they wanted to stake him and yet couldn't. The Wizard Council knew that Sturtagaard was off limits to staking, beheading, or fire. It was the way it had always been, though no one in the Wizard Council was aware of why—until now. Annie could see Cham's back as he read the decree. She knew without a doubt that the coven descendants had always known what was in it.

"We can stake him when this is over?" Cham asked for clarification.

"Yes. Tell her you love her, but you have to let her go," Ryan said.

Footsteps crossed the hardwood floor. The back door squeaked opened and shut again. Cham came to the foot of the stairs.

Annie looked down at him, still crying. Cham sat beside her, placed his arms around her, and let her cry.

CHAPTER 14

ANNIE STEPPED OUT of the shower, wrapped herself in a towel, wiped the steam from the mirror, and took a look at herself. She was tired. Her muscles ached from fighting the demon and from attacking Sturtagaard. She was tired of crying.

She shuddered and wiped tears from her eyes. The thought that she could die or not make it through the portal either way gave her pause, and yet, she knew the regenerating demons weren't alive now because she had done this in the past.

She dried herself off and slipped into her pajamas before wrapping her hair in a dry towel.

Cham lay in bed reading one of the books Annie had kept on portals. The rest of the books had gone back to the library. He noted something and scribbled in his notepad.

She entered the bedroom, dropped the wet towel on the floor, too tired to care and climbed into bed.

"Engrossing, isn't it?" she asked as she slipped inside the covers and lifted the blankets to her chin.

"It doesn't seem hard to build the portal. Talismans use blood-to-blood to direct the time. We just need to link blood-to-blood, Kolgaar's to Sturtagaard's, coven-to-coven."

"But how do we know I'll get back to the correct time and place? The coven was around for hundreds of years, and there's a lot of coven members to connect to over that time."

"I'm still reading up on that. I'm hoping they can use the portal energy to figure it out," Cham said.

"So that might be why they needed Sturtagaard alive," Annie murmured.

"Maybe. With everything so messed up, I wouldn't be surprised if the coven sent a vampire to turn Sturtagaard. But that's not the issue. The descendants of the coven had to be directing it. They knew what time to go back and where to go. They had to have conjured them here," Cham said.

"Gila Donaldson," Annie said.

"She knows more than she's willing to say. I think we need to take another run at her. We can bring Ryan with us to force her to give up what she knows." Cham floated the books and notes to the window seat and lay beside Annie.

Cham turned on his side and touched her cheek. His eyes were wet with tears. As time was speeding up, neither could hold off the inevitable: Annie was leaving for the past and might not make it back. He gently kissed her lips.

Annie felt herself sinking into to sleep and fought it. All she wanted to do was remain awake, look at him, take in his scent. He pulled away.

"Annie," he whispered. "Don't sleep yet."

Reluctantly, she opened her eyes. In front of her, Cham held a red velvet box with a large solitaire diamond ring at the center. She sat, her eyes wide with surprise. She was no longer tired.

"I think I fell in love with you the day I met you. You were so fun, so free, and all I wanted to do was hang with you. The greatest thing I ever did was to tell you I love you, to become us. Will you marry me?"

He held the ring for Annie.

"Yes!" she squealed and laughed. He slipped the ring on her finger. "I would be honored to be your wife. I love you." She placed both hands on his cheeks and kissed him, slow and soft.

He wrapped his arms around her. She leaned against him. "It's your beacon home because I believe you will come back," he said, kissing her again.

Reluctantly she finally pulled away. "I wish you could come with me," she murmured.

"Milo won't let me," he said.

"But if we couldn't get back, we'd be together," she said. She spread her fingers and stared at the ring.

Cham lay down, she snuggled beside him. "I'm sorry. I'm scared," she admitted.

"I am, too. I know you. You'll go and assess the situation, and you'll come up with a plan." He kissed her palm and started rubbing it with his thumb. "You need to sleep."

"I don't want tonight to end." She sighed and closed her eyes.

"If everything goes as planned, you could actually be back tomorrow," he joked.

"You're hilarious," Annie murmured as she fell into a fitful sleep.

◆

Annie offered a wan smile when Kolgaar looked at her. He lay on the thin cot mattress. Though she knew it must be an uncomfortable sleep, he seemed relaxed with his legs up against the wall.

"Hi," she said.

"We're wasting time. I need to bring you back," he growled and looked away.

"How do we get there and how do I get back?" she asked.

"The talismans together will open the portal," Kolgaar said.

"How did this originally happen? In the past? It doesn't make sense."

"It's a time loop." Kolgaar glanced at her, his eyes black, his lips pursed.

"So, the energy of your time and my time is connected. By who? How?" Annie asked.

She didn't wait for an answer and instead began walking an unfamiliar hallway. She was no longer in Tartarus Prison, and she was certain it wasn't Wizard Hall. Her confusion grew when Kolgaar caught up to her and matched her stride.

"You need Gila's blood," Kolgaar said. "You asked if I saw anyone who seemed odd or different. Gila Donaldson. Ask her what she knows."

Annie continued to walk, this time by herself and no longer down that hallway.

She scanned her surroundings and found herself in the middle of a small village surrounded by a thick forest.

"Where am I?" she asked. At first glance, the village appeared to contain about twenty small cottages. At the center, a large fire burned brightly. Attending the fire were two women. From the distance, she could tell one was a young girl, the other an older woman. Together, they fanned the large flames, added magic, and watched the fire move at their command. Curious, Annie stepped out from her hiding spot and strolled to the fire.

"Hi," Annie said, but the women either didn't hear her or they were ignoring her. Annie felt foolish standing there with her mouth wide open. She reached out and watched her arm. It was hers, but not; it was ghostlike, hazy. She touched the old woman's shoulder. The woman glanced through Annie as though she was not there.

"I'm not, yet," Annie murmured.

The old woman muttered under her breath. Though Annie didn't know the language, she knew the cadence of the words. The old woman was chanting a lengthy spell.

The size of the fire should have produced warmth, but Annie felt nothing. She thought it was probably because she wasn't really there. Curious, she positioned herself next to the dancing flames and touched the fire. It buzzed against her fingertips. Acting on instinct or moved by a force she couldn't see or explain, Annie stepped inside the fire.

Untouched by the flame, she turned and observed the women as they continued to chant. Suddenly, something changed for them, and their eyes widened in surprise as they saw Annie's face in the flames.

As though Annie knew what to say, she said in a clear, comfortable voice, "My name is… Anaise from the future. The ancient ones will send me to the land of the demons, to help rid you of the evil ones."

She stared at the women who trembled at her voice, her face, the fire. She opened her mouth to further explain, but it was no longer her voice that spoke. It was deeper, harsher. "She will receive the ultimate power; her magic will grow tenfold. And you will owe her your lives."

Annie shot awake, her heart thumping in her chest, her blood flowing, her hands shaking. The clock read 4:45 a.m. "What the hell," she murmured.

Beside her, Cham slept with his jaw and fists tightly clenched.

The dream became fuzzy images. To not forget what she learned, if it was real at all, she ran for a pad of paper and made notes about Gila, about the blood, the time loop. Reviewing everything only confused her and made her shake harder. She summoned her phone and began to make a call, but it was still dark outside and still early.

Keyed up, she sent a text instead, sat at the corner of her sofa, and waited for dawn to cross the horizon.

⋙

"You're up early," Cham said as he stumbled into the den, his pajamas hanging from his frame. He yawned and sat beside Annie. She handed him a sheet of paper.

"I had a dream this morning. I couldn't sleep," she said. The television was on low. The images flickered but didn't register with her. She took a sip of her tea.

"It's just a dream," he said as he read her notes. "Though, if this is true, if each time period still exists in an energy form, you would think it would be easier to get to the past. You could get anywhere," he said.

"The earth is four-and-a-half billion years old. How do you pick the right energy pocket?" she asked.

Cham laughed. "In the dream, Kolgaar said the talismans open the portals. They'd be created in the time you want to go," he suggested.

"Date, time, place," Annie murmured.

"It's closer and it's something. You've never been a good sleeper. Your brain seems to always stay alert and work. It was working through something last night," Cham said.

Annie snuggled against him. "Maybe. I'll talk to Kolgaar at a decent hour." She glanced at her phone when it buzzed. "Ryan and I will talk to Gila Donaldson. I want to know what she really knows."

Cham pulled her close. "I'm not sending Spencer to the past with you. He's got a family. Gibbs and Brite volunteered." Cham didn't look at her, but she could feel his muscles tense against her. His jaw continued to unclench and tighten.

"Really? That was very… generous of them," Annie said. The dim light from the television reflected against the carat stone of her solitaire ring, casting light against her legs. "It's beautiful, by the way," Annie said.

"I believe you're coming home. If I didn't believe that, I'd be a blubbering mess, thinking about losing you. I'm not a blubbering mess," he said.

"No, you're not a blubbering mess, but you're worried. Your jaw is tense and you're shaking slightly," she said and pulled away.

"To be honest, I don't want you to go. If I could, I'd send someone else or send Kolgaar back with instructions on what to do," he admitted.

"You gave me this now because you're worried I won't come back. You want me to know you love me," Annie stated.

"No. I do worry you won't come back, but this ring, use it as a lifeline home. I love you. I should have given this to you weeks, months ago. I trust you. I just don't trust the coven. I worry they're setting you up for their own needs."

"I don't trust them either. I couldn't have gotten luckier that Gibbs and Brite volunteered. They're smart, cautious, and good at what they do." Annie sighed and glanced at the clock. "I need to go to the prison." She kissed him. "I love you," she said and jumped up.

"I love you too," he murmured to himself.

CHAPTER 15

THE CELL BAR jingled when Annie knocked on them. Kolgaar glanced up. "What do you want now?" he asked.

"I... I wanted to know what you know about the talismans opening the portal?" Annie asked cautiously.

It was a dream.

"I told you everything I know about them when you were here a few hours ago," Kolgaar said.

Annie frowned. Her stomach roiled.

It was just a dream.

"I was at home in bed a few hours ago," she said. Her hands shook lightly.

Kolgaar looked at her quizzically. "No. You were here. Right there. I told you we need both talismans to walk through the portal."

Annie held tightly onto the bars. A wave of nausea gripped her. "You told me we're in a time loop and that Gila Donaldson was strange?" she murmured.

"What's the matter with you?" he asked.

Annie shook her head. "A few hours ago, when I was talking to you, I was actually at home in bed. Dreaming."

"You were standing right there. I talked to you, like we're doing now," Kolgaar argued.

"It's not that simple."

"Explain it to me then," he said.

Annie held her breath and released it slowly. "It's called astral projection. It's when your consciousness is separated from your body so that you can be in two places at the same time."

"We went for a walk. Down the hall," Kolgaar said. Annie glanced toward the door of the cell block. She knew it wasn't the same hallway. At least, it didn't seem like the correct hallway.

Where were we?

Annie looked at Kolgaar. "How did you get out?"

"The cell was opened. I just walked through."

Annie leaned against the cell bars. "I remember the conversation, I remember walking. I didn't leave here and go home. I went to the coven. I was there with two women, one young and one old."

Kolgaar looked frightened as she told her story. He seemed as though he would have walked away, but he needed Annie as much as she needed him.

"What do you mean you were at the coven? In the past?" He was confused.

"It had to be. The village was small. A lot of one-room cottages, and there was a fire pit in the center of the village," Annie said.

"That is the coven village." He stepped away from the bars.

"You know I'm magical. Get over it," Annie reproached. "I'm not going to turn you into a frog." She smiled, but it didn't calm him. She could tell her astral projection scared him as much as it unnerved her. It was just a power she didn't have and one that most witches and wizards would never experience. "Just tell me, why you don't trust Gila Donaldson?" she asked.

Kolgaar smiled. "She is… different. Hair, clothes. Not quite like the women in Jorvik or even the coven village," he said.

Annie was becoming increasingly convinced that the two Gila Donaldsons might be the same person, not just two people with the same name.

"Thanks," she said as an elf stepped beside her with a tray piled with food. She didn't wait to see Kolgaar eat. She had another stop to make.

⌇

The vampire lay on the cot, facing the stone wall. He was still and unresponsive even though Annie knew he could smell her as soon as she entered the hallway. If he couldn't have sniffed her scent, he would have heard her footsteps against the stone floor. He ignored both signals that she was there.

Trying to push my buttons.

She held her hands in tight fists. As much as she wanted to plunge a stake through his heart, she didn't. It didn't stop her from summoning her stake and flipping it.

He heard the ash stake smack against her palm and always the sound made him jump. This time, she knew he was really frightened.

"What do you remember about the talismans?" Annie asked. It occurred to her while watching his pathetic show that she really didn't need to know any more from him than she already knew.

Why am I wasting my time?

She turned to leave, not willing to play his game. The bed moved as she took a step away. Sturtagaard stood up.

"The talismans open the portal," he said. He was tall at over six feet, and yet, he seemed so small to her standing in his vampire cell.

"Do you know how they're used or how they were made?" she asked.

"I'm not a filthy witch. I don't have that answer," he jeered. But his sneer, his anger, seemed so weak, so false.

Annie lifted her palm to cast a jinx and thought better of it. She dropped her hand to her side. "Did you meet Gila Donaldson in the original coven?"

Sturtagaard startled at the sound of the name and slowly walked to the bars, standing away from the magical metal. He glared at her, hatred pouring from his eyes. They were dark, black, with fire burning inside. Yet, when he spoke to her, it was small, fearful. "Gila Donaldson is the key."

"Was it worth it?"

"Was what worth it?"

"You're just trying to be an ass for the sake of it," she said.

"You'll kill me when you see my human form. What difference does it make?" he asked.

"And if I do that, what will happen? I come back to my parents both alive, both here? And all those people I saved because you bargained away information to save your life. Was it worthwhile ruining my life? Was yours happier because of the bargain you made?" she sneered.

"My life was never happy, once my wife and son were dead," he said.

"The poor little vampire. We are on a time loop. And I will save the coven and your Viking village. And I will let you live with the pain of your family's deaths. And you will do what you will do and I will stake you when it's over. Because I cannot change one thing that doesn't have to do with killing the demons."

"It must be so hard to realize you've lost again." He smiled for a moment but stopped when he saw the anger in Annie's eyes.

"I haven't lost anything. Eleven hundred years you get to relive your pain." She held up the stake for him to see. "And this end, here, will meet your heart when I return."

"Maybe you will and maybe you won't. You see, I know where the new market is." He smiled broadly and gracefully set himself back on the cot facing the wall laughing.

⁓

"He laughed at me!" Annie said when they landed behind a tool shed in Gila Donaldson's back yard.

"What the hell did you expect? It's Sturtagaard." Ryan poked his head around the shed and looked into the yard, searching for prying neighbors.

"I hate him!"

"You can stake him when you come back," Ryan said.

"He claims he knows where the new market is," Annie said as they stepped into the backyard. She glanced around at the patio, the swimming pool. They were alone.

"You think he's telling the truth?" Ryan asked. Annie looked through the window of the downstairs living area. It was empty.

"I can work him over when you're gone. He bothers me less than he bothers you," Ryan suggested.

"That's up to you." They turned the corner to the front yard. Annie looked up at the large house and saw the attic curtains fluttering. "She's hiding in the attic again," she said. "By the way, Sturtagaard did reiterate what his brother said. Gila Donaldson is the key,"

"I wonder what that means," Ryan said as he rang the doorbell.

"I wonder if she's actually the Gila Donaldson in the past. Like a time traveler."

Ryan chuckled. "You're basing it on a dream."

"I didn't dream about Sturtagaard."

Ryan glanced at her. "Kolgaar insisted you were at Tartarus, huh?"

"Yes,"

"That's astral projection. Have you ever done that before?"

"No." Annie looked at the sky as a thunder clap roared above them. "The rain's coming again."

I'm safe in the thunder.

"Maybe you're getting your powers early?" Ryan suggested.

"She's avoiding us. I know she's home," Annie said, pressing the doorbell a second time. This time they could hear footsteps patter against the wood floor.

Gila Donaldson's eyes grew wide when she noticed Annie standing with the Grand Marksman of the Wizard Council. She nodded and motioned for them to enter. Annie and Ryan exchanged looks and followed her inside. They took seats in the front room across from Gila. "I told you what I know."

"Kolgaar said you were in the past. And both he and Sturtagaard said you're the key," Annie said.

Gila Donaldson looked at Annie, unsurprised by the pronouncement. "I'm not her, if that's what you're thinking."

"It was, actually. So, how are you the key?" Annie asked.

"Someone had to set this up," Gila said, no emotion in her voice.

Annie could feel Ryan's hand on her back. He squeezed lightly. "We understand that Annie has to go back," he said. "We're not finding anything useful in the archives or in the research. How do we guarantee she's going to be safe without you telling us everything?"

"I'm not supposed to say anything. This was a test for you. You will receive immense powers. The ancient ones wanted to make sure you're worthy," Gila said.

Annie sat on the edge of the chair. "Listen carefully. I don't care about the powers. I care about getting back home without dying or changing the future."

Thunder roared and shook the house, rattling the glass panes. Annie glanced outside, a shadow passed across the window. "Tell me what to do!" she implored.

Gila sighed. "I was given very specific instructions on how to handle this—when to conjure the demon and bring Kolgaar back." She stood and waved for them to join her.

Ryan and Annie followed Gila to the back of the house, where they climbed a narrow staircase that led to a locked attic door. Gila cast a spell into the lock and turned the knob when the lock clicked open. With a flick of her wrist, a single bulb at the center of the room switched on with a dim, warm light.

Annie scanned the attic. It was what she would expect from a house large enough for an altar room. Around the room were bookshelves filled with books and jars of herbs. Crystals lay across the flat surfaces and, most importantly, an altar sat at the center of the room with a *Book of Shadows* on top.

Annie joined Gila at the altar, the book was opened to a page with Annie's hand drawn face on it. Under the picture was the name Anaise. Annie perused the passage.

"There's too much here," Gila said as she rummaged through the pages and ripped the necessary sections from the book. "You need this more than I do. If you don't get the powers, I can't guarantee what will happen."

"I'll worry about that later. Thank you," Annie said.

"Is there anything else?" Ryan asked.

Gila frowned and sat on an antique sofa. "If you're okay not receiving the powers, then I might as well tell you the story."

Annie sat beside her on the sofa, the pages of the *Book of Shadows* still in her hands.

"The coven prayed to the ancient ones. I'm sure you've heard of them if not believed in them at one time."

Annie did not. It was an ancient religion that meant nothing to her family. She nodded respectfully though.

"The coven prayers were answered when they saw the face of Anaise in the fire. The face told them that she would come to the them and help them. But they wanted to know more. They called on the ancient ones again. This time, I received the message. It came about a year ago, and it's then that I put the pieces into place based on those pages." Gila touched the pages.

"How old were you when you found out you'd be receiving the message?" Annie asked.

Gila laughed. "I've known since I was a child. It was written in those pages and read to me like a bedtime story. I was instructed from a young age to pay attention and do what I needed to do to make the plan work. I created the talisman and got the statues to the past. I gave the coven instructions. We're on a time loop of some kind."

"I had a dream last night that I was in the fire. In this dream, I told them my name and what would happen," Annie said.

Gila glanced at her with a worried expression. "You were really in the fire?"

"It was a dream," Annie insisted.

Gila shook her head. "Did it feel real, like you were really there? Have you always been able to astral project?"

Annie held the edge of the sofa with a tight grip. "No. I haven't had that power," she murmured.

"The ancient ones. They've set this in motion when the coven called to them," Gila explained.

"Maybe not. You're linked to the original coven through your relative with the same name. They prayed to the ancient ones and you received the message instead," Ryan suggested.

"Maybe that's true. I don't believe in the old magic either. But the coven does." Gila smiled fondly.

"I've heard the same stories growing up. But who are the ancient ones really?" Ryan asked.

"They are the Fates."

"The Fates." Annie looked at Ryan. "Clotho the Spinner, Lachesis the Apportioner, and Atropos the Inevitable."

"You know them?" Ryan asked.

"Zola told me the folktales growing up. The Aloja fairies, they're linked to them. They sent Zola to us," Annie explained. "I always thought they were stories."

"Sometimes, the stories are based in truth," Gila said. "Annie, we are linked to that point in time. Your magic, my blood. They are forever joined, and it seems like you and I have been floating between the two."

Annie glanced at the pages in her lap.

"I can't tell you more. I wasn't supposed to tell you anything. We have to honor our roles in this," Gila said.

"Thank you for this. If I don't get this power, I'll be fine with it," Annie said.

Gila pulled a vial from her skirt pocket. "Here."

Annie recognized the blood and took the vial. She and Ryan followed Gila out of the house and said their goodbyes, teleporting themselves to Wizard Hall.

CHAPTER 16

ANNIE SAT IN a guest chair in her cubicle, which far more comfortable than the desk chair. She placed her legs on her desk and sank into the back cushion, reading the notes from the Donaldson *Book of Shadows*.

"Did she talk to you?" Cham asked as he entered and sat beside her. Annie held up the pages. "And?"

"It's blood-to-blood. And apparently we've both been traipsing through time."

"Your dream really happened then? You astral projected?"

Annie shrugged. "I guess. I don't have that power though."

Cham sat on the edge of the chair and hung his head. "You went back to the past."

"Ironically, I'm the one who gave them the prophecy," Annie said.

Cham chuckled. "Time travel is headache inducing."

It was Annie's turn to laugh. She handed him the page on portals. "It's all here. How to open the portal. We need the talismans. And the Donaldson blood."

"It's that simple," he said.

"Seems to be."

Cham read the pages. "I was hoping we wouldn't find the answer. Then you couldn't go back." He handed her the sheets. "What do you need from me?"

"Do we need permission from England? To go back?"

"To the ninth century? Wizard Halls weren't established back then. Mostly individual covens. I wouldn't think you'd need to. I can check for you."

"Avrum's been around since then. I should probably take some back with me in case I need to make a purchase." She offered a wan smile knowing the highly prized ancient gold coins could be helpful.

"What else?" He let his hand graze hers as she turned back to the pages.

"I didn't know you could open a portal to the past. Ryan was supposed to call a Wizard Council meeting to discuss."

Cham bit his lip as he thought. "Ryan hasn't yet. But you're right. It's like a memory modification. You could change the future, this present," he said.

"Apparently, Gila's been going back and forth."

"That's a problem. I'll talk to Ryan about that and verify if he's talked to the Executive Council."

Annie turned and faced him, taking his hands in hers. "I need to prepare. The sooner I leave, the sooner I'll be back."

"Baby, you could be back in five minutes with time travel," he said.

She reached over and kissed him. "Then I'll see you in five."

∽

The emergency meeting was pulled together so quickly, Annie barely had time to pull out her Wizard Council wool robes. She was hot inside the heavy fabric and tugged at the collar as she waited near the back of the line for other council members to cast their spells into the lock box, gaining entry.

When it was finally her turn, she cast the required spell, which opened the door for her, and she slipped in. She grabbed the agenda and walked into the large auditorium, which fit over five hundred people.

Today, she wasn't sitting in her assigned seat. She took her place beside Cham and Milo at the table on the bottom floor. They were surrounded on all three sides by seats that reached to the ceiling, the Grand Marksman's chair behind them. Today, the second-in-command, James McIntosh took the seat. Annie glanced around and found Ryan sitting beside Gibbs in the Wizard Guard section.

"Why isn't Ryan presiding?" Annie asked Cham.

Cham glanced over at the team. "He recused himself from this vote because of you. He thinks it will be close and doesn't want to have to break a tie," Cham answered as he fiddled with the projector.

Sabrina Cuttlebrink, in addition to being the Wizard Hall librarian, was also the Wizard Council secretary. She made her way to the floor and sat in her seat near James McIntosh. She offered Annie an encouraging smile before preparing her duties.

Annie's palms, neck, and breasts were dripping in sweat. It was the vote, the lighting, her nerves. When the last Wizard Council member took their seat, the lights dimmed, and James McIntosh called the meeting to order.

"Emergency meeting of the Wizard Council is now called into session by myself, James McIntosh, Vice Grand Marksman. I turn the proceedings over to Robert Chamsky, Assistant Department Manager of the Wizard Guard." Cham nodded and stood at the podium. He clicked on the first picture that appeared on the screen above the Grand Marksman's chair.

"This demon and this man were found roaming a neighborhood in Evanston, Illinois, for the past week. After testing their clothing, the Wizard Hall lab determined they came from ninth century England, then known as an area called Northumbria." Cham switched pictures. "In the course of the investigation, we discovered that the demon and the Viking were summoned here by the descendant of an original coven member named Gila Donaldson, who is in the auditorium today. The purpose of conjuring and bringing forth the man was to fulfill an ancient prophecy involving Anne Elizabeth Pearce, who is said to have killed the ancient demons in the past." Cham clicked on the next picture, the prophecy itself.

"This is the prophecy. You all have a copy of it in your packets. Also in your packets are copies of the Donaldson *Book of Shadows*. You'll also find the decree that allows Sturtagaard the Vampire to remain alive, a letter from Jason Pearce to Anne Pearce about the prophecy, as well as a picture of Anne's mother taken eight years after she supposedly died. As per the prophecy, Anne is to receive an ultimate power for her duty. We believe this in all in preparation for the Fraternitatem of Solomon to come back. We believe they are coming back for these powers."

A collective rise of surprise came over the crowd. Cham hit the gavel against the podium. "Please review the items in your packet. When you have questions, use your signals. I also want to inform you that Ryan Connelly isn't presiding over today's meeting due to his relationship with Anne and will not be available in the instance of a tie break."

The din rose around them as Cham sat beside Annie. "You okay?" he asked.

"No. I feel sick," she admitted.

"Yeah, so do I."

When the din silenced, they could see the closest Wizard Council members reading through the packet.

It was almost time for discussion.

It came almost immediately.

"I don't even know where to begin but I have concerns sending our own people to the past." Annie looked up to see a witch named Bertha who was the department manager for the Office of Special Requests. "How do we know she'll get back? What are you doing to protect her?" Bertha remained standing. Her face pale and worried.

"I'm bringing a team to help," Annie said. "But the reality is, there are no regenerating demons in our time, so we know someone killed them. As I'm the object of the prophecy, we believe that means me. I have notes from the original coven, including a description of the magic used. I risk my life all the time for this job. And this is one of those times. I fully accept the responsibility and realize there's no guarantee that I'll come back." Speaking the words made it all too real and Annie felt dizzy.

"What is the plan to get them back?" a wizard in the first row asked.

Cham explained the opening of the portal and that they were still working on the exact procedure.

"What about changing the future? How can we guarantee that won't happen?" It was a council member Annie couldn't recognize in the dim light.

It's a legitimate question.

"We have the pages from the Donaldson *Book of Shadows*. It's pretty clear on those pages what Annie had to do. She'll follow those instructions and perform her duties with as little disturbance to England as possible." Cham said.

"But if not?" asked another.

"The VAU is working on how to monitor the situation," Graham Lightner offered.

"But how will you know?" asked a council member.

The disagreement raged on, as it should. They were all concerned how changing the past might change their present and future.

Graham said, "We will find a way to make sure life doesn't change. I have ideas that might work. How much time do we have?"

Cham looked at Annie. Annie stood again. "I think we need to leave as soon as possible. Kolgaar is getting anxious. How soon can you have something?" she asked.

Graham whispered to his second-in-command, the assistant manager named Sky Allen. He looked up at Annie. "We'll test our theory immediately if the vote is for yes," he said.

"Is that enough?" a voice called out through the darkness.

The discussion continued for another thirty minutes, the longest discussion the Wizard Council had ever had since Annie joined three years ago.

When the voices calmed, James McIntosh said, "I call for the vote on whether to allow the Wizard Guard to open a time portal."

"I want to make conditions to that," Ryan called out. All five hundred Wizard Council members turned their attention to Ryan.

He said, "I think that there should be restrictions to this. Annie's contact must be limited to the Vikings and to the coven. Annie should in no way be permitted to interfere in any other plan or scheme, only what is required to rid the demons from England."

There was a short discussion amongst the council. James used his gavel to bring order to the room. "I agree with those conditions. I call the vote. Please complete your vote in your book at your seat."

Annie could hear some discussion, most were scrawling their notes inside their magical books linked to the original beside James. When the witch or wizard was finished, they lit up the crystal at their place. When all crystals were lit, James opened the book. "There's a tie, 250 to 250."

Annie exchanged a worried glance with Cham.

James wrote something in the book and lit his crystal. When he was done with the tie breaking vote, he said, "251 votes for yes, 250 votes for no. Annie Pearce will lead a small group of wizard guards to ninth-century England to fulfill this prophecy. Meeting adjourned."

⤝

It was late in the day when Annie finally left the special council meeting. While most departments were winding down for the day, she still had things to do and headed to the telecommunications department, not to speak with her favorite computer hacker, but to get a specific supply for her trip.

A special support team had been set up adjacent to the telecommunications department that helped wizard and witches obtain necessary items to assist with their jobs.

The Office of Special Requests worked in conjunction with the telecommunications department to help create nonmagical birth certificates and passports, police or other office identification, driver's licenses, bank records—any paperwork that a magical didn't necessarily have but might need in order to perform his or her duties. It was also a bank that had a complete collection of currency, where Spencer had gone when he and Annie were in France several months prior.

Any of the items in this department required management approval. She looked at her request form, signed by Cham and sighed as she lay it on the counter.

"Hi, Bertha," Annie said.

"Annie." She nodded and reached for the request form. "Just avrum?" she asked.

"Just avrum." Annie smiled.

Bertha frowned. As the department manager, she had been to the meeting. "I don't know how I feel about you going to the past. A lot could go wrong," she said.

"I know." Annie watched at Bertha placed a finger in the blood lock and opened a walk-in bank vault. She returned several minutes later with a leather pouch filled with gold coins.

"I voted no," Bertha said as she slid the pouch through and opening in the window.

"That's why we vote. Everyone has a voice and the majority in this instance allowed for a time portal." Annie picked up the bag, the coins jingled.

"You be safe, okay," Bertha said.

"I promise. In and out. Nothing else," Annie said and waved, leaving Bertha to her books and figures.

⚜

Cham poured another cup of coffee he didn't really want. It merely gave him something to do and was warm on his cold hands. It left his stomach feeling nauseous, and yet he took another sip.

"I got your message," Graham Lightner said as he stepped inside the long narrow cubicle and took a seat.

Cham drummed his fingers on the desk and put his mug on the blotter.Graham swallowed, his jaw tensed. "She went, fought, and killed the demons. All her interactions in the past created the future, our present." Graham sighed and continued. "Time has since caught up to the moment she was summoned to the past. Since she doesn't know what she did and does something different, it could potentially change everything. Even the most innocuous incident. I'm hoping Ryan's conditions will be enough." He was nearly whispering.

Cham let out the breath he had been holding. "So like the butterfly effect? If she steps on a butterfly, she'll change the future?" Cham asked.

Graham shook his head. "No. What if they meet someone they weren't supposed to meet? What if they brought with them an illness and passed it on? To a future leader. Or if someone dies because Gibbs and Brite are there and they weren't originally there?"

Cham's hand trembled as he held the book he was reading. "I would have sent her back with help. Regardless of what the prophecy said."

"I would assume that as well. So realistically, I'm not worried about Gibbs and Brite. To get you up to speed, we've been keeping an eye history books. The problem is, we think if something changes it will be a collective memory shift and we won't know it's happening," Graham admitted.

Cham sat thoughtfully carefully weighting his words. "We... I didn't think about that."

Graham laughed. "What do you think I'm here for? I keep the world moving as it was. I have an idea about that." Graham reached out and dialed his phone, placing it on speaker.

"Hey, Graham. What's up?"

Cham recognized Bucky's unmistakable voice.

"I'm here with Cham explaining the situation. Do you have a minute?" Graham asked.

"I do. We've been watching for something to happen as well. But you know the situation," Bucky said.

Cham sat at the edge of his chair. "Okay. So, what do you think?"

"This is the deal," Graham said. "Energy, magical and otherwise, is all around us. While none of us seemed aware of time portals, we're assuming we can travel in time because that pocket of energy still exists. People, places, the ghosts of the past, are all around us. We tap into that, open a portal, and walk through. That's oversimplification, but that's the general idea. With me so far?"

Cham nodded.

"I'm good," Bucky said.

"The first changes in history will be the first days, weeks, and months following whatever they do to change history." Graham stood up and began to pace from the wall to the desk. After two laps, he stopped and bent over the phone. "Whatever history is changed, the corresponding written and collective world knowledge will change. We won't know it."

Cham nodded.

Graham sat back down, crossing and recrossing his legs while he waited for Bucky to stop typing and for Cham to take a steady breath.

"What if sending them through the portal changed history in the way it should have been? Maybe it was bad before and we just made it better?" Bucky asked.

Graham glanced at the phone. "We wouldn't know that either," Graham admitted.

"It's sounds like we're screwed either way," Bucky said.

"Annie has no choice but to go through the portal because there are no regenerating demons in this present," Graham said.

"So my tracking history won't do anything useful. How do you suppose we track the changes?" Bucky asked with worry in his voice.

"We know for certain that they'll be regenerating demons," Graham suggested.

They could hear Bucky typing on his keyboard. "Good news. Assuming they'd be overrunning England first, I just checked: there are no regenerating demons reported yet," he said.

Cham turned to the book shelf that lined his back wall and searched for a tome. It was thick and covered in worn leather like most of the books he had shelved.

"Is it safe to say that all history books in the world are tied to actual history? That, as history changes, all the history books, all books about history will change with it?" Cham looked at Graham for confirmation.

"That's the assumption." Graham looked at the history book Cham retrieved.

The *World History* was a school book of nonmagical history as it was woven with magical history, a full review of all the events that had taken place since the beginning of written time.

"So, Cham just pulled down his nonmagical history book, the one we all used in school. We had an idea, but honestly, we're not sure if it will work." Graham grabbed the book. "We think we can lock the book so to speak, so what's in here won't change if the rest of history changes."

"Actually. we have that book online now. We can lock it there and I can write a quick algorithm to look for changes against that book," Bucky said.

"We're pushing for them to leave tomorrow. Can you do it by then?" Cham asked concerned.

"It would have been great to know this sooner, but I can have the whole team on it and have it ready tomorrow morning," Bucky said. "My only question is, what would happen to the magical and other energy that we've created here and now if the history changes? Will alternate worlds pop up?" Bucky asked.

Graham glanced at the phone, his eyebrows raised. "Alternate realities." He bit his lower lip while he thought and solution to the problem.

"I'll tell you what. That's a good theory. I wonder if we can track the energy of alternate worlds. But, for now. I think that's getting too deep into this. I think what you should do, Bucky, is create the algorithm. Don't you already have software to track anomalies? Things that seem weird?" Graham asked.

"We do. We'll watch that and look for strange energy spikes. You lock the paper version of the book and send me the spell. I'll lock the online version. Scanning the internet will be faster. And I'll look for the demons," Bucky said.

They said goodbye and left Bucky to search for anything "weird."

"He's right. We could've used more time." Graham said.

"It's just happening so fast. I was hoping we could have avoided sending them," Cham admitted.

"I'll take the book, if that's okay?"

Cham nodded and watched the opening of his cubicle long after Graham had left the department.

∽

Annie and Ryan were the first to arrive in the fifth floor conference room. She stood at the large window and stared at the street below. Cars stopped and started as the traffic flowed in a choppy manner, as was usual for downtown Chicago.

The sun, low in the horizon, cast an orange glow across the buildings. Employees left their jobs for the evening, streaming out of the buildings for restaurants or home. They were completely unaware that a time portal would be opened within hours and that a witch was heading to the past to save them from demons that hadn't been seen in centuries.

Footsteps crossed the carpeting, and chairs were pulled from around the table. Cham touched her shoulder. "You okay?"

She glanced at him. "Are you?"

They sat in the waiting chairs: Cham, Gibbs, Brite, Lial, Ryan, and James McIntosh. Annie sat in between Cham and James, feeling nauseous; it was really happening.

"This is for you," James said as he slid a scroll to Annie. She unrolled the parchment:

Anne Elizabeth Pearce has been given permission by the Wizard

Council of America to open a time portal. Her orders are to return the
Viking to his time and eliminate the regenerating demons in the past.

Annie glanced at James. "I would have been okay if you didn't give permission."

"I suspect that is true." James smiled and patted her hand.

"It doesn't say the demon. Might I ask why?" Annie asked.

James glanced at Gibbs and nodded. Gibbs said, "I requested that we only bring back the Viking. The demon is too unpredictable. I expect we'll be performing some spell to kill them. If it works, it should kill the demon at Tartarus. If not, we'll shoot it with fire when we get back," Gibbs said.

As the minutes ticked away on the clock, Annie felt time running out. It had become fact, that she would be traveling to the past to kill the demons. She had been so preoccupied with figuring out how to get back, it had left her little time to figure out what she would actually do once she got there.

Annie focused on Cham, who handed her a sheet of paper. "I consulted with the law department. You don't need permission from the Wizard Guard in England because you are going at the request of the coven. Not to mention, you'll be there at a time when there was no Wizard Council. On the advice of the law department, I did let the British Wizard Council know what is going on," he said.

"And?" Annie asked curiously.

"I think they were a little taken back that one of their wizard guards wasn't called to do this. I gave them a copy of the file and reminded them that the coven of the ninth century became our original Wizard Council. I think that eased their dismay a bit," Cham said.

"Do they have an expert in English magical history?" Annie asked.

"Actually, they do. They offered to send someone with knowledge of the coven. I thanked them but said no. I worry that working with someone you don't know in this situation would be more difficult. You wouldn't have time to form a trust bond, and that could put you all in danger. They agreed with that. But they did send Lial some interesting things that he can explain to you," Cham said as he pointed to Lial.

"I've been pulling maps for several hours, but I haven't found anything as comprehensive as these." He pulled several scrolls, unrolling them and flattening them against the table. "There is an original map that looks like it's from about 866, which is the later part of the ninth century. They also sent names, dates, events. It's the research they have on that original coven. There's nothing about you, but it may offer some help." He slid three parchments to Annie. She looked at the map from 866. It listed towns and any roads through England at the time. She pulled the next sheet, which listed the names of the original coven members and their family ties, as well as a list of several members of the Viking colony in Jorvik.

"This is good," she said and looked up at Lial. "Thanks."

"Glad to help. The next piece, though, is a little trickier. Opening the portal itself is easy. It's opening it to the right date and time, that's harder. We can't send you too early, because Kolgaar can't return to his timeline while he's still there in the past. We have to return him the day of or the day after he left."

"So, how do we do that?" Annie asked.

"Reverse the portal energy that's near the house using a simple polarity spell. It's already linked to the past. It's where he came from," Lial explained. For reference, he pulled out a book and passed it to Annie. She opened the marked page and read the passage.

"It's really that simple?" she asked and handed Cham the book.

"I don't think any of us realized you could open a time portal. It's not so difficult to open the portal, and reopening that one will get you where you need to go." He smiled.

"It sounds like it could work." Cham's jaw clenched tightly as he passed the book to Gibbs and Brite. Annie couldn't help but notice, and it broke her heart. "Just an update for you: I talked to Graham and Bucky. They're working through ways to determine if events change in the present." He glanced at his phone. "They actually think they figured out a spell to do the job." He sighed.

"Okay. That eases my mind slightly. If there's nothing else, I think we should go home. I don't think I can put it off any longer. We'll leave tomorrow morning," Annie said.

"I think, then, that's the plan," James said, leaving everyone concerned.

CHAPTER 17

ANNIE STOOD ON the porch of her house, protected by a blocking spell that allowed her to teleport without being seen. While her neighbors couldn't see onto the porch, she could see Mrs. Welter watering her plants at the outer edge of her patio and the children on the other side swinging so fast that their swing set swayed.

The world rotated in its normal ebb and flow of the everyday. Her neighbors did what they normally did, and the traffic flowed two streets away.

It wasn't just any day for Annie. She felt unnerved, as if she were being watched, not just by the entire Wizard Council, but by someone else. She worried that no amount of magic could hide her here at home.

She scanned the trees on the other side of the alley behind her house. From where she stood, she saw no movement, no shadows, nothing that looked human, and yet she couldn't shake the feeling she was being watched.

Annie debated whether to search the trees, once a safe hiding place for her and Janie when they were young. They used to take the trail that wound to a small creek and hide in the hollow tree trunk. Hiding back then was merely a formality of play where they could hang out without the interruption of parents. They would read, eat candy, and talk about boys.

At this moment, the trees didn't feel safe. She turned and glanced inside the kitchen window where Zola was cleaning an already clean kitchen. Annie sighed, she knew Zola could feel her pain and wished she didn't need to have this conversation as she pulled open the door and entered her house.

"You told me the story of the Fates since I was old enough to understand. Now I know why," Annie said.

Zola was mid-wipe and stopped cleaning, but wouldn't look at Annie.

"You're hiding something," Annie accused. She watched her Aloja Fairy. Zola's bright emerald green eyes were cloudy with worry, and her thin wings flapped wildly. "I don't care about the powers. I just wish everyone who was there or who knows what's going on would just tell me." Her voice was louder than she anticipated; she couldn't help the anger that bubbled to the surface.

Zola dropped the rag and sighed. She pulled something from her pocket and placed it in Annie's hand. Annie opened her palm and stared at a silver necklace. Hanging from the delicately forged chain was a round, silver charm. The design at the center was something Annie had never seen before: two birds, apparently swans, their bodies curving gracefully to form a circle, their necks crossed as though each watched the other's back. At the center of the charm, surrounded by the swan bodies, a small circle was split in four by two crossed lances.

Annie could only assume it was a protection charm. She asked anyway. "What is this?"

Zola led Annie to the kitchen table and sat. The fairy held her charge's hand and swallowed. "While I am linked to the Pearce family and all of your descendants, I am particularly linked to you. This is my fairy protection amulet, imbued with my blood. It will protect you in the past because I am alive in the past." She glanced at Annie.

"I figured you were alive in the ninth century, but you were there, weren't you?"

She nodded. "I intended to give this to you before you left. When you arrive through the portal, call for me and show my younger self this necklace. I will know and I can help." Behind her smile was a lot of worry, stress, and fear.

Annie placed the necklace around her neck and hid it under her shirt where it lay cold against her bare skin. She reached around Zola, her former nanny and now family friend, and let her arms envelope her. It almost seemed less daunting, knowing she had Zola waiting for her.

"You remember this, yes?" Annie asked.

"I do." Zola kissed her on the cheek.

"Why didn't you tell me sooner?" Annie touched her shirt and felt the design of the necklace through the fabric.

Zola stood and began to pace, very much unlike herself. She stopped in front of the window and faced Annie.

"There was something I was supposed to accomplish for you and I... I was unable to fulfill that request. I'm embarrassed and full of regret. Eleven hundred years and I could not find an answer."

"What was the request?"

Zola shook her head. "I promised I would figure out how to remove the power from you without killing you. I don't have that answer. I should have found it."

"It's just not possible then." Annie let out the air in her lungs. "So I need to prepare for my trip and accept the power. Is there anything else you can tell me? I have no one else who knows."

"You have yourself, my brilliant, beautiful woman. I am so proud of the woman you've become. You must trust yourself and Gibbs and Brite. The demons were wiped from earth because of what you did. You know how to kill them; you just need to tap into your knowledge. I will help you."

"You really won't tell me what to do." Annie chuckled nervously.

"I... I can't tell you the specifics. I will remind you that you know how to kill the demons. You know who is in the original coven. All that information in your folder will help you solve this. Use the resources you have. Trust your team and your magic. While they are forcing you to play their game, you can play it on your terms. Your way," Zola reiterated.

"So I shouldn't worry that the prophecy didn't say anything about a team?"

Zola smiled. "That's correct. I'm glad the Wizard Council put it to a vote though."

"It was a very close vote. But I'm allowed to go back, with conditions of course," Annie said.

"As it should have been. I just want you to remember. Do not trust the coven. They only care what you can do for them."

"You know what's coming," Annie stated.

Zola nodded. "I've seen your life play itself out. I've seen you succeed. I've seen you fail. And yes, I know what's coming. Please don't trust the coven. Stick to your plan."

Annie stood and glanced out the window. "I think they might be watching me."

"You think the Fraternitatem is already here."

"If I was going to kidnap or kill someone, I would want to know everything about that person. They knew how to get to Emily. Whatever they have planned for me, they will know everything about me. They're waiting for the right time. Maybe they came when the demon was conjured because they knew it was time. I don't know for sure."

"I didn't know about the Fraternitatem back then. I should have known. I should have been watching for changes, anomalies. I made so many mistakes." Zola took a deep breath.

"You've been there. You know what happens. But when I go back, I can change things. You told me to do it my way. I can tell you what didn't work. You can change your next eleven hundred years," Annie said excitedly.

"Be careful what you share, even with me. I would hate for you to come back to a world you don't know. Be choosy with who and what you reveal," Zola warned.

Annie looked at her incredulously. "I shouldn't tell you?"

"No."

Only discuss what needs to be discussed as it pertains to the demons.

Annie digested Zola's words and understood how they were connected to the restrictions placed on her by the Wizard Council.

"I feel a little comforted that you will be there with me." Annie reached over and gave Zola a hug. She let her fairy squeeze her.

"I love you, my precious girl. Be safe and be smart."

∾

Kathy folded Annie's T-shirts and placed them in her field pack, silently working.

"At least Robin will be here soon." Annie tried to remain cheery as she mentioned Kathy's only biological child. Though Robin and Annie were ten years apart, they had been close, raised like siblings or cousins. She was sorry she'd miss his visit.

It's time travel. I can come back now if I wanted.

"Do you have enough food, water, clothes?" Ryan asked as he dropped more water bottles on her bed.

"I'm really only worried about water. I can hunt if I need food." It wasn't Annie's favorite pastime, but she had learned how to survive during her training as a new wizard guard.

Kathy frowned as she loaded Annie's field pack with more clothes. "Is it wise to wear your normal clothes while in the past? Shouldn't you blend in?" she asked.

Annie glanced at Ryan.

"They know you're coming. Though if you're not with the coven or the Vikings, it could be a problem. Maybe one outfit for each of you would be appropriate," Ryan suggested.

"So I have to wear a long, heavy dress to kill them? Where the hell am I going to find that now?" Annie asked. She glanced at her phone. Time was ticking away and she tossed it on the bed and lay down.

"Hey, there you are." Kathy, Ryan, and Annie turned to the familiar voice of Robin Price.

"Oh, sweetie, you're home!" Kathy flew up and hugged her son. It had been many months.

"Hi, Mom." He pulled away and turned to Annie. "And you. I heard you're leaving. What's that about?"

"Since you've heard, you really already know," Annie said. Robin nodded. "So, why did you come home? I haven't seen you in ages."

He told them briefly of coming across an ancient grimoire that he was depositing in Artifact Hall at Wizard Hall. It reminded Annie of the Fraternitatem grimoire she had in her field pack.

"Sounds like you've been busy," Annie said.

"Not as busy as you. What's really going on?"

Annie gave him the short version. He stood in her room with his jaw tensing like Cham's had.

"Do you need anything from me?" Robin asked.

Annie shook her head. "And you're staying for how long?" she asked.

"Well, I've actually made some decisions. I think I'll be staying around for a bit. Got myself a real job with Wizard Hall." He smiled.

They all sat, stunned expressions on their faces. He was thirty-four years old, unmarried, and had never lived a conventional life. He was an adventurer, traveling the world looking for ancient artifacts for any wizard hall that requested his services.

"Really?" Kathy jumped up and hugged her son again, kissing his cheeks.

"Mom. Stop." He jokingly pushed her away. "Anyway, I'll be here when you get back."

"So, you'll be here tomorrow?" Annie joked. Ryan and Robin laughed.

"That's not funny," Kathy said. "How can you joke? And you." She pointed to Ryan, raising her voice. "She's your goddaughter! Jason's daughter! You're just standing there laughing!"

Robin and Annie stared at them.

"I'm not okay," Ryan said. "I'm an emotional mess inside." He looked at Annie, the girl he helped raised, the woman he was proud of. "I trust Annie and her abilities."

"I know everyone's on edge. But you two need to stop," Annie said. "You're bickering. It's not helpful. And I need to know you're okay before I go."

Kathy put an arm around Annie. "While I'm glad Robin's home, this isn't okay. This will never be okay. But Ryan and I are fine." She kissed Annie's cheek.

"Actually, Mom, Ryan, I need to borrow Annie for a bit. You mind?" Robin asked. They nodded, confused. Robin walked Annie back downstairs and to her back yard.

"This is ominous," she said.

"Sorry. I wanted to tell you I decided to take the job because of Mom. And a little because of you and Sami. Honestly, it's probably time to start acting like an adult," Robin said.

"Okay. That's not why you brought me out here," Annie surmised.

Robin chuckled. "You're right. I probably could have talked to you upstairs, but Mom is really upset. I'm not crazy about you going to the past either. But I agree with Ryan—you're smart. Scary smart. You'll come back."

"Still not what you want to say to me though." Annie winked.

"No, it's not. I also heard the reason you can't kill Sturtagaard is because he was needed for this?"

"You did hear a lot," Annie said.

"It's all over Wizard Hall. What's he going to say to keep himself alive when this is over?" Robin asked.

"How did you guess that?"

"I've met the vampire on my travels. He manipulates the situation to suit himself. His time is coming to end. He'll pull something."

"He already did. He claims to know where the new Black Market is," Annie told him.

Robin nodded in understanding. "I figured that's what he'd use." Robin pulled a small notebook from his pocket and handed it to her. "There are coordinates in there for markets that have popped up. I know they're not the main market. I have contacts all over the world, and we've been searching for it. I think I know where it is."

Annie glanced at him. "Really? No joke?"

"No joke. I know you. You won't relinquish your life that easily. You'll find a way to get back. When you get back, I'll take you to the market. Don't keep that ass alive on account of the market."

Annie smiled. "Thanks. I was considering listening to him. Knowing this changes my mind."

⌇

It was a goodbye nearly impossible for Annie. She kissed Dave's cheeks and offered Janie a hug. She didn't want to pull away.

"I'll be back in a few days, most likely," Annie said. She pushed them out the door because it was late, nearly midnight, and she had an early morning. She turned and walked back to her kitchen. Samantha looked at her.

"I was going to stay the night," Samantha said.

"No. You need to go. But I need to show you something first. Upstairs."

"You're making me angrier with you," Samantha said when she sat on Annie's bed.

Annie shrugged. "I'm sorry, but this has to be done."

She lay the fireproof metal box on her bed. "I keep it in the closet. Your blood will open it," Annie said as she poked her finger in the blood lock. The lid sprung open. "The mortgage is in here. All of my bank accounts. My will and insurance policy. I might be engaged, but nothing's been changed yet. You still own half the house, and the rest of it goes to you."

"You're coming home," Samantha said.

"And I might not. You need to think ahead, just in case." Annie could feel the tension.

"I can't. You're all I have left."

Annie handed her a USB drive. "If I don't make it back, that's for you too."

Samantha shook her head. "Keep it with everything else."

Annie shrugged and dropped it in the metal box, slamming the lid shut. The sisters remained in the uncomfortable silence as Annie returned the locked box to her closet. There was only so much they could say to each other.

"I love you. Not just because you're my sister but because you're also my friend. I need you to be safe," Samantha choked.

Annie sat on the bed beside her. "I need you to trust me. Please just trust me." She could barely whisper and slipped her arms around her sister. "I love you. Take care of him."

Samantha nodded quickly and picked up Annie's left hand. "He did good with the ring. It's beautiful."

Annie smiled and kissed her cheek. No matter what she told Samantha, Annie worried it would be the last time she would see her sister.

CHAPTER 18

THE PORTAL BURST out between the talismans and whirled like a tornado in front of Annie. Lightning flashed quickly, nearly grazing her. Beyond the whirlpool of air, she could see all the people she loved the most. They looked at her, worried for her.

She stood on a narrow pathway, damp cool air surrounding her, as the sun hid behind a thick layer of clouds. She clenched her muscles as wind whipped across her; it wasn't from the portal, but from the storm that was closing in on her.

Annie reached out to touch the swirling air, out to Cham who stood on the other side. While he was only inches from her, they were really 1,100 years apart, so far away that she couldn't reach him, touch him. She couldn't feel his warmth or smell his spicy cologne. A pained whimper crossed her lips.

"Cham," she murmured.

"Annie!" he shouted.

A strong force pulled on her, yanking her farther from him. Annie felt as though she was falling, falling from the sky, slipping away from him.

"Cham!" she screamed as she began to flail. Her arms flapped wildly, her body twisted and turned as the wind picked up and blew against her. "Cham!" she screamed again, but her voice was gone. She panicked. She tried to scream again, but nothing came out.

Annie whipped her hands out around her to cast a spell. Nothing shot from her palms. She couldn't access her magic. She was alone, as she fell from the sky, without her powers, without her voice.

So close to the ground, she kicked out, trying to make contact with the colors surrounding her. Again, she reached out for something to cling to, but there was nothing above, below or around her.

She looked down. The ground was almost there…

Annie woke, her breathing haggard, her palms and brows drenched with sweat. She looked around her bedroom. Dark shadows covered the floor, her walls, her bed.

Cham lay beside her, his breathing even and steady, though his fists were balled tightly and his jaw was tense. She pulled the covers to her chin as she lay on his chest. She rose up and down as he breathed. She touched his chest, his hair; her hand settled on his stomach, where she could feel it rise and fall. Annie took a deep breath, memorizing his scent, the cologne he used, the shampoo in his hair.

"Baby. What time is it?" he murmured.

"It's still really early. Go back to sleep," she said.

He quickly woke. "I'm awake now. I don't think I can go back to sleep," he said. He wrapped his arms around her.

"Sorry. I… I had a dream. Woke me up," Annie said.

"At this point, I don't want to miss a moment," he said as he stared at the light across the ceiling. "I haven't slept much anyway."

"I don't want to go," she said.

Cham kissed the top of her head. "I don't want you to go either. You should get some sleep. You might not get much once you get there."

They lay there in the darkness, Annie thought of nothing else except the moment she would step through the portal. "I can't."

"You're shaking," he said. He summoned the blanket at the end of the bed and wrapped it around her.

"Fear, not cold," she said. She buried her head in his chest. She couldn't hide her lip that quivered or her eyes that watered.

"Remember senior year, that weird obstacle course? You and I, seventeen years old, and they set up the Wizard Guard training course so we could do first-year wizard guard training."

Annie looked at him. "What about it?" She rested her chin on his chest and memorized the shape of his chin, of his nose, his forehead, committing him to memory.

"We worked as a team when we went in and everything was going well until… there was that fog that covered us, and somehow we managed to get separated."

She smiled to herself in the darkness. "I was scared. One minute you were there, and the next, I was in a different part of the course. I couldn't see anything, and that vampire came out of nowhere. It was intense," Annie said.

"I was scared, too. But the thing is, I trusted you. I knew how smart you were. I knew you'd find me again and we'd finish what we set out to do. I never doubted you, even when I had that prickly little demon waddling around my feet."

Annie and Cham had both been good students, and both had intended on becoming wizard guards since early in high school. As they trained for that goal, they grew closer, relying on each other with school and personal problems. They were so proficient as Wizard Guard students; they were able to enter the Wizard Guard training program their second semester senior year. The final test sealed their friendship for life.

"I've always known you had my back. I never questioned it." Annie rolled onto her back. Her engagement ring caught the light from the moon. "I'm glad you and Ryan have so much faith in me, because right now I'm worried—not so much about the demons, but about the portal, getting there and back."

"It's a good plan. We have good people here who are working through the night to get you safely there and back. Your job is to get rest so you can do your job."

Annie sighed and knew he was right. They had the best people working in the Wizard Guard. "I love you," she said.

"I love you," Cham whispered. Annie held his hand tightly and hoped morning wouldn't come too soon.

෨

Somewhere between three and four in the morning, Annie fell into a fitful sleep. Remnants of her dream still haunted her. When her alarm blared at six in the morning, calling her back to the present, she groaned.

Cham was already awake, leaving her alone in bed. A flash of lightning burst above her as the rain beat against the window.

She climbed out of bed and jumped into the shower, her last one for she couldn't imagine how long. The water was extra hot. She soaped and continued to rub at the bubbles until they were fluffy peaks in her palm. She chuckled at the sight, of the simplicity of the things she would miss.

Only for a few days.

Time travel was such a complex concept. It was difficult to wrap her brain around it. It was impossible to think she could leave this morning and come back tonight while living in the past for days, weeks, or even years.

Annie touched her skin, smooth with water and soap, and let her hand trail her taut body. She thought of all the jokes she had made that week about how she could come home tomorrow.

But what if I get trapped in the past for decades? What if I age and they don't?

The thought frightened her. She rested her head against the cool tile and cried.

"Annie? Are you almost ready?" Cham asked.

She wiped her eyes. "Yeah. I'm coming," she said. She finished rinsing and let the water and soap slide down her body and pool at the drain before being sucked inside. She shut off the water, clean and warm in a clean and warm house with no sickness, no pain, a television, and phones.

A warm towel wrapped around her, she wiped the mirror and looked at her young self before she prepared to leave.

A hearty breakfast waited for her when she entered the kitchen. Her clothes were comfortable, the protection charm Zola gave her hung against her chest under her lightweight sweater, and her field pack was hidden in her waist of her pants.

She sat at the table and took a bite of eggs, then toast. She chewed slowly but didn't feel like eating

Cham sat beside her playing with his food. "You need to eat too," Annie said.

"I know." He stabbed an egg and took a bite.

The kitchen clock ticked away the time quickly. Before Annie knew it, the clock read 7:15 and she felt nauseated.

"You okay?" Cham asked.

"I'm fine. I'm ready," she said as she pulled on a jacket. Annie took a last look at her house and exited to her back porch.

She let Cham wrap his arms around her and teleport her to the spiral portal.

ᴥ

It was agreed that only the necessary people would be there for the portal opening. This included Gibbs, Brite, Kolgaar, Lial, Milo, and Cham. Everyone else was told to stay away. The rest of the group had arrived before her and was waiting anxiously. Annie looked at the portal. In the gray light, the magical anomaly hung in the air and shimmered. Annie felt dizzy, nauseated, and ran to the bushes to vomit.

Milo held his hand up and shook his head. He joined Annie at the bushes.

"I'm okay," she said when he knelt beside her.

"I know. I'd be a little nervous, too, if I were you." Milo waited patiently for Annie to sit up. She glanced at her team, then looked away, embarrassed by her reaction.

"Sorry. I didn't realize how jumbled I am inside."

"Jason was my friend. And, as I always told you, you were like a niece to me. I expect you to come home."

"What if I get stuck in the past for years and come back old?" Annie asked.

Milo chuckled and reached for her hand. "Congratulations." He dropped his eyes, but not her hand.

Annie watched him. She felt he had more to say. "Thanks. Is there something else?"

Milo looked at her. "While you're in the past, I'm going to work with Bucky and see what we can find out about Emily... before she finds you."

Annie held her breath and nodded. "What if... what if I have to kill her?"

Milo shook his head. "No. Don't think like that. We'll deal with her. One problem at a time. You concentrate only on this. This, Annie."

Overcome with dread and emotion, she hugged him. "Take care of yourself," Annie said as she pulled away and joined the others.

The storm rolled across the Chicagoland area and felt as though it was drenching their location in particular. Lighting flashed, thunder roared, and all of their group remained in the clearing to watch Annie, Gibbs and Brite leave. Annie was glad for the thunder. It had truly become where she felt safe.

Both Kolgaar and Annie wore the talismans. The statues were twitchy and active so close to the portal's magical energy.

As the rain pounded on them, Lial set a crystal on the ground below the spiraled energy and summoned the magic where it hung in the air, inches above the rock.

"I'm going to reverse the energy. Kolgaar, stand here. Annie, here." Lial guided them to either side of the portal, held his palms toward the energy, and said, "Revertere." Wind shifted as the magical energy sizzled. Lial held a second crystal and followed the spiral of magic; rather than spiraling upwards to the right, it spiraled up to the left.

"You sure that's going to take us back?" Annie asked, worried.

"Yes. I've been up all night rereading the books. Now touch the talismans to the magical energy," he ordered.

Annie and Kolgaar obeyed. A swirling mass of air began to blow from the portal. Tiny flashes of lightning sparked inside the whirlpool of wind as thunder roared between the talismans. Annie glanced inside but could see nothing more than swirling colors. She took out the vial of Gila's blood and handed it to Lial.

Lial stood in front of the whirling mass of air and said, "Praeteriti aperiri." He tossed the vial inside.

"Come back to me," Cham whispered in her ear. She turned and kissed him.

"We need to go!" Kolgaar said anxiously.

Annie looked back inside the whirling mass. It still was a wild jumble of wind, thunder, lightning, and colors.

"Jump through," Kolgaar ordered.

"You first," Annie shouted over the clap of thunder above her.

Kolgaar grabbed her upper arm as a wind whipped against them, and yanked her through the portal.

She fell.

Her arms flailed about; her legs kicked at nothingness. Disoriented, she twisted and turned to get a look at where she was falling. With each twist of her body, Kolgaar tightened his grip on her as if she could escape from him.

A heavy weight pulled against her waist. She had no idea who had grabbed her as she was dragged into the portal.

The notion of time raced before her eyes in a long blur of colors. Each foot another year, another decade away from the life she knew and the people she loved, away from Cham.

Lightning flashed around her without touching her. A soft roll of thunder pulsated through her as she continued to fall to the earth.

CHAPTER 19

LIGHTNING FLASHED AND thunder rolled.

THUD!

"Oooooff." Parched earth flew up around her. Annie groaned. A heavy thud shook the ground around her. A gentle whimper.

Where am I?

Her body ached. Her head was fuzzy.

Where am I?

Her memory came back to her: a bitter wind, water pummeling her skin and drenching her hair, a clap of thunder, a flash of lightning.

She slowly realized she was warm and dry now. The sun beat down on her back and her hair, warming her. Annie turned her head and closed her eyes against the blinding sun. A hand clutched her ankle. She pulled away, and pain shot through her body.

A man's deep moan came from somewhere near her feet.

Gibbs or Brite?

A warm summer breeze rustled Annie's hair and fluttered her clothes. It kicked up the dust around her face. She coughed, and it rattled her body.

"Crap," she murmured. To her left, a second male voice groaned.

Feeling pain throughout her body, she wiggled her toes in her boots, moved her feet, made a fist and released it, assessing any injuries.

I must be alive.

Kolgaar pulled himself up and limped across the path. He mumbled as he turned and walked the opposite direction, passing her vision for a second time.

Annie held her breath as she pulled herself up. "Shit!" she murmured. Her lungs burned with each breath as she took in her surroundings.

"Get up!' Kolgaar pushed on Brite's shoulders attempting to rouse him. Brite groaned.

Annie turned slightly. He lay at her feet.

"Get up!" Kolgaar shouted again, pulling Brite up by the shoulders.

"Stop!" Annie's throat was dry and sore, her words garbled. She pulled herself across the dirt to her colleague and friend, and pushed Kolgaar away. Anxiously, she felt for Brite's pulse and pulled up his eyelid, looking for signs of concussion.

"What are you doing?" Kolgaar asked.

Annie ignored him and held her hand above Brite, maneuvering across his body from his head to his feet, while chanting a healing spell.

Her hands should have felt a tingle as the magic passed through her, but she felt nothing.

"Damn." She looked at her palms. "Damn."

Annie held her hands against Brite's cheeks. "Brite," she said again. "If you can hear me, wake up. Say something." She lightly slapped his face, rousing him.

He groaned. "Annie?" His eyes were closed, his lips curled.

"Yeah. It's me. Where do you hurt?" she asked, her hand rested on his arm.

"Everywhere," he murmured. Annie couldn't help but chuckle.

"Yeah. I'm achy too. Listen, my magic's down. Can you get up?"

"I think so. Just feel so stiff."

With a hand against his back, Annie pushed him up. Her shoulder stiffened.

"We need to go," Kolgaar said as he still limped across the narrow dirt path.

Annie stumbled as she stood and nausea gripped her. She bent over and fell to her knees. The earth spun around her.

It was a pleasant day: warm, but not hot, sunny and breezy enough for the grasses on either side of the narrow road to wave gently.

When nausea subsided, she stood again and scanned the landscape. The path they landed on was narrow. Barely one car would have fit on it. It stretched across the landscape, twisting and turning through the valley leading to a wide hill.

Grass as tall as Annie's hip covered the land and the hills, all she could see across the miles of England. She continued to look from east to west and north to south. There was nothing in her line of sight: no buildings, no people, no white noise to remind her she wasn't alone.

Where's Jorvik?

She had expected a town of considerable size, the Viking stronghold that should have covered several acres or more of land. She saw nothing. "Where are we?" Annie demanded.

Kolgaar stood at the edge of the narrow path and peered into the distance. His steely blue eyes crinkled in thought. "I don't... I am not sure. We should be just outside the Jorvik. I fear we are not," he said plainly.

"Why didn't the spell work?" Annie asked, but she knew he wouldn't be able to answer that question. She looked behind her.

"Something is wrong. We need to go before nightfall. It won't be safe," Kolgaar said.

Annie glared at him.

"We need to go. Now! You do not understand. The demons come out at night. We need to get somewhere safe before that happens." Impatiently, Kolgaar limped across the path and back again, kicking up dirt, skipping a rock into the grass.

The silence of the countryside enveloped her, unnerved her. They were alone and possibly in the wrong place.

And wrong time?

Annie turned back to Brite, who shook as he limped to her. She turned and looked for Gibbs. He was nowhere in sight.

"Gibbs!" she shouted and walked east through the tall grass. "Gibbs!" Brite walked through the grasses to the west calling out for Gibbs.

Annie thought she heard a low groan and stopped shouting. She followed the sound and ran to Gibbs, who lay at the edge of a small pond.

"Gibbs!" She rushed to his side. "I found him, Michael. I found him!"

she shouted. "Gibbs. Damn. Gibbs!" She checked for a pulse and lightly slapped his face as she had done for Brite. "Gibbs!"

Brite trekked through the grasses to Annie. "Shit!" he said.

He knelt beside Annie as she held her palms above Gibbs's head, to heal whatever might have been wrong. Again, where she should have felt tingling as the magic released from her hands, she felt nothing.

"No magic." Annie stared at her hands, feeling powerless as a nonmagical.

Brite placed his hands above Gibbs's head. "Place your hands on mine. Maybe together?"

She did as he suggested, but even together, there was barely enough magic between the two of them. Still, drawing what little magical energy they could, they continued until Gibbs jerked his head and opened his eyes. He was bewildered and confused.

"What…" he muttered.

"Can you move?" Annie asked.

He glanced at the blue sky and waved her away. But for Gibbs, considerably older than Annie and Brite, sitting up was difficult as dizziness gripped him. He pulled his legs up and rested his head on his knees.

"Girl." He waved her away again. "Just a little stiff," he said. He glanced at her through nearly shut eyes before pulling himself up. Dizziness sent him back to the ground with his head between his legs.

"Stay down," Annie said. He waved her away again. She returned to Brite. "And you're okay?" she asked.

Brite nodded and continued to pace along the roadside, stretching his stiff muscles.

The grasses rustled as Kolgaar marched to them. "We need to leave!" he shouted.

She exchanged glances with Brite who continued stretching. Annie turned and shouted back to Kolgaar. "Listen to me. We're not ready! Go if you want. We'll leave when I say!"

"I only need you. They can catch up later," Kolgaar jeered.

"Enough. We're sore and need a minute to catch our breath. Have you figured out where we are yet?" Annie asked.

Kolgaar glanced to the north and pointed. "It's just over the hill, that way. We should make it within half a day." He glanced at the sky. "The problem is that it will be dark soon. We need to find shelter."

Gibbs hobbled to the path. "What do you mean a half day? We're not in Jorvik? Are we even in the correct year?"

"We'll find out when we get there," Brite said. "Test your magic. Annie and I are down."

Gibbs held out his palm, attempting to summon his field pack. "No. I'm down too." He rubbed the stubble on his chin.

"If we can't get our field packs to original size, we're screwed." Annie sighed.

Gibbs glanced at her. "Such negativity, girl."

"You realize once I come into those powers, I'll be more powerful than you. You can start by calling me Annie."

He grimaced and said, "Such negativity, Annie."

She chuckled. "See, you'll get there. I have supplies we kinda need."

"There's magical energy across the planet. We'll just have to borrow that," Gibbs said.

"This wasn't a problem I expected," Annie said.

Gibbs held his palm up as if he was going to summon an object. "Nothing. How did you wake me?"

"We called for the magic together." She pointed to Brite.

"Are you done discussing this? We need to go," Kolgaar reminded them.

Annie glanced down the path. The valley stretched out for miles.

What if this isn't the right year?

Without her magic, their magic, she was less certain of what would happen, less confident that she could right this ship. "Fine. Let's go." Annie exchanged a concerned glance with Gibbs and Brite as they followed Kolgaar down the path leading to the valley.

It had grown warmer, yet they still hadn't reached the bottom of the valley. Annie was parched. She held out her palm.

"What are you trying to summon?" Brite asked.

"I'm thirsty. I'd like my field pack." She glanced behind them and sighed.

Brite placed his hand on Annie's, together summoning her field pack. The small object appeared. "Do you think we can grow it?" Annie asked.

It sputtered and shook and grew slightly. Annie sighed.

"You can stick it in your pocket for now," Brite suggested.

They continued to walk.

The sun moved again, and soon was several degrees west of high noon. "We've been walking about two hours," Annie said.

"You're right," Brite said, holding up his wrist to show his winding watch.

"Smart," Gibbs grumbled.

They continued to follow Kolgaar.

Another hour passed as they crossed into the valley. Kolgaar stopped at the side of the path and looked out into the landscape. "It should be here."

"What do you mean it should be here?" Annie asked.

"A path to the village."

"We're not where you thought we were? Terrific. And we're without magic," Annie said.

"What do you mean you are without magic?" Kolgaar asked.

Annie explained their difficulty in using magic. Kolgaar growled. "Why did I risk my life to come and get you if you are useless?"

"Figure out where we are." Annie pulled out the small field pack and lay it in her palm. Brite held her hand, Gibbs placed his below as they slowly grew her field pack to normal size. They glanced at each other.

"Are you feeling exhausted, too?" Brite asked.

Annie slung her field pack across her shoulders. "Pretty much." She sat down in the grass.

Gibbs opened her pack. His fingers grazed one of the water bottles and pulled it out for her. "Thanks." She took a sip and passed it back.

"Well?" Gibbs asked Kolgaar.

"Near the trees is a house. We'll head there for the night," he said. He slung his bag across his back and walked at a quick pace.

"I guess we move on," Annie said as Brite helped her up.

While the path continued north, they stepped into the grass heading

East. Here the ground was uneven and thick with long grasses, wildflowers, and hay. Annie felt a twinge in her back.

On constant alert, she scanned the landscape. Something—an animal or demon—was winding its way through the grasses, getting closer and closer to them. As the grass fluttered, the creature's sniffs and snorting grew louder. Annie estimated the creature was about one hundred yards away.

"I think we're being followed from the south," she said.

"It's the demons," Kolgaar said angrily.

"Do they crawl?" Annie asked.

He picked up his pace. His strides were long, and Annie was nearly running to keep up. Again, whatever was following them snarled.

"Run!" Kolgaar shouted as he pulled Annie with him. She was nearly dragged, unable to keep up with his long strides; he threw her over his shoulders. She watched helplessly as Gibbs and Brite ran after them, the distance between them growing.

Annie struggled to release Kolgaar's hold on her, but he was determined to keep her safe. Ahead of them, the house loomed larger. Behind them, Annie watched as the creature lunged for Gibbs.

"No!" Annie screamed and wiggled from Kolgaar's grasp. Gibbs threw the creature off of him and cast a jinx. While the magic was feeble, it was just enough to make the creature think twice about chasing them. Brite helped Gibbs toward the house. Once inside, Kolgaar slammed the door shut, plunging them in darkness.

CHAPTER 20

ANNIE DUG IN her field pack and pulled out a flashlight, illuminating the house. It was nearly empty except for a pile of loose hay, a primitive ladder leading to a loft, two water buckets, and a table.

Kolgaar saw her light and reached for it. "What is that?" he asked.

"It's called a flashlight. I'll show you how it works later," she said, irritated and tired. She searched for a window and unlatched the shutters that locked them in darkness.

Just outside, a catlike creature paced the edge of the grass. It turned toward them; orange eyes glowed in the dim light of sunset. Annie flashed the light at the creature. It was long and low, covered in long, thick orange hair. Two teeth poked out from each side of its mouth.

"No way," she exclaimed as she watched the magnificent creature pace and growl.

"What is that?" Brite asked.

"That is a Cath Palug. They died out a few centuries ago. Well, a few centuries before our time," Annie explained.

"I knew what you meant," Brite said, seeming entranced by the creature.

Kolgaar stood at the window with them. The rain was thick. When it touched the dried ground, it sounded like steaks sizzling on a grill. "We have a lot of magical creatures that roam this land," he told them.

The creature hissed as lightning struck the earth and thunder burst above them. Annie glanced at Brite, at Gibbs. "Far away for a Welsh cat," Gibbs said.

"It's attracted to magic. There must be a lot of magical energy in and around England," Annie said.

The creature stopped and slunk its way inside the grasses where it found a spot to lie and wait out the rain.

Annie closed and locked the shutters and illuminated the house.

"I'm going to see how safe the loft is. We should sleep off the ground," Brite suggested as he moved the rustic ladder to the loft. He climbed slowly, exhausted from the trip through the portal and the unexpected walk. The thin and brittle ladder shook with each step. Brite walked the hay filled loft.

"Well?" Annie called out.

"It's safe unless you're allergic to hay. Can you climb up, Gibbs?" he asked.

Annie glanced at Gibbs's shoulder where a small patch of leather had been torn.

"It got you," she said as she pulled away his jacket to examine his wound. The Cath Palug had scratched his shoulder with a long claw. The wound was about four inches long but not deep.

"There's a little blood, but it's not deep," Annie said.

Gibbs pulled away. "We have no magic. Just cover it."

Annie led him to a bucket, turned it over, and had him sit. She cleaned the wound with bottled water, rubbed antibacterial cream on the remaining wound, and added a large bandage on top. "We're inherently magical, whether it's our time period or not. We need to figure out how to harness the magical energy around us," she said as she shoved the garbage in her field pack.

"So, what do you suggest gir—Annie?" Gibbs asked.

Annie smiled. "Just keep summoning it, just enough to feel the tingle, to feel the magic awaken within us. We're still magical."

Gibbs pulled his shirt back over the wound and grimaced. "The problem is that we're not alive right now. This isn't our timeline. Our magic might never fully wake up."

"We don't need it to fully wake up. We just need to tap into enough to make the plan work. We have the coven for the big stuff," Annie said.

At the mention of the coven, Kolgaar frowned.

He doesn't like the coven.

They climbed the ladder to the loft, seeking out their spot for the night. Brite pulled up the ladder and set it against the wall.

"I have food," Annie said as she passed out several sandwiches. She was hungry, nearly starved from the travel through time. She finished her sandwich in a few bites and washed it down with water.

At loft level, Annie opened the shutters, staring out at what she believed to be ancient England. Without landmarks, street names, or even people, she hoped they landed where they were supposed to be. She sighed. The moon rose slowly casting a blue light across the landscape. Just below the window, a fuzzy sheep strolled across the grass.

They continued to eat in silence. When they finished, they put their garbage in a plastic bag and shoved it in Annie's pack.

"Now what?" Brite asked. He sat at the window and looked outside. With darkness covering them, there were no buildings or people to see. Annie felt unnerved at the lack of white noise, that noise that came from traffic, airplanes, or train whistles that she was used to hearing but not paying attention to throughout the day. Annie hadn't realized until this moment how very important that noise was. Without it, the world felt lonely and unfamiliar—and extremely scary.

"There's nothing out there," Brite said dismayed. "Can you guess if we're in the right time?"

Annie shrugged. "Based on this building, I think we're close if not actually here." She reached for her pack and pulled out a book on ancient England. "It looks like we're in a barn or house."

Brite perused the book quickly. "Still, that's not much." He handed the book back to Annie.

"I'm guessing the polarity spell and the portal energy took us back to where we wanted to go. I'm just concerned the location was wrong," Annie said.

"Our presence could have affected the portal location," Gibbs said. Annie glanced at him quickly.

"You think that could be why our magic is off?" she asked.

"Maybe. I suspect we've already changed something by being here," Gibbs said.

Annie glanced back out the window and sighed with a loneliness she had never experienced before. "We should get some rest. It's been a long day." She leaned against the wall and held her palms up. "Just a little practice," she murmured as she closed her eyes. Her muscles relaxed and went slack. Annie summoned the magical energy that floated in the air around them. It was there, that small twinge in her fingertips, a familiar warmth. She found the magic.

"It's here," she said as she let the magic go, feeling extreme exhaustion. "How's your shoulder?" she asked Gibbs.

"Throbbing. Got any meds?" he asked.

Annie dug in her bag and tossed him the bottle. "Well, how about that," he said.

"I'm too tired to get into my sleeping bag if someone else wants it," she murmured and then remembered nothing else until morning.

⋙

The portal opened before her—the blinding light, the whirlpool of air. It sputtered and sparked with lightning, and multiple colors swirled inside like a kaleidoscope. Annie was mesmerized by the movement and stepped closer to touch the whirling mass of brightness and warmth.

As she neared the portal, the air sped up and the lightning struck rapidly. In between the lightning strikes, the thunder roared uncontrollably, leaving the portal to shake and sputter violently. She pulled her hand away. Instantly, the portal calmed to a minor storm.

When it settled, Annie reached for the portal again. For a second time, the portal grew restless and forceful as it grew unstable beside her.

"Annie, no! Don't touch it. Your magic is too much for it. The portal's going to implode!" he screamed.

Cham!

He loved her so much and she would do anything for him, but she couldn't stop. She needed to get through the portal to go home to him. She reached out to touch it. The energy tickled her fingertips at first, but then the swirling winds picked up again and yanked on her arm. The portal grew more unbalanced with her and her power inside.

"No! No, The portal! Please make it stop!" she cried. She dug her feet into the earth, but the strength of the tornado-like wind was so strong, she felt herself being dragged inside the vortex. "Make it stop! Please, make it stop!"

"I told you not to, Annie. The portal is too unstable to hold you and your magic. Why didn't you listen to me? I'll miss you so much," he said as she fell through the portal. It stretched and tugged her. She screamed as the portal blew apart with her inside.

Annie flew awake. It was nearly dawn. She was no longer against the wall; she found herself inside her sleeping bag and covered to her chin. Her flashlight had been tucked in beside her.

Through the slats in the shutters, she could see thick clouds flying across the sky. Cold air blew into the cracks. Annie shivered from the damp chill and a full bladder.

Crap!

The last twenty-four hours came rushing back to her. She knew she couldn't go outside without backup, not with her magic so weak. She wiggled in her bag and sat up. She opened the shutters. The air smelled of rain, and thunder rolled softly in the distance. Annie climbed from her bag and found the ladder.

I can't wait.

"Where you going, girl," Gibbs growled.

"Sorry, go back to sleep. I'm finding a spot to pee."

"Not alone," he said and pulled himself from his own bag.

"You found your magic?" she asked as she slid the ladder to the ground and began to climb down.

"Just enough to get at our packs. It's too exhausting," he said.

"Stay up here, I'll find a dark corner in the house," Annie said. She trembled with each step from the toll the trip was taking on her. She steadied herself on the dirt floor and opened the lower window, peering outside. The Cath Palug was still there: awake, alert, and sitting within feet from the house waiting for them.

"I think I'll use the corner," Annie said as she pointed outside.

"We're going to have to kill it," Gibbs said as he reached the floor.

Annie found a dark corner and relived herself, chuckling softly and then loudly. If she didn't laugh, she thought she might cry.

"You okay, girl?" he asked when she returned.

"No. I'm really not." Still exhausted, she held out her palm and summoned her field pack and her sleeping bag. She dropped the items when the magic burned her palms.

"Damn, that hurt," she said.

"That's a good sign. Your magic must have come back," Gibbs said.

Most magical children got their magic at around two years of age. Annie was one of the oddities—hers had come in at three days old. First magic always left scorch mark across the palms. Experiencing it as an adult felt strange.

"Maybe, yes," she said.

A light rain dripped on the roof. "It's going to be a long day," Annie said. "We should eat and get moving."

～

The cat lay just inside the grasses, unaffected by the rain and singularly focused on the house. Annie stared at the creature, which stared back at her.

"It's still there?" Brite asked.

"Yeah. Gibbs thinks we're going to have to kill it to get out of here," Annie said.

"Does this fall under our restrictions?" Brite joked.

"We could wait for it to leave." Annie sighed. "I can't imagine what will change if I kill this beast."

"Well, maybe it's supposed to kill someone it hasn't met yet," Brite said.

Annie glared at him. "Really not helpful."

"Sorry. It's hard to know what changes we'll make when we do anything. Everything has consequences. I've never worried about it like this before," Brite admitted.

"We can teleport," Gibbs suggested.

"I can barely summon an object," Annie said.

"We have to kill it," Gibbs reiterated.

The rain hadn't let up in the last hour. In that time, they cleaned and repacked their items, wiped away their footprints, and now watched the storm through the lower window.

Neither the rain nor the thunder and lightning seemed to affect the Cath Palug. It glanced at the sky and rested its head back in the wet earth, keeping its gaze on the house. Annie closed the shutters.

"Is it still out there?" Kolgaar asked. He heaved his bag over his shoulder.

"Yes," Annie said.

"We will kill it," Kolgaar said.

With their field packs across their shoulders, they followed Kolgaar out of the building and headed northeast through the grass.

The cat followed, slinking along a path parallel to theirs. Annie pulled the sword that was tied to her pants and held it out. They walked beyond the building and continued toward a clump of trees where they would, if they were in the correct location, find a river that would take them into Jorvik.

If Kolgaar knows where we are.

The Cath Palug growled, low and soft as if trying to intimidate his prey. Annie stopped and found the orange eyes observing them. She raised the sword as the magical cat lunged for them. Gibbs and Brite waited with their palms open. Together, they shot a jinx. The beautiful beast yelped as it fell to the ground. Angry and hungry, the cat scrambled up and paced as it readied itself to pounce. Annie, Gibbs, and Brite stood strong and waited.

The cat lunged at them again and they shot off another jinx, pushing the beast back into the grass. In her anxiety, Annie felt the sword buzz and hum. A shock of white light glowed from the blade as she connected to the sword that was meant for her. As if in slow motion, the cat ran and lunged again. Annie really didn't want to kill the majestic beast, but as it flew down to her, the sword made contact, pierced the thick fur, and penetrated the skin. Annie felt the sword give way as it slid easily into the beast. It shrieked. Annie dropped the sword as the cat fell to the ground.

Annie leaned over to catch her breath.

Gibbs ventured to the Cath Palug that, in its death, saturated the ground with its blood. He touched the cold, dull hilt of the sword, and slid the blade from the animal. "It's a shame to kill such a beast." He wiped the blade in the grass and held it out for Annie. When she touched the metal, it again reacted to her.

"It definitely belongs to you," Brite said. She holstered the sword and they headed east, leaving the carcass of the Cath Palug behind. "Do you think we overstepped?" He pointed back.

"No. It got me once. It could have killed us," Gibbs said.

The rain continued to pour as they followed Kolgaar to Jorvik.

⁓

Kolgaar led Annie, Gibbs, and Brite into the trees. They were drenched from the rain and cold, shivering to their bones. Rather than entering the thick of the forest, they hugged the edge of the trees where the canopy still protected them from the elements. Annie glanced inside the trees. Several large mounds were piled inside. It occurred to her that they were probably sleeping demons.

Annie continued to count the creatures they passed. As the number of demons rose, her anxiety rose. They had left in a hurry because Kolgaar demanded it and Ryan believed that because the plan had been set in motion. They were on a clock and needed to leave. It left her little time to create a perfectly prepared plan, and that made her a jumble of nerves and fear.

"How do I get the fire to each demon?" she murmured. She had been so busy thinking about how to open the portal, she hadn't had any time to figure out how she was going to kill the demons when she got here.

"Did you say something?" Brite asked.

"Just talking to myself," Annie replied.

The natural choice would be to set them all on fire using a spell to ensure all the demons would be killed. It was suggested using a spell similar to the one they used when they returned all the shapeshifters back to their human selves after the fall of the Black Market.

But how do I reach all *of the demons?*

The shapeshifter spell had been easy because the creatures had all been imprisoned in the Black Market and could easily be surrounded by the spell.

Do the demons all live in one location?

Annie would need time to determine where the demons were located. If they were scattered across England, Wales, Scotland, and Ireland, it would become more problematic since their magic was still so weak. Annie's thoughts churned as she remembered the memory modification spell they used at the top of Mt. Rinehur in Amborix, using crystals to surround the small country. The magic had found all of the crystals and blanketed the country in the magic, affecting everyone within its borders.

She sighed at the thought of crisscrossing Northumbria with crystals as they attempted to kill all of the demons. Without their magic at full strength, it seemed like a bad proposition. She formed a fireball above her palm. Even in the heavy breeze and pouring rain, the flames remained strong as they danced quickly.

Annie's thoughts turned to the memory modification spell they had used in France. It had been cast on a rod in the ceiling of the French Wizard Hall. The spell had flown up the rod and out of the Eiffel Tower. The magic had stretched across France and across Europe as it searched for the French Wizard Hall lapel pin all employees wore. It didn't matter where the pin was located—the magic had found it and attached itself to the person wearing it.

But they were all linked to the pin. What would link the demons?

The river wound around a bend. The fast rapids bounced around the curve and down the hill. The small group trekked up it.

Annie released the magic to the fireball. Expending even that small amount of magical energy was exhausting. They turned again, adjusting their direction and heading northeast again.

Her thoughts turned to Gila Donaldson telling Annie how she'd found the coven. She had told her it was through Donaldson blood. Gila could find her ancestors through her familial link.

Blood!

To find the coven, Annie had been given a vial of Gila Donaldson's blood.

Blood was life, history, the past, and the future all wrapped up in tiny little veins and arteries that linked families or groups of people from the same region.

It's always blood!

Annie relit the fireball. As her heart beat faster, the flames danced more quickly, keeping rhythm with her.

Blood-to-blood.

For Annie, it was the first time since she learned of the prophecy that she discovered an answer that had been in front of her the whole time. If there was something in the blood that all demons possessed, then maybe she could burn the blood of one and the magic would stretch across the land, searching for the demons with that blood, and lighting them all on fire all at the same time.

Even the demon in Tartarus!

Annie smiled.

"You okay gir—Annie?" Gibbs asked.

"Awesome!" Annie said.

Kolgaar turned. "We'll stop here and eat."

They found a small patch of open, dry land and lay out a sleeping bag. There Brite passed out lunch, and they took a much needed rest.

CHAPTER 21

THE FOREST THINNED and eventually was fully behind them as they climbed the final hill. There at the crest, they could see Jorvik spread out in the valley. It was surrounded on two sides by fields and farms that stretched to the south. To the north, it was bordered by more forests and the river that ran through it.

Annie stared at the village, which was larger than she expected. Streets wound through the town haphazardly, and yet they all led toward the center where a large longhouse stood. Smoke billowed from each chimney, so Annie assumed it was currently in use.

On either side of narrow streets were simple cottages amongst two-story buildings. People led horses to the stables at the edge of town and pushed carts carrying goods to the market near the longhouse. Smoke billowed from what Annie could only guess was a foundry, a black-smith's booth.

Beyond the longhouse, the village tapered off into fields that, in the midst of growing season, were thick and full of grain. Several large buildings, appearing to be something akin to barns and accompanying cottages, were scattered across the fields.

Kolgaar picked up his pace, anxious to return home. Annie, Gibbs, and Brite followed closely. As they got closer to the town, the ancient smells of close quarters, animals, food, smoke, and human waste wafted to them.

"I'm…" Annie began. "This is a lot larger than I expected." She stood in awe.

"We need to keep moving," Kolgaar said.

"It looks very English," Brite commented.

"If I know English history, the Vikings first conquered England in 793. They seem pretty well established. I wonder how far out we are from that date," Gibbs whispered.

Still unaccustomed to the silence that had surrounded them, Annie was pleasantly surprised by the noises wafting from the longhouse. Singing, shouting, and music played as if there was no demon threat at all.

They entered Jorvik, passing the first cottage. Annie glanced inside the window and caught a glimpse of a mother, father, and small child eating a midday meal at the table. She continued after Kolgaar, taking a passage into the center of the village.

I wonder where Sturtagaard is now?

Cottages were occupied, as shown by the smoke billowing from chimneys. They passed the blacksmith's building where he pounded against metal in a fiery hot space. Carts rolled through town. Horses left droppings everywhere or else were fenced inside stalls along the narrow street.

Women carried baskets filled with laundry or food, while the men carried tools and headed to work or home. Despite their busyness, the residents of Jorvik watched them with fear on their faces, staring at them, at their clothes, at their bags.

Brite pulled closer to Annie. His left hand rested on her lower back and his right hand faced out should he need to shoot off a spell.

They soon reached the longhouse, which vibrated with life and energy. On either side of the heavy wooden doors were cold sconces Annie was sure would be lit at sunset. Her stomach lurched as she recognized the carvings that were currently on the thick doors. These doors would be brought to the new world and would one day hang at the Wizard Hall Library. For now, the door was nearly empty; much wizard history hadn't happened yet.

She swallowed hard. "The finished product sits at the library entrance," Annie said as she touched the heavy doors.

"Really? I didn't know that," Brite said as he looked at the earliest carvings, eyelevel to the left.

"Yeah. It's obviously not finished, but these here... I recognize them," she said.

Kolgaar glanced at them, unaware that this precious building would soon be dismantled and shipped off to a foreign land. He opened the thick doors.

Annie squeezed Brite's hand and reached for Gibbs. Her emotions tormented her. She would soon set eyes on Sturtagaard.

What will I do if I see him?

They followed Kolgaar inside. She could feel all eyes set upon them as they stepped through. A man as tall and as wide as Kolgaar raced toward them and wrapped Kolgaar in a bear hug.

"Kolgaar!"

"Svenson," he responded.

"You made it safe, my friend, and so quickly too," the man said, a large smile on his face.

"Did you understand him, too?" Annie whispered to Gibbs.

"Talismans work," Gibbs said.

"So, we're in the correct time and place," Annie surmised aloud.

"Of course. He just left just yesterday. I see you brought the witch. Good work, man," Svenson said in a jolly voice.

How do we understand him too?

Kolgaar led Annie, Gibbs, and Brite through the longhouse. The din grew silent and the crowd parted. The intense scrutiny left Annie with extreme anxiety and a sense of hopelessness. Gibbs squeezed her hand.

With so many people, two fireplaces, and a central fire pit, the room was warm, smoky, and suffocating. The fires were attended to by people Annie guessed had a lower social status, given their plain clothing and lack of adornments.

Everyone stared at them as they walked toward the far side of the longhouse.

While Annie and Gibbs held hands, Brite kept a firm grip on her upper arm. Gibbs and Brite scanned the crowd looking for any person that might harm her; Annie looked for Sturtagaard.

The Vikings were curious above all else and began to inch closer to them, choking off their already narrow path. Annie felt strangled and batted about. Gibbs tightened his grip; she could feel the heat from his skin. He whipped his palm out, a motion the Vikings apparently understood—most backed away.

A baby cried out and the crowd turned toward the wailing. The mother turned away, patting the baby's back, and whispering sweet nothings to her young one to quiet the child. With nothing left to see, the room returned their focus on Annie. Meanwhile, Annie returned her attention to the longhouse, taking in the wooden walls, the posts that held up the ceiling, the iron sconces that lined the walls.

She couldn't place the familiarity of the sconce design as she continued on what was becoming the longest walk she had ever attempted.

The pathway parted, revealing the king on his wood throne. It was thick and the high back was carved in three points. Annie held her breath as she took in the wood, the shine, a newly carved structure that in the present day was nearly eleven hundred years old.

"That's the chair in the Wizard Council room," Annie said with wonder.

Gibbs, not typically one to be impressed by much, said, "I'll be damned. It is." He waved his palms, forcing the crowd back.

"Really?" Brite asked with much curiosity. Of the three of them, he was not a Wizard Council member and had never been permitted inside the Wizard Council chamber.

"It is," Annie said.

While she was well familiar with wizard history, she had never realized how much of it was tied to the Viking community of Jorvik. The things she grew up with she knew were old, but not this old, and she had never known that the coven was linked to Jorvik.

As they continued through the crowd, Annie realized that she was observing history in real time, and she was so much a part of it. She suddenly understood the connections from the past to the future, making her task all the more real.

She turned her attention to the king, the formidable man sitting on the throne. Even if she hadn't seen him sitting there, she would have known he was the king; he wore the most furs and wore a gold crown on his shaved head except for the lone braid that sprung out of the back of his skull.

They were separated from the throne by a long wooden table covered with wooden bowls brimming with dried fish and bread like the kind Kolgaar carried with him. The food smelled rotten. Annie refrained from making a face and concentrated on the family that surrounded the king on either side of the throne. His wife sat on his left, a slender woman with a long, thin face and lips that were pursed so tightly that Annie couldn't tell for sure if she actually had lips. Either the queen was fearful of them or just annoyed.

Annie estimated she was thirty-five. Her hair was white, braided in multiple ropes that hung down her back in one plait. On the top of her head was a crown of golden flowers. Her steely blue eyes stared at Annie. As Annie returned the woman's stare, she knew this wasn't someone to underestimate.

Refocusing, Annie observed the girl to the king's right. She was young—Annie estimated twelve or thirteen—and her golden hair shined in the fireplace light. Her hair was braided from the temples to the back of her head, and the rest flowed down her back. Her dress was well made of a shiny material, more fitting to a princess than a warrior, and yet she too stared at Annie with a glare that wouldn't back down.

Sensing no fear or unease within the royal family, Annie turned her attention to the cause of her current anxiety, and scanned the crowd for Sturtagaard. His dark eyes, pale skin, and tall, lean frame were etched in her mind, but here all the men were tall and wide, dressed in tunics, pants, and boots. There were too many of them, too many sets of eyes watching her every move.

The king observed the three travelers. His gaze stopped on Annie and he smirked. To Annie, it was offensive and creepy; she felt as though she were a piece of meat or a potential mistress. She grew uncomfortable under his glare and tensed.

Svenson took a place behind the king as if he might be a member of his royal guard. He fondled the ax tied to his belt.

Annie wouldn't have recognized him if she hadn't been looking so carefully for that familiar face. But she eventually spied Sturtagaard sitting with his pretty, young wife. He had a human smile, devoid of the familiar fangs and sneer. His eyes were dark blue and sparkled as he smiled at his baby boy, who was an exact copy of the father.

Sturtagaard's eyes are blue!

Sturtagaard looked at Annie. She could sense the soul he carried her heart skipped a beat. She found it hard to breathe as she looked at his human form, knowing that in several centuries, he would set in motion the plan that would destroy her family, turn her mother against her, and set one of the most dangerous ancient societies on her. Sturtagaard in that moment had no idea what he would become and how much Annie loathed him.

"King Hrothgar." Kolgaar bowed to his king. "I have brought the girl who will save us from the demons," he said.

"I see this lovely creature in front of me. I have a difficult time believing she is the warrior who will rid the land of the demons," he said.

Annie glanced at the king, her face stony, her hands balled in tight fists. If she could get away with it, she would have liked to punch the chauvinist in the mouth.

"I assure you, I'm far more capable of ridding you of the demons than you are," she said.

With that, King Hrothgar laughed heartily. It was followed by the laughter of his men behind him and the general audience around her. Annie's cheeks flushed. That seemed to entertain the king further.

"Anaise. You are welcome, as are your friends. Welcome to Jorvik."

The noise in the longhouse grew louder as those still in attendance returned to their previous machinations. Annie, Brite, and Gibbs were led to a table and offered seats.

"Now what?" Brite asked. Annie watched the others. There was no silverware, just metal plates and knives. She reached for a piece of dried fish and took a sniff.

"I'm not sure I can do this," she said and placed the fish on the plate.

The king sat across from her and placed a cup cut from a horn in front of her. "Have this," he said and smiled at her. She offered a wan smile and looked at the Queen, her pursed lips deepened, her eyes angry.

"Thanks," Annie said. Her voice was gravelly and her mouth parched. She took a sip and coughed. It was far stronger than she was used to. She felt her cheeks flush in embarrassment for a second time when he laughed at her.

"Leave it to the coven to bring me a little scrawny nothing and two witches that couldn't last in a fight." The king took a swig of his mead.

Annie looked to Gibbs and then to Brite, their eyebrows raised at the insult.

"This is John Gibbs and Michael Brite. It would be unwise to underestimate us," Annie said.

The king took another sip of his mead. "Tell me. We were only expecting you. Why should I not kill them?" He pointed to Gibbs and Brite. His smile was jovial as if he were teasing them, bullying them, showing his power.

Annie played with her mead and took a sip. The second time, it went down a little smoother. She observed the king cautiously and matched his stare. "You won't kill them because as much as you fear the coven, you need us." She took another sip and quickly felt the effects of the drink.

"We do not fear the magic," the king scoffed.

She held her hand out and formed a fireball. As she added more magic, it grew to the size of a basketball. She wiggled her fingers, and the flames danced at her command. King Hrothgar's eyes grew wide with anticipation.

"I can burn down the entirety of Jorvik with one flick of my wrist. I can burn the forests and the grass and scorch the earth. I am Anaise." The longhouse grew quiet as everyone watched the exchange. Annie could feel the heat of the king's gaze on her. It was not completely fearful and definitely not friendly.

The fire roared above her palm, pulsing with life. Through the flames, Annie watched the princess smile, almost giddy at Annie's interaction with her father.

It was Sturtagaard's reaction that intrigued her the most. Just minutes ago, he was happy with his family, but in this instant his face radiated fear. Fear of her and the power she wielded. He held onto his wife and child tightly. His son squirmed, far more interested in the lady with the fire. Annie stood and tossed the fireball into the already raging fire in the fireplace. It brightened and settled.

King Hrothgar raised his glass and said, "Skol!" toasting them as if this were some sick joke. The others joined in. A musical pipe began to play somewhere in the corner as the rest of those in attendance returned to their festivities.

All except Sturtagaard, who continued to look upon Annie with fear and curiosity. Even in the past, her presence pushed his buttons.

Nothing's changed.

The king removed himself from the table and sat beside his wife, still laughing, still leering at Annie. He raised his glass to her.

She returned the action, but took no more of the mead. Her head already pounded.

"You okay, girl? Annie?" Gibbs asked.

"When in Rome." She took another bite of food, but her stomach roiled at the strangeness, at Sturtagaard's reaction to her magic.

"Sturtagaard's afraid of us," Annie said. She reached for a bit of bread. It was dry and rough. She swallowed the mass that sat in her stomach like a rock.

"Where is he?" Gibbs asked.

"To the right by the wall."

Gibbs and Brite took turns searching, both finding the future vampire.

"He's helpless, he's human," Gibbs said.

Annie pushed the food away, anxious to be gone from the longhouse and the people within. "I'm not going to kill him. I'll wait until we get back. I'm really pissed at the Sturtagaard rotting in Tartarus."

While Annie believed that when she said it, she remained obsessed with Sturtagaard the human and couldn't stop watching him. Even when Kolgaar joined his brother and had an animated discussion, she couldn't look away.

"Do you think he's asking how Sturtagaard got to the future?" Brite asked as he reached for more food.

"I don't know. He can't tell him." She stood. "The coven did him a disservice by not preparing him or the people of Jorvik for this. Makes me trust them even less." She walked to the brothers. "Kolgaar, a word, please." Annie pulled on his arm, dragging him with her.

"He doesn't remember," Kolgaar said when they were far enough away from Sturtagaard.

"We told you he was a vampire. A demon who can live forever. He must never know what his future holds. You cannot tell anyone what you saw in the future. No one must know what's to come."

Kolgaar stared at Annie. "Did I cause damage?"

Annie stared at Sturtagaard, protectively holding his child and glaring at her—a more familiar look to Annie.

"Tell him you were mistaken. There was a person in the future who looked just like him. You were confused. I don't care what. He must never know!" Annie said.

Kolgaar ambled toward Sturtagaard and said something. They had harsh words before Kolgaar slinked back to Annie. The future vampire scowled at her, just like he would in the future.

Sturtagaard watched his brother return to Annie. "I told him I was mistaken. There was someone in the future who greatly resembled him. He does not seem convinced."

"Would you be?" Annie asked.

"No. I guess I wouldn't," he said.

Annie observed him carefully. He nervously glanced at his brother and then back to her.

"Are you okay?" Annie asked.

"You have been here less than a day, and you and your people are nothing but trouble."

"Good. Take us to the coven and you'll be rid of us," Annie said.

"You will stay in Jorvik tonight, and I will take you to them in the morning," he said and walked away.

"Why?" she asked but he was already immersed in the crowd.

CHAPTER 22

AS IT NEARED nightfall, the narrow streets emptied as the villagers retired for the night and stayed inside, fearful of a demon attack. Kolgaar led them to the edge of town twenty feet from the forest, to an empty cottage. Through the darkness, orange eyes looked out at them, blocked by a protection spell. Annie first saw the spell before entering the small cottage. It was woven into the trees, and fluttered as the wind blew through them.

The golden mist shimmered in the moonlight. Though it started at the ground and worked its way to the canopy, there were thinning and missing spots in the protection spell. She hesitated as she entered, concerned that the protection spell was tearing and would soon be unable to hold back an attack.

The cottage consisted of two separate sides. The first was a small home with a bed, table, a storage chest, shelves on the far wall, and a fire pit at the center of the room with a pot hanging from a tripod-type hanging system. At the far wall, an open doorway led to an empty room that was still filled with hay and tools, with a loft above. Annie glanced inside, sniffed a strong stench of animal. The family must have stored their livestock here as well.

"I'll take you to the coven in the morning," Kolgaar said and left them alone without inquiring if they needed anything.

"Thank you," Annie mumbled as she watched him leave. "Stuffy in here," she added as she opened the shutters that faced the trees.

Gibbs began loading firewood into the pit and fumbled with the fire-lighting implements, grumbling as he attempted to light the fire sans magic.

Annie chuckled as she looked out the window. Thick gray clouds rolled across Jorvik, bringing chilly air and a fine mist. While she was cold and wet from the hike over, she left the window open and breathed in fresh air.

"What are you looking at?" Brite asked as he joined her at the window. She leaned against the window jamb, completely mesmerized by the protection spell and the holes scattered through it.

"The protection spell is ripping in areas," Annie said. She glanced east and west. "I'll have to watch it as we leave."

"What protection spell?" Brite asked.

Annie glanced at him. "You can't see it? It's woven along the forest perimeter."

Brite scanned the trees and shook his head. "I don't see it. Gibbs, take a look."

Gibbs used his magic to create a spark and lit one of the twigs. He placed it into the pile of wood before joining them.

"Annie sees a protection spell. Do you?"

Gibbs squinted as if that would put a magical spell into sight. He shook his head. "Nothing. What do you see?"

Annie explained the shimmering rose gold magic that was intertwined throughout the branches. "Seriously? You don't see that?" she asked.

Both men shook their heads.

"Should we worry?" Brite asked.

"Maybe you've tapped into powers that aren't yours," Gibbs suggested.

Annie shrugged and returned to staring out the window. She shuddered as another pair of orange eyes glared back at her.

"Do you see the eyes at least?" Annie asked as she pointed.

Both glanced out. "Yeah. I see those," Brite said.

"Demon?" Gibbs asked.

"That would be my guess." Just above the eyes, she could make out a large rip in the spell.

Brite peered through the trees. "It's really dark out there. I see another set of eyes."

"They are nocturnal," Annie said.

"I'll collect the magic along the tree line when we leave tomorrow. I'm guessing you're right about it being a protection spell. However, why only you can see it is a mystery," Brite said.

Gibbs fumbled with the table, pushing it against the door. He flipped the chairs and lay them on the top, making room for them around the fire. "We should eat something and get some rest. Come morning, we'll need to be ready." He dug through his bag pulling out sandwiches and fruit. "Eat," he said again.

The fire popped and crackled, quickly warming the small cottage. They covered the floor with a sleeping bag and sat to enjoy their cold sandwiches. Annie played with hers before taking a bite.

"You can have the bed," Gibbs said as he cleared away their garbage, leaving it in his field pack.

"I can sleep on the floor," Annie said, though she was too tired to argue the point. He helped her up, she crawled on to the bed and let him place her sleeping bag across her shivering body.

Gibbs and Brite unrolled their sleeping bags on the floor. "I've never been this tired before," Annie said as her eyes flickered closed.

"Not even during your Wizard Guard test?" Brite asked.

"Not even that." She pulled the blanket to her chin, but the bed was nowhere close to comfortable. "What I wouldn't give for a futon."

"I'd take a cot from Tartarus," Brite said.

"No point complaining," Gibbs said as he punched his pillow to find his comfortable position.

"Just lightening it up a bit." Annie yawned as they each settled in, the sounds of the demons growing louder as they would be awake for most of the night.

⇜

Annie startled awake. Her heart pounded so quickly, she felt lightheaded and nauseated. Outside, the rain fell in a steady stream and the chilly air had snuck into the cottage, making Annie shiver under her sleeping bag.

She lay awake on the straw-filled bed, listening to the demons' growl and their footsteps stomp across the earth as they paced against the protection spell that, for the time being, held them back.

Gibbs snored softly beside the window, Brite kicked out and made contact with the bed. Annie sighed and pulled the blankets around her to warm herself. But the dampness of England seeped to her bones and she couldn't warm up. Annie stared at the fire, which by now was nothing more than smoky embers. She held her palm toward the firebox and cast a gentle spell to ignite the wood inside.

The magic didn't take. Annie sighed and closed her eyes, stretching her hand out, reaching for the fire pit as she imagined the magical energy around her. She summoned the energy until her hand tingled. She felt the surrounding magical energy as it joined with her own. She let another spell fly from her fingers; it hit the lone log still in the pit and set it on fire. Annie fed the fire additional magic and watched the log become consumed by the flames. Confidently, she directed another log into the fire and watched it light.

At home in her time with full magic, the fire would have been roaring and burning through a large pile of wood. Here, her magic trickled slowly as she placed another log in the fire. Finally feeling warmth, she rolled to her back, exhausted from the magical output, and listened to the wood burn and pop until she finally fell back asleep.

᠅

Annie didn't wake again until the light outside was turning gray. Gibbs and Brite were still asleep but moving slightly inside their sleeping bags.

The fire was low. Annie climbed out of her warm sleeping bag and added another log, stoking it with magic and watching the flames grow. Still chilled, she closed up the shutters and sat back down on the bed.

Knowing she should only use magic when necessary, she dug through her bag, found her portable *Book of Shadows*, and searched for the memory modification spell and the one she had used to turn all shapeshifters back to their human selves.

How can we use this to kill all of the demons at once?

Rain began to fall gently against the thatched roof. She would have enjoyed the sound had she been home. Instead, she glanced at the ceiling and wondered if the roof was waterproof.

Too late if it isn't.

Wind whipped against the cottage, which creaked and groaned against the storm. She returned to her *Book of Shadows,* reviewing both events as she worked through how to disseminate fire to an unknown number of unpredictable creatures in a large area.

"I can't corral them into one place." Annie murmured. "How do I use their blood to link them?"

"What girl?" Gibbs grumbled in a sleep haze.

"Sorry to wake you. Just working out a problem. Go back to sleep," she said. She found an empty page and found a pencil.

"What's the"—Brite yawned— "problem?"

"Sorry. Just figuring out how to use their blood to link them and kill them all at once," she said.

"And?" Gibbs unwrapped himself from the sleeping bag and joined her on the bed. His long, thin hair fell to his shoulders; he tied it with a rubber band.

"Remember the setup we used when the Black Market fell? The one to turn the shapeshifters back to their human selves?"

"Yeah. We corralled them into the pen, surrounded them with crystals, and chanted the spell over the main rock that sent it to all the crystals, enveloping them in magic," Gibbs said.

"We can't do that with the demons because I don't know where all the demons are. I suppose I could summon them, but then we don't know how many there are either. You mentioned using a spell to do whatever we have to do. That got me thinking about linking the demons somehow. I can only think to link them with their blood."

Gibbs glanced at her. "We know their blood is… different," he said.

"How different?" Brite asked.

"Part human, part demon. I'm assuming it's similar enough because they're pretty much contained to this island. If they're reproducing, it's mostly from the same genetic pool," she said.

"Okay. So we would need blood from one of them," Gibbs said.

"Cast a fire spell on that blood? We'd need to use a spell to link the blood," Brite said.

"In theory, if we can link the blood, we should be able to toss a fire on that linked blood and it should, in theory, burn all of the demons," Annie said.

"Have you slept?" Brite asked.

"Not much. I was so worried about how we were going to get here, I never thought about how we were actually going to do this. And now with the limited magic, I'm hoping we can actually pull it off," Annie admitted. She summoned her crystal and waited several seconds before it landed in her palm. She touched her finger across the grooves and cuts of the crystal.

"The Vikings or the coven might have it on weapons or clothing. Otherwise, we'll have to find one in the forest and bleed it." Brite grimaced.

"I think it might work," Gibbs said.

Annie sighed. "And if it doesn't work?"

"One problem at a time," Gibbs said.

Light crept into the cottage through a slit in the shutter slats. When Brite opened them, cool, damp air and rain fell through the window.

"Heavy rain again," Brite said.

Jorvik was already awake. Soft voices wafted through the air, doors squeaked, and smoke rolled across town. "It's about six o'clock, you think?" Annie asked.

"About that. Eat something. He's bound to come around soon and send us off to the coven." Gibbs said. He pulled the morning's provisions out. Annie summoned an apple; it came more quickly this time and smacked into her palm.

"Keep using magic. It gets stronger," she told Brite and Gibbs. She took a bite of her apple and peered out the window. The forest was silent. The orange demon eyes were gone, and the grunts and growls had stopped. Lightning flashed and thunder boomed. Annie sighed.

I'm safe in the thunder.

The unmistakable scent of men's cologne wafted to her. She sniffed again. It was so familiar, so safe. She knew Gibbs didn't wear cologne and she didn't think Brite did either. The memory of who belonged to that scent came to her. She kept the unused portion of her father's cologne in her medicine cabinet, and she knew it was that scent—plus something else. A mixture of the cologne and the smell of him, almost like he was here with her now.

Dad!

"Do you smell that?" Annie asked excitedly.

Both men sniffed. "Just smoke and cooked meat. Why?" Brite asked.

"I smell cologne. It's so familiar." She looked at Gibbs who watched her with worry.

"It smells like the scent Dad wore." She answered Gibb's question before he could ask it.

He stood beside her and took another sniff before looking at her. "I smell it too. Right here next to you," he said.

"Sturtagaard told me I'd be safe in the thunder."

"Maybe he wasn't blowing smoke up your ass," Gibbs grumbled. He glanced outside and closed the shutters as a shadow of a man came toward the small cottage. "I think it's time to go."

CHAPTER 23

KOLGAAR SHIFTED WEIGHT between his feet as they finished gathering their things from the small cottage.

"Good morning," Annie said as she passed him. He barely acknowledged her with a quick nod before he stepped away. She bit her tongue to keep from laughing, fully understanding that, after he deposited them, he was done.

Annie pulled her hood over her head as thunder roared and gray clouds rolled across the sky. The scent of the next storm mixed with her father's cologne filled her nostrils as they walked east to the coven.

Brite walked the edge of the trees, examining the magic. His rock glowed a bright, hot white light. The magic use unnerved the villagers as they watched them march away. Annie watched them watch her. Some seemed frightened, others didn't seem to care or were too busy. She sighed and turned back as they trekked toward the narrow trail that linked Jorvik to the coven village.

Annie's thoughts were scattered. While she was here to kill demons and the plan was coming into fruition, she couldn't help be curious about the relationship between the coven and Vikings. Why didn't a coven member come for her? Why were there Viking artifacts in Wizard Hall? Something seemed... She thought of the dark wood walls, the throne, the sconces that hung on the support beams in the longhouse.

The sconces in the library!

Annie knew the design had looked familiar. She wondered if they had been brought over with the longhouse doors, electrified, and hung in the library.

Why did the Vikings let the coven take their things with them to the new world?

Or did the Vikings join the coven?

But Jorvik had been a Viking stronghold for decades and would remain the stronghold for another two centuries until William the Conqueror raided England in 1066.

They passed through the protection spell onto the narrow path through the forest. Annie reached out and touched the veil that protected the village. It shimmered and swayed gently at her touch. Kolgaar swung an ax, removing low hanging branches as they made their way through the trees.

"I don't think this trail is used much," Brite whispered.

"You're probably right. I get the feeling neither group is fond of the other, but something about it is odd," Annie said. Thunder roared above and the rain pelted the canopy.

"Still smell your dad?" Gibbs jested.

Annie chuckled. "It's not strong, but I smell his cologne," she admitted.

The path narrowed, cinching them together until they walked single file. At the end of the path, Kolgaar slid between two trees, entering the coven village.

"We're here." Kolgaar stepped aside to let them exit the dryness of the trees into the clearing, where the storm whipped against them.

Annie recognized the village from her dream. It was much smaller than Jorvik; only twenty cottages had been built along the perimeter of the clearing. At the far end of the village was a longhouse. While it was larger than the cottages, it was much smaller than the one in Jorvik. Annie assumed it wasn't the center of coven life, as the chimneys on each end of the building weren't billowing out smoke. She thought maybe the villagers were tucked away in their own cottages, dry and warm and out of the consecutive storms.

A large fire blazed in a pit at the center of the village, fighting mightily against the raging winds and rain. It was tended to by two women who were pouring magic into the flames. They turned when Annie, Brite, and Gibbs entered the clearing. Annie recognized the women from her dream.

"You'll stay with them until it's done," Kolgaar said to Annie. She nodded absently as the familiarity of the village hit her like déjà vu. She was walking the same path she had the day she entered the fire and proclaimed the prophecy.

The older woman reached for the girl, whispering in her ear. The young girl stopped and held her hands behind her back, her lips pursed anxiously. A smirk broke across the older woman's thin wrinkled lips.

"You are here, blessed be," the girl said and curtsied low. "Welcome, Anaise. We are so glad you are here. I am Bega. This our coven elder, Etheldreda."

"Etheldreda, I've brought her here. I am released of my obligation," Kolgaar said and dumped his pack at Etheldreda's feet. He ripped the talisman from his neck and tossed it on the pile, walking away without saying goodbye, without looking back to ensure that, in the least, Annie was fine. She watched him leave, unsurprised by his actions.

"At least he brought you here," Etheldreda spat. She took Annie's hands and offered a smile that was neither warm or friendly. "We are so very glad you are here. Though I must admit, we did not expect others," she said.

"This is John and Michael." Annie pointed to each of them. "They are here to help me with this task," Annie explained.

Etheldreda and Bega glanced at each other as if communicating silently, their lips curled in apprehension. "I did not see them in the fire," Etheldreda said after a moment. "But what is done is done. We must meet with the coven."

Annie stood close to the roaring fire but felt no warmth. The rain fell against her skin, and yet it didn't affect the flames.

It's a cursed fire. Why?

Etheldreda waved her palm through the flames, which burst with energy and grew.

"It is a protection spell for you, and it allows you and I and the others to communicate. That is why we tend to it," Bega said excitedly. Etheldreda gave her a stern look of warning.

They were left in an uncomfortable silence. Whether it was from their anguish or the lack of food and sleep, Annie felt dizzy and wished to find an isolated spot to sit and think. "Is there a place we could rest before speaking to the coven? I think the trip has worn me out, and there's much to do," she said.

"Of course, dear," Etheldreda said. "We will let you rest first."

"I will take you there," Bega volunteered.

"You will meet with the coven when you are ready." Etheldreda said. Her forced smile revealed twisted, yellowing teeth. Annie nodded and held her breath as they were led by the young girl, whose yellow hair was plastered down her wool cape.

The cottage was at the far end of the village. Again, they'd be staying only a few feet from the edge of the forest. Annie stared into the trees where the protection spell shimmered against the darkened forest.

"The protection spell needs a magical boost," Annie commented as Bega led them inside a small cottage. It was smaller than the one they had stayed in overnight. This was just one room, with no bays and loft.

Bega moved about, placing wood in the firebox and starting a fire. "How do you know that?" she asked as she added magic to the flame.

"I can see it. There are worn spots. It won't hold for long," Annie advised. She dropped her field pack on the floor by the bed and sat by the fireplace to warm herself.

Bega frowned and glanced at Annie. "I will alert them of the protection spell." The fire sputtered as she continued to observe Annie.

"Is there something else?" Annie asked.

"I was there… when your face was in the fire. I am so glad it was you who came here," Bega said.

Annie smiled. "You don't know me yet." She reached for Bega's hands. "Are you married, or do you live with your parents?"

The girl looked down at their hands. "I am not married. My parents were killed in the last attack," she said.

Annie glanced at Gibbs and Brite and sighed. "I'm so sorry. Do you know anything about the demons? Maybe how they were created or for how long they've been around?"

Bega looked up at Annie and offered a slight smile on thin lips. "They've been around since before I was born. I… I am not aware of where they are from." She returned to the fire and added more magic, making the flames jump and the fire expand.

"You know something," Annie said.

Gibbs and Brite pulled back and began unpacking items, placing them on a chest in the corner while carefully observing Annie and the girl. Bega pulled another log from the pile and placed it on top of the fire.

"What do you know?" Annie asked.

Bega wrung her hands, picked up a small stick, and poked the fire.

Annie tried again. "Ever since I found out about the prophecy, I have lain awake at night worried about coming to the past. Could I do it, can I get back? I have spent so much time researching, looking for the actual prophecy, and reading about portals and the demons. The future coven refused to offer me needed help until I had to beg, and now I find it odd that the ones who actually called upon the ancient ones for help also chose not to help me." Annie took a breath. "Thanks for the fire. Let us know when the coven wants to meet." She stood and grabbed her bag and pretended she was looking for something.

"The demons came when Vikings first attacked Northumbria. I do not know why. I'll get you some food and drink." Still wringing her hands, Bega ran from the cottage.

Annie unlatched the shutters from above the bed and peered through them, watching Bega enter a cottage several away from theirs. Within minutes, the girl raced back through the rain carrying a basket that was almost too large for her. Annie closed up the shutters as Bega slipped inside and placed the basket on the table.

"I do not know why the coven of your time refused help. I just do not see why you need to know where they came from. Or how," Bega said.

"I know that it's a test so that I can earn the powers." Annie frowned. "I don't want the powers. I just want to kill the demons and go home. Telling me the truth about the demons will make it easier for me to kill them."

"The demons killed my parents. I would very much like you to kill them all." Bega's voice was harsh as she spoke.

"I can't bring your parents back, but I can make sure no one else dies. But I need help."

Bega nodded. "If I can find out anything, I will let you know." She pulled up the hood of her cloak and left through the rain.

"You okay, Anaise?" Gibbs asked.

Annie watched Bega run through the muddy earth to her cottage. The girl looked back at Annie before entering. Even after Bega was safely inside, Annie remained at the open door and watched the village.

"At least, you're not calling me 'girl'." She rubbed her hands against her arms, closed the door and sat beside the fire. "No. I'm actually not fine. I'm dizzy and tired. I need to eat and somehow take a bath."

Brite opened the basket and pulled out dark bread, cheese, and a jug of ale. "I'm going to get sick of this food," he commented and tossed each of them a small loaf.

"I've got some peanut butter in my bag. That should help," Annie said as she sniffed the dry bread.

Gibbs lit several candles and set them around the cottage. While it looked warm, Annie couldn't shake the damp chill. She wrapped a thin blanket around her shoulders and took a sip of strong, bitter ale from the jar Bega had left. "Ugh. I think I'll stick with water."

"I packed enough. We should be fine." Gibbs took a bite of his bread and chewed slowly, washing it down with the ale. Apparently, it was too bitter even for him; he put the mug on the table, splashing some as he did. "What are you going to tell them?"

Annie tossed the rest of the bread in the fire and watched it burn. "I'll tell them the truth. We'll collect demon blood, link it, and set it on fire."

"We might not have enough magic," Gibbs said. He took the last bite of his small loaf of bread and looked inside the basket for additional food, finding some dried fish. He took a piece, sniffed the meat, and took a bite.

"I'll tell them that too. We'll need magical help. Whether it's that girl Bega or someone else, we'll need help with teleporting and possibly also with the spells. I'm drained. I'm not sure how much more I have in me," Annie admitted.

With her elbows on the table, she placed her head in her hands. The necklace she wore moved inside her shirt. She had nearly forgotten she had it. She pulled it out and stared at the design.

"What's that?" Brite asked.

Annie explained the protection charm that Zola had given her and how she needed to give this to Zola's younger self when she called for her.

Gibbs took a closer look at the charm. "Having Zola's magic on your side is a good thing," he said. "When were you planning on calling for her?"

Annie shook her head. "I don't know. Maybe once we get a lay of the land, so to speak. I want to walk through the forest mid-morning and see what the demon population looks like. On our way here, I saw maybe twenty, thirty of them sleeping on the ground. I'm guessing a majority of them are here." She placed the necklace back inside her shirt. "I think I should change."

As she finished pulling on dry clothes, there was a soft knock on the door. Brite opened it for Bega, who stepped inside. "The coven has gathered to meet you. Did you have a nice rest?" she asked almost too cheerfully.

"As nice as it could be," Annie mumbled. Even though she was dry, Annie couldn't shake the dampness as she put on her drenched jacket. She wrapped the laces of her hiking boots around her ankle, securing them, and raised the hood of her raincoat, tying the strings tightly under her chin. Protected from the rain, she followed Bega outside.

Bega led them through an empty village, where they passed the fire still roaring in the heavy rain. A different coven member tended to the fire and watched them as they walked to the longhouse where smoke now billowed from the chimneys.

CHAPTER 24

A COUNCIL OF COVEN elders took their places at a long table
that stretched from one end of the longhouse to the other. As
Annie shrugged off her wet raincoat, they stared at her, leaving
her uncomfortable.

Annie, Gibbs, and Brite walked to the center of the longhouse. Its
interior was far different than the one in Jorvik; it was much smaller, had
less décor, and there were no festivities, little conversation, and no food
or mead. Rather than having sconces lining the walls, candles were laid
across the table and a fire pit at the center of the room was blazing. Annie
still shivered.

The coven members stared at her with no expressions of happiness or
gratitude. They were stone faced, intense, and far more formal than she
had expected from this smaller group.

Annie stopped at the fire pit to warm her hands.

"You okay?" Gibbs asked.

"Perfect," Annie groused. Feeling their eyes on her, she turned, offered
a smile, and sat across from Etheldreda at the center of the table. She had
a sense that this was possibly a place of importance in the coven order.
Nervously, Annie folded her hands and set them on the table.

The old woman smiled at them and said. "Dear Anaise, John, and
Michael, welcome to the coven. I trust you had a nice rest," she said.

Annie nodded.

"I would like to introduce the coven elders. I am Etheldreda

Browne. Starting from this end, William Cockburn, Gila Donaldson, Henry Debenham, Anaise Gladwyn, Jacob Reeves, Jacob Rhodes, Gila Rutherfurd, Henry Turnbull, Samuel Vahn, Gwendolyn Townsend, Angus Wickham, Alastair Willoughby, Callum Wortham, Bryony Voxall, and Rhys Younge." Annie tried to commit their names and faces to memory. She was just too tired to remember the information for anyone.

"It's nice to meet you. My name is Anne Pearce. With me is John Gibbs and Michael Brite. They are part of my team and traveled with me to keep me safe and help rid the land of the demons. Having said that, we're formulating the plan and we think we have an answer."

She observed the elder coven members as she spoke, paying especially close attention to Gila Donaldson, matching her gaze, and rendering the woman uncomfortable. For now, Annie could see nothing in her hair or clothes or mannerisms that screamed twenty-first century, though she knew this woman was somehow the key.

"Anaise, how will you go about this?" The question came from a man Annie believed to be Jacob Rhodes, though her memory of their names had quickly faded.

"We plan to create a spell that will link the demons by their blood. Once we do that we can set fire to that blood and, with a separate spell, search out the creatures with the same blood. It should rid all of the demons at the same time, throughout Northumbria and other realms," Annie said. The coven elders didn't react as Annie thought they might. "So, do you have any questions?" Annie asked.

"Now, Anaise, we expect that this will be done soon. Yes?" Etheldreda asked.

"As soon as we can collect a blood sample from a demon and get a lay of the land. If this doesn't work, we'll need to come up with a new plan," Annie said.

Several members of the coven frowned and started muttering.

"I see. That is disappointing. We assumed you knew what you were doing," said a male member of the coven. Annie believed it was Rhys. She took in his gaunt, sickly face and bald head. His lips were so tightly pursed together, he looked like he had just eaten a lemon.

Annie shook from the cold. She sat on her hands but felt like a small child hiding something. She pulled herself from the bench and warmed her hands by the fire. "I realize you assumed the ancient ones would send you someone who knew how to do this, but unfortunately, at some point in time between now and our time, the coven determined I shouldn't receive help. When I finally did receive help, the information was incomplete."

"What do you mean the records are incomplete? Surely, we wrote down the necessary spells and potions for you." It was a woman, possibly Byrony, with long dishwater blonde hair, rolled into a bun on her head. Her dress was tight across her large breasts, and her frown hung low on her face.

Annie laughed, shocking Gibbs and Brite. She held out her palm and attempted to summon the pages from the Donaldson's *Book of Shadows*. A spark flew from her palm as she waited.

"What's wrong, girl?" Etheldreda asked.

Annie held up one finger as if asking them to wait as she syphoned more energy to summon the documents again. The pages finally materialized on her palm. Slightly dizzy, Annie said, "Our magic is down. We're taking longer to perform magic, and it's just not as strong. We will need assistance from the coven to complete the plan." She passed the pages to Gila Donaldson. "This is all I received. Anything else is being guarded by your descendant. Her name is also Gila Donaldson, and she was reluctant to assist. Why would that be?"

The Gila from the past reviewed the words on the page. Annie watched her. Her braided hair was rolled upwards into a bun and the color almost seemed too yellow.

Maybe.

Her face seemed smooth, less hardened by life and the sun than the other women assembled at the table. But the eye color... Annie couldn't read it in the dim light.

Gila Donaldson of the future had admitted to traveling to the past to give them the plan, the spells, and information.

Would she really live here for any length of time or come back here on this day to help me? I could be very wrong.

She stared at Gila Donaldson. Regardless of who she might be, Annie knew the woman was hiding something. Annie could see it in the way Gila wouldn't make eye contact with her.

Gila Donaldson reviewed the notes. Her fingers trailed the words on the page yellowed with age. She stared at the picture of the face of Anaise. She summoned her familial *Book of Shadows* and opened to the picture of Annie, just like the one Annie produced for her. She summoned a quill and ink jar and placed it on the table, beginning to write. It was the plan as Annie laid it out for them at the top of the page. When she finished the entry, she handed back the torn pages to Annie.

"I do not know why my family would feel the need to hide this from you in the future. It is a disgrace, I assure you. As you work through this, I promise it will be recorded and handed down for you to have in the future," Gila said.

Annie read the pages. What Gila had written was inserted at the top of the first page. The rest of the items had been moved down.

"Thank you," Annie said.

The members of the coven were glancing at each other with concern. *Maybe they're not responsible for this problem.*

A bolt of lightning quickly flashed above them; bright light flickered around the spaces between the windows and the walls, the doors and the ground. Though Annie expected the thunder, the boom made her jump.

She sniffed the air for her dad's familiar scent. It hovered to her left, where she felt a soft pressure on her shoulder, much like a protective hand. For a moment, Annie felt safe.

"Can we expect the coven's help?" she asked.

They fidgeted at the suggestion. Etheldreda spoke first. "My dear. We are grateful to the ancient ones for sending you here. We are uncertain why they have seen fit to bring you unprepared. We assumed you would do this without assistance."

The ancient ones?

Annie wondered if the coven was aware it was the future Gila Donaldson and not the ancient ones who was leading this scheme. Again, she glanced at the past Gila and tried to ignore the sinking feeling in her gut. Not wanting to beg, she said, "Fine. Do you have a map of the area? I'd like to know where the demons roam and live."

"We have those." Etheldreda pointed to Bega, who sorted through a basket of scrolls. Finding the relevant maps, Bega brought them to Annie.

"These shall help you," she told Annie and turned to the elder council. "If there is nothing else for the ones of the future, I will take them back and get them ready."Etheldreda waved them away.

"Before I leave, you should know the protection spell is wearing thin. There are holes in it. Granted, the rips are higher up, but you need to add juice to the magic," Annie said.

Etheldreda and the other coven members nodded. Again, the old woman waved them away.

The rain hadn't let up since they entered the longhouse; to Annie, it seemed to have gained in strength. Although they were surrounded on all sides by the trees, violent winds and heavy rain battered them. They held their jackets and hoods against their bodies as if the thin layers of fabric could protect them from the onslaught. Unaffected by the storm was the fire raging in the pit. The man tending to it did so efficiently, ignoring the rain. As they ran past him, he glanced up but quickly returned to his work. By the time they lunged inside the cottage, they were thoroughly drenched.

Bega busied herself with their fire, replacing logs and relighting the pile. The fire took quickly with a magical boost, warming the room.

Though they had just arrived in the coven that morning, to Annie it felt like they had been here for days, if not weeks. She found a towel in her backpack and began to squeeze water from her hair.

Bega watched with interest and touched the fabric, pulling her hand away, confused by the texture. "What is that?" she asked.

Annie glanced at Gibbs and Brite. "It's called a towel. Here." Annie handed it to her. Bega may have been impressed with turquoise, not a common color during this time. Or maybe it was just the texture.

Bega held the damp towel. "What does it do?"

"It helps dry us."

Bega nodded. "Everything you own is so… different." She handed the towel back. "You wear men's pants," she added.

Annie chuckled. "Actually, this is what most people in our time wear.

Very versatile. Comfortable and warm." Annie dug in her backpack for another pair. She handed it to Bega, who touched it carefully.

"I would very much like to learn more," she said expectantly.

"I wish we could tell you more. I really do. But we can't share too much. It wouldn't be... wise."

Bega nodded sadly, slipped off her heavy wool cloak, and wiped her hands on the apron tied across her waist. She was painfully thin; her collarbones stuck out harshly. Even wet and dirty from the mud, her skin was clear and creamy and glowed in the low light.

She opened the basket she had brought earlier in the day and pulled out the rest of the candles, lighting each and placing them around the room. Annie had to admit the effect was warm and lovely. If only it wasn't here.

"You asked me if I was married. I'm not. My betrothed... was killed during one of the early attacks. There are not so many of us anymore. I fear I will die alone." As if embarrassed, she looked down, her cheeks flushed with color.

"I'm sorry. What was his name?" Annie inquired, generally concerned for the young girl.

If only she could come with me.

"William Jacoby. He was..." she took a breath. A tear fell from her eye. "He was beautiful. Perfect, really. But the demons were so strong and he could not... his magic was not strong enough to move them away. He died to save me." Bega wiped the tears from her eyes.

"I'm so sorry. I wish there was something I could do to make that right." Annie stopped and looked at Gibbs and Brite. "I wish I could have come sooner, when the demons first came, but we were limited to where the talismans and the time portal could bring us. They brought us here. "

"I wish you could have also," Bega said.

"I fear more will die and that I can't change that." She thought of Sturtagaard. She had wanted to kill the human but couldn't. As much as she hated to admit it, he had saved hundreds of people over the centuries and, in turn, more survived or were born. She couldn't go back farther in time to save Bega's love, just like she couldn't kill the vampire before he turned.

Annie watched Bega clean up their mess, toss old food in the fire, and brush off crumbs from the table. "You don't have to clean up after us," Annie said.

Bega looked at her. "It is nice and warm and interesting in here. I do not mind, really." She offered a smile, but Annie could read the sadness on her face. For only a teenager, she had suffered much in her young life. Though in this century, Bega really was middle aged. Annie sighed.

"You're welcome to stay. We'll just be working." Annie held up the maps.

"I should leave, then." Bega bowed quickly, wrapped her cape around herself, and scurried from the cottage, slamming the door shut. Annie opened the shutters above the bed and watched Bega run through the mucky earth toward her cottage. Even after Bega lunged inside, Annie continued to watch the cottage as a dim light emanated from it and smoke billowed from the chimney.

When rain began to come through the window, Annie closed the shutters and sat on the bed. She pulled out the maps of the area and began to plan.

✦

The table was covered in the maps from both the coven and the modern British Wizard Guard. Gibbs and Brite continued to mark up the modern maps with areas of demon occupation while Annie continued to observe the village from the window and saw two blonde women enter a cottage.

"I'm going for a walk," Annie said as she slipped on her jacket and headed out the door, leaving Gibbs and Brite to stare at her.

She ran for the cottage next to theirs, slinking her way along the back wall. At the corner, she ran for the next house, making her way to the edge. *One more.*

She could hear a pair of coven members speaking in hushed tones as they entered the next cottage. Annie positioned herself under the closed shutters, which were thin enough that she could hear two familiar voices speaking to each other: the voices of modern Gila and ancient Gila.

"It was a magical agreement passed down from generation to generation. Every family member who received the information took the oath that it would be passed on until the time Anaise would need to go to the past. That ended with me, and I did what I was supposed to do. I took a magical oath." As modern Gila spoke, her voice climbed several octaves.

"On whose orders? The girl doesn't know what to do," the ancient Gila said.

Annie stared through the slats. Modern Gila paced the empty cottage.

"She's being tested. This is what is supposed to happen. She isn't to know. She must figure it out," modern Gila said.

"The coven is dying. The ancient ones promised us a girl who could fix this. You came and promised me we would be strong and grow again. I've lied to them, to my family because of you." Ancient Gila, frustrated and fearful, cast a spell that blew apart the shutters above Annie. Annie ducked low and moved to the edge of the cottage.

"Because there is a prophecy that told you so, she will figure it out, she will get the power. You must trust the ancient ones, and they will provide for you," modern Gila said.

"You are the ancient ones, are you not?" ancient Gila asked.

"I did not send you the prophecy. They did, and I got the message. There's a difference," modern Gila argued.

"If you weren't my descendant, I would strike you down now. Do you even know what happened? How she did it?" ancient Gila asked.

Modern Gila walked to the window and looked outside. "I gave her what we had. It wasn't much, but it got her here.

"Who made this determination that she should not know what to do? Who decided it was a test?"

"I don't know," modern Gila said.

"What if she doesn't pass and we die? Our descendants, you, will also die. You said she would save us and we would grow to great numbers, and in return, the powers would come to save you. Did it occur to any of you that maybe you should have told her how to go about this?" Annie could sense ancient Gila's fury.

"She will save you. If she didn't, I wouldn't be here," modern Gila said.

"It doesn't absolve you from the fact that you are hindering her ability to do her job," ancient Gila reminded her.

Modern Gila paced the small cottage, stopping again at the window.

She tapped her fingers against the window frame. "A seer saw a vision with Anaise. It was around the year 1901 or 1902."

"And?"

"She saw the power. Annie's power and what she will do with that power."

"According to the prophecy, we know that her power will increase tenfold. This is nothing new."

"The power will destroy us all. She will destroy us all. The seer was insistent on this and, as a result, all information pertaining to Annie coming here was destroyed. Except for what I gave her."

Annie heard a slap of palm to face and jumped.

"What the hell was that for?" Modern Gila demanded.

"So, who determined that she shouldn't have the powers promised to her? That presented with the gift, the girl couldn't control it and use it to benefit all of us?"

Annie sat in the mud, dumbfounded by the revelation. They had purposely, willfully, decided her future and her destiny without her input. She trembled.

"Annie must save you, and we must make sure she doesn't return back to my time. We expect she will die trying to save you or she will not be able to return home because the magic will kill her. Either way, matters not. That girl will be too strong to stop, and it will be the death of us all."

"If this doesn't work, you will be recalled and killed. You promised us," ancient Gila said as she left the cottage, slamming the door.

Annie turned. Bega stood at the next cottage, her face an ashen grimace. Annie shook her head as she snuck toward the cottage and stood beside Bega.

"What did you hear?" Annie whispered and wiped tears from her cheeks.

"Enough to know what I did not know before," Bega said.

"Don't tell them what you know," Annie said. She peeked around the corner. Ancient Gila crossed the village to her cottage.

Modern Gila exited next and ran for the trees. Annie followed, not sure what she would say if she caught up to the witch. Bega ran after. Annie ran through the trees and caught Gila's sight. The older woman looked horrified as she touched the portal with the talisman and stepped through.

"What the hell?" Annie ran for the portal, but it closed before she reached it. Annie could still feel the magical energy. She reached for it, then, in her anger, kicked the foliage and marched from the trees.

"What are you going to do?" Bega asked, still following.

"Get the blood, say the spell, and go home. When we get back..." Annie shook her head. "When we get back, I don't know. Maybe talk to the Wizard Council. I'm not sure what they can do to her. She's a liar or someone lied. I don't know."

"The coven survived?" Bega asked.

Annie glanced at her. "Yes. It's the largest wizard community in the world with the largest Wizard Council. You'd be proud of us." She smiled. It felt fake.

"So, you save everyone?" Bega asked.

"I can't tell you much more than that, but whatever I did, it worked. I just hope it's what I'm going to be doing."

⁓

Annie told Gibbs and Brite about the conversation between the two Gilas and how the modern Gila had opened the portal and stepped through.

"She said you are meant to die?" Gibbs asked for clarity.

"They expect it." Annie paced by the fireplace on the far wall, turned, and walked back again. She looked out the window and turned again.

"That won't happen. We'll find a way to get you home safely, and you won't die saving them. I'll make sure of it," Gibbs said. He placed his hand on Annie's shoulder. "Call Zola."

Annie took out the necklace and stared at the charm. "Not yet. They can't know she's coming. I can't show my hand," Annie said and placed her hands on her face. She shuddered from emotion, from the wet, cold air. She sat on the bed and let Gibbs envelope her in his arms. She lay her head on his shoulder and cried.

"Come with me," Brite said to Bega. They left the cottage and returned several minutes later. When they entered again, Annie was at the fireplace warming herself, her cheeks still wet, her eyes red.

"The portal is just inside the trees. I have the magic. There's a lot of it. Gila's been coming and going on several occasions. We needed permission to do this; I'm pretty sure the Wizard Council didn't approve her secret trips," Brite said. He handed Gibbs his crystal. Gibbs waved a palm across the rock several times staring at each new spell used to open the portal.

"They set you up. You have two choices. Stay and help them, or we leave now," Gibbs said.

"Do you have enough energy to find the portal and teleport there? I don't. My magic is so weak, using it gives me a headache."

"Then we stay. We do this job and get you the hell out of here," Gibbs said.

Bega reached for Annie's hands. "You are very brave to stay here knowing what they hid from you. I thank you for trying to save us. I do not think I would stay here if I were you."

"I can't leave. Not when I know what will happen. Those demons will overrun the coven here and they will spread. That I can't live with."

Annie looked at the table covered in maps and set the original map beside the modern map. While the distances on the original map weren't completely accurate, it contained other valuable information.

"They mostly live here." Brite pointed to the forest outside their window.

"If we knew they only lived in this area, we could put crystals around here." Annie touched the map and drew an imaginary line around forest.

"What would that do?" Bega asked.

Annie explained how casting a spell into one crystal would scatter the spell across an area in search of other crystals. Bega nodded in fascination.

Gibbs examined the map and pointed out the window. "To do that though, gir—Annie, you have to do the spell from the center. That's a lot of fire."

"That's an issue," Annie said.

Brite walked to the open window and stared into the forest. The rain finally stopped but another storm was brewing from the west. "I'm guessing the rain will be here by evening," he said.

Annie pulled open the shutter on the window facing the center of town just enough to peer out. Etheldreda was tending the fire, occasionally stopping and staring at their cottage. "Etheldreda seems upset you're not out there," Annie said.

"I best be going." Bega pulled on her cloak and ran through the muddy village, expecting Etheldreda's admonishment. She glanced at the cottage and returned to her work.

"The demons should be asleep. Wanna go for a walk? See how we should get the blood?" Annie asked.

"As good a time as any," Gibbs said.

"I think we should climb through the window. Not let them know what we're doing," Annie said.

Gibbs climbed out of the window; Annie and Brite followed.

Before entering the trees, Annie observed the protection spell. "By the way, the protection spell is incredibly thin. We don't have much time," she said.

"Good to know." Gibbs found a narrow opening in the trees and entered the forest. They found themselves surrounded on all sides by massive lumps. Shadowy figures rose and fell with each breath. Several demons lay right by the protection spell, so close they should have been able to feel the magic buzzing against their skin.

Annie, Gibbs, and Brite carefully maneuvered around several large demons until they found a narrow path away from the village.

The uneven, muddy path was covered in animal, demon, and human-sized prints that crisscrossed the path in all directions. The human prints caused Annie's stomach to roil. She felt a sense of being followed. Annie continually scanned the forest, several times turning back, partly to see if they truly were being followed and partly to determine how far they had come. Whether she was being paranoid or if she really saw a person lunge inside the trees, she mentioned it. "I think we're being followed," she said.

"It doesn't matter," Gibbs said as they continued toward the river. Just outside this patch of forest, the swollen river rolled downhill, crashing into the corners and creating white caps that in the present day would have been perfect for whitewater rafting. Annie watched the water. "How many do you supposed we passed?" she whispered.

"Hundreds, if not thousands," Gibbs replied.

"It's too many if the spell doesn't work..." Annie's voice trailed off.

"If the spell doesn't work, we burn down the forest. Don't think about that yet," Gibbs ordered. "Do you have an idea of how you want to collect the blood?"

Annie glanced back down the empty path. Whoever followed them had either left or was well hidden in the trees. She scanned the sleeping demons. "From what I can tell, they sleep closer to the villages. Let them settle for the day, and then we come back out here, freeze the forest, and cut one of them with the sword. I'm assuming it's sharp enough to pierce their skin." Annie caught the view of a demon stirring on the ground. "Once I cut one of them, I'll summon the blood." Annie exited the trees and bent over to submerge her hand in the icy water. "Once we have the sample, unfreeze the forest, and teleport out," she added.

"It's a lot of magical use. We could use a least one additional witch or wizard to join us. I'll freeze the forest. Annie, you can collect the blood. When you're done, Gibbs will teleport you out. Then I'll unfreeze the forest and be teleported immediately by whoever we bring with," Brite suggested.

"It's a good plan… if our magic was at normal strength." She glanced into the trees. The demons were waking. "I say we teleport back to the coven," she said, and they each teleported away.

CHAPTER 25

ANNIE LANDED BEHIND the cottage first. Nausea gripped her. She bent forward and sucked in the air until her stomach settled. She heard two pops of air behind her as Gibbs and Brite pushed air from the spot where they landed. They, too, doubled over from an attack of nausea.

"There's no way we can teleport on our own," Brite said.

Annie looked at Gibbs and Brite. Both of them radiated grayish, greenish skin. "You're right. We need the coven to perform the magic." She peered around the side of the cottage and saw Etheldreda and Bega stoking the fire, raking bits of charcoal, and casting spells. The flames stretched upwards. Occasionally, one of them would glance at the cottage.

While Annie spied on them, a familiar man joined the women at the fire. She knew they were discussing them as he repeatedly pointed to the cottage while using large hand motions.

Gibbs and Brite climbed back through the window. "I think that guy is reporting back to Etheldreda," Annie said.

"Who is he?" Brite asked as he unloaded their next meal.

"I think it's Rhys." When he finished, he glanced at the cottage before heading for his own, leaving Etheldreda to tend to the fire and Bega to come to them.

"We have company," Annie said as she slipped inside the window and took a seat on the bed.

Rather than knocking on the door, Bega, strolled around the cottage and knocked on the back window. Annie unlatched the shutters.

"What's up?" Annie smiled at the girl.

"They want me to place a spell around the cottage. They're worried something might happen to you," Bega whispered.

"They want to spy on me," Annie said.

Bega nodded.

"Do they know I'm supposed to die?" Annie asked.

"I do not know if Gila shared that with them. I know they're frightened," Bega said.

"Tell Etheldreda and the rest of the coven to back off and not get in my way."

Bega nodded.

"Oh. Tell them if they don't fix the protection spell, there's going to be another attack. The rips are nearly at the ground," Annie warned.

Bega glanced back at the trees. "How can you tell?" she asked.

Annie looked at the trees, at the leaves and branches. "I see a golden pink mist that's weaving in and out of the branches. Some areas have thinned considerably and other areas have holes. The demons sleep at the edge, just against the spell," she explained.

Bega walked to the perimeter and touched the trees at the edge. She seemed surprised to see how many lived so close to the edge of the trees. When a demon woke and lunged at the protection spell, Bega cried out and ran for the cottage, slamming the door shut behind her.

"At least the spell held," Bega said as she breathed heavily.

Annie chuckled. "Yes. That is a good thing. We're about to eat. Would you like to join us? It's not much."

Gibbs and Brite ate at the table, easily polishing off their sandwiches. Annie and Bega sat on the bed. Bega stared at the sandwich, pulled the top slice of bread off, and looked at the meat inside. "What is this?" she asked.

"It's called a turkey sandwich," Annie replied. She took a bite of her own and chewed it slowly.

Bega watched Annie take a second bite and tried what she did. After swallowing, she took another bite. "It is good," she said when she swallowed.

"We have more." Brite crumpled up his garbage and tossed it in the fire.

"This is good. Thank you," Bega said again. "They want to know what you were doing in the forest."

Annie raised her eyes brows. "They seem to care an awful lot for not wanting to help."

"They are worried and want to make sure you are safe," Bega said.

"They only want the demons killed. They just want to make sure the deed is done," Annie said. "We're planning to collect the blood tomorrow morning and we needed to plan how that was going to happen. If they want the demons gone and us back to the present, then we need three witches or wizards to help with the plan. The magic is just too much for us. I'm not asking."

Bega nodded. "I can arrange that for you."

The rain was momentarily replaced by pea-sized hail, which beat against the thatched roof and mud walls. After an instant, it stopped and the rain returned, bringing with it clouds so gray, the village was plunged in darkness.

The rain whipped through the tiny village, blowing the rain sideways into the trees and awakening the demons. They grunted and growled angrily, as if forced awake. Annie stood at the window peering into the trees, growing anxious at the sight of their orange eyes staring back at her.

"What do you see?" Brite joined her.

"They're nocturnal and go by the light of the sun. It's very dark," Gibbs said.

"I don't like this," Annie said. In theory and principle, weather shouldn't affect magic, and yet, she could clearly see the winds battering the spell and ripping through protection. "Tell the coven they need to place more magic at the perimeter now." Annie looked at Bega. "Go!" she shouted.

A terrified, naked shrill echoed from the distance, followed by rumbling of the earth and chaotic hollering and screeching.

"What the hell was that!" Annie shrieked.

Brite yanked open the door. "It's coming from Jorvik!" They ran from the cottage, joined by the coven, and rushed down the narrow path.

Mass chaos met them when they entered the city limits. Men, women, and children scurried from the demons, their terror-filled cries seeming to fuel the beasts' determination. Creatures easily snatched the humans, snapping their necks, and biting into their fresh flesh. Mutilated bodies were tossed to the ground.

Annie, Gibbs and Brite ran into the fray and threw fireballs at the nearest demons. While their magic was not at its normal strength, the flames easily burned through the demon's skin and flesh. The demons shrieked in pain. "Burn them with fire!" Annie screamed as she threw another fireball.

As they spread themselves out around Jorvik, the fireballs roared around her and demons burst into flame, popping like a grotesque video game. Vikings retreated from the demons in a haphazard manner, running in circles with no protected building in which to hide.

Annie frantically scanned the chaos for Kolgaar and Sturtagaard, for the king and his family. In the bedlam of the attack, she couldn't find any of them.

They should be going somewhere safe!

She ran for Brite, "Corral them into the longhouse." Brite nodded and left for the Vikings pulling them to safety.

Thunder clapped above them. The rain pounded Jorvik as if it could wash the scene clean. Annie glanced at the darkened sky.

Safe in the thunder. Wait a little longer, dad. We need to burn them.

Annie ran and tossed a fireball at a demon as it reached for an elderly man. The Viking male was thin and fragile in appearance only. He was determined to beat the demon off of him with a sharp stick. The weapon reminded Annie of a javelin, but she knew it was something else. The demon burned beside the elderly man. Annie helped the man up. "Run for the longhouse, now!" she shouted. The old man limped away, injured and bloody, his left arm hanging beside him.

Annie reached for the magical energy around her, gathering a strong and large fireball. It hung above her palm. Her heart sped up as she released it on the next demon. It howled in pain.

With each new fireball that hit a demon, thick, sodden ash billowed upwards and rained from the sky in wet clumps, covering her hair and clothes. Annie scanned the fight and the forest; hungry, angry demons flooded Jorvik, focused specifically on killing the humans.

Her fireballs grew in strength and accuracy. The more the demons ran, the more the fire consumed them, the more they brushed flames and embers from their thin linen clothing, and the faster they burned. They cried, shrieked, roared with the pain, and the sounds hung in the air.

Annie stumbled across the blood-soaked earth.

A child's distressed wails pulled Annie away. Reaching him felt like she was in a slow-motion film. All of two years old, the boy shrieked when he was torn from his mother's arms. Annie ran for the demon and threw successive jinxes at the massive beast, hoping it would release its hold on the boy.

She was joined by the boy's father, who pounded at the creature with a large, wooden bat. The demon ignored the screaming father and the crying mother and bit into the boy's neck. He shrieked. In desperation to save him, Annie cast a fireball and threw it on the demon's foot. But the little boy was already dead when he hit the ground.

Blood seeped from the deep wound in the boy's neck and swirled in the puddle beside his dead body. It mixed with the ash becoming a thick soupy mess. Reluctantly, Annie looked at his parents; the father's face was eerily familiar. Long, black hair, dark blue eyes devoid of life, skin so pale he could have been…

Sturtagaard glared at the girl who was meant to put an end to this madness. His pain and anger exploded in that moment. Annie felt vulnerable in his gaze.

Sturtagaard told me his wife and child were killed.

"You need to go to the longhouse. Now!" Annie shouted, pushing them away from their son. "Go!"

Sturtagaard finally moved his feet as he held his inconsolable wife and ran with her to the longhouse.

Annie wiped away the tears and pulled the boy from the stampede of humans and demons. She gently lay him against the cottage wall.

I was supposed to end this!

She looked at the scene, at the death, at the unstoppable force of the human-demon hybrid. Annie's chest tightened, and she stumbled in the mud. The world spun around her, causing colors to swirl. She fell to her knees with the weight of the boy's death choking her.

When she looked up, Jorvik was still being overrun by demons.

Rain pelted Annie's face, she stared at the sky as the thunder clapped and rang in her ears. She closed her eyes and sniffed the air. "Dad," she whispered; she felt his hand on her shoulder pulling her up.

Fire lit up Jorvik as the demons burst into flames. Fire crackled their bones and left a rancid stench of burnt flesh enveloping them. The one-sided attack didn't kill the coven's determination to not die that day. They linked their arms, becoming a human wall, and used their strength to corral and surround the demons. Annie joined the end of the line. The coven became one with the magical energy surrounding Jorvik, creating a large conduit for the magic. Full of energy, fear, and anger, they cast their fireballs.

The creatures, too unsophisticated to understand anything but the pain, scattered across Jorvik. Hot, orange flames ate away at their flesh. Annie felt their screams in her bones.

The massive fire was enough for the remaining demons to retreat into the forest.

The coven and the Vikings watched in stunned silence as the demons were eviscerated. Annie shuddered and trembled as the rain assailed her skin. She held herself against the nearest cottage. Coven members walked through the village searching for demon parts, digging with sticks through thick piles of mushy ash. What they found, they set on fire. Human bodies were removed and laid at the edge of town in a field of wildflowers.

Annie let go of the cottage, faltering across the muddy paths. Vikings cautiously exited the longhouse to assess the damage and deal with the dead. Annie was singularly focused on the boy, Sturtagaard's son.

Whatever hatred for Sturtagaard that she came here with was momentarily pushed aside as she found his son where she left him. With what little strength she had left, Annie knelt beside the body and gently cradled the toddler as she carried him to the edge of town.

"My boy!" Annie jumped. Sturtagaard yanked him from her. "You've done enough," he growled at her and lovingly held his son, crying into his muddied hair. He placed the boy next in the line of bodies that would be burned tonight. She stepped back, growing more fearful of Sturtagaard's rage.

"Annie!"

She turned.

Brite ran for her, protectively putting an arm around her shoulders. "We get the blood tomorrow and end this," he said.

She nodded. "I watched a demon kill Sturtagaard's son," she said and shuddered.

Brite enveloped her. "There wasn't anything you could do. You knew he lost his family to the demons. We can't change things." Rain pelleted them for several more minutes as the cleanup continued.

CHAPTER 26

A LOW, SOFT DIN filled the longhouse. Images were dark and blurry as they whipped across the room. Annie slumped against the wall in an empty corner and waved away help and food. She closed her eyes, but it did little to erase the memories of the battle.

"We could use your help," Gibbs said when he found Annie turned away from the room.

"I failed." Annie began to cry. The sight of the blood and the injured and the memories of the boy taken from his mother left her nauseated.

"Boo fucking hoo. You didn't create the monsters," Gibbs reprimanded.

Annie looked passed him, finding Etheldreda and Bega administering care to the coven and Vikings. The old woman healed wounds with skill as the young girl kept up, mopping foreheads, and cleaning wounds.

"Girl, what the hell's your problem?" He pulled her chin toward him and stared at her, leaving her uncomfortably vulnerable.

"I failed. This is my fault. I should have forced them to fix that protection spell," Annie said.

"Get over yourself."

"Go to hell," she countered.

Gibbs sat beside her. "Someone created those demons. It wasn't you. You're up against a Viking stronghold that invaded England and a coven that created the demons, probably to get rid of the Vikings. Now both hate each other and find themselves stuck with each other. We killed a lot of demons today."

"A lot of people died today and a lot of demons escaped," Annie said. She rubbed her temples.

"They understand the nature of the fire and retreated. We should be safe for now," Gibbs said.

Annie wiped rainwater and tears from her cheeks and turned from him.

"Get a grip. You look like hell. What happened to you out there?" Gibbs asked.

"Exhausted from the magic," Annie said.

"Bullshit, girl. What happened out there?" Gibbs touched her shoulder. She looked at him with red, watery eyes.

"I watched a demon kill my enemy's son." She took a breath.

"He said they died during this time," Gibbs reminded her.

The weight of history felt heavy in her chest; she couldn't breathe. "I now understand what I should have before I came here. Everything, everything that I touch can change the future. Before we left, I had Sturtagaard under a stake, ready to kill him. Ryan stopped me. And as I left, I implied I'd just kill his human self to make up for what he started." Annie wiped mud from her engagement ring. "It was the first time I ever saw Sturtagaard scared. And knowing that made me feel strong. But here, seeing history unfold in real time, I know I can't. I know his wife and child die now. I can't kill him just because of what he did. But knowing all that doesn't make it any easier watching that boy die." Annie sighed.

"So you've matured in the last few days, girl," he said.

"You can start calling me Annie," she groused.

Gibbs never chuckled until that moment. "Fine... Annie." He took her hand. "You weren't supposed to save his child. You knew this. You also know this is the trigger for what's to come. Even if that means your parents are still dead."

"Ouch," Annie said.

"Do you want me to coddle you?"

Annie chuckled. "No. I hear you. It just doesn't help."

Gibbs grumbled and placed a thin yet muscular arm around her shoulders.

Annie lay her head on his shoulder and scanned the longhouse.

Unexpectedly, she met Sturtagaard's glare and shuddered. "He held onto that anger and fury for eleven hundred years. I can't imagine living with that for so long. That's all he is—pain and fury. I guess when you only live a natural lifetime of, what, maybe seventy-five years, you might appreciate the time you have more and in that and learn to do something good with anger," Annie said.

"Like you did after your dad died." Gibbs found Sturtagaard and his unmistakable sneer; his jaw tightened and the cords in his neck throbbed when he saw the future vampire. "You need to have either me or Brite by your side at all times. Sturtagaard's becoming a problem," Gibbs said.

"I'm okay with that." Annie shivered and rubbed her arms for warmth. "Ironically, had I saved his son, his anger and fury wouldn't have consumed him and my parents would be alive." She chuckled softly.

"You're not responsible," Gibbs said.

Annie pulled away. "I'm not saying I am. I'm just saying that my inability to do this started him down a path. My astral projection in the fire marked me for the prophecy. It's just maddeningly ironic. I didn't have to kill the man, just save the boy."

"And now we see just how much damage we can cause by being here," Gibbs said.

"Yeah. I'm guessing when I did this the first time, or… damn, this is weird."

"It is. So, when this went down in the ninth century in the first place…" Gibbs tried.

"When it happened in the ninth century, I probably didn't have what I needed to do this job. I'm guessing that didn't change. The seer said I should die because of the power." Annie said.

"That can be changed," Gibbs said.

Annie rested her head in her hands.

"Play on your terms. You know their end game, so don't let them win. Concentrate on what you can control. The blood, the spell. That's it," Gibbs said.

She had never known Gibbs as a comforting sort, but tonight, she found him to be so. "Thanks," she said.

"You need to eat. Gain your strength. We have a final battle to wage.

Sooner rather than later, I think." Gibbs helped her up and she teetered with her first step. "You're already smarter than them. Don't forget it."

She leaned on Gibbs as they joined Bega and Etheldreda assisting with injuries.

"Bega, Etheldreda," Annie said.

"Anaise, are you feeling better? We were rather worried," Bega said.

"I'm fine. How bad have the injuries been?"

They sat Annie at the bench beside them.

"It's not as bad as the last attack, now that we know how to stop them," Bega said. The girl offered a wan smile, hiding her fear and exhaustion. She continued to nurse a small child in her care. "Over here. Sit over here," she murmured to the child as she guided him to the ground.

"I knew the protection spell was waning. I should have insisted you fix it when I saw it or I should have fixed it," Annie murmured.

"What's done is done. We expected too much from you. You will heal and then kill them. We'll send you home," Etheldreda said. She held the arm of a young man whose forearm had been cut when a demon lashed out. She held her hand above the deep gash, attempting to heal the skin.

"Don't misjudge your descendants. I'm perfectly capable." Annie leaned in to look at the deep wound. "He needs stitches," Annie said.

"What, dear?" Etheldreda asked.

"It's…" Annie began. Etheldreda stared at her with anticipation. "You mind if I take a crack?" Annie took Etheldreda's spot and summoned her field pack. Inside, she found her basic medical kit. She examined the man's deep gash. She cleaned the wound with water, administered a numbing agent, set up the needle and thread, and began to stitch up the wound. "What's your name?" Annie asked.

He glanced at her with fear and confusion, then said, "William."

"William. I know this looks scary, but it will help the cut heal. You'll be fine." Annie turned to Etheldreda. "In a week's time, remove the threads. The cut will be healed." Etheldreda watched intently as Annie finished with the stitches.

"Amazing," Etheldreda said. "And that works better than magic?"

"Sometimes nonmagical procedures are better. Most still aren't, though," Annie said as she cleared away the kit and placed it back in her field pack. She glanced up, still weak but more energized than before.

"Sturtagaard needs attention," Annie said and stood to heal him. Gibbs took her hand.

"Not without a bodyguard," he said.

"He's not a vampire yet. But come if you want," she said and headed across the still crowded longhouse. She felt the stares, the whispering, the pointing. Any goodwill she might have created was gone. There was a chill as she neared Sturtagaard.

Sturtagaard glared at her when she arrived. "You need healing," Annie said.

"Not from you," he jeered.

"Well, I'm all you have right now. Sit still," she ordered as she examined his face. Blood dripped from his temple and his chin. Neither cut was deep and could be healed easily with magic. Annie summoned water and warmed it in a puddle above her hand before placing over the wound. When the wound healed, she worked on his chin.

"I'm sorry about your son. What was his name?" Annie asked.

He sneered. "His name was Tyr," he said. "My wife Astrid is missing."

Annie dropped the healing water to the ground, splashing her boots. She knew he lost everything here and now, and she felt sorry for the human sitting before her. "When did you last see her?"

"I came out to find my son. I placed him with the rest of the dead. When I came back here, she was gone. Dirty witches will not let me leave."

Annie glanced at the door. Guards had been stationed to keep the villagers inside while a patrol walked the perimeter of Jorvik searching for stray demons.

"I'm sure she's here. As soon as the coven determines there are no more demons outside, they'll let everyone out to find those who managed to escape and hide." Annie's hollow attempt to reassure him only made him harden more.

She checked his hands, his pulse. "I think you're fine for now. Rest and eat and we'll begin searching for..."

"Where is she?" An angry screech came from the king's throne. Behind

King Hrothgar, Queen Signe was hysterical, her maidens attempting to calm her.

"Gyda, my daughter. She is missing!" The king's cheeks were flushed, his mouth turned in anger as he spoke to Kolgaar. Annie turned toward the commotion and met Kolgaar's eyes. For a moment she felt relief until he glared at her and motioned for her to join them. She cautiously walked through the longhouse, all eyes on her. She shuddered with anxiety and exhaustion.

"This is your fault!" the king shouted at Annie.

She jumped at the verbal attack. "I didn't create the demons, nor did I send them to attack," she said.

"Your coven did. And now my daughter is gone!"

"I got here two days ago." Annie stopped. It wasn't the time to make excuses or pass blame. She took a breath and felt her hands shake from hunger and emotion. "The coven sent the demons?" she asked.

"They created them. This is their fault!" The king pointed to Annie.

"Has anyone gone out to look for the princess?" Annie asked. With a tilt of her head, she turned and walked from the king. Gibbs and Brite joined her as she stopped at the longhouse doors. "It's time to search the village for anyone hiding after the attack. Send the Vikings to look for their families," Annie ordered the guard at the door. He nodded and left his post.

"I saw Sturtagaard help his wife inside the building. He came back out to find his son and when he went back to her, she was gone. I think she left. I'm wondering if she went home. He's even more angry now," Annie said as they systematically walked the first street, passing several male bodies scattered in the mud. Blood covered the ground and clung to their boots and pants. Annie couldn't describe it as anything other than a real-life horror movie.

I didn't ask for this.

"You're not safe," Gibbs said. Annie ignored him and bent over the first dead female in the path. With respect to the body, she slowly turned the woman and examined her face, noting the bite marks across the chin, neck and shoulder. She grimaced at the mangled muscles, ripped tendons and pool of blood as it drained from the deep wound. Annie touched the woman's cheek. "I know I'm in danger. Sturtagaard is at his breaking point. This isn't Gyda," she said. They moved on to the next female body.

Gibbs and Brite followed closely, palms out and ready, as Annie knelt beside another girl who wore her golden hair in a plait behind her back as Gyda did. The roughly woven gray fabric didn't seem suitable for a princess at this time. Annie turned her over nonetheless and examined the face of the dead girl.

She knew immediately it wasn't Gyda. "She was so young." Annie removed a chunk of mud from her creamy skin. "Tomorrow morning, we collect the blood and this stops."

Villagers cautiously exited the longhouse and spread themselves through the village, pulling the dead from the muddy puddles across the narrow streets. Behind them, several carts were pulled around and were soon filled with the bodies.

Annie knelt at another dead girl.

Kolgaar trotted to them, his expression grim.

"We should have left sooner. You should have taken care of this already," he said.

Annie stood up. Though she couldn't match his size and height, she knew she was formidable. "It didn't matter when we walked through the portal. We could have only returned when we did. I won't say it again. Do not talk to me. Do not look at me. Go protect your king. I don't care where. Just go!"

She turned and knelt beside the next female body, bending over to observe her young face.

Kolgaar followed. "You need to take care of this!" he shouted. Annie stood again.

"Tomorrow when the demons are down for the day, we'll collect their blood and perform the spell. Now go protect the king. I never want to see you again!"

Annie stomped off, searching for Princess Gyda. She bypassed older women, men, small children. The princess wasn't along this road.

"I'm ordered to stay with you and ensure you finish this," Kolgaar said, still following her.

"You'd best use your time to protect the king. Move him outside of Jorvik." Annie faced him. "Go protect him. I don't need you to spy on me."

He grabbed her wrist. Gibbs and Brite held their palms up, prepared to jinx him. "I am staying with you as I was ordered. We will go to the forest, and you will get the blood you need. Now!" he said. Together, Brite and Gibbs cast their jinxes, releasing Kolgaar's hold on Annie. He stumbled backwards into a cottage door.

Annie backed away and bumped into a tall, thin man. Even before turning around, she knew it was Sturtagaard. When she faced him, his expression was so familiar, so angry, as it continued to build. He would never be the same. "We were told by the coven that there was someone who could save us from the demons," he said calmly.

"I can save you from the demons," Annie said as she took a step back.

"Look at this. Does this look like you saved us?" Sturtagaard jeered.

She stared into Sturtagaard's eyes, which were blank, as if he'd given up and let the pain numb him. "I understand your anger and fury. I have my own. There's a... man who is responsible for the death of my parents. He ruined everything, but I didn't let the fury consume me. You can't either," she said. It was difficult to have this conversation; she knew it wouldn't accomplish anything. She knew what he was to become.

"We were promised you would stop this," Sturtagaard took a step closer to her. She was trapped between the angry brothers.

"I have a plan. We'll put it into motion and we'll kill the demons," she said. She bumped into the cottage and felt the rough edges of the mud wall. Gibbs and Brite again had their palms up and ready.

"We believed you were the one," Kolgaar said.

Annie's jaw tensed. "I didn't create the demons; I didn't create the failed protection spell and I most definitely didn't volunteer for this. I'm doing the best I can without my magic at full power, and I'm dealing with two groups who can't stand each other. Don't place all of the fault on me!"

Sturtagaard lunged, pinning Annie against his body, holding her with a thick arm. With his other hand, he held a knife to her neck. Gibbs and Brite dropped their palms. Annie's heart pounded, he could feel her pulse at her neck. It wouldn't be the last time he bested her.

One night, almost five years ago, a very new wizard guard had been paralyzed with fear, locked in the arms of one of the most dangerous vampires ever recorded. He had licked her neck and sniffed her skin, instilling terror in her. In that moment when she had let her defenses down, letting him get so close to her, she learned to hate him and worked on controlling her emotions when he was around.

He knew this was coming.

Because of his agreement with the Wizard Council, she couldn't touch him and he couldn't touch her. All he could do was play with her, torment her. She sensed he enjoyed the torture more than he would enjoy actually sucking the life from her. The Fraternitatem, her mother, her father may have been his way of getting even with her when the opportunity presented itself.

She held her breath, lulling him into thinking she was afraid of him. He loosened his grip on her, dropping the knife a little lower. Annie turned her palms backwards and blasted him twenty feet. He landed in the mud.

Kolgaar backed away when he looked into her eyes. Annie turned and walked to Sturtagaard. "Search the bodies. Astrid may still be alive. The princess is missing too. Where might they run to?"

Dazed, Sturtagaard blinked rapidly as he sat in the mud. "To the coven." He thought again. "My farmhouse." He pointed north of Jorvik where several farms had been established.

Annie walked back to the end of the street. "Go home then. She might be there with the princess," she said.

Sturtagaard scampered up and ran for his homestead. Annie was certain he wouldn't find his wife there.

Returning to Kolgaar, she said, "Clear the village of the bodies. If the princess is not here, then she ran away. Do not follow me, do not talk to me." Annie turned and marched through Jorvik for the narrow path to the coven village.

CHAPTER 27

ANNIE RELISHED THE sounds of the softly falling rain as it hit the thatched roof, the crackling fire, the slight breeze that rattled the shutters. She stared into the forest, her feet resting on the window jamb. A demon snored softly inside the trees.

Maybe it will be a good night.

Upon returning to the cottage, Annie was filled with anger, fear, and anxiety. She ate to satiate the pain. Hours later, the food sat like stone in her stomach and Annie was now only angry.

The pages from the Donaldson's *Book of Shadows* lay in her lap, but the words told her nothing new. They were useless scribblings from a group of people afraid to accept the responsibility of their actions and resolve the situation themselves. Annie felt like a sheep being led to slaughter.

"You should go to bed," Gibbs said. He pulled the second chair beside her and looked into the darkness.

"I'm fine," Annie replied curtly.

"You need to keep up your strength," he said.

Annie shrugged. "I hope they'll still be tired tomorrow."

"Odd how they attacked during the day," Brite commented as he stoked the fire with his returned magical strength.

"Sneak attacks are planned," Annie said.

"The demons aren't smart enough to plan," Brite said. He leaned against the bed and took a sip of water. "Who's controlling them?"

Annie looked at him. "We know they're human-demon hybrids created with strong black magic. Old magic. The Vikings pretty much accused the coven of doing something with the demons. If they can control them, why did they call for help?"

"They can't control them. Which means, either the demons are able to think on their own or someone in the coven is controlling them, and they refuse to do something about it," Gibbs said.

"So they're either protecting someone or they don't know who's doing it?" Brite asked.

"There aren't that many coven members. We guess what, seventy-five total? They know who is controlling them."

"They just can't control that person. We need to have a little conversation with the coven elders." Brite yawned and stretched his arms above his head.

"One problem at a time. Gir—Annie, you need sleep," Gibbs said.

Annie yawned. "I know. I think it's time to summon Zola." She pulled out necklace and stared at the design before placing the book pages in her backpack. Something moved in the darkness. Annie stood.

Brite startled. "What is that?"

"Footsteps?" she whispered. She hung out the window and watched the shadows.

"Human or demon," Gibbs asked.

"Human, I think," Annie said as a tall, slim man holding a lantern, entered the trees.

"Now, why would someone head into the trees so late at night after a demon attack?" Annie asked.

"Let's find out," Gibbs said.

Annie, Gibbs, and Brite slipped out of the cottage window and slunk toward the path, following the man inside.

∽

The wizard guards held small crystals in their palms, creating a magical light that was strong enough to see inside the thick foliage, but would not be noticed by anyone or anything around them. Up ahead, the lantern light bounced toward the roaring river. If the man knew he was being followed, he ignored it.

The lantern light turned left and it disappeared behind the trees; Annie, Gibbs, and Brite picked up their pace until they were jogging down the path. At the river's edge, Gibbs peered west as the lantern light continued to jump about in the darkness.

The footsteps were easy to track in the mud, and they stopped when the lantern stopped. The lantern disappeared and reappeared on the other side of the river, then headed back inside the trees.

"Why the hell didn't he just teleport to his final destination?" Gibbs asked.

"He wants us to follow?" Annie asked.

They continued to the teleportation spot and looked across the river.

"Do you have enough magic to teleport?" Gibbs asked.

Annie took out her flashlight, illuminated the river and noted its flow and width. "I'll be fine," she said. In an instant, she teleported away and landed on the other side. She bent over from the exertion and dizziness, and sucked in air.

Gibbs landed next, also exhausted. He leaned against the tree, closed his eyes, and said, "Not good."

When Brite landed, he fell on his ass in the mud. "That's a lot of energy," he said.

"Can you make it?" Annie asked.

"Yeah. Yeah." Brite looked down the narrow path where the lantern light was barely visible. "He's getting away. We should go."

Wasting no more time, they followed the light.

While they believed the demons would be tired and satiated enough to leave them alone, orange eyes still followed them in the darkness. Annie held her palms out, ready to cast a fireball should she need to.

"The demons are awake," Brite said.

"I'm trying not to think about it, though I'm hoping that one's just not hungry," Annie said.

Lantern light hovered in the air for a moment, turned right and disappeared. "Watch for paths to the right." Annie jogged down the path in complete darkness, nearly passing the path she was searching for. She hid behind a tree and watched the coven member being received at the door of a hidden cottage.

Gibbs and Brite joined her as the door was closed. "Let's see what he's up to," Gibbs said. They crept closer to the cottage; Brite walked to the left, Annie to the right; neither side contained a window. They met at the front door and positioned themselves near a crack between the door and wall.

"Everard, she is here to get rid of the problem you created, old man," said the coven member. Annie pressed her face to the open space wide enough to observe the tall, thin man with shocking red hair and long thin nose. His mouth was pursed together in disgust. She couldn't remember his name.

"You cannot. You must not kill them. That is genocide." The man called Everard's spoke up, his voice quivering.

Annie's mouth opened when she caught sight of Everard for the first time. He was withered, skin and bones, with deep wrinkles across his forehead and around his mouth and eyes. White wisps of hair sprung from his head in patches. Life expectancy during the ninth century might have been anywhere between age forty-five to sixty-five; Everard appeared to have lived well beyond that. He peered at the coven member with fear in his eyes.

"They are dangerous. You can't control them. You haven't been able to control them in decades. And the demons didn't free us of the Vikings like you promised. They are in control. It failed. And it is time for this experiment to end," the tall man said.

"You... you must not. Please do not kill them. They are a species now and must be protected. You wouldn't wipe out the Cath Palug, would you?"

"It does not matter. The girl is here to clean up your mess."

"Wha... what will happen to me?" Everard asked.

"We think you should consider stopping the potion. You've outlived many lives. I suggest you end it tonight," the coven member said.

Everard rested his head in his hands.

"Do it tonight," the man ordered. Without waiting for Everard to respond, he turned and came to the door. Annie, Gibbs, and Brite slipped around the side of the cottage. The man slammed the door behind him without saying goodbye.

The lantern swung as he walked. When he turned, Annie, Gibbs, and Brite stepped back into view.

"So, he created them." Brite pointed to the cottage.

"I'm going in," Annie said.

"Annie, it's late. We should go in with a clear head," Gibbs said.

She shrugged and opened the door, standing face-to-face with the man who started it all. Everard stared at Annie, his mouth and eyes agape.

"Everard. I'm An—Anaise. The girl." She offered a wan smile.

His eyes darted from her to Gibbs and Brite as they entered the cottage after her. "It's okay. We're not going to hurt you," Annie cooed and took a seat opposite him. While Annie thought she could take Everard with one hand tied behind her back, Brite sidled up to her. She could feel his sleeve on her arm.

Everard quivered. Close up, he appeared even older than she had originally thought. She stared into his translucent skin, marked with age spots and dark veins. She thought if she held him up to the light, she would see right through him.

"You created the demons," Annie began.

He nodded quickly. Annie now understood that the demons had been created to remove the Vikings from England, but they clearly hadn't done so. Annie also knew the Vikings raided England for several centuries before they assimilated into English society. She asked anyway. "Why did you create them?"

Everard wrung his hands, his knuckles swollen with age.

"When the Norsemen came..." His voice cracked. "When the Norsemen conquered us, they ravaged the land, our people."

He coughed. Annie summoned a water bottle and poured it into a glass on the table and handed it to the wizard. He took a sip and coughed again. Annie glanced at Gibbs and Brite.

When Everard's cough cleared, he took another sip. While thumbing the lip of the cup, he said, "They raided our treasures, killed our people. My mother was a witch and my father was human. They had me, a hybrid human."

He looked at his hands.

"Under that definition, I'm a hybrid human too. I'm not sure why you'd use that as a model for demons because we don't go around raiding and killing magical settlements. Why create the hybrid demons?"

"No!" he shouted. "It was not like that. We needed help. We were trying to create stronger warriors. I experimented with adding demon blood to the warriors, using magic on them. Dark, dark magic."

"What worked?" Gibbs asked. He held Annie's shoulder with a firm grip. Annie didn't want to hear the answer to the question.

"Nothing. Nothing worked! The magic changed the men. They had children and their children were beastly. And each generation since had children more feral and horrible than the generation before. They grew in numbers and we could not stop them."

Annie drummed her fingers on the table. "And you don't want to see them killed," she said.

"No, they do not deserve that. It is not their fault. They are still living creatures," Everard pleaded.

"They don't exist in the future," Annie informed him.

He seemed surprised by the revelation. "That cannot be," he said softly.

"You created unnatural demons, with magic. They don't belong and they need to be stopped," Annie said gently.

"They are living beings. They deserve so much more. And I will stop you if you try to kill them," the old man squealed.

His eyes bore through her. For a moment, he appeared strong and virile, and she felt that even with his age, he could strike her down. He blinked and that moment passed, leaving behind an anxious old man who glanced from her to Gibbs to Brite.

Annie grabbed a blanket and draped it around his shoulder. "It's late. You should sleep," she said gently and moved him to his bed.

He obeyed and lay down. Annie pulled additional blankets over his frail body. When he looked at her, his eyes were clouding and confused.

"They follow a pretty light," Everard said. He fell asleep instantly.

"What does that mean?" Brite asked.

"It's like he's suffering from dementia and is only lucid periodically. I'm not sure it means anything," Annie said.

"It could be an act. He created them, so he must control them," Gibbs said. "Maybe he uses a light and the demons react to that."

"He's really old. That guy said something about a potion. He's outlived his time. He's got to be over one hundred years old," Annie murmured.

"A potion to keep himself alive unnaturally. Now I've seen everything," Gibbs said.

Annie glanced around the cottage, found Everard's storage chest, and looked inside. It was a dump of items: one pair of pants, a shirt, old shoes, fabric, loose herbs, and crystals. She pulled up another blanket and handed it to Brite. When she looked back inside, she saw his *Book of Shadows*. Annie reached inside and opened the tome, quickly perusing the first two pages. "Think he'll miss this?" she asked and turned back to the old man. He was shivering under the thick blankets, his legs twitched, and he snored.

"Maybe," Gibbs said. "It's time to go, Annie. Now."

❦

Although Annie was exhausted by the time she climbed into bed, she woke before dawn to the sound of Gibbs snoring. Soft light streamed through the shutters. She rolled over and groaned. Brite was gone.

Warm, stuffy air choked her. She opened the window and peered outside. Rain fell again. She lay her arms on the window sill and rested her head as she watched villagers completing their morning chores. As always, Bega and Etheldreda tended the fire.

"What's going on?" Gibbs mumbled and sat up. He ran his hand through his morning hair.

"Nothing out of the ordinary. Brite's gone," Annie said.

"Never heard him leave," Gibbs said. He pulled off his long sleeve shirt and tossed it in his bag.

Annie pulled her hair into a ponytail, letting the air cool her sweaty neck. "I could use a shower."

Gibbs grumbled and stretched his arms above his head. His back popped. "So, did we learn anything last night?"

"Besides the fact that back in the day the coven was into black magic?"

"Aside from that." Gibbs sat. He stretched out his legs and touched his toes.

"We know who created them, how they were created, and why they were created," Annie said. She returned to observing the village. People she hadn't even met stared at the cottage and turned away. She wondered if the coven kept her contained on purpose, with limited contact with only certain members. Annie felt very alone as she watched the villagers prepare their morning meals, haul in laundry, conduct village business. Three small children ran about, splashing in the mud and laughing as they tagged each other.

"Everard is an unexpected problem," Gibbs said.

Annie summoned Everard's *Book of Shadows* and stared at the cover.

Gibbs opened the opposite window and glanced inside the forest. It was still silent in the trees. "It's been generations since Everard created them. At this point, they really are their own species. He believes it's genocide to kill them all."

"I killed them, though." Annie sighed.

"Yes, you did."

"He's going to be a problem," she added.

"Yes, he is."

The cottage door opened. Brite entered with an iron skillet filled with food and placed it on the small table. "I thought we could use something more hearty," he said.

They gathered around the table, each picking up a knife and scooping up the food.

"You're a good cook," Annie said.

"It wasn't easy procuring these delights," Brite joked.

"Did you learn anything out there?" Annie asked. She scooped more eggs into a wooden bowl and sat back on the bed.

"Our man of last night was Callum Wortham. I got a good look at him when he left Everard's cottage. He was out and about this morning. I don't think he realized we followed him last night." Brite dug into the shared eggs and potatoes in the pan.

"And?" Gibbs asked impatiently.

"He told Etheldreda that Everard wouldn't be a problem anymore," Brite offered. He chewed a mouthful. Annie and Gibbs waited. "Etheldreda asked if he killed him. He said no and explained what he had told Everard.

She tossed a spell into the fire, and it blew upwards and nearly exploded. Not only is that woman damn powerful, she's pissed."

Annie crossed her legs, placed her bowl between them, and took another pinch of eggs. She chewed slowly and finally said, "So, the old lady wants someone to kill the problem. All Everard needs to do is stop taking whatever potion or stop whatever magic he's using to keep himself alive. At least that's what I gathered from the conversation between him and Callum."

"You realize they fucked up and now you're cleaning up their mess," Gibbs said.

"Yeah. The thought had crossed my mind," Annie said. "I wish I could say it's coven business and leave it alone, but I'm really worried he could get in the way. And I don't mean by stopping us from killing them."

Brite put down his bowl. "What's your concern?"

"He might be old, but he knows serious magic. He could be what the future Gila Donaldson is hoping will stop me. He said he'd stop me," Annie said. She pulled out the protection charm and stared at the design. "I think it's time to call her."

"We can use the help," Gibbs said.

Annie stared at the charm again. "Let's get the blood this morning and set everything up for tomorrow morning. Does that sound okay?"

"We do this, we do it right," Gibbs said.

"And Everard?" Brite asked.

"Keep him away from Annie," Gibbs said.

CHAPTER 28

THEY ENTERED THE longhouse and stood before the Coven Council as if on trial. "We expect to have it all over by tomorrow. For today, we'll be collecting demon blood. As we've stated before, we need coven help," Annie began. She observed members with anxious expressions on their faces.

"What is your plan?" Etheldreda asked.

After Annie explained the plan, a low din broke out among the council. Annie waited patiently for them to discuss and release the shock they felt.

Etheldreda held up her hand. "Are you absolutely certain demon blood is required?" she asked.

"Yes. It is the only item that links the demons together. We can't guarantee the demons are contained in the forest. So yes, this is the plan, and the demon blood is required to fulfill it." Annie tapped her fingers against her pant leg, no longer patient with the coven council.

Again, Etheldreda held up her hand and spoke. "What exactly do you need from us?"

"Three wizards with strong magic. Someone who can think quickly in case something goes wrong." Annie held her breath.

"Why?" Etheldreda asked.

"We've managed to tap into the magic surrounding us, but using magic is exhausting and challenging. If three coven members could assist with certain spells, the plan will more likely succeed."

Etheldreda thought for a moment. "That is well thought out."

Again, the coven stopped to speak with each other, gesturing as they discussed. Annie glanced at Brite and Gibbs and sighed deeply.

Finally, Etheldreda raised her hand again and said, "You shall have three wizards. When should they be ready?"

"Soon. Midday. The demons should be unconscious by then."

Etheldreda frowned. "There is a man. He may try to stop you. We are trying to stop him," she began.

"We've met Everard."

Etheldreda squinted at her. "How?"

"We followed Callum to his cottage." Annie glanced at the ancient Gila Donaldson. "I expect that this is what your counterpart explained to you yesterday. He will try to kill me, or stop me, or keep me stuck here."

Gila Donaldson blanched as the coven looked at her.

"What does this mean?" Etheldreda asked.

"The girl is imagining people that are not here," Gila said quickly.

Annie walked to her and bent over the table. "I expect your secret will catch up to you," she hissed in Gila's ear. She got up again and moved to sit across from Etheldreda. "I expect you won't appreciate the lies that brought me here and that are meant to keep me here. When this is over, deal with Gila Donaldson. You will be very interested in what she has to say."

Etheldreda glanced down the table. Gila looked as though she wanted to earth to open up and swallow her.

"What does that mean?" Etheldreda asked.

"I've been set up to die or to remain in the past. I'd like to keep both scenarios from happening. You should have dealt with Everard decades ago. Since you did not, make sure you keep him from coming here. Callum was wrong. Everard will not stop whatever is keeping him alive. He will fight to protect those demons. Deal with him or keep him away. And whatever happens, I want three witches or wizards by the fire when the sun is overhead," Annie said.

"Is that all?" Etheldreda asked.

Annie nodded. Etheldreda waved them away and they returned to the cottage.

"I didn't think you'd tell them," Gibbs said.

Annie shrugged and dug inside her field pack. "I think we need a large vial for blood. I want to make sure we have enough to do the job right the first time." She pulled out several different sizes of plastic bottles, settling on an empty water bottle and placing it in the deep pockets of her cargo pants. She summoned the sword. It smacked against her palm and gleamed in the firelight. As she raised it above her head, yellow light burst from the metal and exploded across the cottage. Gibbs and Brite ducked low. Magic tingled through Annie's body and then, in an instant, stopped.

"It's like that thing was made for you," Brite said.

Annie felt dizzy and sat on the bed.

"You okay girl… Annie?" Gibbs asked.

She nodded. "Too much magic," she said. "So the plan." She glanced at Gibbs and Brite.

"As we discussed once, the coven will have to freeze the area, let us collect the blood, and teleport us out quickly," Brite said.

Gibbs sat beside Annie. "Since the blade loves you, you cut the demon and summon the blood."

Brite glanced outside. "When they unfreeze the demons and the one we cut shrieks, how do we prevent any of them from attacking?"

"Have one of the coven heal the demon before we take off. Best you can do," Gibbs suggested.

"I hope you're right." Annie returned to the window and continued to watch the village from the safety of the cottage as they waited for midday.

∽

As promised, Etheldreda had three coven members waiting for them by the fire; Annie recognized them as Bryony Voxall, Rhys Younge and, ironically, Callum Wortham.

"Anaise. Who will be doing what today?" Callum asked. He pushed his red hair from his face and folded his arms across his chest impatiently.

As Annie explained what each pair would be doing, Byrony and Rhys pursed their lips together in apprehension.

"That is fruitless and dangerous," Callum said incredulously. His jaw tightened and flexed.

"Of course, it's dangerous. If the coven hadn't let Everard get away with what he did, we wouldn't be doing this at all," Annie reprimanded them.

Callum tensed. Bryony and Rhys seemed apologetic but said nothing.

Annie looked at the protection spell. Whatever was left hung in the trees like laundry on a line, tattered and torn. "We'll be cutting a demon and summoning blood. I want to make sure if there's a problem, the demons can't attack." She looked at the tree line. "You need to recharge the protection spell."

Etheldreda shook her head. "It is the energy surrounding us. It is limited. The three of you are draining us of our magical energy. We do not have enough to create a strong barrier."

Annie frowned. "You give up too fast. Create whatever perimeter of protection you can muster—spell, potion, fire—along the tree line." She looked at Etheldreda sternly.

The old woman shrunk back and nodded. "We will pull what we can." She bowed her head and backed away.

"That's everything. Are we ready to move?" Annie asked.

"I think we should look for a demon away from the river. It will be more inconspicuous if we do," Callum said. His look was stern and determined.

"Do you really think Everard will find us there?" Annie asked.

All three coven members blanched. Bryony's lips were pursed so tightly together, Annie thought she might be holding in vomit.

"You were never to know about him. This is not why we brought you here. Can you not do what is required of you?" Callum argued.

Annie, unafraid of Callum and his magic, strode to him. Though he was taller than her, she looked him in the eye. "Do not tell me what to do. If you had all been forthcoming when I arrived, had you taken the time to care that I was here, or had you controlled Everard in the first place, all of this would have either gone smoothly or not happened at all. But you insist on hiding things and hindering the success of this whole process." She was inches from him. He backed away.

"Are we ready then?" Bryony asked.

Annie held out the sword. "Yes. I think we have everything we need."

They stood in awe as the sword glistened in the light. Annie shoved the sword into her belt and led them to the forest.

᳘

Gray clouds hovered over the coven, bringing with them a new storm. They stepped inside the trees.

"Feeling safe?" Gibbs whispered.

Annie sniffed; the air smelled like demon, rain, and a hint of her father's cologne. "Yes. I smell my dad, if that's what you want to know," she whispered back. They walked cautiously, methodically, as they followed the path to the river, their palms out preparing to strike if one of the sleeping demons were found awake.

At the river, the group turned right and headed east. They remained close to the tree line, still under the canopy of trees, as rain pelted the river and its bank. Each time thunder clapped, the scent of Annie's father was strong when it hit her nose. She took a deep breath to calm herself.

"I smell that," Gibbs whispered. He glanced around him. "I suppose his energy could easily move from time to time, location to location."

"He knew it was coming. He died for this," Brite said. "Sorry, that was blunt."

"It's the truth," Annie said.

Callum turned and observed the river and the distance they had come. "We are far enough from any potential massacre and far enough from…" he looked in the direction of Everard's cottage. "There will be plenty of demons to choose from here."

Annie agreed and stepped back inside the trees, scanning the landscape for a smallish creature that would be easy to control should they need to. Callum followed Annie as they sidestepped a demon; Brite and Rhys walked through the trees farther northeast while Byrony and Gibbs walked southwest. They observed the demons breathing and snoring, watching for any that might be stirring, ready to wake.

Annie and Callum both pointed to one demon at the same time. He glanced at Annie, sighed, and motioned to the others. Byrony and Rhys nodded, held their palms up and froze the area. The spell was tricky, and only worked on nonmagicals and non-humans. And while they could attempt the spell during an attack, it was much harder to contain the magic when the objects of the spell were not stationary. In this case, hidden well inside the trees, they were able to freeze all creatures that were inside, leaving the witches and wizards free to work.

Once Annie and Callum observed the frozen creatures, Callum reached for the demon's wrist and pulled it up for Annie.

"Ready?" Annie asked.

He nodded quickly and summoned water from the river, holding it above his palm and warming the liquid.

Annie pulled out a bottle, twisted off the lid, and cut across a blue vein in the demon's wrist. She held the bottle against the cut and summoned the blood to the container. Callum blanched beside her. Annie's stomach churned. When she felt she had enough, she put the lid back on.

"Your turn," she said.

Callum placed the water on the demon's wrist, sending a healing spell to the open wound. Beside them, a demon snored softly. Annie turned and watched its chest rise and fall with each breath. "Hurry! The spell is wearing off," Annie whispered loudly.

Flustered, his hand shook wildly spilling some of the puddle. When the skin healed, he dropped the water, grabbed Annie's forearm, and teleported her from the forest.

They arrived to the fire pit and were pelted with the wicked storm.

Brite arrived with Rhys next.

"Well?" Annie asked.

Gibbs and Byrony arrived minutes later.

"It's done." Rhys said as he walked to his cottage and slammed his door. Byrony pursed her lips as the village was blanketed with pouring rain.

"And why are you worried?" Annie shouted over the thunder.

"They are his children. Everard will know." Bryony turned and marched across the village, entering her cottage, and leaving them alone in the rain.

∽

"That was the first thing that went well," Annie said. She glanced at the new protection spell. It was not as strong as the first but would be secure enough to keep the demons inside the trees.

"It definitely helped having their magic." Brite passed Annie a sandwich.

She took it but didn't eat right away, choosing instead to watch the forest. Water found its way through the window moistening her hair and skin. She let it hang on her; the closest to a shower she had since they arrived.

Absently, she bit into the sandwich as she met a demon's stare through the window. "They're waking up," Annie said. She turned toward the other window facing the coven and glanced out. Rain didn't hinder the coven from their chores as they crisscrossed the wet earth with baskets or carcasses. As always, Etheldreda and Bega tended the fire that allowed Annie, Gibbs, and Brite to communicate with the coven and the Vikings.

Annie wadded up the plastic wrap and held the ball. She closed her eyes, her mind wandering to Jorvik, to Sturtagaard and his missing wife, to the missing princess.

"So, how do you want to work this?" Brite asked.

Annie glanced at Brite and summoned her crystal. She touched the crevices and stared at the center. "I'll pour the blood on here and say a linking spell. When that's done, I'll set fire to the blood." Still holding the crystal, she wrapped herself in a heavy blanket, sat on the bed, and returned her attention to Everard's *Book of Shadows*. While she believed in her plan, she hoped he might offer a clue on how to kill his "babies."

"We need a safe place for you to perform it," Gibbs said.

"Uh-huh," Annie said as she turned another page.

"You listening… Annie?" Gibbs asked.

She held up the *Book of Shadows*. "Sorry, engrossed in the coven black. I heard you. We need a safe place to perform the spell. I'm thinking the longhouse," she said.

"Byrony said Everard knows. I suspect he'll be there," Brite said.

"If we were home, I wouldn't doubt you and Gibbs could take him easily. He's old. But his magic is strong and we aren't consistently at full power," Annie said.

Gibbs summoned a vial of clear liquid and stared at it. "Graham

Lightner gave this to all wizard guards to use in those instances we come across a vampire attack victim close to death. Just one drop," he said.

Brite looked at him with his jaw opened.

"No. Find another way to keep him from me," Annie said.

Gibbs pocketed the poison. "Fine, we'll rely on protection charms and spells. And what's your plan if it doesn't work?"

"I don't know." She dropped the book and closed her eyes. Zola's protection charm rested between her breasts and she pulled it out of her shirt.

"Zola told you to summon her when you arrived," Brite said.

"Wizard council restrictions," Gibbs reminded him.

"Yes and no. Besides the restrictions, you two were a surprise they hadn't expected, but are well aware of now. They know we aren't at full strength, and I stupidly hinted about Gila Donaldson's secret. I have no secrets, no way to protect myself from Gila's plan. Zola is my secret weapon, and I want to bring her in when it would impact us the most." Annie pulled the necklace off and held the charm in her palm. "I think it's time to summon her."

CHAPTER 29

I T WAS WELL past sunset. Gibbs stood like a sentry at the open cottage door and glanced around the empty village. It had been two hours since any coven member had ventured outside and an hour since Etheldreda and Bega had switched places with a coven member, Henry Debenham, at the fire. Periodically, he'd look to the cottage, see all was well and return to keeping the fire burning strong.

"Only Henry Debenham at the fire. You're good to go," Gibbs said.

"Okay. Wish me luck," Annie said. She held the necklace and stared at the design. "I should have called her sooner."

"Don't second-guess your decision. Just call for her," Gibbs said as he watched Henry carefully.

Annie wrapped the necklace around her hand and held the amulet in her palm. She closed her eyes and pictured Zola, her petite frame, her golden hair, her bright green eyes. She said, "Zola. I need you. Zola, please come and help me."

It took very little time for young Zola to come from the fairy region of Spain to the small cottage in Northumbria.

Unfazed, Zola glanced at the woman who summoned her. She smiled politely. "May I ask who you are?" Her bright green eyes sparkled with happiness in a way that was so familiar to Annie. The fairy unfurled delicate, transparent fairy wings that sparkled in the firelight. She placed her hands together and stared at Annie.

Annie handed Zola the amulet. Zola held her necklace in her palm and stared at her insignia stamped in the center.

"Where did you get this?" Zola asked in a gentle, yet mildly accusing tone.

Annie stared at Zola, the same fairy she would know and love in the future and yet who now didn't know her.

"You give that to me in eleven hundred years," Annie said. Her hands shook slightly at the strangeness of having Zola here, and yet, she didn't really have *her* Zola. This Zola had yet to witness the Black Plague, the discovery of the new world, the Revolutionary War, even Desert Storm. She didn't know Annie or have any feelings for her. Annie held her breath as she observed Zola and wondered if summoning her was a good idea.

"You are my charge," Zola said.

Annie nodded. "I'm Annie Pearce."

Zola's wings flapped wildly, as she processed the news.

"I felt something... odd for the last few days. How long have you been here?" Zola asked.

Annie explained the last two days. In the telling of it, she felt dizzy and weak. If she hadn't lived through it, she might have believed the storyteller was lying or crazy.

"I only have one charm. I can feel my magic running through it," Zola said. She kept focused on her protection charm, her mouth twitching as she attempted to piece together what Annie had told her. "Why you?"

Annie summoned the written prophecy, the seal still attached to one side of the parchment scroll, and handed it to her.

Zola read quickly and said, "Most know that when Aloja fairies are born, they are linked to their future charges." She looked at Annie. "But that's not quite what it is. Even if a medium or the Fates see the future, the future is fluid and can change for any big or small reason. As an example, I might be linked to a future charge, but if the parent dies before my charge is born, then the future changes."

"What does that have to do with Annie?" Brite asked.

Zola chuckled. "I've known from my birth that Annie was one of my charges. But had one of her parents passed before she was born, the future would change and I would receive a new charge." The protection amulet swayed as Zola looked at it. "I am very glad to meet you now. It's just… I wasn't expecting to meet you for another eleven hundred years, give or take." She placed the necklace back around Annie's neck. "You must be in grave danger if I sent you back with this."

Annie's lip trembled and her eyes welled with tears. Instinctively, Zola reached for Annie and wrapped her arms around her future charge. Annie hadn't expected the rush of emotion at seeing her Aloja fairy, especially a version of her that didn't know her, but in that moment she was overcome. She took in Zola's familiar scent—wildflowers on a spring breeze, so familiar to her. Annie shook and cried.

Zola held her tightly, like she would in her future after her mother's funeral or when her father died, or even when Dave broke up with her their senior year of school. Annie's pain and fear were Zola's pain and fear; the fairy understood her more than anyone.

"You will be okay. I feel this," Zola said.

Annie pulled away and wiped her eyes. "It's weird. I've been smelling Dad's scent when the thunder roars. Like he's here with me. But seeing you and touching you is so much more comforting."

Zola placed her hand on Annie's cheek. "How can I help?"

"I wasn't sure what to expect when we came here. I'm restricted in what I'm allowed to do and who I speak with, including you." Annie chuckled, her nerves brittle as she wrung her hands. "I only trust John Gibbs and Michael Brite. Which, if we were at home and at full strength, would be more than enough. But our magic didn't come through the time portal at full strength. We're back to almost normal, but performing magic is so draining and it's depleting the coven of necessary magical energy. I think I could complete the spell fine, but there's some things that are a bit troublesome."

Annie explained what they had learned while in the coven, about Everard and the demons and the future coven.

"And I didn't tell you any of this?" Zola asked.

"No. You only told me you were supposed to do something for me but were unable to do so. You warned me not to tell you what that was for fear of changing the future," Annie said.

Zola paced along the window, deep in thought. "You should be angry with me too." She stopped and leaned against the fireplace. "I can see why you do not trust this coven. Had they done their job, none of this wouldn't have happened."

"You didn't record anything for Annie," Brite reminded her.

Zola looked at Annie. "I guess I thought the charm would be enough. That I should only help you with this." She bit her perfectly curved and plump bubble-gum-pink lips. "I'm sorry you were forced to clean up someone else's mess. You need protection. All of you. And you will need help getting through the portal."

Zola waved her hand across the table, summoning their three field packs.

"What do you need?" Gibbs asked.

"Herbs and crystals. Seeing that you are all feeling the ill effects of the magic while here, I should create a protection spell for you," Zola said.

Each emptied their packs of crystals and herbs and watched as Zola searched for specific ingredients. She pulled sprigs of Angelica from Gibbs's pack, sage and rosemary from Brite's, and bound them together with the spine of a mug wort plant from Annie's. "You do keep yourselves well stocked," Zola commented.

Zola summoned their crystals and broke off a small piece from each. She placed the pea-sized shards into the cooking pot that hung above the flames and dropped the herb bundle inside, covering it all with water. The water bubbled and smoked and turned the crystal from light pink to a dark green. Zola stirred the potion, examined the rocks, and pulled them off the fire when they turned black. She cooled them with a flick of her wrist and held them in the palm of her hand. "They'll be more effective if you swallow them," Zola said.

Annie glanced at Gibbs and Brite, who looked at her in return. They each swallowed the hard rock. It rolled down Annie's throat slowly. She felt the rock hit her stomach and sit there. The magic quickly warmed her, spreading from her middle to her arms and legs to her head.

"And you feel good?" Zola asked them.

"I'm warm and tingly," Brite said.

Gibbs cast a large fireball and held it above his palm. He made the flames dance and move before dropping the magic. "Good here," he said.

Zola looked at Annie. "And you, my sweet?"

"All warm and protected," Annie said. "You'll stay with me?"

"I'm not leaving you. I fear what will happen when you receive magic not meant for you. It may have been taken from someone else, it might not…" Zola stopped.

"What?" Annie asked anxiously. As her time in the past was rolling to a close, she felt her anxiety rise. "Zola, it's almost over, please tell me before I have to do this."

"Every magical person is born with that extra magical chromosome. And when the magic comes in, it is the magic that the witch or wizard was meant to receive. It forms to them, molds to their DNA."

"We all know this," Annie said.

"Magic isn't given as a reward. You don't receive additional magic as you get older. That magic you received as a child was yours. It was the only magic you were meant to receive. I fear the additional magic could harm you."

"I never asked for it," Annie whispered.

"I know." Zola placed both hands on either side of Annie's head and looked her in the eyes. "I will stay here until you go home. We will figure out what to do if there is a problem. The prophecy doesn't say when you'll get the magic or how. Just pay attention around yourself and your body. From all you've told me, I don't trust any of them."

Annie nodded. "I've already started getting new magic."

Zola glanced at her, her eyes grayish-green with worry. "What magic?"

"Astral projection. I can see the magic spell in the trees," Annie said.

Zola sighed. "That's disconcerting." She held on to Annie's shoulders. "Can you pull yourself together and do this?"

Annie nodded again.

Zola kissed her charge on the forehead. Annie could feel herself calming. She breathed slowly. "You must sleep because, in the morning, everything will change." Annie felt a spark at the fairy's touch and shivered.

"I was right to send you to me." Zola smiled.

✧

Annie tossed and turned through the night but, as she promised, Zola remained by her side, gently touching her cheek and calming her with kisses to her forehead. Still, Annie woke before dawn.

"I should have given you a sleeping draught," Zola said when Annie sat up in bed.

"You'll come to learn, I'm not a great sleeper," Annie said. She summoned her field pack and pulled out an apple. When she finished, she tossed the core in the fire and reached inside for another item.

"I'll stay beside you. Let your team do their jobs."

Annie nodded and reached for a sandwich. "I can't wait for a shower and real food."

"I'll make you your favorites when you get back," Zola said.

Annie chuckled. "I love you. You are very important to me. I don't think I've ever told you that," she said.

"I feel it. But it's nice to hear," Zola replied.

Annie took a bite of a sandwich, chewed slowly, and felt the food sit in her stomach. "I'm really scared."

Zola sat beside Annie on the floor. "If you weren't, I'd be worried." She pulled Annie's hair into her hands and combed it with her fingers, pulling out knots and smoothing the curls. Annie summoned her protection amulet, a gold barrette Zola would give her when she turned four, and handed it to Zola.

"Should I know where this comes from?" Zola asked as she clipped up Annie's curly hair.

"No." Annie lay her head on Zola's shoulder. "You know what's coming, don't you?"

"I live with the Fates. I know enough. Just remember, I will always be there for you," Zola said.

They sat on the floor in silence, waiting for the sun to come.

❧

"It's quiet," Gibbs said as he continued to watch the village. He searched for the old man, Everard, for the coven members, for the demons.

"That's positive," Annie said as she gathered her supplies and repacked her bag. When she had what she needed, she took in a deep breath and looked at Gibbs.

"Ready?" he asked.

She nodded once and let Gibbs lead them from the cottage.

The villagers had heeded Annie's concern over Everard and the demons attacking, and were patrolling the perimeter of the village. The protection spell had been reinforced again and several protection amulets now hung in the trees.

As they walked to the longhouse, Annie noted coven members she had never seen before. She searched out familiar faces, making eye contact with Byrony, Rhys, and Callum as they stood beside the longhouse doors. Etheldreda and Bega opened the doors and led them inside.

"Blessed be," Bega said. The young girl lunged for Annie, wrapping her arms around her.

Annie smiled and touched Bega's hair and cheek. "Thank you for everything."

Bega nodded and stepped back, giving Annie a large berth inside the building. Annie turned and looked out into the village. She shuddered, seeing the intensity with which the villagers watched her enter. She couldn't wait to leave this crazy time and place.

"This is my Aloja Fairy, Zola," Annie said to Etheldreda and Bega. They exchanged quick glances and closed the doors behind them.

"Over here." Gibbs led Annie to the center of the longhouse. He looked up at the ventilation hole in the roof and back at the long table. He whipped his wrists and pushed the table across the room. Standing under the hole, he raised his palms and blew a larger opening in the ceiling. Thatch and wood rained down. When the debris stopped falling, he whipped his wrist and scattered the wood and thatch away from the center of the room.

Annie sat at the center, the open hole above her. She summoned her crystal, demon blood, and the spell, laying them on the floor. Zola took a protective position behind Annie, with a full view of the longhouse door. Annie nodded to Gibbs. He and Brite closed the door and locked them inside.

Shrill, panicked cries broke out in the village. The earth vibrated with heavy footsteps as demons exited the forest.

Gibbs ran to the window, peered through the slats in the shutters, and watched the demons flood the village. Fireballs flew through the air and demons burst into flames as the coven protected the longhouse. Annie caught the stench of burning flesh. She glanced at Zola.

"Keep going," Zola ordered as she changed her position to guard Annie.

Brite observed the action through a crack between the door and wall. "Hurry, Annie!"

Annie fumbled with the crystal as she lay it in her lap. The terror outside the building rattled her. She took a breath, picked up the blood, and poured it over the crystal. It collected in the crevices and cracks. Annie blanched.

A heavy thud hit the wall and the building shook as much as Annie's hands. Thunder rumbled, she sniffed the air; her father was near.

"You're doing well," Zola said.

"Annie, now!" Gibbs shouted.

Annie held her palm above the blood-soaked crystal and said,

Oh ancient spirits, I call to you
Hear these words now.
Connect this life force
To all that live in this land.
Connect the blood to the blood of the masses
So that they may be the same.
Kill the one and the rest will follow.

Annie held her breath as she waited for the spell to work. She shot more magic into the crystal until it finally glowed a bright white light. She let out the stale air in her lungs.

I hope they're linked.

"Annie, now!" Gibbs yelled again as the demons pushed on the longhouse doors.

"Check Jorvik!" shouted an unfamiliar voice.

Annie held her palm above the crystal and cast the spell. "Fiero!"

The fireball sparked against the blood. While Annie expected the spell to billow from the crystal and up into through the hole in the ceiling, it didn't. As she set fire to the blood, the spell exploded up and out with such force it blew apart the remaining roof and sent Annie sliding across the floor, hitting the center fire pit. Magic flew out of the roof in search of creatures with the demon blood.

"It worked! Anaise! It worked!" Bega shouted from outside the door.

Gibbs opened the shutters. Demons squealed and shrieked as the fire consumed their flesh and bone. The scent of burnt flesh hung heavy around the village.

Annie glanced at the ceiling; her head pounded from crashing into the stone around the fire pit. "Zola? Zola!" Annie shouted.

"Here." Zola limped to her charge. "Hi, sweetheart." The fairy helped a woozy Annie sit.

"It was stronger than I expected." She held her pounding head.

"Can you get up?" Zola asked.

"I think so." Annie stood and leaned against Zola as they walked gingerly to the window.

The demons burned to death outside. Hundreds of them cried out, their suffering echoing across Northumbria long after they became piles of ash. Annie scanned the clearing, impressed by the number of piles scattered across the coven village. The ash hung in the trees, across the thatched roofs, along the walls of the cottages, covering the entire village in a layer of gray.

"What do we know about Jorvik?" Annie asked as she leaned against the window. Her arms and legs shook; she held the wall to steady herself.

"We sent a scout. Jorvik is fine. The demons came here to stop you," Bega said breathlessly.

"Everard must have set them loose," Annie said.

He failed. And that makes him dangerous.

"It's not over," she added.

Zola placed her hands on Annie's shoulder. "Everard is their problem now. It's time to get you home."

"He can't get you in here. The lock on the door is strong. We have Zola's protection spell," Gibbs said.

As he finished his pronouncement, a cursed fireball flew through the air, landing on what remained of the thatched roof. Though it was wet from rain, it caught fire quickly, sending flames around the perimeter of the roof and down the wall. Embers blew into the longhouse. Annie swatted a piece from her hair.

"Damn," Annie shouted as the longhouse filled with smoke. "We need to leave!"

Zola grabbed Annie's hand as Gibbs blasted the doors open.

"We need to get you to Jorvik," Gibbs said.

Annie nodded quickly. Zola held her shoulders tightly as Gibbs and Brite walked on either side of them, their hands open as they stepped into the village and headed to the narrow path to Jorvik.

Everard blocked their path. While he was old and appeared feeble, Annie knew the coven had misjudged him; he'd had a century to practice and hone his skills. He whipped his hands around, freezing the coven mid-step, mid-curse, mid-running around and, most impressively, he left them aware of what was happening.

Annie stared. "What the hell? Magicals can't be frozen!"

Zola chanted a protection spell, adding more magic to the crystal lodged in Annie's belly. The good fairy magic warmed Annie as it radiated from her belly down her arms and legs.

Annie wasn't sure if Zola's good magic could rival Everard's dark magic. He held his hands out, and while they shook with age and dampness, he nonetheless forced Zola to drop her hands, binding them against her body.

Gibbs and Brite tossed jinxes at Everard, but the old man in his determination, held Zola still with one hand and whipped the jinxes away with his other. He walked forward with a slight limp and his back hunched over. He smiled wickedly, pushed his arm out and sent Zola flying into the burning longhouse, slamming the heavy doors shut.

"Zola, no!" Annie screamed and ran for the burning building.

Zola pounded on the doors, her spells to unlock them and to teleport failing. "Annie, I can't get out!" she screamed.

Gibbs and Brite barreled down on Everard. So strong and practiced, he whipped his hands at them, forcing them to their knees. With his magic pressuring them, they involuntarily retched until they coughed up the protection stones. Once they were free of the protection spell, Everard froze their bodies, leaving their heads available to watch.

Annie turned as Everard shuffled toward her. He flicked his wrist, his strong magic pulling her forward and down on her knees. She resisted, but his spells were too strong. Annie turned and vomited with such strength, the stone flew several feet from her. Gibbs and Brite, stared in horror as Everard yanked Annie up in one swift motion.

Fear overtook her.

In the distance, thunder rolled. Annie sniffed the air, but her father wasn't there. She tried to pull away from Everard, whose grip was surprisingly strong. She glared at the old man. His eyes seemed soulless, black with fury. While she could see him touch her, she couldn't feel him.

Astral projection!

In his raspy voice, he said, "It's not over." In an instant, he shot a jinx at Gibbs.

"Annie," Gibbs said as he fell backward. It was the last thing Annie saw before she was teleported away.

CHAPTER 30

THE FREEZING SPELL broke when Everard left with Annie. Brite scrambled up and ran for Gibbs. "Get Zola out of the longhouse!" he shouted and checked Gibbs for a pulse. He began chest compressions and continued feverishly to revive his friend, but Brite knew.

Callum ran for the longhouse, cast a spell, and burst open the doors. He raced inside and fetched Zola, who lay on the floor unconscious. He threw her over his shoulder and ran for the center of the village, laying the fairy on the ground.

Holding his hands over her head, he cast the first healing spell. Her skin glowed. She coughed and looked at him.

"Where's Annie?" she whispered.

"Are you okay?" Callum asked as he quickly examined the fairy. Her face was covered in smoke. She coughed as she breathed in the fresh air.

"Everard got her," Brite said.

"It didn't work? It should have worked." She sat up and scanned the village, her eyes stopping on Gibbs, who was lying in a puddle.

"What happened to him?" Zola asked. She pushed away Callum's assistance and crawled to him.

"Everard cast a jinx before he left," Brite said as he tried to breathe.

"His magic..." Zola placed her hands on either side of Gibbs's head. Her magic flowed from her body and into him. "Wake up!" she shouted.

Brite wiped away his tears as Zola finally removed her hands from Gibbs.

"I can't. Everard's magic is too strong. We need to find Annie," Zola said. She stumbled up and closed her eyes, concentrating on her charge. Her face contorted and twisted as she reached out for the charm Annie wore around her neck.

The longhouse, completely consumed in fire, crashed in on itself, sending sparks to the cottages on either side of it. No amount of rain could diminish the size of the fire. The coven members began digging trenches to hold the fire back from destroying the forest.

"I can't see her. She's blocked," Zola said with despair. "It should have worked."

"He used black magic," Brite said. "The fire's cursed." He searched for Etheldreda, grabbing hold of her robes as soon as he found her. "Where did he take her!"

She quaked at his touch. "I… I do not know where Everard took her." Her eyes searched his face. "Maybe his cottage," she said.

He released Etheldreda's robes. "Take Gibbs to Jorvik. Keep his body safe. We'll take him back to the present with us." Brite glanced around them. "This village is destroyed."

The heat was building in the clearing. Brite wiped his forehead with his sleeve and summoned a crystal, using it to scan for any magical trace around Annie's last location. His crystal glowed a black light, indicating several dark spells. Brite followed the dark magic to the center of the village, where it stopped at the fire pit. He walked the perimeter and climbed inside, unaffected by the magical fire.

Zola and Etheldreda observed his actions. Etheldreda grew anxious and stepped back as if she were leaving. Zola placed a firm hand on her shoulder, holding her to the spot.

"What do you know?" Zola asked.

Etheldreda shook her head, her lips pursed together as Brite reached down and pulled up a hex bag, a small burlap bag containing magical herbs and cast with a jinx with the intent to cause harm.

Brite glared at Etheldreda and pulled himself from the fire pit. He shoved the hex bag in her face.

"When did he put this in the fire?" Brite asked.

She shook her head quickly. "I do not know."

As fire continued consuming the cottages in the village, coven members congregated at the center. Fearing the worst, Etheldreda pointed to Rhys. "Make sure everyone in the coven escaped. Settle them in Jorvik." Rhys enlisted Bryony and Gila as they began knocking on doors, pulling them open, and pushing villagers toward Jorvik. Others left their protective holes in the ground, escaping the smoke and fire.

In anguish, Etheldreda watched them leave and turned to Brite. "I will take Gibbs. But we need to leave. Please," she begged.

"What is he going to do with her?" Brite's face was so close to Etheldreda, he could smell her breath, the body odor, the remnants of black magic.

"She killed the demons, so she should be receiving the power. Maybe he wants the power for himself. It might be strong enough to make him permanently immortal," Etheldreda suggested.

Brite looked at Zola briefly. A tear rolled through the ash on her creamy skin. He scanned the remaining coven members and found Callum still at the longhouse.

"Take Gibbs and go," Brite said. He ran for Callum, whose eyes grew wide as Brite wrapped his arms around him and teleported from the village. They landed at Everard's cottage. There was nothing but a burnt shell. Brite kicked at the stone foundation. "Where would he go?"

Zola landed gracefully beside them and stared at the cottage foundation and the lump of ash beside it. "There must have been a demon nearby," she said thoughtfully.

Brite whipped out a map of Northumbria and shoved it in Callum's face. "Where did he take her?" he asked again.

Callum took the map and summoned his own crystal. "I need something of hers," he said sheepishly.

Zola wielded a large knife in one hand and cut through her palm. Her blood flowed from her hand and dripped to the ground. "The amulet she wears is imbued with my blood. That is how I knew I gave it to her; that Annie is mine. Take this." She held out her hand for Callum, who captured the blood on the crystal. He maneuvered the crystal across the map. The crystal remained cold and dull, as if Annie were no longer alive.

Brite turned to Callum. "Where would he take her?" he repeated.

Callum looked at the map. "The caves here. He might have taken her there. It would be easy to block his magic and cloak her."

"If Zola couldn't sense her, and the crystal didn't find her amulet, then he definitely has her blocked. We need to hurry. I think Etheldreda was correct. He wants her power," Brite said. He sniffed the air as smoke billowed around them. "Do you smell that?" He glanced inside the trees. A large fireball raced toward them.

"Fire! We need to go!" Brite shouted. Callum reached for Brite, teleporting them to Jorvik. Zola turned and disappeared through the trees.

⌇

Residents of Jorvik dug channels at the edge of the village near the trees. The coven whipped their palms across the trees, creating a fire barrier of the strongest spells they could muster.

Smoke from the cursed fire blanketed the town.

"Go to the longhouse! Callum shouted. "You'll be safe there." A stream of Vikings and coven members not assisting with fire prevention headed to the longhouse, stunned and anxious as the fire ate away at the trees and headed toward them. It might have been a useless cause as a storm battered Jorvik.

Brite looked at the sky and felt the rain pelt him with such an angry, bitter force. He almost believed it was Jason letting go of his fury. He wanted to chuckle at the lightning as it flashed in consecutive bursts, as the thunder roared with rage. "She'll be safe in the thunder," he said, though this time he was unsure that would be true. Zola stood beside him. "She smells the scent of her father when it thunders," Brite said.

"Well, if he's here now, he's extremely angry," Zola said.

This time, Brite laughed. "I thought that myself," he said. "We need to find her." He turned and stared at the door, where a new carving had been added. It was the girl that looked like Annie, wielding her sword, and at her feet lay the dead demon.

"How in the hell did that get there?" Brite asked.

"It's magic," Etheldreda said. "We created the doors for Jorvik to protect them from the demons. It seems to add new stories as they happen."

Brite touched the girl on the door.

"We've laid Gibbs out," Etheldreda said.

Brite looked at Etheldreda, who looked to have aged years in the last few days. "Thank you."

"The queen's body was found," Etheldreda added.

Brite saw the queen, her body laid across the table near the throne. She wore a dark crimson dress, her golden crown atop her head. A wound across her neck was fresh and purple.

The king knelt beside the table, acknowledging nobody as he mourned his loss. Kolgaar and Svenson joined Brite at the door. "Princess Gyda is still missing," Kolgaar murmured.

"If you have something of the princess's, we can search for her," Etheldreda said.

Svenson left to speak with the king, whispering quietly in his ear. The king frowned at the coven. Desperate to find his daughter, he reached inside his robes and pulled out a necklace. Svenson returned and handed it to Etheldreda.

"I'll search for her now." The old woman shuffled toward the first table, took out her map, and began to scry for the young girl.

"Annie is missing," Brite said. His watched the rain fall in near white-out conditions, beating against the cursed fire. "The coven will search for the princess, but we need help to find her." He handed the map to Kolgaar. "The coven thinks she might be in the caves."

Sturtagaard strolled to the map, looking over his brother's shoulder. "If she's missing, she'll be dead too."

"She hasn't received her powers yet. She's safe until she does," Brite said.

Sturtagaard pulled away and sat at the nearest table. "My child is gone. My wife disappeared, and when she returned, she was injured; a large piece of flesh had been eaten away. There is nothing I can do for her. She is dying." He spat. "Why should we care where that girl is? She was supposed to save us. For not doing so, she must be punished."

Brite wanted to argue for Annie, lay out her sacrifices, explain all the good that she accomplished, but he could see that Sturtagaard was in distress and unreachable. It would fall on deaf ears. "Go care for your wife. There's nothing more you can do here," Brite said emotionlessly. He felt a heaviness in his chest as he saw Gibbs lying on a table in the corner of the longhouse. He knew Gibbs's death would be hardest on Annie.

Kolgaar tapped the map. "We know these caves. We will come with you." He glanced at the king as if he would be ordered to do so, but the king was lost, deep inside his grief.

"Keep someone with him," Brite ordered. "He's not in his right mind." He tapped Etheldreda on the shoulder. "Anything with the princess?"

Etheldreda shook her head and then hung it low as if shamed.

"We're going after Annie," Brite told her.

She nodded quickly and moved to a table on the other side of the longhouse.

Brite took one more look at the monsoon outside the doors and pulled up his hood. He was followed by Kolgaar, Svenson, and, at the last moment, a reluctant Sturtagaard. They bent their heads low and headed east for the caves.

಄

Annie slumped against the stone wall. Her head rolled forward.

Where am I?

She opened her eyes. Her pants and her hands were stained with mud and blood. She lifted her head. Her vision was fuzzy and dark. She closed her eyes again, took a deep breath, and was assaulted by the smell of burnt flesh, smoke, and the musty smell of water. The stench covered her hair, her clothes, her skin.

What happened?

She felt hard stone, bumpy yet smoothed by age and water, dig into her tender flesh. She ached from her feet to her head.

Pictures formed in her head—demons, fire, Gibbs falling forward—but she couldn't make sense of the images that rapidly flipped through her memory. She pulled her head back up; lightheaded, she turned her head and vomited.

Annie closed her eyes again and let the images come back to her. Brite and Gibbs watching in horror.

Why?

"Zola," she groaned and blacked out.

⚭

Metal pinged against rock in a slow, repetitive cadence and reverberated off the stone walls. The sound bounced around in Annie's head. A musty, sour smell wafted to her. She grimaced at the puddle of vomit beside her.

She was so exhausted; she could barely raise her arm to pull herself up. Instead, she pushed backwards against the stone wall until she stood. There was a heaviness around her waist. She glanced down and saw a metal chain strapped around her. As she moved, it clinked against the wall.

Where am I?

A heavy boulder blocked her view. She stumbled forward and held onto the rock as her eyes grew accustomed to the dim light. She found herself in a cavern of some sort. She scanned the small area, which included several niches filled with candles and a table on the far side. She blinked her eyes rapidly and looked at the table again. It was covered in items she couldn't quite make out yet.

Annie leaned against the boulder. She shuddered violently from wet clothing and the damp, cool air. She rubbed her arms for warmth.

Again, she heard the sound of metal pinging.

I'm not alone.

The thick chain pulled on Annie's waist. She turned and followed the chain up the wall where it was embedded in the stone. She yanked, but the chain was firmly attached.

Fear gripped Annie. She closed her eyes and held her palms out to syphon any magical energy around her. She felt no tingling in her fingers, hands, or arms. The effort left her with a pounding headache and deeper exhaustion.

Annie held the chain as she scooted around the edge of the boulder. Now accustomed to the low light, she could see the roaring fire in the fire pit and a work table covered in herbs, crystals, potion jars, books, and scrolls. Upon closer inspection, she noticed a basket of uneaten food on the floor where mice squealed in delight at their found feast.

She heard another ping of metal, but Everard wasn't in this part of this cavern.

Where is he?

She walked around the boulder as far as the chain would let her. She closed her eyes and listened to the cave sounds. The pinging continued off in the distance, water dripped from the ceiling, the fire roared, and a soft moan reverberated off of the stone walls.

Annie slid to her knees and scanned the cave searching for the owner of the moan. Nausea and dizziness gripped her again. She turned and threw up against the rock. When her stomach emptied, she returned to the search. Unable to see in the darkest corners, she bitterly tossed a spell at the chain where it was embedded into the wall. Magic bounced across the metal and sent sparks everywhere. When the magic stopped, she tried again with the lock on the chain. Again, it bounced across the metal and flew against the walls.

Of course.

Annie leaned against the rock as she examined the table. There were too many shadows blocking a clear view. She held out her palm anyway and summoned keys, not expecting Everard had any. Her eyes widened when a set of heavy keys landed in her palm. Nearly giddy with relief, she placed the key in the lock at her waist and turned. It gave way easily. She pulled off the chain and ran toward the moaning sound. It came from the frail body of a girl dressed in thick robes. Her yellow hair fell around her face. The girl moaned again.

Princess Gyda!

"Gyda. It's Anaise. I'm going to release you and get you out of here." Annie knelt beside the girl who was attached to the wall like Annie had been. She fumbled with the key, found the lock, and released the girl.

But how do I get her out of here?

Annie summoned her flashlight, left the girl, and searched the room until she was back where she started – at a passageway that led to the cave system.

I could be lost in there for days or weeks.

A low menacing laughter echoed off the walls. Everard's feeble form entered the cavern from the other side.

"Where do you think you are doing? Do you really believe you can get her out of here?" Everard asked. He pulled the stool out and sat beside the table, pulling herbs and dumping them in the mortar. He picked up the pestle and began to grind them into a thick paste.

"What are you making?" Annie asked as she leaned over for a better look.

Everard dumped the ground herbs into a larger bowl and said "Fiero," lighting the ingredients with fire. He turned to Annie. "You killed them. All of them. I am recreating them. Just like I did before." He reached for another ingredient and dumped it into the stone bowl. The old man began to pound at the ingredients, the stone pestle scratching against the bowl. Princess Gyda moaned.

"I can't let you do that," Annie said. She whipped her palm up at him, sending the mortar and pestle across the table and onto the floor.

"You bitch! How dare you come here and kill my babies!" He picked up the broken stone and potion ingredients, placed them on the table, took his candle lantern, and shuffled to Annie.

"What keeps you alive, old man?" she asked. She looked at his wrinkled face and the blackness of his eyes.

Demon eyes?

Everard smiled a crooked, yellow smile. "I'm an alchemist. I have secrets that you are not privy to. And now to keep you from ruining my plans any further..." He blasted Annie with a jinx. She flew backwards, her head bouncing against the rock, and slid to the floor.

New pain radiated across her back and down her legs, through her arms and to her head. She let out a groan.

The world floated away from her, leaving her in an unfamiliar void. Princess Gyda moaned in the distance. Annie tried to speak, but she couldn't make a sound. Trapped in her body, there was nothing she could do when she felt a spark of electricity and blacked out.

✧

When Annie woke again, she was incapacitated against a hard board, her arms above her head, a strong magical rope binding her hands together. She attempted to move her legs, but they too were tied tightly and immobile.

The old man shuffled across the floor and knelt beside Princess Gyda, reconnecting the chain around her waist. Annie turned and watched as he poured a potion down her throat.

"What are you giving her?" Annie shouted.

"Oh good, you're awake. This is nothing for you to be concerned with." Everard smiled and pulled himself up, his joints creaking and popping. His advanced age made it difficult for him to move with ease, but it didn't hinder his ability to perform strong magic.

Annie watched in horror as Everard easily floated a heavy stone above her. She feared he would bash her head in. "You can't do this. Not until my powers come!" she shouted in fear.

He laughed as he directed the large rock to her hands and let the magic go.

"Ahhhhhhhh!" Her scream reverberated across the stone. She couldn't help the tears that followed as she felt the pain from her two broken hands radiate down her arm to her shoulders. Her body shuddered as she cried out.

"Shut up. I need to continue," Everard said as he returned to the table and to his potion.

CHAPTER 31

STURTAGAARD ANGRILY MARCHED with purpose as he, Kolgaar, and Svenson led Brite and Zola across the countryside in a blinding rain to the hidden caves where they might find Annie. Brite observed him carefully. He distrusted him immensely and was curious as to why Sturtagaard chose to leave his dying wife to assist in finding Annie.

Whatever he does, he does for a price.

They took a path around the coven village, which had once been completely hidden inside the forest. Now the forest had been burnt and its trees were mere sticks, charcoal, and ash. The longhouse was nothing but a rock foundation, the walls had crashed in and were piles of rubble. None of the cottages remained. Even the fire pit at the center of town was empty; whatever remained inside was smoldering as the rain drenched the last of the fires.

The group slipped as they headed down the slope toward the river, which was heavy with white caps as it overflowed through the landscape. The riverbank was thick with mud. Their boots stuck in the muck with each step. They followed the brown, muddy river as it swung around and changed direction east.

Sturtagaard pointed across the river. "The caves will start there," he shouted over the pounding rain.

Brite acknowledged him with a nod. They found a shallow point in the river and crossed. Icy water rushed up their legs, drenching them to their waist. Each step was painful as the water pounded them. By the time they reached the other side, they crawled along the bank, exhausted. Brite and Zola sat at the edge, breathing heavily. Sturtagaard staggered up and pointed.

"It's here!" he shouted.

Brite and Zola scrambled to the cave entrance and clawed at the foliage, releasing the hold the vines had on the opening. What remained was a cave entrance, at ground level, only two feet wide and three feet high. Brite lay on the ground, his flashlight illuminating the short, narrow entrance. "Everard is too old to drag her through here. Is there another entrance?"

Sturtagaard nodded. "This way." They rounded the corner, rejoined the river's edge. He led them to a narrow fissure in the rocks. Brite glanced inside with his light, estimating the narrowness at the beginning of the entrance expanding as they walked inside.

Maybe he could bring her through here.

Brite glanced at the Viking men. "Thanks for your help. You can go if you'd like," he said as he turned sideways and entered. Zola entered next, shuffling sideways through the narrow space until the tunnel expanded.

Kolgaar, Svenson, and Sturtagaard followed. Brite turned. "I said you can go." He turned back and examined a long tunnel.

"You might need our help," Kolgaar said.

Brite and Zola glanced at each other before Brite led them through the cave system. They stopped at an intersection between two passageways and listened. "Do you hear that?" he whispered. Kolgaar pointed to the right.

Brite nodded and flashed his light in both directions before switching it off, turning on a low-level crystal and heading toward the sound. At each passage, they'd stop, listen for a clanking sound, and turn toward it, winding their way through the cave that languidly snaked through the earth. The sound grew louder. Brite pointed and Kolgaar nodded.

A low, dim light emanated from a cavern up ahead. At the entrance, Sturtagaard, Svenson, and Kolgaar wielded their swords, staying behind Brite and Zola as they looked inside the opening. Brite entered, crouched behind a boulder, caught a sour stench, and looked down. He thought of Annie, grimaced, and returned to scanning the cavern.

Princess Gyda lay motionless on the floor. Behind her, Everard was forcing something from his bowl into Annie's mouth. Brite sprung up. "Get away from her!" His panicked voice reverberated around the stone walls and floors. Everard looked up, glared at him and continued with his business. Brite angrily whipped his hand toward the bowl. It flew from Everard's grip and crashed against the stone wall. The potion splattered and dripped to the floor.

Kolgaar lunged for Everard, knocking the old man to the ground. The wizard cried out as his rib cracked.

"You're not using her as a vessel," Brite said. Kolgaar sat on Everard, holding his hands against his body with his thick legs. Brite summoned a vial, unstopping it. He grabbed the old man's jaw and wrenched it open, pouring the clear and odorless liquid down his throat.

Everard knew from his long life's experiences what Brite had done. Within seconds, the old man went slack; his magical powers had been bound by the powerful potion.

"What was that?" Kolgaar asked.

"I bound his powers. He's nothing more than an old man waiting to die," Brite jeered. He ran for Annie. Brite released her arms from the bindings, her wrists were red and raw, her hands mangled and bloody.

"What the hell did he do? Brite asked.

She looked at him with puffy eyes and wet cheeks. "Gyda. She's drugged over there." Annie motioned with her head. Brite removed the straps from her legs and helped her sit, leaning her against the wall.

"You okay for a minute? I'll deal with her," Brite said. Annie nodded and rested against the wall as Brite returned to Gyda. After checking her vital signs, he said, "She's alive. Barely." He motioned for the others. He checked the chain around her waist, found the lock, and waved a palm above it. When it wouldn't open with magic, he summoned the keys, opened the lock, and tossed it across the cavern.

"Take her back," Brite said. Kolgaar lifted the slim princess, her clothes weighing more than she did. "Tell them she was drugged. The coven can give her an antidote." Kolgaar nodded but stayed in place as he glanced at Annie. "Go," Brite said again, waving him out.

"What can I do?" Svenson asked.

Brite led him to Everard and began the chore of tying his hands behind his back. When he finished binding the old man's ankles, he yanked him up. "Bring him back to the coven. Tell them his powers are bound and inform them of what he did to Gyda and Annie."

Svenson nodded, pulled Everard from the floor, and flung him over his shoulder. Everard moaned. Brite couldn't have cared less about the old man's comfort.

After the others had gone, Sturtagaard watched Annie intently; his eyes bore into her. Brite shuddered at his expression. Zola caught his reaction to a weakened Annie and stood between her charge and the future vampire. Sturtagaard stood still, his fingers twirling a knife behind his back. He placed the knife back in his scabbard and walked away.

Relieved he was gone, Brite ran back to Annie. "You okay?"

"Yeah." She looked at them and held her mangled hands for them to see, gritting her teeth.

"What did he do?" Brite asked.

"Broke them so I couldn't use magic against him," she murmured.

"Hang in there. We'll get you out of here." Brite gently lifted her from the floor. Unable to teleport through the thick cave walls, he carried her back though the cave paths. Annie, succumbing to the pain, closed her eyes and leaned against his chest.

At the cave entrance, Brite and Zola exchanged glances as they entered the torrential downpour.

Svenson and Kolgaar ran from the caves with the princess covered in Kolgaar's cloak and Everard haphazardly tossed across Svenson's shoulder without the benefit of protection. They followed the path they had taken to get there, first crossing at the shallow point in the river. It had been a tougher experience returning to Jorvik as both Vikings were entrusted with bodies unable to care for themselves. The extra weight made the walk through the whirling water most difficult. The waves continued to crash against their legs, and they were unable to fully see where they were going as they maneuvered across the water. At the river's edge, Svenson tossed Everard to the ground, fell to his knees, and climbed from the water.

Kolgaar grunted, lay the princess on the bank, and pulled himself out of the water. The rain blinded them as they gathered their charges again.

"Do we wait?" Svenson shouted above the storm.

"We need to get them back now!" Kolgaar shouted.

Svenson nodded and pulled Everard up, tossing him across his shoulders again as Kolgaar gently picked up Princess Gyda. As Jorvik came into view, they ran faster into the wind and stepped inside the town. The streets were empty as they ran for the longhouse. Kolgaar threw open the doors, and they lunged inside where the air was warm and dry. Spotting the coven in the far corner, Svenson marched to them and dropped Everard on the ground.

The old man cried out.

"He was in the caves with Anaise and Princess Gyda," Svenson said.

Etheldreda glanced across the longhouse where Kolgaar lay the princess on the table closest to the king. King Hrothgar rushed to his daughter and cried over her lifeless body.

"Is she alive?" Etheldreda asked.

Svenson glared at Everard. "He drugged her with something. Brite said he bound his powers." He touched the man with the toe of his shoe and glanced at the king, who wailed. Svenson nodded once and left to offer comfort.

"Be thankful they only bound your powers," Etheldreda jeered as she followed Svenson.

"What is wrong with her?" the king shrieked.

Etheldreda touched the princess on the forehead and placed her hand over the girl's chest. "She's been drugged." She summoned a bag, engorged it to its original size, and summoned a smaller bag filled with leaves.

"What is that? Don't you touch her!" the king shouted.

Etheldreda held her palm up and glared at him before she took the herbs and placed them in the girl's mouth. The old woman held her gnarled hands above Gyda's stomach and syphoned out the magic that blocked her. She moved her hands to her chest and then to her throat, and held it there. The girl woke, turned her head, and began coughing until she spat out the herbs. In an instant, she retched, throwing up the potion. Her body quivered and she vomited again.

Despite the stench of stomach bile and the rancid potion, Etheldreda continued to hold her hand above the girl's neck. Gyda continued to cough and vomit until nothing else came up. When Gyda no longer felt the need to gag, she rolled on her back, and looked from Etheldreda to the king.

"Father," she murmured. The broken king bent over his daughter. His thick body heaved and quaked as he cried.

∽

Rain and wind assailed them as they ran to the river. "This is where we crossed earlier," Zola shouted.

Brite grumbled as he held Annie tightly. The river had swollen to twice its size in the ten minutes since Kolgaar and Svenson must have passed. "We can't cross here," he said.

Zola motioned for Brite to follow. They walked along the river's edge until the river narrowed again. They stopped and watched the water squeeze into the slim passage; the current was strong there. "I can't walk through this," Brite said.

"Can you teleport her?" Zola asked.

"The wind's too strong." Brite glanced down the river. The rain fell sideways. They continued down the river and entered the burnt forest.

Lighting flashed.

"I get the feeling this is Jason's doing," Brite said.

Zola glanced up at the gray sky as the thunder boomed and vibrated through them.

Brite stopped for a moment and glanced up at the dark sky. "She's safe now, Jason! You can stop!" The rain and wind continued to pelt them. "Maybe not," Brite joked, but it didn't feel funny.

Zola pointed. "It's flat down there," she said as they walked down the slope.

"It's too fast," Brite said.

Zola looked at Annie, unconscious in Brite's arms. "If we don't get her back, she might die. We need to cross."

Brite pointed at the narrow spot and took a cautious step. Zola held him steady as the current beat against his legs. On the opposite side, Zola nudged him with magic, helping him step onto the riverbank.

They said nothing as they sprinted across the barren landscape. When Brite found the path to Jorvik, he took it and ran Annie back to town.

✥

Brite left Annie unconscious by the fire pit, covering her in a thick, dry blanket. "I'll be right back," he said and left Zola beside her as he wandered to Gibbs's lifeless body.

He touched the other man's three-day-old beard and felt the death chill across his skin. Brite shuddered, summoned and unfurled a blanket, laying it across Gibbs's body. "Sorry, old man. You deserved a better death."

Brite wiped the tears from his eyes. He hadn't worked with Gibbs much, but he respected him, as did all of the wizard guards. His death would crush Annie.

"I'm sorry for your loss," Bega said.

"Thank you."

"Can I get you anything?"

Brite shook his head, sighed, and returned to Annie.

"Is she up?" he asked Zola.

"No."

"I need to wake her. We need to leave before her powers come." Brite peeled off the blanket and looked at her mangled hands. He touched her right wrist carefully. Her eyes flew open, and she cried out in pain.

"Sorry. I think I need to repair as much as I can before we go back," Brite told her.

She nodded in understanding. "Where's Gibbs?" she asked. Brite and Zola exchanged glances. "Where is he?" she asked again.

"Let me heal your hands," Brite said.

"Where is he?" she screamed out, her voice shrill and panicked.

"Everard..." Brite began.

Pictures filtered in Annie's mind. She knew she had seen a flash and Gibbs falling forward. He had fallen. "No. No. NO!" Annie began to hyperventilate. She couldn't breathe. "No!"

"Come here." Brite held her arm and helped her up. She leaned against him and shuffled as she walked, her hands dangling in front of her. He guided her to the end of the longhouse where Gibbs lay under the blankets. Brite pulled the wool blanket away, exposing Gibbs's cold, gray skin. His eyes were closed.

Annie reached out for him, but her mangled hands were useless, painful. "Bring him back," she said.

Zola held her shoulders. "I tried. It was black magic. I couldn't."

"Bring him back!" Her voice, filled with pain and anger, reverberated across the wooden walls. Everyone still inside watched Annie. She didn't notice the spectacle she was making made, and she wouldn't have cared if she did.

"Annie. We can't," Brite said.

She fell to her knees, bent her head, and cried.

CHAPTER 32

ANNIE SAT ACROSS from Gibbs as he lay on the table. Brite and Zola tried to heal her, but she shrugged them away. They offered her food, but she glared at them.

Brite sat several seats from Annie, observing her patiently. Zola fiddled with Annie's backpack.

"I need to heal you before you go back," Zola said.

"Later. I need to protect him." Annie wiped the tears away with her forearm.

"You can't protect him without your hands." Zola knelt beside her and picked up Annie's left hand.

Annie resigned herself to Zola's care and let Zola blanket her hand with Aloja fairy magic. It was warm and familiar, but at the same time, it hurt like hell as the magic knitted her bones back together. Annie grimaced, sweat gathering at her forehead and behind her neck. Her breath was quick, and she bit her lip to keep from screaming.

"It's almost healed," Zola said.

Annie closed her eyes. Her arm shook as her magical energy depleted. She shivered uncontrollably and Zola stopped.

"Rest for now." Zola placed her hand above Annie's heart and waited for her to calm. Instead, she began to cry.

"How is she?" Brite asked.

"So much magical energy is gone," Zola said. "I suspect with love and care, she'll move on."

Zola prepared food and passed it to Brite. He made a face at the charred meat but took a slice and chewed slowly.

"Are you okay?" Zola asked him.

"I didn't know him as well. But he didn't deserve that. He was a good wizard guard, and underneath his gruffness, he was a good man and he loved her." Brite took another bite. "I'll be fine. Thanks."

Annie wiped more tears. "I'm ready for my other hand."

Zola returned, placed both hands on Annie's right hand and began the healing spell. Annie felt numb. She barely registered the pain she should be feeling as Zola fixed her broken hand.

"Make fists," Zola ordered. Annie obliged. The action was slow; her hands were stiff and sore. "When you get home, have them continue with treatment."

Annie nodded and began shaking violently.

Calmly, Zola wrapped Annie in a thick blanket and added warmth with her magic.

"I can't stop shaking," Annie said.

"You've used so much magic and are still pulling energy from around here to help heal. My poor dear," Zola said as she wiped Annie's forehead.

"Has anyone seen Sturtagaard?" Annie asked.

Brite stood and looked around longhouse. "He's not here. Last I heard, his wife was dying. He's probably with her," Brite said. "I can look for him if you like?" Brite put his arm around her. Annie shook her head.

"I don't feel so good," Annie said.

"You just need rest," Brite said.

"No. I really don't."

Brite jumped when her skin began to glow. A light mist billowed around her. She reached out and pulled it from the air, the earth, and the water around them. Annie was regenerating; she was receiving her power.

"Annie?" Brite shouted. He reached for her, but he could not touch her. He and Zola stepped back as the magical energy filled Annie with life, with power.

Everard, tied to a chair, watched with fascination and a crooked grin across his thin lips. "It is here!" he shouted.

"Nooo!" Annie shouted. The blanket slipped from her shoulders as her body twisted and jerked. Painfully, the magic gripped her muscles and bones; every cell in her body burst from magic that didn't belong to her.

The Vikings and the coven stood in fear of the magic that swirled and twinkled as golden light around them while the magical energy that existed in the longhouse was siphoned for Annie.

Energy rushed through her; her body could barely contain it. Losing all control, she rose in the air, seizing with magic. Brite grabbed her, but the magic burned his fingertips and she slipped from his grip.

"There's nothing we can do," Zola said. She watched with concern as Annie rose to the ceiling, shuddering as she hung in the air.

Annie let out a wild, frenzied scream as the light around her burst forth.

"What if she falls?" Brite asked.

Zola levitated herself in the air as the light exploded around them. She reached for her charge, holding Annie tenderly as she floated back to the ground. Ignoring everything around them, she walked Annie to the table and lay her down, folding Annie's arms across her chest.

Annie opened her eyes and smiled before her head rolled sideways and she blacked out.

⁓

The rain fell, but it was no longer violent, angry, or hard. It was the type of summer rain that would fall and wash the humidity from Chicagoland, leaving everything smelling clean. Brite left the window of the small cottage open, letting fresh air inside. There was no more forest to the north, only smoldering embers and smoke that, luckily for them, had been driven away in the storm.

The fireplace was dark. Soft candles glowed around the cottage. Brite stared out the window. Had there been moonlight, he could have seen across the fields of England.

Annie tossed and turned in bed, rolling on her side and moaning as she slept fitfully. Zola touched her forehead and hovered over her heart, but there was nothing she could do to calm her. Annie would have to feel the pain and work through it.

As the dawn neared, Annie began to scratch at her arms feverishly as if she were trying to remove something. Brite and Zola exchanged glances.

"Why is she scratching? She'll scratch herself raw," Brite said.

Zola held Annie's hand. Her skin felt hot. "The magic doesn't belong to her."

"You think it's her body rejecting it?" Brite asked.

"I don't know. I can't think what else it could be. If she were allergic to something in Northumbria, she'd have reacted already." Zola raised Annie's sleeve. Her skin glowed, except where she had scratched; there, it was red and raw from scratching.

Annie murmured and twitched. Her eyes flew open. Her breathing was shallow and quick.

"Hi, sweetheart," Zola said. Annie's eyes darted between Zola and Brite.

"Where am I?" she asked.

"We're in a cottage in Jorvik. We're going back in the morning," Brite tried to smile. He was finding it hard to be happy.

"Here. Drink this." Zola offered her a bottle of water and helped Annie sit. Annie took small sips; the water sloshed in her stomach and made her queasy.

"How long was I out?" She took another swig of water.

"Long enough. I'm very sorry the spell didn't keep you safe," Zola said. She held Annie's hands in hers.

"It's not your fault. Everard used black magic." Absently, Annie scratched at her thigh.

"You're itchy?" Zola asked.

"Yeah. It feels like something's crawling inside of me." Annie scratched faster, but it offered no relief.

"I think it's the magic," Zola said.

"I don't like it." Annie shook out her hand as if that could dump the magic out. Sparks shot from her palms and hit the shutter, smashing it against the stone walls. For a short moment, the magic stopped itching. "Damn." She stared at her palm.

Zola opened the second window. The streets of Jorvik were empty.

The survivors had returned to their homes and the coven remained at the longhouse. The silence was stifling.

"Where's Gibbs?" Annie asked.

"He's in the longhouse. We prepared him to travel."

"I don't trust them. I should go watch the body." Annie turned to get off the bed.

"No. You need to sleep. To rest. Kolgaar made a solemn oath to watch over him," Zola said.

Annie slumped against the wall and scratched at her temple. "I'm sick of the rain. I'm already sick of the magic." The itch was deep inside her body. As much as she scratched, she couldn't reach it. The powers were taking hold and molding to her. The thought made her blanch.

"I imagine so. How can I help you?"

Annie looked at her Aloja fairy, overwhelmed with the knowledge that she had known Zola her whole life, just not this version of her. While it was familiar, it also was not. "You can remove the powers," Annie said.

"Ask me when you get home. I'll have had eleven hundred years to figure out how." Zola offered a wan smile.

Annie wanted to tell her that eleven hundred years hadn't been enough to figure it out, but Zola had warned her not to discuss it with anyone, including her younger self. Instead, she offered a hopeful smile and said, "Okay." Annie scratched the skin on her head and rubbed her face. "I think I'd like to go for a walk."

"I'll come with you," Brite offered.

Annie shook her head. "No. I think I need to be alone."

Gingerly, Annie pulled on her jacket, turned on her flashlight, and left the cottage.

Her flashlight lit up Jorvik as she followed the narrow streets packed with buildings for business and homes. She passed a blacksmith's forge and followed the road to the stables and beyond.

She wandered aimlessly, eventually reaching the longhouse. She stood at the door and touched the carvings. Immediately, Annie saw the new one that had been created. She touched the girl that looked like her before holding the door handle. She wanted to see Gibbs, to touch his hand, to talk to him. She shuddered and turned away, unable to bear his loss, and walked on.

At the edge of Jorvik, Annie found herself staring at an empty cottage. The door was open and gently swung in the breeze. She looked inside. It was clearly a family home, and yet it looked as though it had been recently abandoned. She stepped inside.

Uneaten food lay on the plates on the table and a pot rested in the now-cold coals. Annie ran her fingers across the table, touched the edge of the plate, and looked inside the cup of mead.

They must have run off in the last attack and never came back.

Annie shuddered and opened the chest at the foot of the bed. Inside were linens, thick woolen blankets and extra pillows, a new dress, a pair of pants. She gently closed the lid and sat at one of the four chairs at the table.

"They may have died," she murmured.

Annie stared at her engagement ring. It was mostly intact, even after Everard had crushed her hands.

It needs a good cleaning.

Butterflies filled her belly when she thought of Cham. He had been in her life since they had first met at Parents Weekend during their siblings' first year at Windmere School of Wizardry. That day had forever changed her life. Through all the good and bad, she'd always had him.

Annie itched with magical energy. It made her restless, so she took to strolling the small cottage. The rain that she'd thought would be ending soon began to pound against the thatched roof and dripped on her head. She moved to the window as lightning struck, bringing with it a soft roll of thunder and a familiar scent.

"Hi, Dad," she said out loud.

"You did it."

The disembodied voice was so familiar to her, she thought she had imagined it. She twirled around and jumped when she saw her father standing there.

"Dad?"

A shimmering white shadow in the shape of Jason Pearce stood in front of her. His face was clear and crisp as if she were staring at a picture of him.

I could be dreaming.

She took a breath. His cologne overpowered her.

"I'm here. But only for a short time. It's not over yet," he said to her.

"I still have to get home."

"With those powers overtaking you," he reminded her.

Annie chuckled and shook her head. "I don't want them. Can we talk about something else?"

Jason laughed just like she remembered, low and jolly. Her heart tugged.

"You'll need those powers to bring down the Fraternitatem. Accept them," Jason said.

Annie observed him. She hadn't thought about that, about her mom or about the Fraternitatem and how they related to the powers. She changed the subject. "Are you okay, Dad? Are you in a good place?"

The white mist that took on his form moved closer to her. "It doesn't work that way. I don't actually remember where I was before coming here. That's beside the point though," he said, sounding a little confused.

"So I'm dreaming you," she said.

"You summoned me."

Annie frowned. "Not on purpose."

"So, what powers do you have?" Jason asked.

Annie shrugged. "All I know is, I'm terribly itchy and a little nauseated." As much as she wished she could remove the powers, the thought of the Fraternitatem made her realize the extra magical boost would help. She clenched her fist and looked at her hand. Golden magic pulsed from her fist.

"You'll learn what you have and you'll master them. That's your way." The Jason-shaped mist stood beside her. "Did he hurt you badly?" He reached for Annie but, as an apparition, he couldn't touch her. He was close, and she could feel the ghost chill as his hand tried to touch her cheek.

She glanced down at the dirt floor and kicked a leaf with the toe of her boot. She glanced outside and wrung her hands before sighing.

"What do you want to ask me?" Jason asked.

Annie shook from the chill, from the momentous task before her.

She didn't know if she really wanted to know. She sighed deeply. "Is Mom still alive?"

"You found the file." He smiled proudly.

"Sami's good," Annie said.

"I do know this. And yes, Mom is alive. She traded her life for yours."

"I know. She shouldn't have done that."

Jason looked out the window. "I wish I could touch that rain," he said.

Annie opened the window without her magic, letting the rain fall against the window sill. Jason put his hand out into the night air, but the rain fell through his mist.

Annie moved instinctively and waved her hand across his back. He shimmered away and she groaned lightly; it wasn't what she expected or wanted. She enjoyed talking to him even though he wasn't really there.

But within seconds, he began to reappear, fully corporeal. Annie jumped at the sight of the fully human man beside her.

He glanced at his arm, flexed his fist and stuck it out the window. He sniffed the wet earth. "Could you have done that prior to receiving the powers?" he asked. When his arm was good and drenched, he brought it inside and shook off the water. Fully dry, he placed his arm around Annie.

"I never tried before. I don't know." Annie leaned into her father and took a deep breath, taking in his scent to always remember long after she returned home.

"She'll be coming for you," Jason began. "Just remember she's not the mom who left. She's different."

Annie wrapped her arms around her father's waist and lay her head on his chest, like she used to do when she was younger.

"I'll be careful." She held her breath to keep the tears from falling.

"No. You'll hit them first. As soon as you return. If it comes to it, kill her. Protect yourself." Jason Pearce held his daughter tightly.

She nodded against his chest and let the tears fall. He rubbed her back and kissed her forehead.

When the tears stopped, she wiped them from her cheeks and pulled away. "I'll deal with it when I have to. For now, I want to pretend that you're real and not going away."

"I'm always with you." Jason kissed the top of her head, and together they stared out the window and watched the rain fall until the sun came up.

✍

Annie entered the cottage just as Brite and Zola finished packing all three backpacks. Gibbs's bag looked lonely on the table.

"You were out all night. Did you clear your head?" Brite asked.

Annie nodded and absently scratched her arm. Magic billowed from her hand.

"Did it ease any when you shot the spell?" Zola pointed at the shutters that lay in splinters.

"I don't know." She looked at her palms and tossed a spell into the firebox. Magic burst from her hands and ignited the remaining wood inside. She made note of the itching. The magic was still there, still coursing through her. "Maybe a little."

Shaky, Annie sat on the bed, pulled her legs to her chest, and wrapped her arms around them. Laying her head on her knees, she watched them finish clearing the table and tossing the remains in the roaring fire.

"They're ready. We'll join them when you're ready." Brite told her.

Still hugging her legs, she said, "I found myself in a cottage. My dad appeared to me. First, he was ghostlike. I could speak to him and he spoke to me." Annie stopped for a moment.

"A dream?" Brite asked.

"No, I was awake. I felt the chill off of him."

Brite sat beside her. "What did he say?"

"Besides making me promise to kill my mom when she comes after me?" Annie tried to smile, but her stomach flipped.

"The Fraternitatem are definitely coming, then?" Brite asked.

Annie nodded. "It was confirmation of something I pretty much could guess. I acted as if I knew what I was doing. I waved my hand across his back and I made him corporeal."

Brite's lips twisted in concern. "You sure it wasn't a dream?"

"It was very vivid, if it was." She still smelled her father's scent on her clothing. "Smell this," she said.

Brite frowned, and yet he did as she asked because he believed her no matter how odd it sounded. "I smell cologne. Could you always do that?" he asked.

Annie shrugged. "Never had a need to turn a ghost corporeal." She turned to Zola.

"You aren't meant for these powers. Be careful while they attempt to possess you." Zola stood. "It's time to send you home."

CHAPTER 33

ANNIE STARED AT Gibbs. He was attached to a board, tied down to keep him from moving as they jumped through the portal. She pulled back the blanket and stared at his pockmarked face with its large scar across his cheek to his chin. She removed a piece of hair that kept falling across his face and tucked it behind his ear. His cold skin unnerved her.

"Kolgaar gave the coven the location where we fell through the portal. We'll reverse the magic and go back to where we came."

Annie raised an eyebrow.

"At least in theory," Brite added.

"He has no family," she murmured.

"He had you. He came here for you."

Annie wiped tears away. "He was like that grumpy old uncle who'd slip you a vampire stake under the table and take you to a vampire fight behind your parent's back."

Brite chuckled. "Your dad must have loved that."

Annie shrugged. "Dad... Dad did that kinda stuff too. It's just, Gibbs did it after Dad died. It always pissed off Kathy, though. Ryan understood it and eventually Kathy backed down." Annie straightened the blanket. "He wanted me to be safe. He wanted me to know stuff. You know?" She looked at Brite.

He nodded and put an arm around her. "Let's go home."

Annie placed the blanket over Gibbs's face and let Brite lead her from the longhouse. Kolgaar and Svenson picked up the board and carried Gibbs after them.

Waiting for them at the entrance, they found Zola, Etheldreda, Bega, King Hrothgar, and Princess Gyda. Annie did not see Sturtagaard.

Am I really surprised?

"Where's your brother?" Annie asked Kolgaar.

"I do not know. Astrid died last night. No one has seen him since."

"I'm sorry for your loss," Annie said as she scanned the village for anyone lurking behind a house, a cart, a barrel. She saw nothing of note, and yet her anxiety rose.

"Are you ready?" Brite asked.

"Sturtagaard's gone," she said.

Brite glanced through the streets, uneasy. "We need to go," he said and held Annie's upper arm as he led her to Gibbs. "We need to leave now."

His tone startled Etheldreda. She nodded quickly.

Svenson reached for Annie. "Thank you," he said and stepped back. Gyda ran at Annie and placed her arms around her neck. "You saved my life. Thank you." The king stayed back and nodded with a sad smile, then led his daughter from the group and back into the longhouse.

Brite and Zola held Annie as Etheldreda, Bega, and Kolgaar held onto the board that carried Gibbs. Just before she was teleported away, Annie saw him. It was just a second, a small moment in time, when Sturtagaard peered around the nearest cottage. Because Annie was searching for him, only she saw him. He offered her that familiar jeer, cold with fury and anger towards her. She shuddered because it wouldn't be long before he was turned, when he would become consumed by blood lust. For now, his skin was pink with life and his eyes hadn't taken on that blackness she would come to know. There was no more time to worry about the future vampire as Brite and Zola teleported her away.

∽

Kolgaar directed them to the magical energy of the portal that carried them to the past, down the narrow road that ran north and south through England. Annie recognized the location, the tall grasses, the landing spot where she had found Gibbs.

That was four days ago!

Annie looked to the south, down a lonely, empty road that they had not been able to explore. She glanced north, where they had walked up the long hill and into the valley where the Cath Palug still roamed the earth, and toward the medieval home that kept them safe and sheltered for the night.

I won't miss this.

"How'll you get him through?" Annie asked Brite. She looked at Gibbs under the blanket with such sadness, she thought her heart would break.

"I'll levitate him through," Brite said. "You look nervous."

As she watched Bega levitate in the air with a crystal to summon the portal's magical energy, Annie thought back to the dream she'd had while in England, the one in which she couldn't return through the portal because the power racing through her was too strong.

Annie knew the future coven hoped she would die here, or at the very least, be trapped in the past where the magic couldn't harm them.

I'm not going to make it through the portal!

Bega siphoned the portal magic and levitated back down to the ground.

"I'm scared," Annie whispered to Brite. Her limbs itched. She balled her hands in tight fists as she refrained from scratching her already raw skin. The magic billowed from her palms and circled around her fists, up her arms, and around her face. She tried to wave it off; it shimmered instead.

"Why?" Brite looked at her.

"I'm… I don't think I'm going to make it through the portal," she said.

"You don't know that," Brite said. "Let's get it up and ready, and we'll see. And we'll figure it out."

Annie sighed and slipped the talisman from her pocket. Kolgaar took out his and they handed the pair to Etheldreda. It would be the last time Annie could communicate with them. It left her feeling naked, vulnerable and very much alone. She watched expectantly as Etheldreda placed the talismans three feet apart, with the crystal at the center. Bega waved her palm over the crystal and chanted the spell, which they no longer understood.

The portal sprung forth. Wind blew strongly, like a tornado blowing around them. Lightning struck as the portal became active. As in Annie's dream, she took a step closer to peer inside. She reached out as if she were going to touch it.

Just like in her dream, the portal sped up and vibrated wildly as she came closer. Lightning struck in quick succession, striking the ground at Annie's feet. Scorch marks covered the dirt.

Kolgaar spoke, his words incomprehensible without the translation powers of the talismans. Annie shook her head and took several steps back. The portal slowed, the lightning shrunk in size and force, and the wind decelerated.

She looked at Zola. "I had a dream about this."

"The power's too strong. I feared this might happen," Zola said.

"This is what the coven wanted. They must have known I'd be stuck here if they didn't give me all of the information." Annie glanced at Gibbs. "You have to take him home," she said.

"No. Not yet. There has to be a way to get you back," Brite said.

Kolgaar spoke rapidly to Etheldreda and Bega as they watched anxiously, unable to offer assistance.

Annie took a step forward to study the portal. Again, it grew unsteady. She stepped back again. Etheldreda spoke, but Annie had no idea what she said and shook her head again. The woman looked at Zola.

"I can't translate for them," Zola said.

Annie felt the necklace around her neck and thought of what Zola told her in the future about not sharing. "You were supposed to find a spell or potion to remove the magic without killing me. You couldn't do it. But you did know what happened here and now. How would you tell yourself what you needed to know?" Annie asked.

"I… I'm not sure."

"Zola, think. You gave her a protection charm to keep her safe and to find you. Figure it out!" Brite shouted.

Anxiously, Annie gave in to the itching and began scratch her torso, her legs, her arms. "I can't take it anymore."

Etheldreda and Kolgaar spoke, knowing they were not understood. Bega watched them, then returned to the portal, her tongue sticking out from her mouth while she thought.

"The charm. I had to leave a clue in the charm," Zola said. Annie whipped it off of her neck and handed it to Zola.

Bega watched as if she understood what was happening. "Everard," she said.

Zola, Annie, and Brite looked at her.

"Everard? What about him?" Annie asked Bega, but they had no way of fully communicating without the talismans.

Bega crossed her arms across her chest and held her own shoulders, making eye contact with Annie.

"What, Bega?" Annie asked.

"Everard," Bega said again, repeating the gesture.

Annie glanced at Brite. "Brite?"

"We bound his powers," Brite said.

Annie looked at Zola.

"No. That leaves you vulnerable," Zola said.

"But that will get me home?"

Zola looked at the charm close up. She found a latch on the back of the charm, so small, it wasn't surprising they had missed it. She popped it open. Inside was a vial so small, she had to levitate it from the hiding spot. It fell to her palm.

Bega placed a hand on Annie's arm. It was cool to the touch, comforting. She nodded toward the vial.

Zola handed Annie the vial. She summoned the stopper and drank down several small drops of clear liquid.

The effect was immediate. The itching stopped as warmth spread across her limbs and torso. Zola placed the protection amulet around Annie's neck.

"I will be there when you arrive to unbind the powers. Take care, my brave girl." Zola kissed her cheek.

Annie walked to the portal and reached for it once again. This time, she didn't appear to cause any ill effect. "I guess we're good," she said.

Bega came to Annie, placed her arms around her. "Anaise," she began, but that was the only thing Annie understood.

Annie pulled away and turned to Etheldreda, fully aware she was glad to be rid of her. Etheldreda placed a gnarled hand on Annie's cheek. "Anaise," she said before stepping back again.

Annie met Zola's glance. Her eyes were moist and grayish green filled with sadness. Annie ran to her.

"I love you. No matter when or where." Zola kissed her cheek. "Be safe, my dear girl."

Annie wiped away a tear. Her last goodbye was the reluctant Kolgaar. She gave him a hug and offered a smile. He returned one with his own.

Brite levitated Gibbs, and he and Annie each grabbed an end of the board he was attached to. As Brite stepped through the portal, the force of it dragged Annie and Gibbs after him. Annie held on tightly as the portal took them back to the future.

⌘

Annie lay with her face in the grass. She moved her hands and wiggled her feet. When she opened her eyes, she saw that it was night. The moon was full, the air warm and dry.

"Are we home?" Brite asked.

She pulled herself up and scanned their location; they were not in the forest beside the house in Evanston. Annie glanced across the location. It was a desolate landscape, with dried grass at their feet and a sparse clump of trees beside them.

"I'm not sure where we are," Annie admitted.

"I wonder if we're even in the correct year," Brite said. He pulled himself up and wandered away from their landing spot.

Annie stood gingerly and found Gibbs several feet from her. While he was still strapped to the board, face up, the blanket had been lost in the trip through the portal. "We need to find the blanket. It's from the ninth century," she said.

Brite ran his flashlight across the bushes and found the single tree beside them where the blanket had been caught. He summoned it. "It looks like we're in the bird sanctuary," he said.

Annie scanned the desolate landscape. Tartarus Prison had been built on a magical island and was surrounded by a bird sanctuary. With the help of strong magic, nonmagicals rarely ever ventured to the tiny island, and if they did, the magic around the borders always seemed to make them leave immediately.

Annie twirled to look around. "I've never been to this side of the island," she said. She summoned her phone. She was aware how useless it had been to bring it with her, but it had comforted her knowing she had it. She switched the phone on and waited for it to load.

"Why would I expect we'd land where we started?" Brite asked rhetorically. He found a trail and stood on the narrow path. Sure enough, Tartarus Prison and its depressing surroundings sprawled across the landscape.

Annie's phone booted up. The screen from the carrier lit the small clearing.

"How do you feel?" Brite asked as her phone finally beeped.

"Like I need a shower." She glanced at her phone. "Damn. We left this morning," Annie said and handed him her phone.

"No shit? I could never get used to that. Tartarus is that way," he chuckled, pointing.

"Let's get Gibbs to the hospital." She wiped sweat from her forehead with shaky hands.

"You look like hell," he said.

Annie grunted as she grabbed an end of the board. "Not now. Let's just go," she said.

Brite took hold of his end and teleported them to Wizard Hall, landing just outside the front doors of the wizard hospital. Dizziness gripped Annie. As much as she didn't want to drop Gibbs, the board slipped from her fingers as she slid to her knees.

"Annie!" Brite screamed. He ran for the front door of the hospital. "Help! We need a doctor! I need a doctor now!"

Emergency room staff ran outside; they instantly recognized Brite and Annie, who had both been patients on several occasions.

"Michael! Bloody hell, Annie!" said the night nurse, Maisy Burke. She ran for Annie. "What's the matter with her?" she asked.

"We had to bind her powers to get back through the portal. The extra magic is affecting her." Several orderlies brought out wheelchairs for Brite and Annie and a stretcher for Gibbs. As they attended to Gibbs, Brite said, "No. He's… he died in the past. Please take him to the morgue and let Milo Rawley of the Wizard Guard know." He watched, devastated, as Gibbs was gently loaded to the stretcher and pulled away to the morgue.

"Get them inside. Call Dr. Andrews. Now!" barked Maisy Burke as she settled Annie in the chair. Annie couldn't watch them leave with Gibbs; she turned her head and cried.

Brite refused the wheelchair and followed after, his fingers typing on his phone: *Come now! We're at the hospital.*

CHAPTER 34

THE HOSPITAL BED *was warm, and hard; she opened her eyes. Jason Pearce sat by the bed and watched her sleep.*

"Hi, Dad," she said.

"You need to rest. Those powers are strong inside of you." He smiled and pulled the blankets up to Annie's chin.

"I'm not five anymore," she said.

"Give me a break. I haven't cared for you in eight years." He touched her forehead. "You're burning up."

"Meaning?"

"Your body can't handle the extra magic. Your powers are still bound."

"Yeah. They did that to get me through the portal." She looked at her father. "That could be a problem."

"All of those demons and vampires and evil wizards would love to know you're defenseless. But I'm still here. They'll have to get through me to get to you," Jason said.

Annie pushed herself up and sat against the hospital bed. "I don't recognize this room." She saw a woman at a table in the corner. Familiar red hair, creamy skin, petite and pretty. "Why's Mom here?"

"It's your dream, you tell me," Jason said.

"I'm worried because I don't know where she is so I keep her close with me?" Annie asked.

"Maybe. I worry that she's on her way to you."

"When are you leaving?" She observed her dad. He hadn't aged in eight

years. He still appeared youngish, no gray hair or lines on his forehead. He looked well and relaxed.

"You're returning to the present and dealing with the extra powers, plus this part of the world is currently a little nutty with the weather. I'll be here, at least until you're safe."

Annie looked out the window of her hospital room. It was a deluge of water as lighting flashed and the thunder rattled the windows.

"And her?" Annie pointed to the representative of her mother. The woman hadn't looked at them, just continued packing medical supplies in a box.

"On one hand, she's still your mother. She once loved you. So much so, she left to protect you. It was misguided, but that's what she did." He took Annie's hands in his own, which were strong and warm and protective. "Don't trust her. She's been with them for nearly twenty-one years. We don't know what they've told her about you or what she's planning to do to you. I suspect they've brainwashed her and they know you have these powers. They'll come after you through her." Jason Pearce looked at his youngest daughter. "I'm always with you. And you will know how to call when you need me."

Reluctantly, he stood from his chair and kissed Annie on the forehead. "I love you." He backed away, still looking at her.

Brite hugged the wall as Dr. Christine Andrews ran from the second floor into Annie's room. Her stethoscope bounced rapidly as she entered, she glanced at Annie quickly and back to Brite. He had resisted medical assistance and insisted on remaining by Annie's side. In the three minutes it took for Dr. Christine to reach the ER, Annie had slipped into unconsciousness.

"What the hell happened?" Dr. Christine asked. She opened Annie's eyelids, but Annie was unresponsive.

"The immediate issue is that we bound her powers to get her through the portal. Zola should be here with the potion soon," Brite said, just above a whisper. He glanced down the hallway.

"Annie! Annie!" Dr. Christine shouted. She checked Annie's pulse, listened to her heart. "Why are the bound powers rendering her unconscious?" she asked him. She wiped sweat from Annie's forehead and temples. "She's heating up! What happened? You were gone for a day!"

"Zola should be here…" Brite began but was interrupted by a stampede of Annie's family.

As expected, they had all arrived, their voices loud as they ran from the waiting room. While Cham, Samantha, Ryan, and Kathy ran down the hallway, Zola, normally graceful and docile, pushed her way ahead of them and handed Dr. Christine a vial. "Here. I would've been here sooner but I didn't feel her arrive," she said as she looked down on Annie, lying small and battered on the bed.

"Oh, hell," Cham said as he entered the room. He began to shake at the sight of Annie lying unconscious.

Dr. Christine unstoppered the potion, opened Annie's jaw, and dropped in the liquid, coaxing it down Annie's throat.

"What powers did she receive?" Dr. Christine asked as she examined Annie's eyes again.

"We don't know the extent of it. We know it's powerful though," Brite said. He leaned against the back of the wheelchair and closed his eyes. "Be prepared when the magic comes back."

As the magic unbound, Annie's body jerked and bounced on the bed. Her eyes flew open; they were wild and frightened as she scanned the room. She seemed confused by the bright lights and the faces watching her.

"Annie. Annie, look at me." Dr. Christine said. She forced Annie to focus on her face. "You're home. You're safe. Your powers are coming back. Do you understand me?"

Annie focused on the doctor. Panic over took her and she cried out. Dr. Christine waved Cham inside. He sat beside Annie and took her hand.

"Oh, man," he murmured as he looked at her. Four days of rain and dirt covered her hair and face, her ring was dirty, her hands swollen and stiff. "Hi, babe," he said as he pecked her lips. He touched her hair. He looked at Brite.

"I'm sorry," Brite murmured.

Annie groaned as she began scratching at her arm. "It's back," she shrieked. "I can't make it stop!" She held her hands to her temples. "Make it stop!"

"What's happening?" Cham looked at Brite.

"As soon as the magic came in, she began itching. We need a potion or something on her skin. She's rubbing it raw."

"It stopped itching when you bound the power?" Dr. Christine asked.

"Yeah. But binding the power was making her sick. That's why she fell unconscious," Brite said.

Dr. Christine touched Annie's moist forehead. "The fever's down considerably." She looked at her patient. "I can give her something for the pain. I don't know what to do for the magic."

Zola waved Cham away and sat beside Annie. "Hello, my brave girl."

"Did you figure it out?" Annie asked. She closed her eyes; the light of the ER was the brightest she's seen in days.

"There is no way to remove the magic," Zola said.

Annie grimaced, disappointed. Magic billowed from her palms. She reached for her chest and scratched.

Zola held her hands. "You did change the future."

Annie looked at her through squinted eyes. "How? You can't remove the magic and Gibbs is…"

Zola looked at the expectant faces, appearing hesitant to reveal what she knew. But then she looked back at Annie, there and alive. She touched her cheek. "My dear girl. I told you in the past that lifelines are fluid. They change continually. When I learned you would be my charge, your lifeline was long and strong." Zola stopped and met Annie's look.

"When did it change?" Annie asked.

"After you left for home through the portal in the past, it shortened. Then again, quite severely, around the time the Fraternitatem learned of the prophecy. And even shorter when Emily disappeared. The coven made it so; they believed you needed to die in the past or not get back home. But you changed your future when you were there. Do you remember when?" Zola asked her.

Annie searched Zola's face, hoping it would reveal what Zola was trying to explain. She shook her head.

"You were not supposed to tell me anything unless it pertained to the demons. You didn't heed to that and gave me enough information to protect you. I sent you back with the protection spell and your way to get home because you told me too much."

"Gibbs died instead," Annie said.

Shocked, Kathy held her hand to her mouth and Ryan sat down hard in the chair.

Cham looked at Brite. "How?" he asked.

Brite shook his head; there would be time later.

"He did. But he went there to protect you and he did what he set out to do: keep you alive and bring you home." Zola offered a smile, but it did little to comfort Annie.

"You told him," Annie said.

"Yes. I had eleven hundred years to figure out how to help you. I told him. He would have gone with you even if I hadn't."

Annie didn't hold back the tears. It was too overwhelming knowing she was responsible for Gibbs's death.

"It will get easier. But in the meantime, I can stem the flow of magic, so it won't affect you as badly." Zola held her hands to Annie's head and let her fairy magic envelope her in warmth and light.

Annie's breathing slowed and evened out. She closed her eyes as Zola kept a light stream of magic flowing through her.

When Zola finished she asked, "Your head?"

"It's better. I still itch though," Annie said.

"It will still itch, just not as strongly." Zola turned to Dr. Christine. "I suggest you give her a sleeping draught for the night. She and Brite have barely slept in four days." Zola smiled. Her eyes were green and sparkled in the harsh light of the ER—her charge was home.

She stood and walked from the bed, letting the medics and doctors continue stabilizing Annie. When they finished, Annie and Brite were admitted to the hospital for their first good sleep in a week.

⚜

The shower Annie had before climbing into bed was the single greatest moment of her life. As mud and dirt flowed down the drain, she felt her muscles relax. She climbed from the shower, put on dry clothing, and climbed into bed. Between the heated blankets and sleeping draught, Annie didn't open her eyes again until nine the next morning.

"Hey, sweetie," Kathy said when Annie woke up.

Kathy had stayed the night watching over her, no one in the hospital could have dragged her away. Cham hadn't left Annie's side either; he still held her hand, now naked of her engagement ring because her hand had swelled up to twice its size. As sleep left her, she made a fist. Her fingers were stiff and swollen.

"They'll continue healing you when you're stronger. Zola said she could only do so much before you came back home. You expended too much magical energy," Cham told her.

Annie didn't want to think of her last hours in Jorvik; it was much too painful to remember. While they offered some healing, she just couldn't bear the pain of it and was suffering the consequences with painful, stiff hands now. She pulled her hand from Cham and held it in her other.

"When is Gibbs's funeral?" Annie asked as she rubbed her fingers.

"When you and Brite are released," Kathy said. She touched Annie's forehead.

Annie fumbled with the bed controls until she was sitting upright and could examine her darkened hospital room. She pulled the blankets to her chin as she shivered. "Where is everyone?"

"Brite is in his room with his parents and Shiff. Sami and Ryan went for food," Cham said.

"Dad was there with me in Jorvik," Annie said.

"He's always with you," Kathy said.

She shook her head. "No. Not like that fake stuff we say. Every time I heard the thunder, I smelled his cologne. He... I hate this bed." Annie fiddled with the controls again. She was uncomfortable in the hospital gown and the mattress was lumpy. She would have said it was more comfortable than the beds in the past, but all she wanted was her own. Finding a spot, she looked at Kathy. "He was there. I saw his ghost. He was translucent white and I smelled that cologne he always wore." She smiled at the memory. "He spoke to me. It was his laugh." She debated for a moment if she should tell them more.

"Are you sure it wasn't a dream?" Kathy asked, cautiously.

"It wasn't a dream," Annie said.

Cham rubbed her palm with his thumb. "What did Jason say?"

"It's not so much what he said. It's what I did." Kathy and Cham glanced at her anxiously. "It's like I knew what to do. I don't know how, but I waved my hand across his back, he disappeared and then he… reappeared in a corporeal form."

Kathy and Cham looked at her curiously. "You didn't sleep well. You were tired. Are you sure it wasn't a dream?" Cham asked.

"It wasn't." She pulled her legs up and hugged them.

Now that Annie was fully awake, the itch returned to her body as new powers attempted to take hold of her. She gave in to the urge to scratch, continuing when Ryan and Samantha entered.

"The power is moving again?" Ryan asked. He placed a bag of food on the hospital table.

Annie lay against the propped up pillow and closed her eyes. She caught a whiff of Jason's cologne. "Yeah. I think it will be like this for a while."

"Annie saw Jason in the past," Kathy said.

"It wasn't a dream," Annie said.

"Okay?" Ryan said.

"Is Mom alive?" Samantha asked.

Annie glanced at her sister and chuckled. "Yes. He warned me to be wary of her. He's here now actually. I can smell his cologne." Annie sniffed the air and thought she could feel his arm around her shoulder. She touched the spot to be sure and remembered the empty cottage, touching him, resting her head against his chest. It filled her with emotions she hadn't expected. She wiped the tears away with her sleeve.

"I smell him too," Samantha murmured. Annie nodded.

"Did he say anything else?" Ryan asked.

It's too soon to discuss this.

"She's coming for the power." Annie scratched her left arm. "I feel it crawling under my skin." Her voice rose a few octaves. She rubbed her legs.

Dr. Christine entered the room. "Good morning, Annie. I think everyone needs to leave so we can do a little more healing. Okay?"

Annie nodded and watched them reluctantly leave as she let Dr. Christine heal her broken body.

᥍

They stuffed themselves into the waiting room as Annie was being healed. Cham paced along the front wall; his mother, Marina Chamsky, attempted to soothe him with a touch to his shoulder, but he shrugged her off. Dejected, she joined his father, Don Chamsky, sitting beside Ryan, Kathy, and Zola.

Along the back wall, Samantha sat quietly with her husband John, Cham's older brother. Their combined hushed tones bugged Cham. He paced and stopped, then paced again, wishing he could be inside Annie's room with her. He leaned against the wall, stared at his phone, and waited.

Cham's younger brother, Danny, a medical student, exited her room.

"Hey," Danny said.

"How is she?" Cham asked.

"Restless. She still has a high fever. They think blocking the powers and having them rush back is causing her body to reject them." Danny turned back and looked at something of interest in the room.

"What's wrong?" Cham asked.

"It's... the magic is really, really powerful."

Dr. Christine had been working between Brite's room and Annie's room all night. She was tired and pale as she exited Annie's room and found Ryan and Kathy.

"What happened?" Ryan asked.

"Annie's not great, but she'll eventually be fine. It'll take time for her to acclimate to the magic. The magic." Dr. Christine laughed. "Oh, the magic. She holds up her hand and magic flies out, busts the cabinets. Electronics go blank, buzz, and flicker."

"So, what does that mean?" Cham asked.

"There's more." Dr. Christine glanced at Danny. "She's feeling a bit of discomfort with the hospital and the bed. She's exhausted and weak, but she... Oh, hell. I need to show you something." Dr. Christine returned to the room and brought out a man.

Kathy, Ryan, and Samantha looked at him. Their eyes grew wide, Samantha cried out. Marina Chamsky said, "Oh my."

Jason Pearce, dead eight years, stood before his former colleagues, his friends, and his family, not as a misty ghost but as a corporeal man, pink with health.

"Dad!" Samantha rushed forward and wrapped her arms around her father. "You're here. Why? How?"

Gently, Ryan pulled Samantha from Jason. "Where did you come from?" Ryan asked. Once a wizard guard, always a wizard guard; he summoned his crystal and maneuvered it over his dead best friend.

The magic surrounding Jason Pearce was a bright, white light; he had been conjured with good magic. Ryan tossed the crystal to Cham who glanced inside, reading the magic. He drew in a breath and sent a text.

"Dad?"

"Sami, not yet." Ryan warned.

"It's okay, Sami. I'm not sure how she did it, but Annie summoned me." He beamed proudly.

"But you're corporeal," Ryan said incredulously as he poked Jason in the chest.

Jason chuckled. "She made me corporeal in England. Just waved her hand and poof. And now I'm here."

"You're supposed to be dead," Ryan said.

Milo entered the waiting room, having come from the morgue. He stared at Jason standing there, alive and well, warm and healthy.

"It's really me," Jason said to Milo when he joined them.

Cham handed him the crystal. Milo stared at the magic in awe.

"Annie did this?" Milo asked.

"Yes," Cham said.

"As stunned and happy as I am to see you, you shouldn't be here. It's messing with the natural order of things. This magic..." Milo started to say.

"Annie's in trouble. Subconsciously, I think she knows this. I'm here to protect my girls," Jason said. "So, how do we do that?"

"You're dead, Jason. It's been eight years." Milo ran his hands across his stubbly chin. He was supposed to retire completely when Annie, Brite, and Gibbs returned. But it all went wrong when they came back; Gibbs was dead, Annie had magic coursing through her that could kill her, and now Jason was back from the dead.

"I'm here, though," Jason said.

"Besides bringing you back, we don't know yet what she might have changed. If anything, the changes might be subtle and we won't know it right away." Milo frowned. "I'm not sure what your presence here will do to the magical energy around us."

"I'm dead, so technically, I'm just taking up space." Jason waved his hand through the air attempting magic. "I can't perform magic. I'm not taking from the magical energy."

"You're here because of magic. You are inherently magic. You'll be a drain on the magical energy wherever you go," Milo said. Still in ill health, his hands shook as he pointed to Jason.

"You can't send him away," Samantha said. "He's here. He can help Annie with the Fraternitatem."

"If this is all she changed, we can control this. But if there's a magical shift, we send him away," Cham said. He looked at Samantha, nearly jumping out of her skin at the sight of her newly reconstituted father. But he knew Milo was right. Jason shouldn't be here.

"We keep him out of sight," Milo insisted. "He can't go home; his neighbors can't know he's here. I say you can stay at the hotel across the way. It gives you access to the entire Wizard Hall. But that's it."

"No. He can come home with me," Samantha said.

"He's better away from the wizard community. If this gets out to the Fraternitatem, any use he is to protect Annie and Sami will be lost," Cham said.

"Hey. I'm here. I can speak for myself," Jason said.

They all looked at him. Milo asked, "Fine. What's your thought?"

"I want to go home. I can stay hidden. I don't want to leave Annie. Her magic can protect me. And I agree with Cham. We can't let the Fraternitatem know I'm back."

"We keep this mum," Milo said to the Chamskys and to the hospital staff. He turned back to Jason. "If this gets out, if you cause trouble, if your presence endangers the magical order, I will send you back to wherever you came from. Do I make myself clear?" he asked, as if Jason were responsible for his own presence.

"I'll do whatever you say." Jason looked at Samantha and waved her over. She looked at Cham as if asking for permission. Cham nodded.

Samantha touched her father's cheek and wrapped her arms around him, laying her head on his shoulder.

"I missed you, Dad."

"My sweet girl."

Cham glanced at Ryan and Milo. None of them felt good about this.

CHAPTER 35

BRITE WAS RELEASED in the morning after a shower, food, and a good night's sleep. Annie fitfully slept the day after returning. After receiving hydration and medical care, she was released from the hospital a day after Brite and placed on medical leave.

She stood in front of her full-length bedroom mirror and looked at herself in her black dress. She smoothed the fabric and held her hands in tight fists as she held back tears. For the moment, she pushed those feelings away and brushed her teeth, applied her makeup, and held her brush loosely in her hand. While the bones had healed, both hands were stiff and swollen. She sighed as she struggled to tidy her tangled mess of hair.

"Need help?" Kathy asked.

"Maybe put it up. I don't think it matters much," Annie said.

She let Kathy gather her hair into a ponytail and brush it smooth. "You okay?" Kathy asked.

"I still can't believe Gibbs is dead," Annie said.

"I know. I thought he'd outlast us all, that stubborn ass," Kathy said.

Annie laughed at the perfect description of him. "I need to pick someone up and bring them to the funeral. I'll meet you there, okay?" she asked.

Kathy nodded as Annie left.

There were very few nonmagicals who knew of the existence of magic. It was a tightly kept secret, one that was protected at all costs, unless something happened that caused a nonmagical to know. In Jason's case it was Emily Worthington, a young nonmagical he couldn't help but fall in love with. In Annie's case, it was FBI Special Agent Jack Ramsey. An unexpected meeting had led to the investigation into the death of the nonmagical Princess Amelie. Because of that, Jack would forever be linked to the magical world, whether he wanted to or not.

He said nothing when Annie met him in their usual location, a parking lot in an abandoned industrial park.

"You okay?" Jack asked when he saw her.

"Everyone keeps asking me that. Like I tell everyone, I lost someone very important to me. I'm not okay yet," she said softly as she held onto Jack and teleported him to Wizard Hall.

It was another experience Jack had an opportunity to view: a wizard funeral. He had worked with Gibbs and Gibbs had tolerated him. Jack had been honored when Annie asked him to attend Gibbs's funeral. Like Brite, Jack had told Annie that John Gibbs deserved a better death than at the hands of a lunatic in another time.

Jack walked to Spencer, who stood with his wife, Melinda. His face was blank, stunned.

"Hi, Spencer. I'm sorry for your loss," Jack said. It seemed like a feeble thing to say, but Spencer had been Gibbs's partner for years and just being there was something.

"Thanks," Spencer said as he hugged Jack. "It's a little surreal that he's gone."

"I wouldn't have expected it. I know you two were close." Jack touched Spencer's shoulder and moved on, finding an empty spot in the back. "I'll stay here," he said to Annie.

"Find me after," she said and took a place near Cham at the front.

The funeral pyre was a four-foot-high wooden platform with Gibbs lying on top. He wore a simple black cotton cloak; he wouldn't have wanted anything more. The edges of the cloak had long tails that wrapped around posts at each corner. The posts stood eight feet high, leading to a canopy of ferns that spiraled downward, wrapping around the posts.

Annie scanned the crowds. The entire Wizard Guard from all five offices stood around the pyre. She saw the teams from telecommunications department, including Bucky Hart and Max White, the VAU department with Graham Lightner, the morgue and Perkins Abernathy, and Mrs.

Cuttlebrink from the library. Even a large contingent from the Wizard Council were jammed into the courtyard of Wizard Hall.

Gibbs had no living family and had never been married, but he had a wide circle of coworkers and acquaintances. Annie spotted so many people she hadn't seen in a while. Even Arrowhead, a former merchant at the Black Market, was there. He spotted Annie and nodded before returning his gaze to the pyre.

For all of his gruffness and his apparent lack of warmth, Gibbs was, if not well liked, well respected. It showed at the ceremony. Even members of the hospital staff were present, many of whom had worked on all of the guards at one time or another.

It didn't offer Annie solace, as she, Ryan, Milo, and Spencer picked up a torch to light the barrels of fire surrounding the pyre. Each of them held their torch as the wizard priest chanted ancient words that Annie paid little attention to. She focused on the flames, and when it was time, she and the others lit their corners of the pyre, watching the fire take hold of the wood.

Flames ate away at the corners and slithered up to the base, enclosing Gibbs in fire. Annie cried out softly when it reached the tails of his cloak. It quickly consumed the cotton fabric, and soon he was engulfed. She let herself cry as the fire took him away forever.

Gibbs wouldn't have wanted a funeral. He would have said, "Burn me and bury my ashes on a mountain." But everyone wanted to honor him in some way, so they all made their way to the Witches Brew, the all-wizard bar that was run out of the house of Douglass Rand, an adventurer and now barkeep and entrepreneur.

Douglass laid out a table of refreshments: free beer, sandwiches, cookies. Annie found a table at the corner and sat with Cham, Spencer, Milo, Ryan, and Jack. Other guards sat at the surrounding tables. Annie played with her mug of beer and smiled as she saw Arrowhead raise a glass in Gibbs's honor.

"When I was seven, he gave me a stake for my birthday," Annie said. The memory made her smile. Her age hadn't matter to him, just her desire.

"I remember that. Jason made a fuss and took it from you," Ryan said.

"Dad gave it back to me. It sat on my shelf for years. Gibbs took me on my first vampire hunt when I was thirteen. Dad was out of town and Gibbs snuck me out of the house. I watched him kill a vampire. I had never seen it before."

"Were you scared?" Milo asked.

"Terrified. He wanted me to be, so I would always remember they were scary," Annie said. Absently, she sipped the bitter beer.

"My first case as his partner, we were chasing this demon," Spencer began. "It was one of those weird, blobby things with no name. The ones that are afraid of water. We stumbled into their nest. We ended up hightailing it out of there. He's screaming at me as five of these things are coming after us. We find a small bridge over the Des Plaines River, and he pushes me. I go over the bridge into the water. He jumps over the other side, and as he's falling toward the river, he shoots a fireball. We're on a well-used trail, with demons grunting and growling, and he starts the whole thing on fire." Spencer starts laughing. "Calls Graham to come over, and let's just say, Graham wasn't amused. He starts yelling at Gibbs. And all Gibbs did was shrug. I think Graham would have punched him out for the trouble it caused, but Gibbs had that look. It scared me the first few months I worked with him." He finished his story and took a sip of beer.

The stories continued through the afternoon as the beer and food were consumed. Eventually, Annie had had enough and joined some others in the front room.

"Hi, Mrs. Cuttlebrink." Annie said.

"If you're up for it, I need to show you something," the librarian said.

Annie nodded and followed her to a quiet corner at the front of the bar where Mrs. Cuttlebrink held on to an accordion file. "I suggested to the Wizard Council, and they agreed, that the sword you used in England, along with the other artifacts you brought back, should remain at Artifact Hall. I don't know if you knew, but Robin Price found the talismans in England." She pulled out the pictures and handed them to Annie.

"I hadn't heard that."

"You were still in the hospital. He found them at the..." she referred to a note pad. "The Jorvik Viking Center in York, England. The VAU created fake ones and Robin made the switch."

Annie shook her head and chuckled. "What does that have to do with me?"

Mrs. Cuttlebrink offered a knowing smile. "Well, since you saved the coven and allowed them to come here with the Vikings, it has everything to do with you," she said.

Annie shrugged. "I'm still not following."

"Well. All of the artifacts will be placed in a special exhibit in Artifact Hall. I was helping Robin. You know, sorting through the ancient coven documents and other artifacts. We found this." She pushed the file to Annie.

Annie untied the rope that held the folder together and pulled out a pile of papers, a small *Book of Shadows* on the top. She looked at Mrs. Cuttlebrink. "You need to see what's in there," the librarian said.

Annie opened the front cover. Inside, the words were in an ancient handwriting; she waved her palm across the page and said "Translate." The words shimmered out and reappeared in English.

Anaise,

There is not a day that goes by that I do not think of you and all you did to save my people. You were a wonder, and because of you, we freed ourselves of the damage done and made a harrowing trip across the sea to our new home.

With us came the Vikings, as they too had been traumatized and needed a fresh start. We decided as two groups to become one and brought with us many things you might recognize in your time. I hope they bring you joy as they have to us.

I married when I arrived to the new world. You might remember Svenson. He has been so lovely to me, and we worked very hard to survive, to raise our family, and begin growing the new wizard community that you promised me would grow in great numbers to be the largest in the world. It wasn't easy, but I want you to know, I was loved and I loved and I had many children. One I named for you—Anaise.

I made Anaise promise to continue to add to our Book of Shadows, to record all of our adventures and our family names and to have each generation do the same, so that someday you could see the good that you have done and all the people that came to be because you were brave and strong and so very smart.

We never forgot you. Stories were written for you and you will find them here in this book. I hope the coven and the Vikings left a beautiful legacy for and your family. Blessed be.

Bega

Annie pulled out several long sheets of parchment written in an exquisite cursive writing. It started with Bega and Svenson and listed their children and their children's children. Annie turned another page of the family tree, finding her way to modern day. She continued to page three and stopped when she saw the names of her great-grandparents on her father's side: Simon and Laurel Pearce. "Whoa," Annie said and looked up at Mrs. Cuttlebrink.

"I thought you'd find that interesting," Mrs. Cuttlebrink said.

"How? Where did this come from?" Annie asked.

"I don't have an answer for that. I just know it was found in the original paperwork and items from the first Wizard Council. Of course, it was documented and substantiated, and there it is," Mrs. Cuttlebrink said.

"I don't know what to say. I met her. Bega helped us, a lot. I... wow." She touched Bega's name on the front page and smiled. "This confirms the original coven and the Vikings came to North America far sooner than history reveals. Too bad, we can't share this with historians."

"Yes. We had thought about that. But it would be very tricky to explain where the new evidence came from." Mrs. Cuttlebrink offered a soft laugh.

Annie stared at her family tree. Like Bega had promised, it grew additional branches. Annie sighed deeply, thinking Gibbs would have found it interesting. She wiped a lone tear, tucked the family tree inside the *Book of Shadows* and packed it back inside the accordion folder. She pushed it to Mrs. Cuttlebrink.

"I'll keep this in the library until you're ready to delve into the documents. Okay?"

Annie nodded. Mrs. Cuttlebrink picked up the folder and entered into the remaining crowd to celebrate Gibbs's life.

A majority of the bar had cleared out several hours ago. The only people left were those closest to him. She found a seat beside Kathy and Samantha. "Holding up okay?" Kathy asked.

"Yeah. My heart hurts though." Annie played with a straw still wrapped in paper.

"It will for a while," Samantha said.

"The last thing he said to me was 'Annie.' He keeled over from a death curse as I was kidnapped by a madman," Annie said.

Cham was the only person she'd told how Gibbs had died. Remembering that moment haunted her, she shook at the memory.

"He called you by your name? He never did that," Samantha said.

Annie chuckled. "I was giving him a hard time about it. I told him since I'd be so powerful, he should start calling me 'Annie.' He tried."

"He was like a grumpy uncle. He loved both of you," Kathy said.

The party, after several hours, was breaking up. Annie was unsure of what would happen to all of them during the next few weeks.

∽

Annie stood in her closet. She hung her dress, slipped on her sweats and a T-shirt, and marveled at the electric light above her. Footsteps crossed the hardwood floor and she startled at the sound.

She stepped inside her bedroom.

"Sorry. I didn't mean to bother you," Jason said.

She sat on the bench at the end of her bed and wrapped a blanket around her shoulders. "I'll never get used to you being here," Annie admitted.

Jason chuckled and looked around the room. "I like what you did with the house," he said as he fumbled with his hands.

"Thanks." She observed him carefully. He was nervous in the unfamiliar year. Everyone he knew had moved on without him, and he was stuck in the same place he was when he died. She saw the anxiety in his body movements and in his eyes when he looked at her.

"I won't be here for long. At least until I know you're safe," Jason said.

"I didn't mean to conjure you. I can send you back," Annie suggested.

Jason sat on her bed and picked up her hands. "I know you didn't. And honestly, I wish you hadn't. I've missed so much and I don't belong here. Everyone has moved on and I'm just… here. But I *am* here. And I know what's going on. I want to help you. Send me back when it's done."

Annie nodded. Jason looked at her left hand, where her newly cleaned engagement ring sparkled.

"So you and Cham, huh?"

"Yep. Me and Cham." She smiled and showed him the ring.

"All those times I took the two of you out on vampire runs and training. I always knew." He chuckled at the memory.

"No, you didn't," Annie replied.

"Yes, I did," Jason said.

Annie and Jason fell into an easy silence for several minutes, the only noise from her television. It was enough for Jason to see things he never would have known if he remained dead. "Can we switch off the television? I don't want to know these things," he said.

Obliging, she shut off the television and turned to her father. "I don't remember Mom. I have no emotional attachment to her. When I think 'Mom,' I see Kathy," Annie said.

Jason hummed. "That could bode well for you. No attachment to her means you can see clearly. She won't be able to trick you."

She watched the pain in her father's eyes. "You're advocating that I kill your wife. How can you do that?"

"She's not the woman I fell in love with. I knew that when I saw her eight years ago. I want you to fully understand that."

"I'm sorry. I shouldn't have conjured you," Annie said.

"It's done. So I was thinking. I haven't eaten in eight years. I'm kinda hungry. Got food?"

Annie chuckled and dragged him to the kitchen for dinner.

᷼

"I never got to say congratulations. I wish Cham had told me after you left." Samantha sat beside Annie and pulled her into an embrace.

"There were a few other things to worry about."

Samantha reached for Annie's left hand and examined the ring. "It's beautiful. He's got good taste."

Annie began to scratch at her arm and stopped when Samantha watched.

"It's not getting better?" Samantha asked.

Annie shook her head and returned to watching the television.

"So Mom's alive and Dad's here. Have you talked to him?" Samantha asked. She ran her hands through Annie's newly washed hair.

"Yeah. He lives with me. We talk. I fed him. Have you ever watched someone eat for the first time in eight years?" Annie lay her head on Samantha's shoulder.

"No. It couldn't have been pretty."

Annie enjoyed the silence after a long, emotional day. She didn't want to be around those who worried about her safety, and she especially didn't want to think about the woman who was coming for her.

"Mom's coming after you." Samantha broke the silence between them and Annie rolled her eyes.

"No. Emily Worthington Pearce is coming to kill me or trap me for the powers. My mom died when I was three," Annie said defiantly.

"She gave birth to you. She's still Mom," Samantha argued.

Annie pulled away from her sister, waved her hand across the lamp, bringing up the light. She took Samantha's hands and looked her sister in directly in the eyes. "Listen to me. I was barely out of babyhood when she 'died'. I don't remember her. The only mom I remember is Kathy. She was the one who took me shopping, cleaned my skinned knees, brushed my massive curls. Kathy and Zola. They raised me. Not Emily. I can't think of her as my mom. If I do, she'll be able to hurt me," Annie said and leaned against the sofa cushion.

"How can you shut it off?" Samantha asked incredulously.

"I don't remember her. I'm sorry. But I don't. She's nothing but an image on paper. I have to keep it that way. I have to," Annie said.

Samantha kissed her cheek and settled in beside her. "I'm sorry," she whispered.

"There you two are." Jason entered the den and sat beside his girls for the first time in eight years. For a few hours, they pretended nothing was going to happen.

⁓

"Is your answer still yes?" Cham asked.

Annie turned her head and kissed him. He pulled her into him and pulled the covers to their chins. "Yes," she whispered.

She closed her eyes and sighed, comfortable under the white comforter on her bed and beside her love. It was a few minutes' respite when she didn't feel the prickling under her skin, like a thousand crawling ants. When she felt her scratches burning, she was reminded of the itch that couldn't be satiated.

Dr. Christine had left her with a sleeping draught. It was warm and Annie felt the effects, nearly ready to fall asleep.

"I missed you terribly." Cham kissed her ear, pulled her long hair off her face, and returned his arm around her waist as if he could protect her from the outside world.

"I was gone less than twenty-four hours your time," Annie murmured.

"It was a long twenty-four hours. Did you have a nice time with your dad and Sami?"

"Yeah. Thanks for giving us time. It wasn't real, but it was something." She lay her hand on his bare chest.

"Rest now. I'm afraid it's going to get bad soon," he said.

"I can handle her." Annie took a deep breath and let it out slowly.

"I have no doubt. I'll be here anyway, whether you like it or not."

Her breath slowed and evened out. "I know. I wouldn't want it any other..." sleep overtook Annie, and for now, it was good.

⁓

Cave of Ages, Middle East, 2019
Blue light radiated from the cave walls without the help of artificial

lights or even the sun. It illuminated their skin making them appear ethe-real. It scared most who saw them.

Melichi, in his robes, looked menacing. To Emily, he once had been. She no longer feared him, only knelt down and bowed her head when he entered the large cavern. She took his hand and kissed the ring that had once belonged to King Solomon.

She knew Annie Pearce had returned it to him.

Anne Elizabeth Pearce.

Emily knew the name; it was a whisper from the past.

She knew the girl was once her daughter, but Annie had been abusive of her power and needed to be stopped. She had stolen a great power that belonged to the Fraternitatem. It would be Emily's responsibility to seek her out and take the power from her, at any cost.

"You may rise, my child," Melichi said.

Ever obedient, Emily rose and straightened out her robes. "What may I do for you, Melichi?" She bowed her head and waited for her direction.

"It is time, Emily. The girl has received her powers."

Emily nodded and smiled. "I'm ready."

The End

www.ingramcontent.com/pod-product-compliance
Lightning Source LLC
Chambersburg PA
CBHW030928260626
47169CB00002B/400